Thank you, Alice

Anna Marie Alt

Queen's Man:
Into The Inferno

Queen's Man:
Into The Inferno

AnnaMarieAlt

Library of Congress Control Number: 2016900690
ISBN: Hardcover 978-1-5144-5058-1
Softcover 978-1-5144-5055-0
eBook 978-1-5144-5053-6

Print information available on the last page.

Rev. date: 03/17/2016

To order additional copies of this book, contact:
Xlibris
1-888-795-4274
www.Xlibris.com
Orders@Xlibris.com
726369

Queen's Man: Into The Inferno

Blackness . . . it surrounded him, cloying, squeezing, suffocating. Pain crashed through his head. A tiny ironsmith slammed hammer to anvil between his ears.

He pushed back at the smothering void, but his limbs wouldn't move. *Why not?*

Am I dead, and this is Hell? He tried to kick, yell, twist and turn. Nothing happened.

Panic grabbed hold, swirled and pulsed through him. *Oh my God, where am I? Why can't I see or feel anything . . . but pain.*

Movement . . . it's what I do. It's everything and I can't move. Blast it, why can't I?

His eyes might penetrate the blackness. But he didn't know where they were.

He fought to contain the panic and the debilitating crush of the awful blackness, breath jerking and jamming in his chest. *I have to get out. Get me out!*

An evolution arose within him, remembered but forgotten, an answer to his anguished call. A force to wage the battle—maybe more atrocious than the blackness. But on his side. A contained rage that lived inside him. The rage would push back, carry him. It exploded in his chest, embraced him, became him and he became it.

What's that? Something touched him, dragged across his belly. *Can't allow it. No! No more darkness. No touching. Leave me alone!* The rage burst forth. Smashed through the dark barrier. Grabbed that invading touch. Twisted it away.

His eyes snapped open. *I can see.* The blackness receded. The rage ebbed, fading away back to its containment—to wait.

Deep, gorgeous green eyes met his, surrounded by the strong, lovely face of a woman with long dark red hair. *An angel? Yes, an angel. But why? If I'm dead, no angel would await. I've killed too often . . . Killed? Who? Why?* He sucked in a deep, quavering breath. Who was this woman, this dazzling angel?

He held her arm. It must have been she who touched him.

The green-eyed woman stared at him, her eyes round and startled. Fear flamed in them.

Why is she afraid?

An old crone—a short, wrinkled, vintage old crone—stood by his legs, gazing at him, a cryptic, assessing smile stretching her lips. Bright blue eyes peered, seeing all, knowing all, as ancient and elemental as the mountains and the sea. No fear in those eyes; those eyes would fear nothing, ever.

He tried to speak, but no sound issued from his throat. The merciless hammer pounded in his head.

The lady with fear-filled eyes ripped her arm from his grasp. She stumbled away and yelled. He didn't understand.

More women swarmed forward from behind the angel, armed women, swords drawn and shields up. Several leaped between him and the green-eyed woman, his angel.

Do they think I'd harm her?

The swords pointed, their piercing tips within inches of his body. The rage roiled inside him again, rolling and expanding in his chest like a dark thunderhead. Its sinister laughter grated. "*Swords? We can handle swords. Let them try. Just let them try!*" He recognized the rage, understood it; it was part of him, but separate.

He glared at the helmeted faces behind the swords. *Neither you nor your swords will put me back into the blackness.*

The rage spread, sending searing lava chasing through his limbs. Surprised, he dropped his gaze to his heated legs. *Oh my God! I'm naked, stark naked in front of all these women.* A blanket lay near his hips. He lunged upward and toward it.

The ironsmith's hammer struck between his eyes. Agony blasted though his head. The blackness surged, reclaimed him.

* * *

Queen Rejeena stared into a pair of dark blue eyes emitting a powerful, exultant craving to kill. The passion struck her essence as the force of a potent buffet of wind.

She snatched her arm from the man's grasp, floundered away from him. She screamed, "Guards!"

Five guards rushed into the tent, sprang between the queen and the naked holdee. Swords out, they threatened him with the slashing ends.

Rejeena peered at the man between two guards. She started. Only a few beats of time had passed, but now those kill-crazed eyes shone deep and dark as a bottomless mountain lake on a dazzling, cloudless day, displaying only quizzical innocence. Did she see lust and rage, or did she imagine that which did not exist? *No . . . I know what I saw.*

The man's gaze flicked to the guards with their menacing sword tips. Some dark thing moved in his eyes, curled as a snake coils to strike, revealing but contemptuous anger. *What kind of man did not know fear of swords?*

He glanced down at his body, his mouth dropped open and his eyes flared. Red flashed to his cheeks. He lunged for the blanket lying beside him—so fast, faster than the eye could follow. His lunge jerked to a stop as though he smashed into a rock parapet. He crumpled and dropped prone, unconscious again.

Seconds passed, and no one moved.

The old woman standing by his legs hobbled forward. She pointed to the guards then stabbed her finger at the tent flap. "You, out. All of you, out."

Line Leader Locin, the head guard, gazed at Rejeena. "My Queen?"

The queen frowned but nodded, releasing the guards. They retreated.

Rejeena wrapped her arms around herself. "LaHeeka," she said to the old woman, "I know you are the ancient conjurah, wise and all knowing, but why have you sent away my guards? We stand alone with that . . . whatever ghastly thing that is."

"Do not dramatize, Rejeena. He is but a man, unconscious and helpless."

"Did you not see his eyes? I have confronted enemies, stood against them to do battle with weapons, but never have I faced eyes such as those."

LaHeeka drew her diminutive frame to full height, crossed her arms, tapped one toe. "I observed, Rejeena, a pair of eyes abruptly hurtled from a deep trance, more startled by what he saw than we women. That which lies behind those eyes poses no danger to you."

The queen's mouth worked wordlessly for a moment. She stopped and coughed. "You did . . . you did not perceive the . . . the . . ." She hesitated again. "LaHeeka, I read the desire to kill in his eyes."

The ancient conjurah grimaced and flung a dismissive hand. "Oh bosh, you read too much." She pointed to the prone figure. "This is the man LaSheena has chosen for you as queen's man. She holds reason for that choice. It is not for you, even as a queen of our island of Kriiscon, to question the wisdom of our goddess."

"Why him?" Rejeena shivered and stepped back. "Has LaSheena seen those eyes?"

"LaSheena stands omniscient. She is the consummate goddess and will not hold you forever to that contemptible curse." LaHeeka struck her demanding pose again. "I have traveled long. I am old and tired. Understand, either take this man as queen's man or spend the remainder of your life acceding to the curse. Until this moment, that curse controlled your destiny. For all your days remaining, your fate will hinge upon the decision you render today. This man—and this man alone—will grant you daughters and fulfill other needs your imagination cannot yet grasp."

"Have I no choice? If LaSheena wishes that I be blessed with Queen's Line, I can take him to skindown. He need not be queen's man."

LaHeeka shook her head. "No, he is powerful and strong"—her brow furrowed as she contemplated—"and far too dangerous."

"You stated he embodies no danger. Will you now reverse upon that?"

LaHeeka's old face split into wrinkles upon wrinkles, an effect that passed for a grin, a deep grimace seeming to encompass all that had occurred before this time and all that would occur hereafter. "I said, O Queen, that he offers no danger to *you*." She stared directly into Rejeena's eyes. "I did not say he offers no danger." She shook her head. "No, he holds power and menace, but also much virtue and decency. Only you, Queen Rejeena, can rein this one to harness. You must make him queen's man. LaSheena grants you this opportunity. Grasp it.

"I must return to my Lair of Serenity. I have found him and instructed you. Heed my words." The old woman paused and gently stroked his genitals. "Other women will want the pretty one, but they hold not the fortitude, the required vitality and integrity, to constrain the forces that roil within him. To protect him from them—and more direly them from him—you must make him queen's man." The ancient conjurah hobbled to the tent flap, hesitated and turned. "Once you have indulged the pretty one at skindown, you will not share him with other women. He cannot be a mere holdee." She stabbed her finger at Rejeena. "Make him queen's man, now, today!" LaHeeka left.

* * *

Rejeena stood alone and stared at the prone man. *I am queen. I must conquer all fear.* She sucked in a deep breath, straightened her spine and whispered, "You will not frighten me. You are but a man, as any other."

She clenched her eyes shut. "Go away. Be gone when I open my eyes. Should you not exist, I needs not decide whether to have you." She opened her eyes. He lay there still, the most beautiful man she had ever seen—long, muscular body, dark hair, handsome face—a fitting prize for any queen. Indeed he displayed sufficient manly beauty to enchant three queens at once. *Viewing him, I do indeed want to own him. What woman would not?*

Still, to make him queen's man? Conjurahs and goddesses, how they managed to complicate one's life. How effortlessly they dismissed that ruinous curse, which stood staunchly between Rejeena and her ability to conceive live daughters. Foisted cruelly upon her by malicious actions of others before her birth, the revilement doomed her Queen's Line, which had endured through generations of worthy women, to perish. She defied the curse, and each time the stalking plague claimed her daughters at birth or in infancy. When the third, chubby, healthy Arliva died, Rejeena could bear no more. She yielded to the calamity, allowed her dreams of Queen's Line, all her hope for the future, to wither away like fallen autumn leaves skittering forlornly in the wind.

Oh, LaSheena have mercy. Why must I do this? By taking a queen's man, she declared before all women, before LaSheena and LaHeeka, and more acutely before herself, that she would once more arise and battle the horrific bane of the curse. *Dare I rip open those barely healed wounds? Dare I again prepare to be completed, conceive daughters and establish my Queen's Line? Dare I . . .*

She had submerged the realization that she could never attain the state every Kriisconian woman sought—from the most exalted of the hierarchy to the lowest denizen of the backways—that one absolute must, to be a mother, bear daughters, build upon the legacy of lineage. Burying her pain beneath scar tissue piled ply upon ply through misery, the queen stifled the agony of unending failure, sleepless nights filled with hopeless regret, anguish like the claws of wild cats ripping her heart and inner woman to shreds. Her dread and regret, her agony did not affect the outcome; she did not control fate.

LaHeeka declared she could yet have daughters, this man her chance to be finally a whole woman, a whole queen with Queen's Line. *Oh, to be whole.* LaHeeka was never wrong. Still . . .

She regarded him, this man who, excepting his incredible male beauty and those predatory eyes, seemed as any other. Her gaze slid to his manhood, that vital apparatus necessary to the conceiving of daughters, with both pique and curiosity. *What evil deity decided to assign that instrument to mere men, making women thus dependent upon them forever?* She chose not to touch it. Queens did not engage in the unnecessary hefting and judging of a man's genitals, as did common allway women. He appeared well equipped to perform the function of liberating her from this state of squalid, daughterless misery, should she assign it to him.

She stepped forward and tentatively touched his hip with a single fingertip. When he did not move, she slid her palm onto his abdomen. An exciting, spiky current slithered up her arm. From him? How could it be? The man lay unconscious. *It is surely my imagination. Perhaps a trick LaHeeka plays?*

Still the current coursed and spread through her chest, into her stomach. Her knees trembled and her breath paused in her throat then fluttered out. She wanted to shriek with budding hope, weep in frustration and scream for help at the same time. Help, though, would not come. As queen, as always, she alone must decide.

She gulped breath into her lungs. Could she assuage these baleful forces and conquer this curse? If only she could. If forced to choose Queen's Line or breath, she would choose Queen's Line.

Suppose she should try and fail again? If this one time LaHeeka were wrong and this man did not possess daughter-creating power, would she writhe once more in the agony she suffered at the death of Arliva—and the others? *I could not live through that again, absolutely could not bear it. How can I choose? How dare LaHeeka and LaSheena force me to do so? Why must I hang my heart on a limb to fall and smash again?*

Wracked with fear but consumed by desire to continue her Queen's Line, have daughters, she stood trembling. Choose she must, between the chance of full life with daughters and certain lingering half-life without.

She sighed. Her mind reverted to that morning which had begun as any other, seeming so ordinary.

* * *

At the foot of Tiismara Mountain, Rejeena's Towne flared outward from the great Hearing Hall like a giant dancer's fan. Wide and rock-cobbled, Mainway cut east to west through the center of the towne, stretching from the outtowne ways on one side to the other. A convenient, straightforward route, it beckoned travelers, inviting them to traverse through the fascinating pandemonium that formed this burghal hub, the heart of Quarter Seven.

Vendors lined both sides of Mainway, peddling wares. A band of wander women had settled upon a spot, trading exotic materials from their wagons, items acquired in their travels to distant townes and with Mainlanders along the border. They displayed spices, coffee beans, tobacco, unfamiliar herbs touted to have marvelous healing powers, cloths of many hues and textures, imported jewelry, knives and tools of Mainland steel.

Two wagons set parallel to Mainway. Fastened into the sides of the wagons were rows of large iron rings. A dozen male holdees, naked for viewing, stood chained to the rings. Interest in new holdees always high, women with daughters gathered. They felt the holdees' muscles and checked their teeth, demanded tests of strength, poked and prodded to determine each man's barter value, read their barks for offspring rate, fingered their genitals. Some women behaved so from simple curiosity, having no barter intent. Some sought to buy. Occasionally, barter concluded, a woman would depart with her new acquisition.

One wander woman stood upon the way, calling to passing women. "Holdees for barter. Stop and visualize. We attain but the best, and will barter to your benefit." She gestured and pointed, obstructing at times uninterested women hurrying about their errands and functions.

A woman and a girl stood watching as a potential buyer examined a holdee. The girl covered her eyes, but giggled. "Mama, she grabbed him between the legs. He turns red. Fists clenching. Might he strike her?"

The woman snorted. "If he dares, he will wish he had not. Severe punishment could be meted. Even hanging." Her gaze cut to her daughter. "You well know, Feena, a mere man may not strike a woman, ever."

"I know, Mama, but he appears so . . . upset. Is it not embarrassing?"

"So? He is but a man."

"Why does she grasp him so?"

"Are you daft, child? She must ascertain his package is sufficient, two well-formed gonads and a schlong which will harden properly. From her words, she desires skindown liaison, wishes to rut with him to produce a daughter. She needs determine he stands able to perform."

"She forces his mouth open, peering inside. Why does she do that?"

"To be sure his age is near that indicated upon his bark of enholdment. Also, if the teeth rot, he is likely a user of spoortaa. No woman wishes to waste barter goods on such."

Feena allowed her scrutiny to wander down the Mainway to a vendor's rack of bright-hued clothing. She sighed and turned back. The keeper and buyer now stood nearly toe-to-toe, and their sparring voices ratcheted over the crowd. The daughter gestured toward them. "Why do they yell so?"

"Coercion, my daughter. I see I shall needs grant you more experience in proper bartering. You will be old enough before many seasons have passed to begin the process of acquiring daughters to build upon our lineage. You will require knowledge and skill to barter a holdee at a fair worth. Wander women all stand miscreants, will cheat and mislead for profit."

The mother laughed. "It seems they have found agreement. They exchange kruets and bark of terms." She turned and strolled down the Mainway. "Come, Feena, we have much else to accomplish today."

Her daughter followed, gaze fastening once more upon the clothing display.

Between the wander wagons a small tent squatted, as though huddled for safety. A large woman, armed with sword and intimidating frown, guarded its entrance. Women clustered about a hand-lettered sign hanging on the tent, which read, *Special Holdee. Serious Barters Only.*

The sign and armed guard served to send the probative urges of the curious surging into a headlong gallop. Many inquired; few were admitted, those showing means and declaring intent to barter. When one of the select few emerged from the tent, inquisitive women surrounded her, clamoring for details. The rumor circulated that the holdee within was exceptionally handsome, young, rated at eighty-five, which information caused women figuratively, if not literally, to salivate.

The sorrowful tidings also spread that the man lay unconscious from a hard blow to the head. Despite his condition, the wander women demanded an exorbitant price. Several women of great means, shaking their heads sadly, stated they would have bought immediately had the man been conscious. One rich banquer, face puckered in gloom, declared she might have broken her fingers snatching for her kruet bag had she assurance that enticing piece of skindown goods would live.

* * *

The Queen's Hearing Hall merged with the mountain. A huge hole in the rock face, it had seasons before been flanked by stonewalls, built with holdee labor. The rocks clung together, bonded with clay conveyed by horses and wagons from the Legarne Plaine. A wooden roof spanned wall to wall, the thick planks pitted and cracked from occasional rocks crashing from the mountainside, then repaired. Sliding doors on rails spanned the front. Today, in late spring, the entrance to the hall yawned open to the noise, sights and smells, the bedlam of Mainway and the towne. The hall served as Queen Rejeena's court and as a mecca for meeting, gossiping, bartering, and at times offering entertainment for all women.

Women, those requiring Queen's Hearing as well as spectators, crowded the Hearing Hall to capacity. They gathered singly or in groups, with daughters and male holdees. Dogs roamed unfettered. The crowd surged about from the Mainway into the hall and back out as women greeted each other, chatted and bartered. Some placed sitting mats on the stone floor; others carried in small stools for their comfort. Choosing their places, they waited for hearing to begin.

At the rear of the Hearing Hall, a low-slung rock dais covered with natural deerskins jutted from the floor. On it perched a cathedra, the chair throne-like with its carved wooden scrollwork soaring over the arms and up the back. Layers of white doeskin, draped artfully for contrast with small pieces of black, softened the single seat and backrest. A sitting cubicle, adorned only with smooth black leather, pulled snug, hugged the left side of the big chair. Five small settees swathed alternately in black and white skins formed a semi-circle to the right. Black and white skins randomly covered the rock wall. A large brazier smoldered to the left, pulsing heat against the early spring chill.

The ornate chair enthroned Queen Rejeena during hearing. The semi-circle accommodated the Hearing Council—five wise women learned in the laws, former precedents and preceding decisions of the island of Kriiscon. They advised the queen. The cubicle seated a queen's man.

A woman wearing a black skin dress stepped through a flap in the back wall of the room. After her, six nubile girls dressed in black and white stripes ran into the room, found places along the sidewalls. The girls, who performed errands, were paigae. The woman in black, the heralda, announced important personages and maintained order.

Silence descended as the heralda blew a thin, wailing note on a wooden pipe. "All rise," she intoned, "the Hearing Council of Queen Rejeena approaches."

The crowd obeyed.

The flap snapped open, and five women draped in white skins entered. The councilors' simple dresses fell from around the neck to the floor in a great swirl, held by a single black tie at the neck. A black band, holding her long hair in place, encircled each woman's forehead. They strutted decorously in single file to their settees, but remained standing.

Six uniformly shorthaired, large, muscled women, attired in smooth black leather pants, tunics and steel helmets, marched through the opening. Each carried as armament a small pointed shield, a sheathed sword and a dagger strapped about her hips. Two took positions on either side of the queen's chair, two farther apart, two near the designated spots for the hearing disputants. These six directly protected the queen's person. Other guards, carrying larger shields, armed additionally with crossbows and bolts, already had taken stations throughout the hall.

The heralda blew lustily on her pipe, seven long, measured blasts. "All bow," she commanded, "Queen Rejeena approaches."

All persons within the hall, including council members and heralda, dropped to one knee, the women with heads raised to observe the queen's exalted presence. Male holdees lowered their heads, gazes down, proper for their status. Only the guards remained standing, their function more vital than bowing.

Queen Rejeena entered, moving at a slow, deliberate pace toward her chair. She stood tall, a shapely, handsome woman of full strength, appearing to be in her prime, though young for her august position. Her bright auburn hair swung long, eyes glowed a deep forest green. She paused, exuding an aura of stately haughtiness and scanned the hall with an icy sweep of eye. Her left hand toyed with a tie on her raiment; the right held her power staff, topped by a carved white stag head. Formally attired for hearing, she dressed in Kriisconian deerskin dyed the bright green of summer grass. She wore a solid green two-piece, loose top over skirt. A green cape fell from her shoulders to below her waist, the front flipped back and tied. A broad leather belt sporting a dagger encircled her waist. She observed the hall, strolled to her chair, flipped her skirt to smooth it and sat.

The heralda blew a short blast. "Council members, your chairs. The queen is seated."

The council members took their seats.

"All resume," the heralda called.

With the queen seated, it was time for hearing. Those women not yet in place scurried as quietly as possible so as not to attract attention, calling softly to daughters, taking control of holdees.

Another woman, the reader, seated at a table, arose with a marking prickle and a sheet of sparlin bark. She called the first hearing case before the queen. "Leatha requests queen's punishment, holdee strikes mistress."

A group moved forward. Two women, dressed in mixed skin and costly Mainland cloth, draped in expensive jewelry, led the way. The younger exhibited a black eye and bruises. Two big, strong women handlers hustled between them a hulking, heavy-muscled holdee. Small, angry eyes marred his otherwise attractive features and a sneer twisted his lips. Long hobbles about his ankles and tethers on his wrists limited his movements.

The wealthy pair curtsied and stepped aside. The handlers tried to curtsey, but the man planted his feet. One kicked him in the back of the knee, plunging him down. The women curtsied. Their hands forced the holdee's head low.

The older wealthy woman spoke. "My Queen, I am Leatha. This is my daughter, Liara." She indicated the young woman with the bruised face. "We request queen's punishment for this holdee. He struck Liara while sharing skindown."

"Did you not punish the holdee for striking your daughter? It is permitted by law."

"My Queen," Leatha said, "this is a second offense. He struck Liara previously. I had him whipped. Obviously, it was not enough."

"So why did you not simply skewer him? A holdee who would strike his mistress is not fit to share skindown with your daughter."

The woman colored. "My Queen, the holdee is valuable, young and strong with a good rate, though injudicious. I would save my investment. I feel queen's punishment is deserved."

"Queen's punishment for such an offense will be harsh. You may not save your investment."

Leatha nodded. "I accept that, My Queen."

The man surged to his feet despite the handlers and bonds. "Well, I don't," he yelled. "We're talking about me. I get some say here."

A collective gasp swept the hall. No holdee could speak at hearing unless so requested. Severe punishment could be meted. He spoke Universal Language, though he had to understand Oldenspeak in order to follow the conversation.

As the reader interpreted for the queen, the handlers grabbed him, tried to wrestle him to his knees. The man shoved at them, striking with his bound hands. A queen's guard stepped forward, hand on sword hilt.

The queen raised her hand, stopping all the women. "You wish to speak, holdee?" the queen asked.

"Damned right I wanna speak, Queen."

Again, the queen raised her hand to still the guards. "Speak then, holdee."

He pushed to his feet, smirked and gestured at Liara. "Well, it's like this. This li'l cutie, I call her Li-Li, wants me to roll her aroun' the skindown. Well, I'm willin', but I want more'n she does. So I just slapped her aroun' a bit, helped her see things my way. That's all. No great harm done." His voice turned to an ugly growl. "You women all act so hifalutin, but where I come from, we keep our women in their place. See?"

For long moments, Queen Rejeena observed him, her green eyes glacial. *This man is unbelievably brazen or crassly stupid. As he understands our language, he must realize his speech has just condemned him.* She spoke to Leatha. "Did you not teach this holdee the rules of society, his proper place, how to speak to and about his mistress and a queen?"

"Yes, My Queen. He has been punished upon several occasions. He does not learn and scorns the rites of behavior."

"In that case, he will be immediately taken to locchot for twenty lashes front and rear. After that, he will be castrated. If he survives, he will work his remaining days in the clay mines. He is unfit to live among good women."

The man jerked spasmodically, then bellowed, "You ain't cuttin' my balls off, you bitch." He lurched toward the queen.

One queen's guard sank her sword into his abdomen; the other slashed his throat. As she slashed, she shoved his head down, restricting the spurting blood so it would not spray the queen.

He gasped, staggered two steps, eyes locked wide with disbelief. He sank gurgling to the floor, twitching, his blood soaking into the skins. The man died quickly

The heralda blew a short blast. Servants appeared, rolled the body in the bloody skins and carried it away. Others quickly scrubbed away the splattered bloodstains and spread clean skins.

"In future," the queen told Leatha, "select your daughter's skindown romps more wisely."

"Yes, My Queen," Leatha murmured. "All those kruets," she mourned, as she watched the holdee's body dragged away. She and her party curtsied and retreated.

Women muttered and shuffled, but the Hearing Hall promptly returned to normal.

"Grun disputes Tasa, ownership of a kid," the reader called.

Two women strode forward, granting each other quick, surly glances, one leading a young goat.

The queen stirred in her chair, green eyes flashing an unspoken question to her council members. The middle councilor, Beertana, oldest and most revered, turned both palms up and shrugged.

Grun and Tasa, with goat, halted at disputants' place, two separated half circles of small rocks bound together and to the floor by clay. Both curtsied to the queen then glared at each other.

"Well?" the queen barked.

"My Queen," Tasa said, "I claim this goat kid. It is aborned of my nanny."

"And I, My Queen, claim it," Grun said. "But for my buck, there would be no kid."

"Did you not make arrangement before the mating?" The queen's eyes narrowed; she crossed and uncrossed her legs.

"It was not an arranged mating, My Queen," Grun said. "We abide near each other, but she is demented. I would never mate my goat with hers. I want the kid because it looks like my buck. I hold much affection for my goat."

Tasa spat, "My Queen, she stands the daft one. Had her goat been fettered, as he should have been, no mating would have occurred. The kid springs from the haunches of my nanny and is rightfully mine."

The queen said, "It would seem, hearing your remarks, this dispute has little to do with the kid, but much with your animosity toward each other. Both your claims to half the kid are legal, but your dispute is silly and childish. The queen holds no patience with it. You have three timebeats for one to relinquish her claim for fair recompense from the other."

The queen turned to the time recorder on the reader's desk, then back to the disputants.

Grun and Tasa glared at each other. Neither spoke. The time beats passed.

"Very well," Rejeena said, "the kid will be auctioned immediately on the Mainway. Each of you will receive half the proceeds, then return half her share to the reader for having annoyed the queen with such folly."

Tasa said, "But, My Queen—"

"Silence," barked the heralda. "The queen has spoken." She grabbed the kid's lead and gestured to a paiga, who ran to obey her summons. "Take the kid and perform the queen's bidding."

Leading the small goat, the paiga hurried toward the entrance.

Grun and Tasa, frozen-faced, curtsied to the queen and followed.

The reader called the next case, "Serfa disputes Micia, the tailor, non-payment for goods against poor quality product."

The queen dispensed with this dispute, finding the tailor guilty of poor quality product, citing her with a fine and payment for perfidy to the complainer. The tailor left furious, Serfa satisfied.

Queen Rejeena spent the morning deciding various hearings and making judgments on disagreements as presented by her subjects. Nearing noon, the reader announced, "Tarkan requests queen's punishment, holdee strikes mistress, fourth offense."

"What is this, an epidemic?" growled the queen. "Can women of Quarter Seven no longer control their holdees?"

A tall, heavy woman strode forward. Her young holdee, thin to emaciation, followed with shoulders hunched, eyes flitting about. His mistress halted and he dropped to a bow, snapping chin to chest.

The woman curtsied. "I am Tarkan, My Queen. This holdee has struck me four times."

"Why does he still breathe?"

A strangled moan issued from the motionless holdee.

"My Queen, he strikes me when I wake him. I punished him for the offense to no avail. Any other time, he is meek and mousy, as you can see." Tarkan gestured with a contemptuous flick of hand.

"Why does he strike you when you wake him?"

"He offers no acceptable reason, My Queen. Perhaps queen's punishment will assist his learning."

"Holdee, look at me," the queen said.

The man looked up, eyes wide, gulping, face pale. "Y-yes, O Queen." He used Oldenspeak.

"Why do you strike your mistress? Why do you not learn?"

"O Queen," he said, "I-I can't help it. All m-my life, if s-someone touches me when I sleep, I str-strike out. I'm not awake yet. I c-can't quit." He stopped, sucking in air. His voice strengthened. "Please believe me, O Queen, I would never intentionally strike my mistress. I've begged her—"

"That is most ridiculous, holdee. Be silent. You cannot even fabricate a believable tale." The queen's eyes gleamed cold as an alcohol bath.

He dropped his head.

Rejeena looked at Tarkan. "What would you judge a fair queen's punishment for this infraction?"

"My Queen, I believe a heavy strikepaddle lashing might suffice. He received strokes previously. Queen's punishment as well as public embarrassment may carry the needed severity."

The queen's gaze raked the holdee's skinny frame. "Ten lashes front and rear with the strife paddle to be administered immediately in the punishment room."

"Yes, My Queen." Tarkan smiled, curtsied and hurried out onto Mainway, turning in the direction of the punishment room, followed by a trembling holdee. Two guards accompanied them to ensure compliance with the edict.

Rejeena sat back. With a wave, she signaled the heralda to pipe lunch break. She rose and turned, and her gaze fell upon a young mother smiling tenderly at a tiny daughter, suckling at her breast. The woman's eyes glowed warm and bright with love and contentment. A stiletto blade thrust into the queen's heart could not have matched the crippling burst of agony that stabbed straight into her soul, her inner woman. *Arliva. Oh LaSheena, Arliva. To be that mother. To have a daughter to suckle at my breast . . . an enchanting little one to love.* A familiar great lump of emptiness formed inside her, a grinding mass, more torturous than the worst pain.

She wrenched her eyes from the young mother, gritted her teeth and clamped her lips. For a fleeting second she despised that woman, hated all women with daughters. *I am not a member of their daughtered cliques. Can never be. But oh, to be one of them.*

Rejeena retreated swiftly through the rear skin flap into a side room where she took breaks and dined. No councilors joined her, as they had not been invited. She wanted no companions, grateful no one requested audience. Solitary, sighing, gaze on the far wall, she pushed her lunch around the plate.

* * *

Shortly after the resumption of Queen's Hearing, a great uproar exploded on the Mainway. Women ran to and fro amid yelling, shouts, feet slapping and startled confusion. The noise drowned the sounds in the Hearing Hall.

The queen motioned a guard to discover the cause.

The guard popped onto the Mainway, reappeared and raced to the queen. With a hurried dip of curtsey, she said, "My Queen, it is LaHeeka, ancient conjurah. She approaches on Mainway."

The queen gasped, "Surely not? She has remained in her Lair of Serenity for several season turnings. You must be mistaken."

"My Queen, I assure you, it is LaHeeka."

Rejeena leaped up. "Then I must greet her."

The heralda rushed toward the crowd, blew her pipe and waved her hands to clear the way.

The guards raced to cover the queen as she swept toward the entrance and onto Mainway.

Her subjects fell back, then swarmed out behind.

The queen looked along Mainway.

LaHeeka, ancient conjurah, held in high esteem due to her wisdom and perceived intimacy with LaSheena, indeed approached. None knew the number of season turnings the old woman had lived. A fixture on the island for longer than most women could remember, she seemed to have sprung from the hand of LaSheena as a woman of full maturity.

Surrounded by armed guards, the conjurah rode in an open litter chair carried on the shoulders of four strong, young holdees. Approaching the queen, the holdees placed the chair down gently, then dropped into bows. Aided by a holdee who leaped back to his feet, the ancient conjurah rose slowly from the chair. The guards curtsied in groups so not all dipped at the same time.

LaHeeka stood barely shoulder level to the queen. Bent, moving slowly, she leaned on her holdee and a stout cane. A craggy effect of wrinkles within wrinkles formed her face. Long white hair swept back, looped in a tight bun. Bright blue eyes gazed about, sharp and alert as a small bird scouting for predators. A simple black cloth gown hung on her spindly frame, covered by a thick woolen cape. She shuffled toward the queen, remaining standing. Ancient conjurahs did not bow.

The queen grasped her hand. "Welcome, ancient one, to Rejeena's Towne. You grace us with your presence. Will you take refreshment?"

The old woman's voice grated low and raspy, but surprisingly strong. "I and my group will require refreshment. We journey back shortly. I must speak with you, O Queen."

"Of course. Please come to my home." The queen gestured toward the old woman's conveyance.

"No time," the conjurah grumbled. "I will speak with you in your lunch cave."

"As you wish." Rejeena led LaHeeka through the crowd, who pushed against the guards, impeding their progress. The women had parted for the queen, curtseying, respectfully allowing her passage, but they thronged toward the conjurah. They offered gifts and tokens; some implored conjuring to their advantage. Even a kind word from an ancient conjurah could change a woman's fortunes.

LaHeeka ignored all, eyes focused beyond the women.

They attained the quiet of the break cave. The ancient conjurah sat stiffly amongst the pillows and mats. Two of her attendants placed pillows behind and around her, insuring comfort.

With LaHeeka settled, a paiga entered with a short-legged serving table holding a pot, coffee casters, cream and honey. "Bless you, Ancient Conjurah," she said, placing the table near the old woman. "May I pour and serve?"

LaHeeka waved her away.

"Everyone out," the ancient conjurah called. She pointed a finger at the guards. "You, too. My words are for the queen's ears alone."

The guards exited.

The queen poured coffee and smiled. "What is so important, LaHeeka, to stir you from your Lair of Serenity? You could have sent a missive. I would have come gladly."

"It would have then been too late, Rejeena." The wizened old face returned her smile with a grimace of wrinkles. "Much too late."

The queen waited while the old woman sipped and looked reflective.

"Six days ago, Rejeena, a presence entered the island proper. I could feel it . . . its strength. It greatly disturbed my mind. I could not discern why. So, I tracked it. It entered from the Silver City Port into claimed territory. It, therefore, had to be a Mainlander—a man." The conjurah paused, wrinkled mouth pursed.

"Go on," the queen said. "Is this man a threat to the island?"

LaHeeka shook her head. "I felt no threat, only strength, inner power. He traveled down the Wishing River through Claimed Land, crossing the border near the Mainlanders' Outpost Three.

Fifteen peckats into our territory, there occurred a sudden upheaval and I lost him. That was four days ago."

The queen smirked. "You sensed strength, inner power? Are you sure this was a man? Do men even possess such qualities?"

"Do not doubt LaHeeka. I know what I sense. He is male and holds strength and power. Two days ago, I detected his presence again, fraught this time with weakness. In my mind, his essence flickers, appearing and disappearing. Each time I become aware of him, he is closer." The old conjurah grinned. "He bides within Rejeena's Towne."

"Impossible." The queen started, sloshing coffee from her caster. "No unfettered man resides in this towne."

The conjurah frowned. "Not unfettered—shackled, his presence weak, but stronger than two days ago. He is here."

"If shackled, than what is the problem? A restrained man presents no difficulty."

"Aaaah," the old woman said. "I did not state he presents a difficulty." She paused. "You see, in tracking him—building upon my awareness of his presence and strength—I discerned, through the grace of LaSheena, the use of him." Her face pulled into a wrinkled grimace. "You struggle with a great problem, O Queen. This man holds the solution."

"I respect your knowledge, but"—Rejeena's brow knit—"what problem?"

The conjurah cackled. "O Queen, sometimes you appear so dense I despair leaving Quarter Seven in your hands. There stands a curse placed on you and your mother. Your Queen's Line is to wither, without daughters. You do remember that?"

"Of course I do. I accept my fate and the effects of the curse. What has that to do with some man?"

"A man placed that curse, when his malicious and unfair death forced him to use the only weapon he held." The conjurah's eyes misted in memory and anger flickered in their depths. Rejeena's grandmother, long dead, the cause of both the death and the curse, lay unforgiven.

"Many seasons ago," LaHeeka said, "I told you only a man could remove the curse, one possessing strength and integrity to match the one who placed it."

"And this shackled man?"

"He possesses the power to defeat the curse."

Rejeena stared. "I cannot credit that. The curse stands old and powerful, has proven itself stronger than this queen. Surely you, my friend, would not ask me to rip open those wounds again. Upon my demise, I will flee to dance upon the four winds without lineage. A new Queen's Line may then form with no curse to condemn it." Rejeena's face twisted. "It is best."

"Nonsense, Rejeena. Continuation of Queen's Line is best. You indeed suffered terrible travail when you lost Arliva. You withdrew and closed up in heart. It is not good. With queenly responsibility and duty, you must stand and face this tribulation as you have others. Where is your courage, your mettle? I, LaHeeka, through LaSheena, declare this man your reprieve."

Skeptical green eyes met hers. "Through LaSheena?"

"It is the will of LaSheena. She informed me, as she always does, in a dream. Two nights before I sensed this man's presence, a missive arrived during my slumber, appeared in my mind, blazing with fiery words, stating that your greatest problem shortly would be solved. You must believe, Rejeena, have faith. She sends this man to you."

"This man can break curses?"

"Yes."

"He is in this towne?"

"Yes."

"LaHeeka," the queen said, "you know I hold the greatest respect for your abilities. I accepted your counsel for as long as I have lived. Your advice stands always good, your knowledge great. When I have moved against your counsel, it has been to my regret. You ask me now to accept that which I do not believe possible. I am torn in mind." The queen surged to her feet and paced, brow furrowed.

LaHeeka sipped and waited.

The queen turned. "I would like to believe, ancient one, that the curse could be lifted. My inner woman flames with desire to continue my lineage. I believed the curse, accepted its inevitability. Now you tell me hope exists. I fear to believe because the agony is so great, the price of losing a daughter so high. I want no more of that—but oh, how I do want daughters. I stand, O Ancient Conjurah, unconvinced and terrified."

"We shall unearth this man, bring him to light. Perhaps he may convince you."

"Where would we look? Holdees abound."

"We needs not look far, O Queen." The multiple wrinkles flashed again. "I feel his presence. He is near, just down the Mainway. I shall lead you to him. Call my attendants. He cannot come to us, so we must go to him."

Frowning, Rejeena called the guards.

The conjurah's young holdees returned, gently helped her to her feet. With the queen, the party moved through the Hearing Hall and toward the Mainway. As fast as the old woman could hobble, following her lead, they moved down the cobbled Mainway toward the wander women's parked wagons.

A wander woman, wearing a feathered caplet indicating her to be a leader, stepped forward. She curtsied. "Welcome, Ancient Conjurah, O Queen. I am Poonesta, foredoya of this group. In what way may I assist you?"

The conjurah pointed to the small tent. "We would view the man within. When did you acquire him? Why is he confined?"

"Ancient Conjurah, he lies unconscious, was so when we enholded him three days ago. He suffered a severe blow to the head. We know not how."

The queen asked, "Where did you acquire him?"

The foredoya smiled without mirth. "We took him from a small group of loose men, after we killed them, near the junction of Wishing River and Feather Creek."

The ancient conjurah mumbled, "Ah, yes, unconscious . . . I would lose his presence. The flickering of the essence. It is assuredly him." Of Poonesta she commanded, "Show us this man at once. Come, Queen Rejeena."

The keeper swept aside the tent flap. The queen, the conjurah and guards pushed into the tent. The woman with the intimidating frown snapped and shoved at the curious who attempted to follow.

The man lay on a platform, flat on his back, covered to his chin by a heavy wool blanket. Two small braziers flanked him for warmth and light. The wanderers' healer stood beside him.

The queen's guards spread their arms, restraining the curious from entering. Queen Rejeena and LaHeeka stepped forward, close to the man.

"Uncover him," the queen said.

The healer whipped off the blanket. The man lay naked, clean, face shaven, proper for viewing.

The pure physical beauty of the man struck Rejeena breathless. Still, quiet, face composed and pale, so utterly gorgeous. His hair was dark brown, almost black, cut short with an entrancing stray lock curled across his forehead. The firmly boned face formed strong, clean lines, with a straight nose, and cheekbones curving into well-formed ears. The closed eyes set deep beneath thick black brows, the mouth a bit wide with thin upper lip and full lower lip cleaving an indentation between it and the square chin. Her eyes followed the lean neck and wide shoulders, sloping into seductive trim hips. His chest, arms, flat belly and legs corded with tightly defined muscle, long and lean, strength without bulk, sleek as the tarag cat. He did not appear particularly large but rather harmonized. His chest and belly flowed smoothly, the hair thickening just below the bellybutton, leading the eye straight to his groin. Between his legs rested his manhood, matched to the rest of him. The whole effect cried strength, masculinity—beautiful, sensual masculinity. His body was battered and bruised, but the bruises could not hide the virility.

The queen wanted to touch him, place a hand on that lean, muscular body.

The ancient conjurah moved faster. The old woman leaned over him, murmuring, hands on his left chest. "Aaaaah, yes," bubbled from her lips, "yes, yes . . . we have unearthed you, pretty one. Yes, indeed." Face entranced as though receiving signals, she stroked his chest, ribcage and flat abdomen. Her bony hands glided upward to his neck, then encircled his head. She remained motionless, gripping his head, lips moving soundlessly, eyes closed.

"Strength. I feel strength. You are powerful, pretty one, in mind, body, heart. I sense no weakness. You will be tribulation to the queen, will you not, pretty one? Oh yes, tribulation indeed." She threw her head back and cackled.

LaHeeka snapped her head down and glared at the women in the tent. "Out!" she screeched. "All of you, out." She waved her hands. "Out!"

The queen's guards shooed everyone from the tent then followed, leaving only the healer and Poonesta with the queen and conjurah.

The conjurah glared at the foredoya. "You, out."

"Ancient Conjurah, I am the holdee's keeper. I belong."

"No more," LaHeeka shrilled. "It is not allowed for you to look upon a naked queen's man."

"Queen's man!" gasped both keeper and queen.

"Yes, yes, of course. You, out."

Poonesta retreated, visions of queenly barter dancing before her greedy eyes. The healer stood motionless.

"Queen's man?" Rejeena said. "LaHeeka, I have never owned nor desired a queen's man. I do not now."

LaHeeka moved to the man's groin. She gently cupped his genitals, holding and stroking, humming softly. "Yes," she said, looking at the lean, sturdy body, replacing the genitals tenderly, "this is the one, O Queen. He is most powerful." She grinned and patted his manhood. "Powerful everywhere, O Queen. He will grant you daughters, his beauty will grant you stature when you display him and"—she cackled again—"he will grant you much travail. This one will resist your control, dance in flame by choice, demand his own way." She absently stroked his thigh, gaze roving his body. "LaSheena has conveyed to you a pretty one with abilities. Do not waste her generous gift babbling your desires. LaSheena knows what you need."

"Ancient Conjurah, the man is knocked completely from his senses. He may die, never awake."

"Oh, he will awake. He is young and strong. His return is assured; LaSheena would have it so." The conjurah stepped away from him.

Rejeena sneered at the supine form. "He is but a man. How can he be dangerous?" She reached and ran an exploratory hand over his belly.

When she touched him, her day that had seemed so normal that morning, changed faster than a snake's strike. He grabbed her hand and twisted it away. The dark blue eyes—filled with fervent, killing rage—snapped open.

* * *

Now Rejeena stood instructed by LaHeeka, convinced this must be the will of LaSheena, terrified of the effect upon her life, but needing daughters as she needed air to breathe.

All the while that spiky current chased up her arm, echoed within her, strangely exciting, prickling her skin into goose bumps.

She could not deny something passed between them, she and this inert male, be it the work of LaSheena, LaHeeka or the man. The queen, residing in her, sneered. *How can a mere man have magic, grant me happiness? Men hold no power, are nothing. They are to be used and discarded.* With this thought, a lump formed choking her, a brassy taste smarted upon her tongue. The senseless, cruel using and discarding of a man started this whole dreadful sequence. A man about to die screamed that curse, hurtling her life into ruin seasons ago. That man held magic. Perhaps another could.

Rejeena shoved down the dread, the memory of this man's eyes. Her fear of life without Queen's Line overrode all others.

The ancient conjurah held great knowledge; many proclaimed her LaSheena's mortal tongue. *Is it possible? Can I indeed conceive daughters, Queen's Line? This man lying still, helpless before me, does he hold such power?* She raised her head, squeezed her eyes tightly shut, pressed her lips together then relaxed them. *If there exists a chance to be a true queen for my quarter, to bear daughters, have lineage as women are meant to do, I must take it.*

She pulled the blanket over him and called for the guards and Poonesta.

The keeper returned, curtseying. "Have you decided, O Queen?"

"Yes. He is mine. He must be moved immediately to my home. My guards will guide you through the smallways to bypass the crowd. Take care his body is exposed to no eyes. Should he live, he will be queen's man. You will be amply compensated. Should he not live, his value is of no import."

The wander woman complied. Even this keeper of holdees knew not to challenge a queen who has made her decision.

The queen gestured to her guards. "Locin, show them the way. Place him in my summer skindown room. Find Alea. My healer must care for him."

"Yes, My Queen." The line leader issued orders to her women, and the guards hurried to comply.

*   *   *

Alea, the queen's healer, rushed to the queen's home, bringing an assistant, Renfra, with her. They found two servants whispering, hovering over a supine, covered form on a holdee pallet.

"Women, let us not stare but help him," Alea said. "Renfra, we must stack padding beneath this pallet. It is inappropriate to place him on the skindown until the queen so requests, but he suffers injury. He must be kept warm and comfortable." She gestured to the servants. "Bring two large braziers and light them."

Alea bent over her patient. Turning his head, she examined the site of the bump, probing gently. The skull and neck seemed intact. He had been struck behind the left ear, the site swollen, bruised. "I have seen worse," she murmured. She found his breathing and heartbeat slow and steady. With servants in the room, she did not uncover him, but traced a hand down him beneath the blanket and confirmed him to be naked. "We must change that," she said.

The healer told a servant, "Have the queen's seamstress fix double buttons on a pair of pants, proper for a queen's man. I want them quickly."

The servant dashed away.

Alea pointed at the other servant. "Leave the room, please. We must fully examine the queen's man. Let no one enter without our permission. He lies unclothed, and none may view him."

The servant nodded and left, closing the door.

Alea grinned at Renfra. "As healers we may view that which our queen has chosen to warm her skindown." She lifted the blanket. "Oh, my!"

Renfra whistled softly.

Alea's gaze traveled over the lean, muscular body. "He is magnificent. Such male beauty belongs indeed as queen's man. If he can rut adroitly, our queen will be a happy woman."

Both chuckled and began to check him for signs of infection or broken bones. They turned him gently onto his belly also. Assured that the queen's man harbored no hidden injuries, Alea patted his shapely buttocks. "Nice keister. With properly tailored pants, he will render our queen the envy of all women."

"It is well," Renfra said. "Those women, who have pitied poor Queen Rejeena as she lacks a queen's man, will henceforth needs sing their song of woe for another."

A servant called, "Healer, we have the pants."

Renfra accepted the garment and together they slid the pants onto him, fastening the buttons. "Much better," said Alea. "Now he looks like a queen's man."

Alea sat beside the pallet. "Due to his status, we may take no chances. I want two attendants with him at all times. I will stay. Find Barrina, Gorsa, Chaara and Wecan. Have them see me."

Renfra nodded and rushed out.

* * *

Following Queen's Hearing, Rejeena returned to her home, ate alone and quickly. She wanted to view her queen's man again, assure herself he did indeed exist.

She rose, walked to her winter skindown room where she slept, and changed into a soft dress of Mainland cloth. Only within the confines of her home did the queen wear raiment other than skins and materials natural to Kriiscon. She hurried to her summer skindown room. It felt warm from the smoldering braziers, but not too warm for an injured man.

Alea and Chaara crouched over him. The assistant dribbled water into a funnel held by the healer. The funnel seated on a hollow river reed. Picked, dried and held until needed, the reed when softened became flexible. They inserted it through his mouth into his stomach, enabling them to give him water.

The queen leaned over them. "Drowning him, Alea?"

"My Queen." Alea acknowledged her without stopping, acceptable behavior for healers. "If we do not force water into your queen's man, he will dry away as dust. He can do without food for a while, but not water. One cannot know, with fickle wander women, the quality of care he received. Though he does appear well tended."

The queen knelt beside her. "Has there been change?"

"No change. He just lies here looking like a potential skindown frolic."

"Your problem, Alea," Rejeena chuckled, "is you stand too involved in the skindown process as pleasure, rather than simply means to acquire daughters."

"And your problem, My Queen, is you do not," Alea said. She motioned to Chaara. "That is enough." She extracted the reed and handed the equipment to the assistant, who departed.

The healer sat beside her patient, Rejeena on the other side.

Alea looked stern, mouth drawn. "My Queen, if you can share skindown with this"—she flipped the cover back—"and not find great pleasure in the doing, I hold no hope for you."

Rejeena reached with one hand then hesitated. She took a deep breath and stroked his warm abdomen. She liked the feel of him. "You are healer, Alea. Will he live?"

"That, My Queen, rests in the capable hands of LaSheena. Head wounds are unpredictable. I hold much faith, though, in LaHeeka. That which she desires usually occurs."

The queen sighed and ran her hand up his ribcage. She savored the fine sheath of muscles, flowing smoothly into each other, forming that enticing body. "Now that I have made him queen's man as LaHeeka demanded and felt his body beneath my hands, I wish this man to survive."

"We do all we can, My Queen."

"He is so perfect," the queen murmured. She brushed the hair from his forehead, traced the bone lines of his face with a finger.

"A man more handsome is hard to imagine." Watching the queen, Alea noted the green eyes thaw. Those eyes had been cold, Rejeena's feelings locked away—since Arliva. Though he lay senseless, something in this man seemed to touch the queen, awaken her lost interest. Alea prayed silently to LaSheena to spare this man.

The queen needed him. Alea needed to see her queen and friend happy again.

Alea rose, curtsied and left them alone.

A while later the queen emerged from the room. She smiled at the healers. "Take good care of him," she said and departed.

Rejeena returned to her winter skindown and, for the first time in many months, slept deeply a full night. She dreamed of a dozen lovely daughters dancing about her, and of that gorgeous male body—locking away the memory of the rage that stabbed from his eyes.

* * *

Alea returned in late morning with Gorsa to relieve Chaara and Wecan. The queen's man lay prone and still.

Wecan grinned and gestured toward him. "He may soothe the queen, but he stirs my blood to hot lava. I want to grip those cunning hips between my thighs and rut until neither of us can breathe."

Alea laughed. "Many women will agree. But he is queen's man. The rutting of him will needs await her pleasure. Take care to not speak so crudely before the queen."

"Queens like it when women admire their queen's man."

"Admire, yes, but not such avid lust."

Wecan chuckled. "We have granted him water every four hours. He is bathed and shaved, should require nothing soon."

Alea nodded. "Any change?"

"He did groan once while we bathed him."

"He did?" Alea's eyes opened wide.

"Is that good?"

"Any life sign is important. I have before treated persons injured of the head. Moving, making sounds often signals return of the senses. This is indeed good."

"Will you tell the queen?"

"Not yet. Let us wait and observe." Alea and Gorsa settled down.

At mid-afternoon, the patient cried out, soft, varying sounds in rapid succession. His right arm jerked from under the cover. Alea gently replaced it. The left arm moved. He lay quiet for a while, then uttered a strangled grunt.

"Is there anything we can do?" Gorsa asked.

Alea shook her head. "No, we wait."

His legs moved, jerky, spasmodic. All his limbs shuddered, then stilled.

Gorsa sighed. "Perhaps we took hope too soon."

"I think not. In my experience—"

An onslaught of movement silenced Alea. His head thrashed, legs kicked, arms twitched and waved.

Alea and Gorsa kept him covered, dodged his thrashing limbs.

Again he lay still. In a moment, he began to move, different, slower, controlled, one limb at a time. His facial muscles writhed.

The assistant leaned forward and her bracelet scraped the floor. His motions ceased.

"He appears to be awake," Alea said.

The patient groaned.

"He has done much of that." Gorsa shook her head.

Alea slid a hand under the cover on his chest. "His heart beats faster. He seems awake, but his eyes remain closed."

Gorsa leaned forward. "Queen's Man, open your eyes."

"Even if awake, he cannot understand. He is Mainlander. He will not know Oldenspeak." Alea stroked his forehead.

His head turned toward her.

She breathed, "Well, you must be awake. Open your eyes." Her fingertips stroked his eyelids.

His eyes snapped open.

She looked into a pair of midnight blue orbs, opaque as a starless evening sky—at once aware, confused, questioning—fitting so well with the dark hair and handsome face.

* * *

No . . . please not the blackness again. If I'm dead, let me stay dead. Don't keep drawing me back. Blackness grasped me before, and . . . I saw an angel.

A tiny, hard point of light shone far above him. He needed to get to that light. Out of this desolation.

The blackness gripped him with pain—agony that had rendered him helpless for a long time. He held no concept of himself, a formless being, the mind his only weapon against that remorseless grip. Thought alone moved him upward, pulled his toward the high flicker.

The agony began at the back of his head, radiated around his skull with clutching fingers. *Head. I have a head, some small part of form.* The dark clung. He concentrated, forcing himself toward the gleaming luminescence, and the tiny point grew. He yelled with delight. *The head has a mouth. I can make noise.* He yelled, screamed and bellowed because he could. The sounds rang hollow to his ears in the encompassing murk. *Ears. I have ears. A head with ears and a mouth. I must have eyes, too; I can see the light. Or am I just sensing it?*

His concentration wandered and he slipped away from that alluring shimmer. "No!" he screamed. Heat and cold together flashed through his arms. *I have arms.* He flailed with swimming motions. Mind driving, arms pumping, he swooped toward the light.

The blackness attacked. His head imploded, as the tormenting angry fingers squeezed. He rested for a moment. The light receded. *Just relax, and the pain will lessen. Why am I fighting? Aren't I dead anyway? Where is my angel? If I could be with her, I could rest here forever. Forever, yes . . . No! Forever in this blackness? I see no angel. Angels like the light.*

He set his teeth against the pain, willed the tiredness away. *I must rise to that light.* The pain gripped with white-hot fingers. His muscles burned with agony. He struggled, swam harder, fixated on that faraway beacon.

A hot swell of rage flashed through his trunk as the breath of a dragon to his legs, engaged them in the battle. *I have form. Human form. I'm called a human. I have arms to swim, legs to kick, a mind.* He gritted his teeth, kicked and swam, frantic, compelled the devastated mind to lead. The glow expanded, bright, beckoning. It blinded. *I need eyes to be blinded. Don't I?* He pumped with his newfound limbs.

The glare filled his horizon. *I have to escape.* The rage that he had felt before roiled inside, pushed him. With its irresistible force, he focused, fought the debilitating crush of pain. Face twisting, teeth clenched, he surged toward the summoning starpoint.

Everything changed. He could feel his entire form, lying covered upon soft warmth. Blackness still surrounded him . . . but different. The pain pounded but no longer gripped. *Where are my eyes? I can't see a thing. Where to look for my eyes?* He nearly laughed at the thought. *The eyes did the looking, didn't they? That's it? I can't find my eyes, because I need them to look.* The thought exhausted him. His head ached, hammering behind his left ear.

All his limbs felt heavy, sluggish, moving them an arduous effort. He pursed his mouth, wrinkled his nose and waggled his jaw.

A scraping noise sounded, close. He froze. *What's there? My angel? If only I could find my eyes.*

A soft, feminine voice floated above him. The words wafted against his ears without meaning, but the sound comforted. It belonged to a human. He tried to speak but emitted only a strangled groan. A different voice spoke, feminine, deeper, excited. He didn't understand.

The cover moved and a warm hand touched his chest.

The females talked, voices flitting across him. A hand stroked his forehead. *My angel? Not possible. I wouldn't be in heaven. Why not? Maybe the angel will know.* He turned his head toward her touch. She spoke, and her fingertips slid down his closed eyelids.

My eyes. Right where they belong. He forced them open, meeting a pair of warm blue ones. *Not my angel.*

The women sat, one on each side, legs folded, knees almost touching him. The friendly blue eyes met his. The full mouth curved into a half-smile and spoke.

Her words made no sense. Confusion and the relentless pounding headache obscured his ability to reason. He sensed softness beneath him and a light cover lay on top. He gazed about, assessing his environment. It seemed to be a room, with an ambience of rugged opulence—a square bed of hewn logs but soft quilts, an unlit metal chandelier holding candles for light, chairs of rough-cut lumber with padded seats and backs, chest and trunks to tuck away clothing, hand-painted drawings on the wall. A flowery, haunting scent floated in the air, mixed with the tang of strong soap. With a bed across the room, why was he on the floor?

Intense thirst consumed him. He tried to ask for water, but his dry throat and mouth released only a hoarse croak.

The second woman produced a large earthenware jar.

The blue-eyed woman slid close, gently ran her arm under his shoulders, lifted. He struggled to help, but pain like dagger stabs paralyzed him, seared down his neck, across his shoulders. The other woman slipped pillows behind him for support. He closed his eyes and breathed in shallow jerks until the pain lessened.

He gulped as the woman held the jar, tilting it to his lips. The cold, wet deluge flowed across his parched tongue, through his dry mouth and down his tight throat. He lost himself in the bliss, the euphoria. Sated, he slumped against the pillows and smiled. "Thank you."

The women conversed in that speech he couldn't fathom. His ears pricked as a sentence ended, ". . . Universal Language." That he understood.

"I know Universal," he said.

"Do you?" The blue-eyed one smiled. "I am glad. We can converse. I shall lay you down. Relax. Let me do the work."

She gently lowered him. Agony sliced through his head and neck. He squeezed his eyes shut, gritted his teeth and again breathed in shallow gasps until the pain eased. When he reopened his eyes, the women sat as before, waiting.

"Are you hungry? We have food coming," blue eyes said.

He recognized the empty, burning feeling under his ribs as hunger. "Yes, I am. Thank you." He searched for words in his confused, murky mind to express his thoughts. "Who are you? Where am I? Why am I here? What's wrong with me? How did I—"

"Hold," she said. "One question at a time, please. I am Alea, your healer. This is Gorsa, my assistant."

"Healer?" He tasted the word. "As in doctor?"

"I do not know doctor. A healer helps the sick become well."

"That's as in doctor." He gave her a tiny smile.

"Then we have both learned. You understand me?"

"Well enough. You are Alea." He stumbled over the pronunciation, trying to wrap his tongue around the word as she had. He pointed to the other woman. "She is Gorsa. I am . . ." He stopped and his eyes flared wide; both hands clasped his cover.

His mind lurched in anguish. He squeezed his eyes shut, looking inward, trying to find himself. Before the battle to escape the blackness, his mind was a total blank. There resided in his head no memory, as though time before the blackness didn't exist. He had language, he knew things, the healers to be female, himself male. Certain knowledge lay within him, but the source was a mystery. *Who am I? Where am I? Why am I here?* Vacuum . . . nothing. He began to gasp, unable to suck in a full breath. His throat burned, jaw clenched. Surely time existed before the dark void. But what? Where? Who? He didn't know and the not knowing set his heart slamming into his ribs.

A cry from Alea jolted him from his perplexed dread. Her hand slid under the cover over his heart. It thudded wildly. "What is it, Queen's Man? Open your eyes. Talk to me."

He managed a long, shaky, settling breath, swallowed deeply and opened his eyes. "I don't know who I am." His voice carried an edge of panic. "I don't know where I came from. I only remember being here with you . . . and the blackness. That awful blackness."

"Seek calmness, Queen's Man. This is not unusual. You suffered a grievous head injury, laid unconscious for days. Your confusion is to be expected. Fretting cannot help. Tell me of this blackness."

He told her, but not all of it—not of the vague memory of waking before or his angel. He would hold his angel secret.

She took his hand in hers and stroked the fingers, a soothing, mesmerizing motion.

He relaxed, calming.

"The blackness," she said, "was manifestation of your struggle to return to a conscious state. It will not reappear. You are conscious and will remain so."

Several women arrived, carrying a footed tray containing covered dishes. They brought armloads of pillows.

Alea gestured for them to halt and wait.

They complied, and he noted the newcomers eyeing him with intense curiosity.

Alea said, "Your memory will likely return, in a few hours, a few days, maybe longer . . . when it is ready. You needs be patient.

Your food is here. You must eat to regain strength. Afterwards, I will answer questions. I must lift you again."

He closed his eyes, hoping the pain to be less. It wasn't. He gasped, fought it, vaguely aware of the women tucking pillows around him.

Alea slid her arm from behind him.

The women made quick pillow adjustments and stepped back. He sat almost upright, every inch of his body, hips, back, neck and head, comfortably supported. The pain abated, and he opened his eyes.

Alea gestured.

The woman carrying the tray placed it across his lap. Her eyes lifted shyly, then she dipped into a curtsey and backed away a step. Alea interpreted as the woman murmured in that strange language, "Your dinner, Queen's Man. We provided choice of food and drink." She removed lids from the dishes. "I will feed you if you wish."

He glanced at Alea. "I can eat for myself, thank you. What is this queen's man? Surely, that's not my name."

"No," Alea said, "not your name, your status. We will discuss that later too. Thank the servants and dismiss them. Then you must eat."

"Dismiss?"

"Just thank and dismiss them," she said firmly.

He smiled a tentative grimace. "Thank you, ladies, and you're dismissed."

The women smiled, curtsied and retreated.

"Why are they acting like that, Alea?" he asked. "What do you know about me you're not telling?"

The healer crossed her arms. "I know nothing of you. Eat your meal. I will talk only then."

His stomach rumbled. On the tray lay an attractive array of foods—a portion of light meat; a baked potato, split in the skin; a green leafy substance; a pile of red, oval beans; cheese wafting a pungent odor; several breads, dark and darker, with butter and jams; and a purple, squishy-looking dessert. Four casters offered water, apple juice by the look and smell, coffee and milk. He lifted a wooden utensil, which resembled a fork, speared a piece of meat and placed it in his mouth. It tasted well cooked, lightly seasoned, tender and delicious. He swallowed.

"This is wonderful," he said. "What is it?"

"It is paaerta, a wild pig which lives on this island."

"Island?" he asked, forking another piece of meat into his mouth, manners forgotten, his hunger overwhelming.

Alea motioned toward his food, and he ate. Finally satisfied, she spoke. "You are on the island of Kriiscon, in Rejeena's Towne, in Rejeena's home, occupying Rejeena's summer skindown room."

He glanced at her, still eating. "Skindown? And what is a Rejeena?"

Gorsa winced then rolled her eyes.

"Skindown is a resting place or bed." Alea's voice hardened to threat. "Rejeena is the queen. You belong to her, hence the term *queen's man*. At a wave of her hand, she can have you beaten, killed, or your balls cut off making of you a eunuch. In future, speak with respect."

He lowered his utensil and stared. "I'm sorry. I meant no disrespect, Alea." Bitter bile churned in his stomach. *I belong to a queen? Belong? Something is highly off-kilter here.* Though curious and apprehensive, he held his questions.

Her hand fell gently onto his shoulder. "I am the one to be sorry, Queen's Man. You will require much teaching. I wrongly used the queen's name without her title, so how could you know? Remember to always show respect for the queen. When speaking to her, call her my queen. When speaking of her, always use her title, Queen Rejeena. Do you think you can remember that?"

"Yes, now you've explained."

"Do not be angry, Queen's Man. We will have misunderstandings. Anger will not solve them."

"I'm not angry. You took me by surprise." He drank some apple juice. Eyeing her obliquely, he asked, "Would this queen really make me a eunuch?"

Both Alea and Gorsa burst out laughing. "If you remain properly respectful, I think you need not worry."

He laid his utensil down. "Surely, you don't expect me to eat all this."

"You need not," Alea said. "As queen's man, you were granted choices. In future, you may request that which pleases you."

"Thank goodness. The food is great, just far too much."

She handed him a small mug. "If you are finished eating, you needs drink this."

He stared at the mug, brows drawn. "What is it?"

"It is for pain. Drink it."

He drank it, making a face. "What about my questions?"

Gorsa took his tray and carried it away.

Alea settled back. "I will tell you what I know. A group of wander women brought you into the towne. They acquired you after killing a band of loose men. The queen selected you as queen's man and bartered you from them."

He stared. "Wander women? Loose men? Bartered? You lost me."

She smiled. "You really do not know much, do you? Wander women are bands of women who roam about without proper affiliation or loyalty. They trade, steal when they can, must be watched. They are held untrustworthy, not of good woman status. Loose men are groups of males, not enholded. They are born of this island, and we women hold them to enemy status. We utilize some for the acquiring of offspring, kill others as needed."

"Am I a loose man?"

"No. You are a holdee, with the elevated status of queen's man."

"Holdee?"

"Those are our male . . ." Alea snapped her fingers, appealing to Gorsa, who had reentered. "What would that be in Universal?"

"Slaves?" Gorsa said.

"That is close enough. Male slaves. We use holdees for mating, work, whatever women require of them."

"Is that what I am . . . a slave?"

"Yes, to the queen."

He tilted his head, brows lowering. "Slave? Why am I a slave?"

"On Kriiscon women rule. All men are slaves—holdees—except those who ramble loose, those we destroy. It is the way of it."

Face scrunching, he squeezed his eyes shut. Something heaved into view in his mind for a second then vanished—a confused vision of women ruling, men as slaves, but he couldn't retain or place the thought. But it did support Alea's declaration. He opened his eyes. "If I'm not a loose man, why was I with them? Why did these wander women kill the loose men and not me?"

"We do not know why the loose men held you. The wander women stated you appeared to be their captive, bound hand and foot. Your clothing declared you Mainlander, and a man so handsome as you will always be captured alive."

He sighed, pressed the heels of his hands against his forehead. "The more questions you answer, Alea, the more confused I become. What's a Mainlander?"

"Those not aborned of this island."

He nodded. "Why would these loose men hold me captive? Am I their enemy? Are they the ones who hit me?"

"All stand enemy to loose men except themselves, and often they hate other groups. Consider it fortunate they did not cut your throat. We know not who hit you. The wander women could not say."

Exhaustion descended upon him, eyes growing heavy, mind languid. "Could I ask one more question?"

"One more only, then you must rest."

"What does the queen want from me?"

Alea smiled. "I think we shall hold that question for later. It will require time to answer." She eased her arm behind him.

Gorsa removed the pillows.

"Could I lie on my side, please?" he asked.

"Yes, but it will cause you pain."

"It's going to anyway."

"You just relax. We will move you."

She laid him down, turning him. Gorsa gripped his hips and eased them over. The severe pain wrung a groan from him despite his efforts to suppress it. By the time the pain ebbed, he lay comfortably on his side. They tucked pillows around him for support.

He glanced at his body. He wore short pants reaching halfway down his thighs, made of a soft beaten skin, a double-sided opening at his groin. He didn't recognize the pants. Before sleep overcame him, he wondered who had put them on him and when. He was not even aware when Alea and Gorsa covered him.

* * *

Queen Rejeena conferred with Carlea, her barter stewarda. "Carlea, I have been informed the queen's man has awakened. Determine if Alea feels he will recover. If so, barter him from the wander women."

Carlea smiled. "I already spoke with Alea, who gave her assent, My Queen. However, the wander women show most greedy. I do not advise barter unless they lower their demands."

"I value your barter advice, but much stands at stake," Rejeena said. "I must needs trek to Squalla's Towne to approve a new land leader for that packet. As you know, Squalla has danced upon the four winds for several moonchanges. I have before deferred their needs; I cannot again. I would expect no more than three days will be required. Negotiations rest in your hands. Use any reasonable means to lower the wanders' barter demand. But understand this—I will own that man."

"I understand, My Queen, and will so barter. Consider the man yours." Carlea curtsied and departed.

* * *

Alea returned to the queen's skindown room the next morning with Renfra. The man slept propped on pillows. Gorsa and Wecan conversed and sewed.

"Alea, you did not warn me." Wecan grinned and arose.

"About what?"

"His voice. Soft, warm like a summer breeze along the cheek. And those eyes. A woman could drown in those eyes. Considering his attributes, I weighed rutting him by force right here in the queen's home. He remains too weak to resist."

"You needs take action about your skindown urges, Wecan," Alea laughed. "Get a weighted holdee, and cease lusting after the queen's man."

"Holdees seldom come both weighted and with looks. The sacrifices I make for my queen." Wecan pointed. "He decided upon that position, appeared tired of lying down. He seems not a patient man."

Alea shrugged. "So long as he is comfortable. Did all proceed well last night?"

"He received fitting care. We fed him breakfast. Then we bathed him." Wecan snickered. "That greatly embarrassed him. He turns red in the most fascinating places."

Gorsa said, "He simply closed his eyes and turned his face away until Wecan teased him. Then he turned colors."

"Wecan," Alea scolded, "show restraint. He is queen's man."

"I know, but he is so delectable. Have you noticed that cute keister? It pleads to be rubbed and fondled."

"I did notice. However, rubbing and fondling must be left for the queen. You two scat and get some rest."

Alea knelt beside her patient. She pressed her fingers against the side of his throat to take his pulse, and the midnight blue eyes popped open.

"Alea."

"I did not intend to wake you."

"I'm glad you did. You have some questions to answer."

"This is Renfra." Alea waved toward her helper.

"Hello, Renfra."

Renfra said, "Hello, Queen's Man."

"May I sit up?" he asked.

The women helped him fully upright and made him comfortable with pillows. His face twisted but not as much as the previous day.

Renfra walked toward the door. "I will bring refreshments."

Alea settled beside him, looked into his eyes, deep as a mountain glaalet cave, calm as unruffled water, inexplicably innocent for a grown man. "All right, Queen's Man, ask your questions."

"We left off where I was the queen's slave. You were to tell me what she expects. You said it would take a while."

"I flung falsehood, so you would go to sleep. The answer is short." She gestured toward the queen's skindown across the room. "Do you know what that is?"

"Well, it looks like a bed . . . a skindown, right?"

"Correct. When your head injury allows, you will there serve your queen."

He started, brows jerked low, gaze flicked from the skindown to her face. Scarlet crept up his cheeks. "You're teasing me."

"No, I am not. Your purpose is to share skindown with the queen, causing her to produce daughters."

"My purpose?"

"Well, except for your decorative duties." She grinned.

"My what?"

Renfra returned with the small short-legged serving table. She placed the table across his lap and poured casters of milk.

He and Alea stared at each other, the woman displaying a smug smile, the man with beetled brows.

Renfra took her milk and settled on a pillow.

"Decorative duties. The queen will display you at hearing," Alea said, "Queens' Council and other places where all women may marvel over the striking queen's man she has acquired."

He wrinkled a lip, glanced sideways at the healer, picked up his caster and took a drink. "Now I know you're teasing. That's ridiculous."

She leaned forward, eyes boring into his. "I do not tease. You are queen's man. You will share skindown with the queen, look gorgeous when she wills it, and anything else the queen requires of you, when she requires it, in the manner she chooses. You will bow to her, call her my queen, be respectful, obedient and appear incredibly handsome all the while. That is why you receive such good care, have servants to tend your every whim, abide in the queen's home, warm and comfortable."

He set down the flasket, eyes following it. He looked up. "You're serious?"

"Yes."

"I see." He sat silent, picked up his milk and drank, eyes lowered, crinkled at the corners.

The healer watched him. *What is he thinking?*

He set the caster down and met her eyes, his blank, unreadable. "Suppose I choose not to share skindown with the queen?"

Sensing he tested more than challenged, she maintained a firm, gentle demeanor. "That choice is not yours. You will accede to the queen's desires."

"Why?"

She sighed. *Will this man question everything?* "I will explain, so maybe you may understand. You still remember nothing?"

"No, nothing." A grin tickled the corners of his mouth. "At this moment, what I got myself out of seems pale besides what I've gotten myself into."

Alea smiled. "You are Mainlander. On the Mainland, as I understand it, men rule, are keepers of the power, have most say in occurrences. The women bear offspring, maintain the home fires and are expected to be docile and obedient. Men and women commit to each other for life, an arrangement called marriage, a most unnatural situation.

"I have never been to the Mainland, so I tell you only what garnered from rumor. All persons, particularly men, are free as they call it, run around willy-nilly, doing that which they wish."

"Sounds pretty good to me," he said.

"It seems useless and futile. I cannot see how there would be any organization. But then, with men at rule, what would one expect?"

"What indeed?"

"Do you want to hear this or not, Queen's Man?"

"Yes. I'm sorry. Please go on."

"On Kriiscon, we organize properly. Women grip the reins of power. We do that which pleases LaSheena. Men stand enholded, used for only sensible purposes. Kept under control, men are not granted choices and thus remain harmless. They belong to a mistress, who holds all power. If holdees displease their mistress, she can have them whipped, castrated and sent to work in the clay mines, or put to death."

Alea stopped and took a long swig of milk. "Since we wish to maintain a low number of men, we share. A woman utilizes a man to garner offspring, then passes him to others. Some men live their whole lives sharing skindown with whatever woman desires completion. Big, strong men with no skindown value work on farms or in clay mines. Some we use both for acquiring offspring and for work around the townes."

She poked him lightly on the chest. "Fortunate men may be chosen by a queen to be queen's man. A queen does not share; he is for her alone. The queen holds complete, absolute power. I cannot stress this too much. Should you enrage the queen, no power this side of LaSheena can assist you. You needs heed my words and think only in terms of pleasing her."

He spent a few moments sorting this information. Finally, he repeated, "I see." He pursed his lips. "You mentioned a LaSheena?"

"LaSheena is Goddess. She directs that which occurs on the island . . . and holds women in favor."

He grinned. "I'll just bet she does. What is the queen like?"

"You will meet the queen in due time."

"When would that be?"

"When she deems it appropriate," Alea said. "I do not know the space of time she will allow us to domesticate you, teach you proper manners so she will not kill you immediately." The healer frowned. "The queen is neither patient nor forgiving. She expects instant obedience, complete compliance, is quick and harsh with punishment. She possesses small sense of humor."

"Sounds like a charming lady."

"That is precisely what I mean, Queen's Man." Alea shook a finger under his nose. "Such remarks will garner you severe punishment. And do not call us ladies. That is a disgusting Mainland term. We are women."

"Well, pardon me, I'll try to remember that. Why did the queen choose me?"

Alea sipped her milk. She set the serving table aside and flipped the cover from his body. "Look at yourself, Queen's Man. You stand a most fetching skindown piece. We cannot find a single flaw, and believe me, we have looked." She grinned as he flushed red. "Sharing skindown with a handsome man heightens the pleasure. It is the birthright of queens to acquire the best-looking men. As well, you have a verified eighty-five percent rate. You are heavily weighted."

His brows slashed down.

She continued, forestalling questions. "Most importantly, LaHeeka, the ancient conjurah, instructed the queen to take you as queen's man."

He pushed the air from his lungs. "Why is it, Alea, when you answer a question, you give me more questions than answers?"

She chuckled. "Probably because you know so little. Most holdees, even Mainlanders, know something of our ways. You appear totally ignorant." Her voice gentled. "Perhaps because you lack memory."

He stared at the table. "I wish I could remember . . . anything."

Alea patted his leg. "I cannot pretend to know what you feel. Your memory should return in time. It could be days, weeks, a season turning."

"Or never."

"Or never. Only LaSheena knows. You must be patient."

"It's not easy. I am so . . . so lost."

"We shall guide you until your memory returns."

"As you describe your queen, I'm not sure you offer choice guidance." He frowned. "Why did you call me a skindown piece?"

"The term describes a good-looking man with skindown potential."

"Skindown potential? Skindown piece? Isn't that disrespectful and belittling?"

"Men do not merit respect, Queen's Man. They are not women."

"Assuredly we're not. I disagree with the rest." He heaved a sigh and paused. "What is an ancient conjurah?"

"A conjurah is a wise woman, a mystic, like a witch on the Mainland. Only," Alea added hastily, "a good witch. Conjurahs see and feel beyond the normal ken—possess anomalous powers, stand capable of transcendent acts and functions." The healer ignored the skeptical look that crossed his face. "They spend their lives learning, teaching, conjuring, casting or removing spells and curses, aiding all women. They advise queens, stand respected and revered."

"Why ancient?" A vision of the old crone at his feet when he had previously awakened flashed through his mind. *Did I wake, or was it just a dream?*

"LaHeeka is very old. She conjured before many women were aborned. When a conjurah reaches that age and status, rises to such level of accomplishment—and LaHeeka is very accomplished—then she becomes an ancient conjurah. Only LaSheena holds higher status."

"Why did this ancient conjurah pick me?"

"The queen will answer that question when she so chooses."

"All right." His eyes squinted. "You called me weighted. What does that mean? What is this eighty-five percent rate? Is it important?"

Renfra chuckled and tossed her head. "Explain that, Alea."

Alea rose, her face twisted. "The answer to that I fear will lead into a quagmire."

"What answer hasn't?"

"Some of the information will not please you. If you do not interrupt me, I will explain."

"Fair enough."

Renfra arose. "I will bring coffee and a light lunch." She flicked her gaze at the queen's man. "Somebody shall need it."

Alea took a deep breath. "Since we comprise a society of women, men held to few and enholded, the need to produce mostly female offspring stands vital."

He nodded.

"By studying the results of skindown liaisons over the seasons, a great conjurah of seasons past concluded that the male determines the gender of offspring. We do not know how, but it is so. She developed a concoction, which mixed with a man's offspring shot, indicates what percent of his issue will be useless males or desired daughters. Shot, which will produce males, turns yellow, daughters green. A man whose shot shows mostly yellow will not be sought for mating, useful only for work. A man whose shot shows mainly green is most valuable. Women will rut him hoping to acquire a daughter. The higher the percentage of green, the more valuable the man."

Alea rose and paced before the queen's man. "As you showed eighty-five percent green, you stand very valuable. Only fifteen percent of your issue will be males. Men with seventy-five percent or higher rates are rare. Most women must risk fortune with men testing fifty to sixty per cent. We refer to men with high rates as weighted." Alea smiled, watching him. "Weighted between the legs."

He flushed. "If I am so valuable, how can the queen afford to kill me for some small infraction?"

"She would not actually kill you. But the queen metes punishment quickly and harshly when deserved. She could punish you severely and still have the use of you, so be respectful and obedient."

"That's how you train a dog," he muttered. "Demand obedience, reward good behavior and punish bad."

"You have grasped the concept, Queen's Man."

He peered at her sideways. "How do you determine the percentage of a man's rate? How do you get his . . . offspring shot?"

"Are you dense? There is but one way."

His flush deepened. "You did that to me?"

"The wander women did."

"How do you know those untrustworthy women don't lie, Alea?"

"It is unlawful to misrepresent a man's offspring rate. Punishment would be severe. Misrepresenting to a queen would be suicidal." She grinned. "Of course, if it concerns you for your queen, we could test you again."

"No! No, that's all right. I'll pass."

Alea laughed.

He frowned. "Suppose you have a holdee who tests mostly yellow. He's a skinny little runt, no use for work. What do you do with him?"

Renfra returned carrying a serving table with lunch. She settled the table and arranged the food and drink.

Alea sat also. "That question, I held hope you would not ask. The answer could incite you."

He just looked at her.

She sighed. "He would be executed if he were a loose man. If Mainlander, depending upon the disposition of his mistress, he might be released across the border. If he causes harm or it is inconvenient, he would be executed."

He stared. "Just like that? The guy is an inconvenience, so you kill him?"

"I told you, you would not like the answer."

"If he's a loose man, he has no chance at all?"

"None. A Mainlander can return to the Mainland. We have no quarrel with those who stay where they belong. A loose man is indigene. Our affinity with loose men is ever hostile. If he holds no use, he holds no value. He would be executed so he in turn cannot kill women."

"I see." He contemplated, gaze fixed on the floor. "You referred to a border. I thought this is an island."

"It is. Seasons ago, Mainlanders invaded causing a cruel, costly war. The price in lives, time and effort weighed so heavily on both sides that we agreed to make peace. The greedy Mainlanders annexed portions of the outer lands. There remains a border that none may cross."

"I suppose everyone obeys." Sarcasm etched his soft voice.

"Outposts and border patrols abound, Queen's Man. Skirmishes occur, but a shaky peace far surpasses war."

He nodded. "Yes, of course."

"Let us stop for lunch," Alea said. She placed a hand on his forearm. "I can see you are disturbed."

He stared at her, eyes narrow, voice low and hoarse. "It isn't right for a man's life to depend on an offspring rate or inconvenience."

The healer nibbled at her lunch of bread, cheese, dried meat and fruit. "Right is not considered, Queen's Man. It is our way. It works well."

"I wonder if the men you kill would agree?"

"Men who hold no value are as old shoes, using space, making clutter. That which is no longer useful must be discarded."

He lapsed into silence, face smoothing to bland, obscuring his thoughts.

Alea liked this queen's man, sensed in him a depth, a difference from any man she had ever known. An aura about him of unfeigned innocence made her want to protect him. His midnight blue eyes were guileless, forthright, and his curiosity understandable. He had awakened in a place about which he knew nothing, without memory. How utterly lost he must feel. Considering all, he was handling it well. Some of her answers could not be helping his state of mind.

He must subjugate himself to the queen for his own good. She sensed within him resistance to subjugation. If she could convince him to submerge this resistance before he and the queen clashed, his life would be more pleasant.

The door snapped open. In breezed Wecan. "Such long faces. Are we quarreling?"

Alea sighed. "The queen's man learns of our ways. He is not pleased."

The queen's man didn't respond.

Wecan sat beside Renfra.

Alea tired of the silence. "What are you thinking, Queen's Man?"

His solemn eyes met hers. "I think this isn't a good place to be a man."

The voice and eyes stabbed at Alea's heart. "You need not be wretched. As queen's man, your status protects you. None but the queen may visit punishment upon you. You needs please only her. If you do that, you may enjoy a good life."

"As a slave?"

"As an elevated holdee, yes."

"And my fellow holdees? I can enjoy a good life, while watching them beaten and killed?"

"What is unchangeable must be accepted."

His voice hardened as dried clay. "Unchangeable?" For a tiny flick of time, a burst of feral fury stabbed from his eyes then vanished.

Alea's breath paused as though a sledgehammer slammed into her chest.

A long silent moment passed.

He spoke, voice soft again. "Suppose I don't like your queen, this woman I've never met who has claimed me? What if I can't—or won't—please her?"

Alea, pulling air back into her lungs, wondered if she imagined that flick of ferocity. *Surely I did!* She noted the deliberate inflection in his second question—the *won't* as opposed to the *can't.* "My queen," she corrected. "You say always our queen. You must call her *my queen.*"

"All right then. Suppose I can't tolerate . . . my queen?"

"Then you needs pretend well."

"I've no skill for pretense."

"It is a skill you needs develop if you do not like the queen. Perhaps I described her too harshly. She holds to hard ways, but she is strong and good, can be gentle and affectionate, was once a happy woman. Do not forejudge the queen, but understand she expects obedience and respect. If you learn nothing else, learn that."

"I'm beginning to understand. I can be respectful but obedient is a giant's step away. I will not sleep . . . share skindown with a woman I don't like." His calm eyes locked with Alea's.

A shiver raced through Alea. She recalled that flash of ferocity, remembered LaHeeka's warning, which she had heard through rumor, of his strength and power, the danger of him. This man might stand his ground and test the queen. If he tested beyond Rejeena's threshold of tolerance, confrontation would follow. The healer winced. She liked this queen's man, and dearly loved her friend, Rejeena.

Alea sighed. "Queen's Man, I wonder at LaHeeka's wisdom to demand the queen accept you."

He displayed a lightning mood change, flashed an impudent grin. "She is the ancient conjurah, the most powerful, wise woman. She sees all, knows all." He cocked his head, eyes dancing. "You dare question her?"

Renfra and Wecan snickered.

"You are an ass." Alea rose and handed the serving table to Renfra, who left grinning.

Alea looked down. He watched her, eyes at once innocent and all too knowing. She said, "It is time you rest. Enough questions for now."

"I'd like to get up and go outside," he said. "I'm so sick of this room I could puke."

She crossed her arms. "Queen's Man, you will not get up and go anywhere. It is a lovely day, though, and the queen's garden is magnificent. We shall carry you out."

"Oh, I think I can . . ." He put one hand on the pallet and pushed upward, started to rise. He grimaced and dropped back, sat gritting his teeth, eyes clenched. After a few moments he peeked at her sheepishly. "On second thought, you're right."

"Wecan, please get a pair of long pants and a jacket," Alea said. "There remains chill in the outside air. I will place a pallet."

Wecan took the long pants from a bureau and knelt beside him, pulling the pillows away. She began to unfasten his short pants.

"I can do that," he said hastily.

"You would swoon if you tried," she scoffed. "Now clamp jaw and allow us our function." She finished the unfastening and ran her hands down his hips beneath the pants.

He reddened.

Renfra, just returned, pushed her hands under his back and hips, lifting him.

Wecan slid the pants off. She shook out the long pants, gaze roaming the length of him, deliberately lingering at his groin. She said to Renfra, who still knelt by him, "Now that is the position and status LaSheena requires for a good-looking, weighted man—naked, in skindown."

Renfra giggled. "You are right," she observed from her close vantage point, "he does turn red in the most interesting places."

"Will you two stop it," he growled. "You're supposed to be healers, not lechers."

"We strive to enjoy our function, Queen's Man." Wecan knelt and smoothly slid the pants onto him. She smirked as they helped him into the jacket. "We would have allowed you more dignity if you had not so provoked Alea."

"You laughed. You thought it funny."

"You must still pay a price."

He glared.

Alea broke into their squabble. "If you have finished badgering the queen's man, servants await to carry him outside."

They placed him, lightly covered on a warm pallet in the garden. The jostling sent pain shooting through his head and neck.

"Drink this." Alea gave him more medicine. "Renfra will remain, but do not bother her with questions. I want you to rest." Alea and Wecan departed.

He relaxed and lay quietly, breathing deeply of the sweet spring air, enjoying the weak sunshine on his face. The subtle perfume of early season blooms wafted on the air currents.

When Alea checked later, Renfra sat plaiting a mat from dried flatweed leaves. The queen's man slept.

Alea sat beside Renfra. "I dread what may occur when he meets the queen. We require time to tame this one. If our queen must tame him, he will not like it."

Renfra's hands skillfully plaited. She nodded. "He is much too fine-looking for strikepaddle sessions."

Alea mused, "I needs find an argument to convince him he must follow the queen's edicts. He is but a man. He has not choices."

"He is Mainlander. Mainlanders do not easily adjust to our ways."

"Would that it were merely a matter of adjustment. I sense about him strength, tenacity"—Alea shivered slightly—"a fierceness as though he will expect adjustment rather than to adjust."

"If so, the queen will teach him the meaning of adjustment." The two women sat silent.

* * *

Returning early the next day, Alea heard the click of muskee, a game of throwing numbered blocks, gaining one cull, a small round disk, per point. Whoever collected the most culls won; some combination of numbers granted extra culls. Any gamess who acquired the goddess cull almost certainly won the game. As she entered, the soft voice of the queen's man said, "Give me seven, Wecan."

"Seven? Nobody wins seven. You cheat, Queen's Man."

"How can I cheat? You throw the blocks. They land. You count the points." Sitting on the pallet, upright, pillows askew, he chuckled.

"I see you feel better," Alea said.

He greeted her with a smile.

She dropped to her knees, caught his head and inspected the wound. "Your lump is smaller. The ointment and treatments function. Have you suffered any neck or back pains?"

"A few." He smiled wickedly. "But Wecan jumped right on me."

"I did not jump on you," Wecan said. "Gorsa and I granted you care."

"Isn't that what I said?"

"Ass." Wecan snatched five of his muskee culls.

"Put those back."

She held tight to the culls. "I fine you for badgering of healers."

"That's not part of the rules."

"I make a new rule."

"Well, I'm fining you for patient badgering." He lunged for her culls, a rock eagle swooping upon prey. Then he groaned, grabbed at his neck, and collapsed backward.

Alea grabbed, catching him with both arms. She sat motionless, held him gently.

He crumpled against her and murmured unfamiliar words, gritting his teeth. Breathing in shallow gulps, he appeared to wait for the stabbing agony to pass. Finally he straightened, teeth clamped and managed a weak grin.

"That was unwise, Queen's Man," Alea said.

"Do tell."

Wecan leaned forward. "I did not wish to cause you pain."

"It wasn't your fault." He opened his hand, displaying eight muskee culls. "But you have been fined."

"Why you sneaky, lowdown man," Wecan sputtered. "Give those back."

"Nope. You got five; I got eight. I'm ahead."

Wecan grabbed for his hand. He clenched and jerked it back.

Alea warned, "No more of that. The queen's man is vulnerable. Have you eaten?" she asked him.

"Yes."

"Good. Wecan, take this game away. We have serious lessons today."

When everyone sat comfortably, Alea began. "The island of Kriiscon is governed by queens and land leaders. A queen rules and upholds the law in a quarter; there are eight quarters. A land leader rules a packet; there are eight packets per quarter. The great queen reigns supreme over all."

"Eight quarters?"

Alea frowned. "They have been so called since ancient times. No one seems to know why."

"So everybody obeys these laws?"

"No, there are outlaw bands, loose men, wander women and other miscreants. Some seek contact. Others maintain distance between themselves and all women. It is dangerous to travel without arms. Outlaws stand ever on the lookout to steal what is not theirs. Sometimes they kill. Loose men will attack a small group."

"This is your fine, organized society, perfectly run by women?" His eyes danced.

The healer flushed. "We strive always to improve. Nothing is perfect. Clamp jaw. I speak, not you." She continued. "You abide presently in Rejeena's Towne. A towne is named after the current most-prominent woman. When the leader changes, the towne name changes. This towne carries the queen's name. We also have a land leader, Parria, who runs this packet. You will meet her later.

"It is vital you understand your place," Alea said.

"My place?"

"As queen's man, the rules for your behavior are different than those of a mere holdee."

"Rules for my behavior?"

"That is what I said."

His black brows lowered.

"A holdee must call all women mistress, never use her name. As queen's man, you need only call important personages mistress. All others you may call by name, or shiira."

"Shiira?"

"It is of Oldenspeak used with someone of equal status. Holdees never use that term. All women stand superior to them."

Those expressive brows pulled lower.

"Queen's men are held equal in rank to most women."

"How do I recognize these important personages?" he asked.

"Queens will be so introduced. You need not guess. You must bow to queens and refer to them by title. All land leaders, conjurahs of lesser rank than great, certain commerce women and religious leaders, will be mistress. Usually you will know, when you meet a woman, if she is important. If you have doubt, call her mistress. Should she not require the title, she will feel flattered. If she does, you will not insult her. All others—women of the allways, guards, healers and wander women—will be shiira. If you know them well, you may use names. All holdees and the queen's servants must call you queen's man. The guards, as a matter of respect, will also. It has to do with their guard code. Those of shiira or higher rank may call you queen's man or by your name."

"If I had a name."

"It should come to you in time." Alea continued. "Conjurahs are of four ranks—learner, conjurah, great and ancient. When you meet a great conjurah, you will call her by title. If you ever meet an ancient conjurah or the great queen, you will bow, lower your head, be silent and remain so until reprieved. You must so remember. Is that clear, Queen's Man?"

"Arf. Arf. Very clear."

"This is most serious. Speaking or raising your head without permission before the great queen or an ancient conjurah comprises an unspeakable social gaffe that would greatly embarrass your queen. You could be severely punished. Do you understand?"

"Yes, Alea."

"Good. You have much to learn. I despair teaching you all in the time available. But I must try. Now pay attention."

"Yes, Alea." He heaved an audible sigh.

"This is most vital. Skindown activity with other women—"

"I get to have skindown activity with other women?" His eyes danced with feigned delight, causing giggles from Gorsa and Wecan.

"No!" Alea exploded. "Absolutely not. Will you clamp jaw and listen. You may never, so long as you are queen's man, have skindown liaisons with any other woman. You belong completely to the queen. If you are found to have indulged at skindown with another woman, you will both be executed immediately. It is an intolerable offense. Please understand that, Queen's Man." She stared at him. "We are talking dead—painfully dead."

He raised a placating hand. "I got it, Alea, no playing the field. None. Keep my pants buttoned."

"Well, I am glad you understand something. I suspect you do not take our rules seriously. That concerns me. Though you are merely a man, I like you and pray to LaSheena the queen and you will enjoy a pleasant, comfortable time together."

"Alea, I hear what you say. If something is not clear, I'll ask. If I get in trouble, it'll not be for your lack as a teacher." He added with a flash of pique, "Sometimes you sound like you think you're my mother."

"If you do as I say, you need have no trouble." She paused. "Would that I were your mother. I would have reared you without this atrocious outlook that you intone against proper rules."

She pointed. "Only queen's men wear those pants with the double-button closing. Holdees wear single-closing pants."

He sat quiet, attentive.

"Know that only the queen and healers, when needed, may see a queen's man naked. A woman will be severely punished for viewing a naked queen's man, without due cause. If she touches his manly parts or indulges him at skindown, with or without his permission, she will be executed."

"Without his permission?"

"It is a thing which happens. Groups of backway women have defiled queen's men for fun. Outlaws will kidnap a queen's man and demand ransom. Some do not honor the double-button pants."

"Defile? Can women do that to men?"

"Absolutely. I will not go into details, but we have of necessity developed methods to convince a reluctant male to surrender his offspring shot."

"Being queen's man sounds like a dangerous occupation," he muttered.

"Queens pick the best males, with alluring bodies and handsome faces, and flaunt them before others. All women so expect and must perceive what an excellent man the queen has acquired. Most women are law abiding and follow the rules. They look and admire only, which stands the way of it. But there are women of unscrupulous ways who desire to possess the beautiful one.

"If a queen's man is indulged at skindown by another, even without his agreement, the queen will no longer have him. If not put to death, he will be sold as a holdee. Many holdees live hard lives. A queen's man will strive to preserve his status."

"How do I keep these wild, wicked women from attacking me?"

Alea grimaced at his flippant tone. "You will have guards. The queen goes nowhere without guards, nor will you. It is their function to maintain your safety. If you act this ornery with your guards, they may grant you to the wild, wicked women."

"Or turn into wild, wicked women and attack you themselves." Wecan arose.

"Just like certain healers?" he asked.

Wecan laughed. "Just like certain healers. Alea, I will get coffee."

Alea nodded. "Queen's Man, you must also understand what is permitted. Your pants mark the queen's territory. Other women may touch you above the waistline and below the pant legs. Women may so express their admiration of a queen's man. Such admiration pleases the queen. Women will lay hands on you. Be sure the hands do not stray from allowed limits. I will teach you in Oldenspeak how to discourage such women."

"I thought my pants show I'm queen's man."

"It is your responsibility nevertheless, should a woman attempt to touch you in a manner not permitted, to immediately identify yourself as queen's man."

"Oh."

Wecan returned and served coffee.

The queen's man sipped reflectively then turned to Alea. "You have too many confusing rules. Can't I just go home?"

"I do not think so. The queen desires your presence." Her shoulders flicked in a shrug. "You are Mainlander, but the Mainland has many different nations, bordered alliances and groups. Where would you go?"

He grimaced. "Where indeed? It appears I'm stuck. So what now?"

"Women demand an organized society." Alea's voice rang gentle but firm. "Societal leaders will visit severe penalties upon those who choose not to follow the rules and observe their place, try to upset the balance. You must learn and observe your place as do all women and especially holdees."

He frowned. "I can't go outside unless guards have me on leash?"

"You could so state. I wish you to drop the dog theme. The queen will not be amused and we do not leash dogs."

"Only queen's men."

"The guards are to protect you."

"And keep me from running."

"That, too. I will have Gorsa demonstrate how to bow in the presence of a queen. You will have little time to practice."

"Yes, Alea." He sighed with studied patience.

They spent the next hour teaching him. When Alea sensed his energy and interest waning, she arose. "Would you like lunch in the garden? You can breathe fresh air."

He nodded. "And stop thinking. My head is spinning."

"Yes, you need rest before we start again."

"There's more?"

"Of course, much more. We grant you knowledge to keep you alive and away from the strikepaddle."

"Strikepaddle?"

"It is a most effective form of punishment."

"I don't even like the sound of it."

"You would like the feel of it even less. So pay attention to your lessons." She dropped her hands onto his shoulders and massaged gently.

"Strikepaddles? Is that how you punish dogs, too?"

She slapped him on the shoulder. "I told you to stop that."

He grinned.

"You are most impudent," Alea said. "I hope you hold your tongue before the queen or she will make of you a minced chowder."

"I can use a language my queen won't understand."

"You leave me without hope. I despair teaching you manners."

* * *

Barrina and Renfra had resettled the queen's man inside when Alea returned.

"I don't see why I can't walk," he said. "I'm feeling much better."

"Maybe tomorrow," Alea said. "You make remarkable progress. You must have the constitution of a tricald ox."

"I'd probably be insulted if I knew what that is."

"It is a creature of myth, notoriously hard to kill. The comparison is a compliment."

"Oh." He slumped against his pillows. "What kind of threats will you terrorize me with this afternoon? I'm bored."

"The threats are for your own good. You make light of them and I fear it will be to your detriment. This afternoon I will teach you two vital phrases. Starting tomorrow a teacher, Lateean, will come every afternoon and teach you Oldenspeak."

"Why must I learn Oldenspeak?"

"It is the language Queen Rejeena uses."

He cocked his head slightly. "Wouldn't it be to the queen's advantage to speak Universal?"

"As representative of an old, proud Queen's Line, she speaks only the traditional Kriisconian language. That is her right as a queen, and indeed all women so expect."

"Queen's Line?"

"Queens inherit their position from lineage, their mothers. This flow of queenship is Queen's Line. Normally, the eldest daughter, the staff scion, will become queen following her mother. If the eldest proves unsuitable, the next will be considered. If no daughter seems apt, a woman of expanded lineage will be chosen or a new Queen's Line formed. Queens' daughters are reared to rise to the duty, so usually one is chosen. To assure having the best queen, the land leaders and council must agree to a new queen's staffing. Their choice must be approved by the great queen."

"Queen's staffing?"

"The queen's emblem of power is her staff. Each prospective queen chooses her emblem. When she assumes power, the land leaders and her councilors present her a staff with her emblem."

"And what is your . . . my queen's emblem?"

"A white stag. However, this conversation will not teach you to say, 'Yes, My Queen,' in Oldenspeak."

He flashed an impudent grin. "Will I learn how to say, 'No, My Queen'?"

"You will have no need of it."

"I'll bet this Lateean will teach me."

"Hopefully by then you will have acquired sense enough not to use it. Now listen and repeat."

The phrases in Oldenspeak were difficult to pronounce and remember. Several times the queen's man grew silent and withdrawn, scrunching his face and rubbing his temples. Despite his discomfort, because time pressed, Alea grilled him mercilessly, taught him to twist his tongue to make the correct sounds.

She said, "You seem to lack talent in the speaking of languages. You need learn only two short phrases."

"Short phrases? In Universal you say, 'Yes, My Queen.' Oldenspeak requires enough words to choke your invincible tricald ox."

All the healers laughed.

He frowned. "I'll have you know, Alea, I already speak three languages."

"Do you?" Alea asked. Sounding indignant, he seemed to miss the nuance of his words. Alea did not.

"Yes, I speak Universal, Hill Silicaran and . . . and . . . one other." His voice began strong then dwindled to a whisper. He slammed a fist into the pillow beside his leg. "Blast. I almost had something. Now it's gone."

"This third language, you do not know what it is called?"

"No." He shook his head. "I know the words. It's the one that sits in my head. But I don't know what it is."

"You did remember the Hill Silicaran. What is that?"

He looked blank. "It just popped into my head. I understand and can speak it. That's what it's called, but I know nothing else about it."

"You remembered that, Queen's Man. It is a start."

He slumped, eyes distant, not sharing his thoughts.

Alea spent the remainder of the day teaching him. He learned to say those two vital phrases—"Yes, My Queen" and "I am queen's man. That is not permitted." Unable to twist his tongue correctly, he ended with a charming accent. Alea felt the queen would be pleased.

He grew irritable and uncooperative, tired and upset about his inability to remember. Alea had the servants give him dinner early. Withdrawn and moody, he desultorily played muskee with Renfra and Wecan, then fell asleep.

* * *

The following day, Alea's door banged against the wall. She looked up.

Queen Rejeena stood in the doorway, clad in traveling clothes of tan skin trousers, tunic and long boots.

Her guards stopped outside the door.

Alea jumped up and bowed. "My Queen, you return early."

Rejeena smiled. "The first nominee offered for land leader, chosen by the packet seegarpt, impressed me with her knowledge, loyalty and leadership. I ensashed her. Squalla's Towne is now Heraal's Towne. We departed immediately following the ensashing. I am most eager to meet my queen's man. We traveled through the night."

"Thank LaSheena you arrived safely home, My Queen. Traveling is so dangerous for you, and at night." Alea shook her head, clucking. "I hoped for more time with your queen's man. He knows so little."

Rejeena, at ease alone with her friend, laughed. "He need only know two things just now, how to say, 'Yes, My Queen,' and how to move his hips effectively in skindown."

Alea grinned. "I assure the first, My Queen. The second you will needs discover for yourself."

"How is he?" the queen asked softly. "Has he remembered anything?"

"He remains weak and sore, requires much rest. However, he recovers much faster than I believed he could. He remembers nothing of note."

"He still does not know his name?"

"No, My Queen."

"He must have a name. We cannot just call him queen's man. I have thought of one." Rejeena paused, and a smile twitched the corners of her mouth.

"Which is?"

"Aarvan."

Alea burst into laughter. "Oh, My Queen," she gasped, "that is perfect. Aarvan is fitting."

The two women chuckled together until Alea grew serious. "My Queen, permit me to have coffee brought. We needs talk."

"Could it not wait, Alea, until I have bathed, dressed and seen the queen's man? I have ridden all night for that pleasure."

"It is about him that we must talk."

"I hope you have not unpleasant tidings."

"No, just advice. Please." Alea gestured to a chair. "There are things you must know before you meet him."

The queen yielded and took the seat. "Why do I feel I will not like what you say?" As servants brought coffee, she unlaced her boots and kicked them off. "Those are hot."

"You seldom like what I say as your healer." Alea waited until she and the queen were alone. "Have you inquired of Carlea the volume of your riches she bartered for this man?"

"No, I came straight here. Will you give me barter advice?"

"No, My Queen, but I did talk to Carlea. Your handsome queen's man represents a lavish investment. The wander women knew LaHeeka declared him queen's man. They bartered accordingly."

"I expected that," the queen said, sipping coffee, stretching her legs.

"The man is heavily weighted and LaHeeka said he can break the curse on your Queen's Line. You and I both know how deeply you desire that."

Rejeena waited, one eyebrow arched.

"He stands all LaHeeka foresaw and perhaps more, controlled, willful, much too self-possessed for one so young. I glimpsed in him a wildness."

"Wildness?"

"Yes, a wildness that stood my hair on end for a moment."

Rejeena recalled the eyes she had glimpsed, but did not share with Alea. "You fantasize. He is but a man."

Alea continued; the queen would not accept what she could not rightly explain. "He harbors strong feelings and does not always share his thoughts. If he desires something, he will endure pain to acquire it." Alea thought of his wanting to lie on his side, be in the garden, snatching Wecan's muskee culls, how he calmly accepted pain as the price. "He will be a challenge."

"I have ways of meeting challenges."

"I know that, My Queen. Please let me proceed."

The queen saluted with her coffee mug. "Please proceed."

"You do possess a wicked temper and absolutely no patience, particularly with holdees who are not respectful and obedient."

The queen saluted again with her mug, green eyes amused.

"You have had holdees whipped, clubbed, taste of locchot, dragged down Mainway for infractions. I have seen you hit a holdee with a truchon for being too slow with an answer. You have had men put to death for striking or calling their mistress a vile name."

The queen smiled. "I admit to being a wicked woman. What has this to do with my queen's man, who I have not yet seen with his eyes open?"

Alea sighed. "You are not wicked. You are traditional, of the old school. Your actions always fall in accord with law, but you stand unforgiving and quick to punish. Aarvan is queen's man, not a holdee. Your affinity with him must be different. He will live in your home, eat at your dinner table, and share your skindown every night. Queen's men do not roll off the skindown onto the holdee pallet when the coupling is over. He will be around all the time; your life and his will be entwined and intimate, such as you have never before experienced. Even though you are queen, he merely queen's man, the affinity between you must contain some give and take."

"I visualize no problem. I give edicts; he takes them."

"That is what I feared to hear from you."

Rejeena set down her caster and spread her hands. "I am queen. He will follow instructions."

"My Queen, I present my final argument. Your queen's man received an almost fatal blow to the head. His body absorbed havoc and injury, and will require time for full recovery. Any blow or distress, especially to his head, could cause more severe injury, throw him back into a sleeping state, or even kill him. I must caution you—"

"I am tired, dirty and wish to see Aarvan," Rejeena said. "Let me finish for you. You wish me to hold my temper, keep my open hand, truchon and strikepaddle off my queen's man until you give me permission as his healer." She grinned and replaced her boots. "Is that not the purpose of this session?"

"You know me well, My Queen."

"Almost as well as you know me, Alea. I will, upon your advice as healer and friend, and because your argument is sensible, try to be patient with my queen's man. However, please stay available in case of misunderstandings. I assume he can neither voice nor understand Oldenspeak."

"He begins lessons today. Thank you, My Queen for your understanding; I would hate to see my efforts as Aarvan's healer wasted."

"Come with me. You may begin interpreting now." The two women departed for the queen's home.

Alea waited while the queen ate, bathed and changed.

Rejeena picked up a band of bright green skin and tucked it into her pocket. "Come, Alea."

Walking along the hall, in a low voice, Rejeena said, "I am as nervous as a rabbit on open ground with a hawk's shadow beside me. Why do you suppose that is? He is but a man, like any other."

Alea chuckled. "He is not like any other. He is queen's man."

They entered the room to find Wecan and Gorsa playing muskee. The room was warm. The man stretched uncovered on his pallet, flat on his back, asleep.

The healers leaped up with a clatter of muskee culls, and bowed.

"My Queen," Wecan gasped, "welcome back."

"Thank you," the queen said. "Does that man always sleep?"

"He remained awake and learning all morning, My Queen," Wecan said. "He rests before his language class."

"Then he may be awakened?"

"Yes, My Queen." Wecan started toward him.

The queen threw up an arresting hand. She grinned, her green gaze on Aarvan. "You may take a break."

Wecan and Gorsa curtsied and departed.

Rejeena stood, her scrutiny caressing the sleeping man. "I forget the utter beauty of him. Each time I set eyes on him, I am reminded." She sat beside him, in Alea's usual position. Her folded knees all but touched his side.

Alea sat further back beyond his head, allowing them space.

"Let us see what will wake him." Rejeena closed her mind to the memory of his eyes. *I am queen; no man may be allowed to intimidate me, no matter how ferocious he may appear.* She cautiously laid her hand flat below his rib cage. The man did not move. She slowly traced his chest, shoulders and neck. He slept on, breathing slow, deep.

"He will be a difficult one. Let us see how he likes this." She ran two fingertips across his abdomen under the front of his pants. He stirred, sighed and settled back to sleep.

"This requires stronger measures," Rejeena said, eyes crinkling, mouth curving into a grin.

Alea watched with delight. The queen, for the first time in a long while, seemed to enjoy the moment. *Please LaSheena, do not let it change when he opens his eyes.*

Rejeena slid her fingertips under the front of his pants. Her fingers traced across from one line of buttons to the other. Reaching each line, her thumb flipped the top button loose, allowing her fingers to penetrate further toward the sensitive groin. Then she eased across to loosen the button on the other side, fingers maintaining light, teasing contact with his skin. At the third button on the first side, she got reaction.

She did not see the arm move, but steel fingers clamped her wrist. A quick, lithe twist forced her arm away. The grip, irresistibly strong, imprisoned her arm as gently as it might have a live bird. Her eyes flicked to meet the midnight blue, and his wondrous, melodious, soft voice stated clearly in Oldenspeak, "I am queen's man. That is not permitted." From the corner of her eye, the queen saw Alea clap a hand over her mouth to stifle laughter.

The green eyes locked with the blue—the same eyes she saw before, but they held only inquiry and challenge, no rage, no lust to kill.

* * *

The queen's man had been exhausted. He ate then retired to his pallet and fell asleep. A hand touched him, demanded attention, drawing him up to drowsily floating, eyes still closed. Too tired to care, he tried to sink back into oblivion.

Someone touched him again, unbuttoned his pants. His abdomen tensed and quivered.

He reacted instinctively, grabbed the offending arm and twisted it away. His eyes snapped open and he stated in well-rehearsed Oldenspeak, "I am queen's man. That is not permitted." *Oh, my God! Déjà vu. It's my angel. I grabbed her again. But I'm awake now, not dreaming. What's going on?*

She didn't attempt to break his grip but her eyes calmly probed his.

He studied her. Standing, she would be tall, with all the correct curves in all the right places. Her auburn hair hung straight and unfettered to her waist. Her eyes glittered a deep, solid green. Not beautiful, but a striking woman—*or angel, whatever she is*—with strong, vital features, muscular, solidly feminine, she projected confidence and personal power. Her wide mouth seemed made for laughter and, he thought, deep passionate kissing. *Should I have such thoughts about an angel?*

A powerful craving surged within him, bridging the space between them. He wanted her, wanted to possess this woman. Potent lust dominated the desire; but more than that, it included a hunger he didn't understand. He had never felt such intense longing at sight of a woman . . . or an angel. The craving engulfed him, seated in his bones. He shivered slightly, and his manhood stirred between his legs. He lay there, struck breathless, immobile by the intense yearning flooding through him, seeming to heat his blood and chill his limbs simultaneously.

She spoke, a husky, deep sound, sending a warm vibration through him. The voice suited the woman. Her eyes pinned him, but she spoke to someone else. He recognized Alea's answering voice. *Alea? Alea is here?* His brows lowered. He thought of the hand at his buttons. *Would Alea allow this? If Alea tests me, and thinks this amusing, I'll have words for her.* He couldn't understand their speech, but felt he was the subject.

"You taught him well, Alea," Rejeena said. "He defends the queen's property superbly. However, you might tell him he need not so defend against the queen." Her eyes glowed, mouth twitching.

"He does not yet know you, My Queen."

"Perhaps you needs remedy that."

Alea rose and circled behind the queen. She leaned forward. "Queen's Man," she said in Universal, "I present Queen Rejeena."

He started as though she slapped him. The dark blue eyes flicked to her face then to the queen's.

His breath caught in his throat. *This is the queen? My angel—my queen is the same woman?* The woman who excited him so, stirred within him this unfamiliar craving, this lust? Laying flat on his back, with no memory, no sense of himself, the queen's shapely arm captive in his hand, he cringed. *If I could, I'd run home to Mama.* He shook his head. Where'd that thought come from? *Then again, maybe I'll just claim this woman and make her mine.*

Gaze fixed on the queen, he gathered his senses. He growled softly, "Thank you for the warning, Alea. Am I in trouble?"

"Not if you remember your manners, greet your queen properly and release her arm."

He opened his hand slowly. "My Queen." He started to sit upright. The gentle pressure of the queen's fingertips against his chest stopped him. He remained prone, and waited for her move.

"Aarvan," the queen's throaty voice said.

"Aarvan?" He looked at Alea.

"As you stand nameless, the queen named you Aarvan." An amused quirk lifted her lips.

He frowned. "Does that have a meaning?"

Alea changed languages. "Aarvan wishes to know the meaning of his name."

"Tell him."

Alea lifted the queen's staff from the floor. "This is the queen's power staff, her emblem, that of a white stag. Many tales exist on Kriiscon, stories and characters of myth. Aarvan is a mythical white stag, the queen's power motif."

"She named me after her emblem?"

"I have not finished," Alea said. "This Aarvan descends from the great forest of LaSheena once every five hundred turnings of the season. He bounds through the forests of Kriiscon, completing all the doe deer, so that all the fawns in the forest will be white."

His face slowly turned red. "Is that necessary? That's embarrassing."

Alea struggled with a grin. "My Queen, Aarvan feels the name will embarrass him."

The queen gave a short answer.

"The queen says, misfortunate."

"Then I guess I'm stuck with it."

The queen leaned forward, reaching for his pants.

He froze, abdomen muscles tightening. *Surely she isn't going to do anything in front of Alea.* It would be one thing to feel and indulge desire, quite another to include others. *But if I stop her, what will she do?*

To his great relief, she merely refastened the opened buttons.

Her knowing smile indicated she guessed his thoughts exactly.

Alea and the queen chatted, their conversation opaque to Aarvan. He lay quietly and contemplated his new name. Except for its embarrassing reference, it seemed as good as any. He watched the smooth, graceful way the queen's hands moved as she talked. Her face flashed with chameleon changes to match her emotions. Green eyes glittered as she glanced from him to Alea. The rise and fall of her husky voice, a smooth intoxicating sound, created erotic images in his mind and pushed the simmering excitement outward to heat his veins. He sensed a depth to her that made him want to explore further. Sharing her life might prove interesting; sharing skindown with her would be not be difficult, in fact pleasant. *But . . .*

He squeezed his eyes shut for a moment. *My angel . . . my queen . . . I want her deeply. But how dare she claim me as a slave? What possesses her? Which way do I go? Do I actually have a choice? Oh, blast . . . my head hurts. I can't think past the pain. But I have to deal with this.*

Alea turned and interrupted his reverie. "The queen wishes to know if you have been well-treated, if you harbor unfulfilled wants."

"I've been well-treated and have all I need. I would like to sit up. I feel a fool lying here." He added with a tiny grin, "I could use a longer leash."

"Show respect, you ass," Alea hissed. She passed on all but his last remark.

The queen arched a brow. "A man who desires naught when offered all by a queen. Most strange. He may sit if he feels well enough. I prevented him as I did not want him to suffer pain."

"He is quite capable of sitting, My Queen."

"Have the servants see to it and bring coffee. I would share coffee with my queen's man."

Aarvan levered into a sitting position, quick, graceful, with no assistance from the servants, causing the queen's brow to tilt.

The healer, queen and queen's man remained silent during the flurry of activity as servants arranged Aarvan's pillows, placed and poured coffee then curtsied out.

"That's better," Aarvan sighed. To the queen, he said in Oldenspeak, "Thank you, My Queen." At their looks of surprise, he explained, "Barrina taught me."

The queen pulled the green piece of skin from her pocket. She motioned for Aarvan to lift his right arm. When he did so, she fastened it around his arm halfway between elbow and shoulder. "Now, Aarvan, you most truly belong to your queen." She glanced at Alea. "Inform him that he must always wear his armskin. Only the queen may place or remove it."

Aarvan studied the armskin. "Please tell my queen I understand." That pesky grin flickered. "Is this the accepted type of leash?"

"Aarvan, I swear . . ." Alea said.

"All right, I'll be good. But exactly what does this mean?"

"Each queen's man wears an armskin in his queen's chosen color. Just like the double-button pants, it declares you the property of Queen Rejeena."

"Oh, how I *relish* being property."

"If you do not show your queen more respect, you may be required to *relish* a strikepaddle."

"All right. All right." He turned to Rejeena, and granted her a wide smile. "Tell my queen I will, of course, wear her armskin."

Alea told her, and the queen reached and stroked the armskin, allowed her fingertips to smooth down his arm before lifting off.

Aarvan's nerve endings jolted. The jolt seared down through his abdomen. He pulled his legs together, moved his coffee caster to his lap and hoped neither woman looked down too closely.

"Now that I face my queen's man," Rejeena said, "I can think of naught to say."

Alea chuckled. "Just relate to him the laws and traditions of Kriiscon. You will spend hours explaining."

Aarvan understood an occasional word. His morning session with Barrina had been helpful. He hoped his language teacher excelled at her job. If he were to cope with this strong, handsome, green-eyed queen—this almost an angel—he needed the ability to speak with her.

Alea and the queen talked, at times including Aarvan.

The queen and queen's man observed one another, silently taking measure.

Finishing her coffee, the queen arose. "I must return to my duties." She smiled. "Inform Aarvan I am pleased to finally meet him with his eyes open"—a chill rippled through her as she remembered those eyes filled with rage—"and with his swift recovery."

Alea repeated.

Aarvan returned the queen's smile. "Please tell my queen the pleasure is mine. I am honored." He remembered her as an angel, waking, seeing her and the old crone, but the rest of that short incident had been swallowed by the blackness.

"I am glad you are properly polite to your queen," Alea said.

The queen leaned down and caught his chin in her hand. Her appraising eyes held his.

His, calm and steadfast, met hers without evasion.

She released him. "I must go, Aarvan."

He simulated a sitting bow. "My Queen."

* * *

"Come with me, Alea. We must speak." The queen swept from the room.

Alea followed.

As they walked down the hall, Rejeena said, "Either he gracefully spouts untruths, or he means what he says."

"He appears not the same man from one moment to the next, My Queen. He flips façades . . . I cannot truly explain what I observed. I believe he means what he says, but he possesses a streak of impudence."

The queen absorbed this for a moment. "Exactly how recovered is he?"

"I cannot easily answer that. He remains far from full recuperation. Why do you ask?"

"Tomorrow I move from my winter to my summer skindown room. I wish Aarvan to join me."

"Oh, My Queen, so soon? I do not think him ready."

"When will he be ready?"

"I cannot say exactly, but I feel strongly he remains too weak to romp in skindown."

"He will be prone, Alea. All he need do is contribute his offspring shot and roll off. Surely he can manage that." The queen strode swiftly, eyes fixed ahead.

"Skindown indulgence involves much exertion. If you could wait a bit longer—"

"On the morrow I begin my most completion-positive days. I wish to begin now. If Aarvan finds it difficult, that is hardly significant. He need perform no other duties and may rest as required. I want him in my skindown."

"Yes, My Queen."

* * *

Alea returned to the summer skindown room, where Wecan, Gorsa and Aarvan sat conversing.

"I thought you were tired, Aarvan," Alea said.

"Not anymore. Every nerve in my body is jumping."

"Aarvan," Wecan squealed. "You called him Aarvan?"

Aarvan's mouth twisted in disgust while Alea explained.

"I love it. Aarvan is most fitting. Anytime you desire to bound through *my* forest, Aarvan, follow your urges." Wecan wrapped her arms around herself, weaving back and forth, snickering. Gorsa tried to smother her giggles.

He glowered. "Will I hear this every time that name is mentioned?"

"Hopefully, others will show more restraint," Alea said.

"By the way, Alea, thanks for the forewarning of the queen's arrival. That was embarrassing, to wake up, latch onto this strange woman, and find out she's the queen. After all those warnings about being polite, you let that happen?"

"I stood unaware of the queen's return, until she walked through the door. I did not know you would be asleep, awaken and latch onto her arm."

"What did you expect me to do? I wake up and some woman is undoing my pants. You told me not to allow that, at cost of life."

Both Wecan and Gorsa still giggled.

"The queen complimented your training and reaction. So stop badgering me." Alea smiled. "The queen will have you share skindown with her tomorrow night."

He blinked. "What?"

Alea repeated.

"Tomorrow?"

"The queen has decided."

"I'm feeling better, but I don't think I'm ready"—redness crept up his neck—"to indulge in . . . amorous euphoria with that queenly hunk of woman."

"No one mentioned amorous euphoria."

He frowned, took a deep breath. "Have I misread all these conversations? You use unusual terms, but I thought I understood. Please correct me. Specifically, what is it the queen expects?"

"The queen expects you to share skindown and complete her."

"Share skindown?"

Alea pointed to the roughhewn but opulent bed across the room. "Share skindown, sleep with her, bed her, lay with, spend the night together."

"Complete her?"

"Yes, rut her, cause her to have daughters. In Universal, I believe that is render her pregnant, in a family way."

"Then unless you Kriisconian women are built differently from others, that's called amorous euphoria or . . . making love."

"It is not that."

"Then please educate me. What is it?"

"As I told you, Aarvan, the queen stands very traditional. Traditional Kriisconian women do not engage in amorous euphoria, this making love. They share skindown and acquire completion."

He ran both hands through his hair. "My headache is getting worse. Is there a point to this?"

"Yes. Tomorrow night the queen will enter her skindown, unclothed below the waist, clothed above. She will apply an ointment to herself to make your entry easy. You will excite yourself or, if you are shy about that, a servant or guard may be assigned the function."

Aarvan's blue eyes flamed. "But—"

"The queen may even do it. When you stand hard and ready, you will lie between her legs, enter her, and the two of you will rock up and down until your body releases its offspring shot. You will then remove yourself from the queen, lie beside her and go to sleep. She will inform you if she wishes your attentions again. You will not touch her person otherwise, not *make love* to the queen."

Aarvan stared. "I beg your pardon."

"You heard me, Queen's Man."

He turned and looked at Wecan then Gorsa. They nodded.

"Please say you're teasing, Alea."

"I am not. You will perform as I stated, the traditional way. The queen will insist upon it."

His brows knit, pulled together, eyes chilled. "Oh, no. That's worse than, *wham, bam, thank you, ma'am*. That's revolting. No way, Alea."

Alea tapped his knee. "Queen's Man, you do not make the decision. You will perform as instructed."

"No, absolutely not. I've bedded women. That's not the way it's done. I am to be allowed to touch only my queen, but she doesn't want to be touched. She wants to be"—he searched for a word—"just humped like an animal. Like a pair of dogs coupling. No wonder she named me after a stag. She thinks we're blasted animals."

"Your duty is to serve your queen, as she wishes."

"I seem to have landed here," he said, "stuck in this peculiar society of yours. I'm willing to indulge in amorous bedding with my queen. But there's a limit. If my queen expects what you've described, then perhaps she'd be best served to find another queen's man."

"Aarvan," Alea scolded, "the queen stands capable of causing you such misery that you will beg to serve her."

He stared at her without further comment, eyes calm, unflinching.

Alea stalked to the door. *He means what he says.* "I have tried my best, Aarvan. If you feel the sting of the strikepaddle, it falls to your own stubborn sword point." She departed.

* * *

Gorsa said, "Aarvan, maybe you should—"

"Women, I'd like to be alone."

"Are you ousting us? We are to stay."

"I need time alone."

Wecan and Gorsa crept toward the door. "We will be with the guards if you need anything."

Aarvan leaned against his pillows and closed his eyes.

Contesting with the queen here, in her bailiwick, appeared a control struggle he would lose. She held all the power and advantages. He had glimpsed her guards. They looked big, dangerous and determined, ready to enforce the queen's slightest command. In contrast, he was both mentally and physically weak, vulnerable from his head wound.

He drew in a quick breath, looked inward, inside his mind. It should be sharp, fast. Instead, his head seemed to swirl with impenetrable thick fog. That fog obscured his convictions and blunted his ability to reason.

This situation, this society could not be natural, not right. Even through the fog, he could reason that men and women alike should be allowed to follow their own bent, not be held as slave or captive, enholded and beaten into submission. With no memory, he had only his sense of propriety and Alea's sketchy description of Mainland life to compare, but this society's wrongness seemed clear.

Conversely, suppose this society was natural, that he did belong, a holdee among these dominant women? What if he had always been of this place? Could it be just wishful thinking that he came from somewhere else? But Alea said the wander women found him dressed as a Mainlander, that Mainland society differed from Kriisconian. Wouldn't he feel different, be more accepting, if this were his natural environment?

Blazes, why can't I remember?

One thing appeared certain. Wherever he belonged, whatever his origins, however strange this place, he was here. At the moment, he couldn't affect or change the circumstances. *In order to survive, I need to live within the limits of this female-dominated society until I find a way to control my destiny.* He visualized himself sound, unfettered by injury. That vision—not quite memory, more a flash of knowledge—caused him to smile. In that condition, he need not comply with unreasonable rules. *I simply need to stay alive long enough to heal.*

He could abide most of the rules and encumbrances. The short pants, the bowing, calling women mistress, sitting with the queen in council, comprised mere outward manifestations of his subjugated position. They could not reduce him as a man in his mind. Some of the other practices would be a problem. He would face them as they came; for now his battered mind disallowed him the ability to anticipate, to plan.

This powerful queen wanted him as her night playmate. Though he much preferred deciding when and with whom he bedded, considering his condition, he would not object. He found the queen, at least physically, attractive and desirable. Sharing skindown, as the women called it, would be no hardship. He felt himself to be an adequate skindown partner. He couldn't remember specifics, but he'd bedded women.

The first difficulty lay with the queen's completion ritual. He thought of Alea's description and shuddered. *What an abhorrent idea. Bestial.* Many women of the night performed better than that. At an instinctual level, not reliant on memory, he knew he revered and respected amorous euphoria or making love, sharing that most intimate act with a woman. He absolutely would not reduce it to coupling like a pair of animals. To indulge in such activity would lower him as a man, as a human being. He would not yield on this point of skindown etiquette. He needed to find a way to turn the queen to his point of view.

He considered Alea's description of the queen. To maintain her position in this society, she would need to be a forceful, domineering woman, who expected to have her way. She would hold little patience or concern for the desires of others, especially men.

The head injury rendered him vulnerable. She could cause him great pain, misery and still demand her way of him. His chance of winning this confrontation didn't look good. With yielding unthinkable, stubbornness might be his only real weapon.

He held great value. Not only had Alea told him, but he gleaned as much from snatches of overheard conversation. The queen would be restricted in what she could do to him—*I hope.* The head injury rendered him vulnerable, but could also protect him. The queen would know that severe punishment might kill a head-injured man. He did hold that small advantage—and he would use it.

All the thinking made his head pound. He lowered it into his hands and cleared his thoughts, trying to remember.

Exhausted, head throbbing, he leaned against the pillows and after a while fell asleep.

* * *

Following the time reserved for Aarvan's language lesson, Alea returned. Chaara sat alone in the skindown room. "Where is Aarvan?" Alea asked.

Chaara gestured toward the garden. "He rose without words and walked out. He is far too headstrong for a man."

Aarvan stood outside, leaning against a tree, back to the door.

Alea walked toward him. He did not turn, but she could tell by the slight tensing of his back muscles that he recognized her approach. She spoke gently. "Aarvan, I wish you would not take it upon yourself to rise and walk, until I have so permitted."

He said, soft voice calm but distant, "If I'm well enough to share skindown, I'm well enough to walk."

"I do not know that you are well enough to share skindown."

"But I'm to do it anyway, right?"

"Since you do walk, how do you feel?"

"Fine. No nausea, no dizziness, just a dull headache."

"Good." She looked at his composed, unreadable profile against the green of the budding trees. "What are you thinking?"

He heaved a long breath, instead of answering. She thought maybe he would not.

Finally, he turned to face her. "I wonder who and what I really am, wish I were wherever I came from."

Alea stepped close and grasped his arm gently. "I know you face a dilemma. I do not understand why you remain so stubborn, but I know you feel strongly. I sympathize, but I fear the queen will not. Remember, I am your friend."

"Thank you," he said. "I have a question."

"When do you not?"

He flushed slightly. "Do all women of Kriiscon share skindown as you describe?"

She waved to a small stone bench. "Sit down. This may take a bit." The healer sat beside him. "Kriisconian society writhes in the midst of change, but the change comes slowly. Mainland practices invade our ancient ways. Some consider this good, so long as it is controlled. The most traditional women argue it will end our society. They desire no change, will fight it to their deaths. Queens, land leaders, commerce and religious leaders, the most powerful women on the island, stand staunchly for tradition. Younger, less-powerful women comprise the forces for change.

"Queen Rejeena," she continued, "stands trapped between the two. She leans heavily toward tradition, supports the ancient laws, rules her quarter accordingly. But change advances upon her. She must find a balance that she and her quarter, both the conventional and change forces, can embrace. For her person and actions, she clings to the old ways.

"To answer your question, no, they do not. Some younger women believe in skindown rapture, this making love. They remove their tops, which a traditionalist would never do. They kiss, fondle and seek pleasure. Even some older women, behind closed doors, behave not so conventionally as they would have all women believe."

"Then I don't see—"

Alea held up a finger. "Traditional women share skindown only for completion. Once a woman fulfills completion, she will not share skindown again until she once more desires to be completed. With this system, we need few holdees, as we pass them from woman to woman. Since old times the privilege of having a holdee to oneself remained reserved to queens, land leaders and some seegarpt. Now there exist certain women, some purporting to hold to the old ways, who keep a holdee and share skindown for pleasure. If it becomes known about these women, they receive censure from the deep traditionalists, and many for that reason keep their skindown activities secret."

"Seegarpt?"

"A comprehensive term for high-ranking women, due to riches or placement in the hierarchy."

"I see. What's wrong with skindown pleasure?"

"Nothing is wrong with the pleasure. Seeking pleasure encourages a woman to fly in the face of tradition and maintain a holdee for that purpose. If all women so acted, there would needs be a holdee for each woman. Half of our society would become male, and we could lose control."

That impudent grin flashed. "Then you'd be almost normal. Heaven forbid."

"Aarvan, must you interrupt with jests?"

"I'm sorry. If there's no shame in skindown pleasure, then why can't the queen indulge?"

"She stands as leader of the entire quarter. She must remain beholden to the old ways, not lead the race to change."

"The queen doesn't share her queen's man, right?"

"That is right."

"So why can't she enjoy sharing skindown, indulge in amorous euphoria, since she can do as she wishes? Who's to know?"

"She wishes to remain traditional." Alea noted an odd light flash in his eyes.

"So you're telling me this whole skindown thing with the queen is her wishes, nothing more?"

"Do not take the queen's wishes lightly. That which she desires, occurs. You needs accept that. Now let us go inside. Your dinner is ready. You require a good rest tonight."

He rose and preceded her into the skindown room, a tiny grin lifting the edges of his mouth.

* * *

The following day Alea returned. Aarvan's pallet lay in a corner of the skindown room. He sat on it, motionless, an unfinished lunch before him, watching the servants moving in the queen's belongings.

Alea sat near him. "I hope you have considered, gained good sense and will accede to the queen wishes."

"I haven't changed my mind."

Alea sighed. "You stand beyond hope."

"I need a favor."

"What favor?"

"If the queen is as adamant as you say, I'll need an interpreter tonight."

"What you will need, is a strong deity beside you. The queen will be adamant. However, I do intend to be near. Someone will needs tell you, as the guards hustle you away, how many lashes you are to receive."

"Thanks, Alea. You boost my confidence."

"I try to help. You are much too stubborn. How do you feel?"

"Fine, if I don't make any sudden moves."

"Perhaps the queen will consider your condition."

His smile formed slowly. "I'm counting on that."

Alea glared. "With a bit of effort you could be an utter ass. I erred admitting your value."

His smile widened. "Despite being a mere man, I figured some of it out myself."

"Aarvan, you oppose a strong-willed queen of Kriiscon, who expects to have her way because she always does. I plead with you to reconsider."

He looked at her with calm eyes, his smile fading.

"All right," she sighed and rose. "I must go. If you are tired, rest before your teacher comes."

* * *

The queen had required that Alea and Aarvan dine with her.

Alea arrived to walk with him to the queen's dining room. She observed him. His pants displayed the artistic talent of the queen's tailor, hugging his taut rear seductively and just suggesting a bulge in front. He wore no shirt but had donned a vest, which allowed tantalizing glimpses of hard, solid chest, flat belly and trim waist. Laced skin boots climbed halfway up his calves. With that lean, muscular body, sculpted face, dark hair and midnight blue eyes, he looked exquisite.

"Am I presentable?" he asked with a grimace, scowling at his raiment. "These pants are something a twelve-year-old might wear. The seamstress and Wecan gave me this getup, and wouldn't let me have a real shirt. I'm not comfortable wearing this . . . this . . . skimpy rigout. Will the queen even let me in her dining room looking like this?"

Alea smiled. He seemed to discount his looks. If covered from head to toe with sticky clay, he would be gorgeous. Upon one look, women would wish to possess and indulge him at skindown. "You look fine. It is the expected raiment for a man in our society when the weather is warm."

He curled his lip. "You're sure?"

"I am sure."

He huffed, but offered her his arm. "Shall we go to dinner? The condemned man always gets a last meal."

"Condemned only by stubbornness," she said tartly and took the arm. "Let us go." As they walked, she reiterated proper manners.

"Yes, Alea."

Inside the door, healer and queen's man bowed on one foot and one knee, head raised, proper for their stations. "My Queen," they said as one.

The queen, who sat at the head of the table, motioned for them to rise, beckoning Alea to the chair on her right. "Come, Aarvan." The queen gestured to a spot to her left.

He obediently walked to the spot and faced her, clenching his jaw. Men in this society didn't enjoy high regard. Still, her imperious command and the attitude behind it rankled, but he would comply. His well being, even his life, depended upon this woman's goodwill. He would not quarrel with her over small points. *I will likely find sufficient large points to jeopardize my welfare.*

Queen Rejeena looked him over. Her eyes paused at the bulge between his legs long enough to cause his color to deepen. She motioned him to turn around. He did so. After a moment, she laid a hand on his hipbone, brought him to face her.

He snapped his teeth together, nearly drawing blood when he bit his tongue, in an effort to minimize his male reaction to her touch.

"Tell Aarvan this raiment pleases me. It is most becoming. Ask him to take his seat." The queen indicated the chair to her left.

Alea translated.

He sat. "Tell my queen I'm happy she's pleased."

More pleasantries passed as the servants loaded the table with steaming platters and bowls of food. One servant stood near the queen, placing food on her plate as the dishes arrived. Another served the queen's man, but only after the queen.

Alea served herself.

During the meal, the women chatted in Oldenspeak.

Aarvan recognized a few words and short phrases, but couldn't follow the conversation. He dreaded the approaching confrontation and wasn't sorry to be left out. For a while his hunger and the aromatic seduction wafting from the meats and vegetables on his plate absorbed his attention. His rejection of the queen's skindown method might secure him an introduction to the strikepaddle, as Alea threatened. He hoped to negotiate an acceptable alternative, but he doubted Queen Rejeena would embrace negotiation.

Following the meal, the servants hustled to remove the dishes, wipe the table clean, serve coffee and withdraw.

Enjoying her coffee, the queen watched Aarvan with the intensity of a fisherhawk aligning the angle of a bass rising to the surface. She said, "Tell my queen's man he is most handsome. I much anticipate having him naked and rutting between my thighs."

Aarvan looked quizzically at Alea.

"I can tell him, My Queen," Alea said, "but he will turn red."

"Why would he turn red? It is a perfectly normal act."

"I do not know, but mention of skindown indulgence turns him red."

"You do not suppose he lacks knowledge, do you?" A pained expression crossed the queen's face. "Surely LaHeeka did not saddle me with a meithateran."

"Oh, I think not. He is young, but he has surely indulged at skindown. He indicated he has done so."

"Ask him."

"He will turn red."

"Then let him. I wish to know."

Alea turned to Aarvan. "The queen wishes to know how many women you have indulged at skindown."

Aarvan choked and almost spat coffee across the table. He coughed and gasped but recovered. As predicted, he turned bright red. "Why would my queen wish to know that?"

"She seeks assurance she has not acquired a meithateran."

"A what?"

"One who has not yet indulged at skindown."

Aarvan lifted his eyes and met the queen's. "Please assure my queen that I have skindown experience."

The queen studied him. "Ask him how he can so affirm to his queen, as he lacks memory."

Aarvan smiled. "Certain things a man does not forget."

Rejeena returned his smile. "Since my queen's man possesses experience, perhaps he will demonstrate for his queen."

Aarvan said, "Please inform my queen I am at her disposal."

"Then you will cooperate?" Alea asked.

"I am at her disposal to make love."

"Aarvan . . ." Alea glared. "Paddle your own canoe, Queen's Man."

The queen rose and motioned Aarvan to follow.

"My Queen, I will remain with the guards for a while, should you need me," Alea said as she stood.

"I think there will be no problem."

Alea thought it best not to enlighten the queen. She would stay available to interpret, but hoped, faced with refusing the queen directly, Aarvan would relent.

Queen Rejeena walked toward her skindown room. "Come, Aarvan."

Behind her back, Aarvan quipped softly to Alea, "Arf. Arf."

"Ass," Alea hissed, turned and left.

Aarvan followed the queen into her room, pasting a smile on his face, belying the coldness flooding his chest. He closed the door.

The queen slipped from her long skirt, kicked off her slippers and sat on the skindown, naked from the waist down.

His presence seemed not to concern or embarrass her. He watched as she took a jar of creamy substance and saturated her vaginal area. *Hmmm, angel or woman, she's a natural red head.*

She motioned him to remove his clothing and come to her.

Blast. She followed the pattern Alea described. He would have to refuse her and face the resulting fury. "No, My Queen," he said in Oldenspeak. He sat on the skindown, took her hand, unsure of his wording. "My Queen, I wish I could talk to you. I can't do it that way. I have to tell you no, and I think I may regret it."

She leaned toward him, head cocked, eyes questioning and slid the vest from his shoulders. She again gestured for him to remove his pants.

He rose from the skindown and backed away, shaking his head.

She glared and stabbed a finger at the skindown.

Uh oh, the sweet outlook turns sour. His dinner curdled in his stomach. "My Queen," he murmured, "I want to bed with you, but this is not right." He moved almost within reach, mimed removing his pants and her top.

Her brows pulled to a glower.

Encouraged that she had not yet hit him, he again mimed unbuttoning and removing his pants then untying and dropping her blouse. When she didn't move, he reached for the fastener to her top.

Just before he touched it, she slapped his hand away. "No, Aarvan."

He understood that, but not the rest of her angry stream of words.

She gestured for him to remove his pants, eyes narrowed, body thrust forward.

He tried a tactic understood in any language. He hardened his face, crossed his arms and backed away.

She leaped up, jerked on her skirt and yelled, "Alea, come here!"

Alea raced through the door.

Several guards followed. Seeing no threat, the guards stopped.

"Get out," the queen snapped. "I did not require you."

The guards left.

The queen turned to Alea. "What is wrong with this man? He refuses his queen. I will not have it."

Alea looked at him. "Aarvan?"

He shrugged. "You called it correctly, Alea. We disagree."

"Aarvan, look at the queen. She is most furious. She knows not patience. Do as she says."

"Alea, please tell my queen," he said, choosing each word with care, "that I will be honored to share skindown with her. However, I won't use this traditional method. I wish to share euphoria with my queen, giving us both great pleasure during the completion process."

"I will tell her no such."

"If you won't interpret as I ask, please call someone who will."

"Aarvan, if I relate your words, she will surely have you beaten. This is rank disobedient arrogance."

"Let me face that. Please tell the queen what I've asked."

"Very well. I will so interpret."

Alea sighed and turned to the queen, who stood hands on hips, face drawn tight. The healer phrased Aarvan's words in Oldenspeak.

Rejeena stood, brow tilted. "Is that his difficulty? Did you explain to Aarvan that queens do not share this euphoria, my expectations, the correct procedure?"

"Yes, My Queen."

"Why does he not comply?"

"He is hardheaded."

"Are you certain he understands?"

"Yes, My Queen, we talked at length several times. He understands your requirements. He wants this euphoria."

LaHeeka's cackling voice flashed through Rejeena's mind, "This one will . . . demand his own way." This tendency in her queen's man must be crushed immediately. "Tell my queen's man to remove his pants at once, place himself in my skindown, and indulge in the completion process as instructed. Ascertain he understands this disobedience constitutes a serious offense against his queen and shall exact most severe punishment."

"My Queen, his head—"

"I did not say I shall whip him tonight. Relate to Aarvan my words."

"Yes, My Queen." Alea relayed the message. She finished with, "Please do as she says, Aarvan. She is serious."

He answered, whisper soft. "Please tell my queen I must respectfully decline."

Alea interpreted.

Rejeena stared, icy green eyes boring into the calm, dark blue. If he felt fear or anxiety, neither eyes nor demeanor mirrored it. He appeared completely relaxed.

"Guards," the queen called.

Alea stood, face drawn, eyes flicking from Aarvan to the queen and back again.

The queen closely watched Aarvan as six guards entered the room, four forming a semi-circle behind him. He revealed no emotion.

Aarvan stood quiet. The studied calmness sprang from ability hidden behind the wall between him and his memory, reflecting years of practice. He didn't know the purpose. As the guards entered, a small door seemed to open in that obstructing wall. He couldn't see in, but he could feel a presence, seeded by a contained rage, stalking behind the door. *The rage emerged before with the angel, but what did it do—anything?*

A voice, inside his head, like his own but different, purred, "*You can take them. There are only six.*"

He started. He had seen the women enter—six big, husky queen's guards. *I can take them? Hardly.* The voice had to be crazy. He couldn't fathom what it was or where it came from.

The queen said, "Alea, take the queen's man and furnish him a pallet. I do not wish to see him again this night." She turned to the head guard. "Accompany the queen's man. Have him available in the morning."

"Yes, My Queen," the line leader said.

"That is all." Rejeena's voice dripped ice water.

"Aarvan, come." Alea grabbed his vest and slapped it against his chest. "You gained reprieve."

He performed a graceful half-bow and exited the room, followed by four guards.

"Alea, what's going on?" Aarvan asked as he followed her.

"Do not speak to me."

He halted, nearly causing the guards to run into him. "Why are you so angry? You knew what would happen."

She stopped, hands on hips and glared. "I held hope that you would relent of your daftness when facing the queen eye to eye. Don your vest and come."

He shrugged into the vest. "Where are we going?"

"To my home. You will sleep there tonight. She does not want to look at you."

"Oh, and I suppose the guards will assure I behave?"

"Correct, Queen's Man," a guard answered in Universal, "and to ascertain that you remain available at the queen's pleasure."

He turned and looked at her. "Where else would I be?"

"You might rabbitt."

"To where? Where would I go?"

"Aarvan, clamp jaw and come," Alea snapped.

"Yes, do." The guard gestured with her shield.

Aarvan followed Alea. "I guess I'm out of favor right now."

"That may be safely assumed," Alea said.

They walked in silence to the healer's home. A servant placed a pallet for him in a small, inside room with one door. The guards took stations outside.

Aarvan scowled, stalked to the pallet, snatched off his boots and vest. Lying down, he turned his back on the women and pulled the cover up to his chin.

Alea asked, "Is there anything you need, Aarvan?"

"No."

She left.

A long time passed before Aarvan slept. What would the queen do now? She would not be happy, and he didn't doubt an unhappy queen could be vicious. His actions were necessary and justified. He, and he alone, was the one person he must face every day, every time. He already found this command performance in the queen's skindown degrading. Degrading men appeared to be these women's specialty. Refusing the queen altogether seemed no viable option. That would get him a beating and he would still end up in her skindown. Every time he stood near the queen, that rush of lust almost overwhelmed him. Were he presented a choice of bedmates, he would choose Rejeena. He would fill her skindown, but he would have some say in the performance.

If only he could break into those hidden memories. Jumbled thoughts teased his mind, suggesting interesting but obscure abilities. For instance, that strange voice telling him he could take six, big muscular queen's guards. What had it said? "*You can take them. There are only six.*" *Only six? What sort of idiot advice was that? What about me? I'm only one.* Those guards would surely make buzzard bait of him.

The door had closed, the voice gone. He couldn't recall it. It vanished when the immediate danger to him passed. Take six guards? It wasn't possible. In any case, he didn't want to fight the guards. He wanted to make peace with the queen, but not her way.

He lay beneath his cover, sweating with a clammy chill. Anger and fear churned his insides into froth, one as strong as the other.

* * *

Alone, Rejeena sank onto her skindown. "LaHeeka, why do you so vex me?" she whispered. Her incredibly gorgeous queen's man, with those warm eyes, smooth, lean body—she did not want to hurt him, punish him, watch those eyes fill with fear. She visualized his lean hips between her thighs, manhood deep inside her, them writhing together through the completion process, his seed releasing, completing her. That is what she wanted. She found the completion process, the rutting, pleasurable. Women who claimed to find ecstasy, euphoria in this lovemaking leaped beyond the bounds of civility and tradition. Fools. They harbored fantasy, possessed great imaginations and no sense.

A man and his manhood were tools for completion. The pleasurable sensation LaSheena allowed as atonement for the pain of birthing a daughter or the grinding disappointment of delivering a male offspring.

She arose and slammed her pillow onto the skindown. *I am queen. He will perform my way.*

* * *

The following day, at mid-morning, Rejeena called Locin, the guard line leader. Locin had served the queen for seven seasons and spoke Universal well. The queen trusted her.

Rejeena said, "I wish you to do a chore."

"Of course, My Queen."

"Pick three other guards, big women. Go to Alea's house and secure my queen's man." The queen outlined her desires.

"The queen's man will not be punished?" Locin asked. Handling of a queen's man meant delicate function. She must rightly understand.

"Absolutely not. However, he will watch the punishment imposed upon the holdee."

"And if he objects?"

"You will have four large women."

"Yes, My Queen."

"The queen's man remains prone to injury, and I cannot chance punishment at this time. But his actions comprise extreme disobedience. Use only necessary force. Do not hurt him." The queen stood silent for a moment then continued, her green eyes meeting the gray ones of the line leader. "My desire is to put the fear of LaSheena into him. That is why he will watch punishment. Show no pity." A grin flickered. "See if we can, quite literally, scare the pants off him."

"Yes, My Queen," Locin grinned. "I can do that."

"Meitra will grant tour before punishment. I have instructed her to paste on her most gruesome countenance, act as obnoxious as only Meitra can. She should impress him."

"Without doubt, My Queen."

"Leave your weapons. You may not use them, and if the queen's man resists, none will be at his disposal. Proceed with him directly to the punishment room."

"Yes, My Queen." Locin curtsied from the room.

* * *

Alea and Aarvan spent an uncomfortable morning. Both worried about the queen's reaction, but irritated with each other, refused to discuss it.

The waiting wore heavily on them.

Alea struggled through some of her work, remaining available to observe and perhaps try to mitigate the queen's reaction.

Aarvan alternated roaming the room and flopping into soft chairs, face drawn. Several times he stood before a window, rocking his feet toe to heel, reaching to rub the back of his neck.

When Locin and her guards arrived, an antagonistic relief surged in Aarvan. Now the dreaded action would begin, but at least the tedious wait was over. He sat shapelessly in a chair when the four guards stopped before him. He noted the contingent to be Patea, Tressa and Meta, guards he had seen around and heard their names, all unusually large women.

"You will come with us, Queen's Man," the line leader said, her voice calm with a peremptory bite.

He stared at the four women and studied their leader.

She stood tall, broad, muscular, an imposing bulk of woman. For all its size, her form flowed round and womanly. Her strong-featured face sported clear gray eyes, brown hair falling to just below her ears. Not a pretty woman, she exuded an attractive aura of strength and competence. She regarded him, without obvious feeling, as she might any trivial piece of her day's work.

Who does she think she is? "Where?" he demanded.

"You will do as required, Queen's Man. We follow queen's bidding. Rise and come, now."

"What's the queen's bidding?"

"You will know in due time. If you do not come of your volition, we are instructed to use force."

He flowed to his feet, a lithe twist of motion, at once graceful and threatening.

"Aarvan, go!" Alea snapped. "You have behaved enough of an ass. Do not build upon it."

He dropped his eyes, jerked in a sharp breath and puffed it out. Then he raised both hands in front of his chest, palms outward. "I'll come peacefully, Shiira Guardswoman."

"I am Locin."

"I'll come peacefully . . . Locin."

"You brought this upon yourself, Aarvan. I warned you." Alea's voice trembled.

"I'm sorry to cause you distress," Aarvan told her. Then to Locin, "Lead on."

They turned to go and, behind Aarvan's back, Locin flashed Alea a quick wink.

The healer rolled her eyes upward, blew out a breath. *Thank LaSheena, he is not slated for severe punishment.*

Locin, walking behind and left of the queen's man, watched him. He glided with the sinuous grace of the tarag cat, muscles flowing smoothly. His feet skimmed the ground, as water at midstream pours effortlessly over a rock. *He is not big, but this man will move fast.* She mentally revised her handling of him to compensate.

They approached the punishment room, and Locin touched Aarvan's shoulder. "To the right, Queen's Man."

He took several steps into the room, realized where he was, stopped and looked around. The guards, between him and the door, waited.

The large room stretched before him, one wall holding a display of odd-looking instruments. Made of wood, they hung from long handles, with flat, round heads, in three graduated sizes.

Further along the wall hung an assortment of items—a rolled whip, clubs, loops of rope and knives. Empty bleachers, built in tiers, six high, crowded two sides of the room. Benches filled the third side, to seat seegarpt, judged by the separate padded seats with armrests, indented to hold a caster or tankard. All seating areas faced the center of the room. At that spot squatted a strange, ugly device of ropes, pulleys and bars. The rusty brown of dried blood stained the ground beneath it, spreading for several feet in all directions, kicked and scuffed about. The purpose of the room would be punishment and the observing of it.

Aarvan's stomach lurched. *How did the women use that ugly device? It would be nothing pleasant.* He feared he might soon find out. The queen sent him to pay for his disobedience. He swallowed convulsively, and wondered how bad it would be.

That door in his mind slid open and the voice purred,*"You can take them. There're only four. Take them and run."*

A jolt raced through him, fire in his blood, followed by a frigid chill. He shivered, breath quickened. For a second he listened to the voice before good sense prevailed. *They are four large women. I am one injured man, and can't put up an effective fight. They will treat me as they please—as the queen pleases.*

That strange voice rang familiar, yet alien. He didn't understand it, couldn't believe its raving. It and the rage contained within it, clearly favored violent action, encouraged, demanded it. What was its source? How did it lodge in his mind? His memory might hold the answer, but he had no access to that.

Locin placed the flat of her hand against his back, propelling him further into the room. "Do not be shy, Queen's Man. Take a close look."

He stepped forward, balance shifting to the balls of his feet, floating light as a puff of air.

Locin nodded to Tressa, and as prearranged, they closed beside him. The other two closed behind.

Aarvan stopped as a door across the room opened.

An utterly repugnant woman entered. Not tall, but broad and squat, her blocky form showed no hint of womanly shape. Her long, muscular arms ended in big, square hands. The head seemed a small block riding a big one, neck short, face dark, mouth a wide slit, nose large and broad, eyes deeply sunken pits of black. Dark hair hung short of her shoulders. She walked forward, a menacing roll of movement. The sunken eyes glittered maliciously and locked on Aarvan. Her lips twisted into a hideous effigy of a smile, a deaths-head grimace. An aura of focused evil surrounded her so thick Aarvan felt he could grab a handful.

When she stopped before him, Aarvan strained not to recoil. His stomach flipped over and anxious tremors danced along his nerve endings. That awful aura touched him, as a hot buffet of wind. He stared, face held tightly bland.

She folded long arms across her chest and looked him over, taking her time. Her gaze began at the top of his head, slid to his feet, then back, lingering both times at his crotch.

His skin crawled wherever her scrutiny touched. His breath caught in his throat, muscles tensed.

The ugly woman spoke in Universal, voice grating like a rusty hinge. "What a pretty little queen's man. It would be a shame to lash such a body." She reached toward his chest.

He leaped backward. Pain sliced through his head and neck, but he preferred that to her touch.

Before anyone realized he moved, he was out of her reach. Beside him Locin stood, astounded by his speed. *He is fast all right. He could out strike a snattsnake.* She again readjusted her guard parameters.

"I am Meitra," the evil apparition said, seeming unconcerned by Aarvan's reaction. "Meitra, the meter, punishment meter that is." She chortled, a squeak akin to a door creaking open in a haunted house. "I enjoy my function, pretty little Queen's Man. Queen Rejeena asked me to introduce you to my domain. Come, I will show you around." She walked toward the hanging implements.

Aarvan didn't move.

Locin flat-handed his back, pushed him.

He walked forward.

Locin motioned the other guards to close tight around him.

Meitra stopped before the round-headed implements, several sets of three hanging. She waved a hand. "These are strikepaddles, Queen's Man," she said, lightly tapping her chest, "my strikepaddles. Handsome devices, every one, functional, efficient. Their purpose is to punish. They cause excruciating agony while not necessarily rendering great damage. A queen or mistress can punish a queen's man or holdee harshly while retaining use of him. Once you have felt the bite of my strikepaddle, you will beg to perform the queen's bidding. You will indeed thank her for the privilege."

She lifted the largest from the wall, whirled it with familiarity and smiled fondly. "This," grated the rusty hinge, "is the grand paddle. It need not concern you. No queen's man would ever feel its teeth." She leaned close and leered. "Should you so irritate your queen, you would no longer be queen's man. The grand, my personal favorite, is the harshest, used only for the direst offenses." She caressed the handle and rim of the head, a lover's touch.

Aarvan's brows pinched inward. *Disgusting. What kind of demented women does this island produce?*

Those black eyes, ominous as a roiling thunderhead, lifted to his. "This beauty will flay the flesh and skin from your body. Control is all in the touch. Holdees have died under this paddle, Queen's Man." She thrust the device toward him.

Aarvan winced as the head skimmed his open vest.

"Feel that texture," Meitra said. "Run your finger across that head. Observe how it is made, hard wood bent in a circle. You notice it is covered with skin then heavy padding on the strike side, the beading stretched on top. The skin can be thus torn and flayed by the beading but the woodenhead will not bruise beyond repair. Feel that beading."

Curious, Aarvan touched it. The beading consisted of rawhide interwoven with small jagged pieces of metal. He lifted shocked eyes. "You hit people with that thing?" His voice grated low.

"Oh yes, but never a pretty little queen's man." She replaced the paddle and took the next. "This is the strife paddle. Only rarely would a queen's man meet this one." She waved down the wall where a rack of these items hung without contrasting sizes. "I demolish many applying punishment for medium offenses. Feel that one, Queen's Man."

He touched the beading. It was rawhide alone, stout and taut.

Meitra replaced it and took the smallest. "This is the kit paddle. It is smaller, the beading softer, causing pain equal to the bigger ones but leaving the flesh beneath, rendering less havoc to the body. Applied correctly it will quickly set you screaming for mercy." She chortled. "The kit would be employed upon a queen's man. The wisdom of obedience would dawn upon you. The queen can have you beaten today and rutting in her skindown tomorrow. You would suffer much agony, the queen none at all." She reached toward him.

He sprang backward into the solidity of two large guards. They formed a wall with their bodies. All four guards grabbed his arms and pinioned them.

Meitra's big hand settled on his bare abdomen, fingertips worrying the skin. That mean, mirthless smile displayed, Meitra slid her hand slowly up his ribcage under his vest, hard fingers plucking at the skin. The hand smoothed across his chest, irritating. She paused to squeeze his nipple, moving on to vex the other side.

Aarvan's skin crawled. Her touch, intimate and repulsive, burned. *I won't stand for this.* He slammed up and back, arched his powerful back muscles, trying to break the guards' holds.

One guard could not counter his speed. Her grip slipped and her hand flew upward, striking his left ear.

A white-hot lance shot up the back of his head, around both sides, meeting in front with a crash. Agony seared his spine, turned his knees to jelly. He crumpled.

The guards held tight, kept him from sprawling face first in the dirt. They supported his weight while the worst of the pain subsided, allowing him to regain control of his legs.

He pushed to a standing position, head pounding, breath jerking in his chest. Opening his eyes, he stared into Meitra's smug face. Her hand still violated him, but it would do no good to fight.

Meitra said, "Oh yes, nice smooth skin with fine muscle layering, not just pretty but pleasing in all ways. I wager you to be one wild rut in skindown . . . when our queen convinces you to enter it."

The voice in his mind purred. "*You can take them. Use your feet. You know how.*"

He ignored it; it was crazy.

"Take your hands off me," he growled. He pushed his shoulders back, forced his knees straight.

Two guards released him, but Locin and Tressa held fast.

"So," Meitra said, "perhaps you prefer this." She flipped the kit paddle around so she gripped it behind the head, shoved it flat against his midriff.

The guards pushed forward, so he stood with the paddle pressed against his skin.

"It's less repulsive than you," he snarled.

"So, a brave little queen's man." Meitra pulled the paddle back and popped it sharply against his belly.

Even from that short distance, the paddle stung. His agitated skin tingled, and he winced.

"Felt that, did you, Queen's Man? Think of the bite from a full swing."

Fury surged in Aarvan. They played some game, the object no doubt to force him into compliance with the queen's demands. If he complied, he would receive no punishment. Sweat beaded his skin and he could feel his heart banging against his ribcage. He sucked in a deep breath. *I will not give in.* He quieted the anger, as a practiced mental hand tamping it. *How many times have I needed to do that, and why?* He said, soft and cold, "If you intend to punish me, then proceed. But stop the game."

Meitra contemplated him. She turned and replaced the kit paddle on the wall. "Do you game with the queen's man, Line Leader?"

"No," Locin said, "I am most serious."

"As am I. Since strikepaddles seem not to provoke within him the required concern, perhaps the locchot may."

"Locchot?" He regretted the question as soon as he asked it.

Meitra waved expansively toward the device of ropes, pulleys and bars. "That, pretty little Queen's Man, is a locchot. Come." She walked toward the apparatus.

Aarvan followed.

The guards held his arms and grouped close around him, prepared to use force if needed.

Meitra paused before the contraption, placed a hand on Aarvan's shoulder, her big thumb kneading his throat and collarbone. She gestured at the stained ground. "If you would drop to your knees, Queen's Man, I will show you how the locchot functions. You can thus acquire a personal taste."

"No, thank you," he said.

"Aaaah well," Meitra sighed, "if you will not cooperate, I will needs explain it. The full effect, though, will be diminished by—"

A commotion at the door interrupted her.

They all looked.

Three women handlers struggled with a holdee, his hands tied and feet shackled.

He cursed and fought them.

They heaved and shoved. One cracked him with a truchon when he stepped on her foot. They ended in a tangle near the locchot. The handlers jerked him to his feet.

He struggled vainly then, unable to break free, stopped fighting and spat on the handler nearest him.

She balled her fist and hit him in the face.

He jerked away with an anguished yelp, blood welling from a cut on his cheek.

"Well, pretty little Queen's Man, we can indeed provide you a real demonstration," Meitra said. Her hand slid flattened down his chest and belly, lifting at his pant line. She smirked. "You notice many women, not just queens, have partials to accomplish their bidding."

He couldn't seem to control his curiosity. "Partials?"

"Yes, these women are handlers, sometimes called partials." The punishment meter leaned close, breath wafting against his face. "Partial to women, of course. Armed or unarmed, they protect their mistresses and force holdees to perform as needed. You will find our society well-prepared to deal with men and their odious natures."

Ignoring the lift of lip from Aarvan, Meitra stepped before the holdee and smiled that ugly grimace.

He funneled his mouth as though to spit on her.

"Go ahead, dogshit," she said. "Spit. I wield the strikepaddle."

He didn't spit, and as he looked into those evil eyes, his face paled.

Aarvan looked at Locin. "What's going on?"

"You will see."

Meitra turned to Aarvan. "Now, Queen's Man, while these handlers place this dogshit in the locchot, I will explain." She gestured. "Bring him."

One partial kicked the holdee behind the knee.

He plunged to his knees and yelled, "No, I didn't do it. Let go of me. Let me up. I didn't do it."

The handlers dragged him under the locchot, still on his knees. He bucked and reared, jerked, pushed, desperately tried to pull his feet under him. The women proved too strong. The partials yanked him into position with his lower legs across a wooden bar, flush with the ground.

Meitra stepped forward and snapped the other half of the bar down, locked it in place. The top half curved to accommodate his legs, pinning him to the ground just below the bent knees.

Meitra said to Aarvan, "Locks your legs right in there. That dogshit goes nowhere until we so allow." She gestured to the holdee's handlers. "Place him. Take your time. I want to explain it to this pretty little queen's man. He attends class today." She snickered that repulsive sound. As she spoke, facing the locchot, she absently rubbed that big, rough hand over Aarvan's bare belly

He recoiled, but remained as much a captive as the holdee. *I'd like to send her to class.*

Meitra continued cheerfully. "His hands fasten onto that bar in front of him." She raised her voice as the man alternated cursing at and pleading with the handlers. "The metal holders lock around his wrists. For a queen's man, of course, we pad the holders. We may not tatter wrists you need to hang onto the queen while you rut her." She chortled again. "He is secured. They now raise his arms with those wheels and pulleys." Meitra watched Aarvan as the handlers cranked the man upward. "You granting attention, Queen's Man? If you persist in your disobedience, soon you will return to visit me."

His eyes met hers. "I don't understand. I thought I was here for punishment."

"No locchot for you today. Watching this dogshit have the flesh flayed from him stands as your punishment."

"I'm not going to watch you beat that man."

Meitra shrugged. "It is not your decision. The queen so desires. You will watch, and the guards will assure that you do. Right, Locin?"

"That is right, Queen's Man," Locin said. "You stay and you watch."

He expelled an angry spurt of breath. "For god's sake, what did this man do?"

One partial pulled her knife and sliced down both legs of the holdee's pants. She pulled them off, leaving him naked.

The man shrieked a line of indecipherable curses, jerking and lunging against the restraints.

Meitra said, "As you can see, Queen's Man, he is stretched to the point of misery. Now, we stretch him further. That pulls his skin very tight, so when the paddle lands, it will accord the most painful effect."

The handlers wound the pulleys tighter, stretched the man's body until he bellowed, a roar of fury and abject terror.

A woman approached and handed Meitra one of two strikepaddles.

"My assistant, Sercha," Meitra said.

The holdee hung stretched and moaning.

Meitra removed her hand from Aarvan to stroke the paddle. "We utilize the strife paddle. Unless, of course, he does not scream enough." She glanced contemptuously at the holdee. "I think that will not pose a problem."

Meitra walked to the man and poked him with the paddle.

He shrieked hoarsely and yanked against his bonds.

"This dogshit," the punishment meter said, "forcibly rutted a youngster, still under her mother's protection, without permission from mother or youngster. He will receive thirty strokes, front and rear, for a total of sixty. He will then be castrated. Should he survive, he will toil in the clay mines for what remains of his days."

The holdee screamed and moaned, twisted and jerked. The metal bands sliced his wrists, and blood trickled down his arms.

"He committed rape? Can't you just hang him?" Aarvan's face twisted, soft voice rough. "Why torture him?"

"It is our way, Queen's Man. Should he survive, we retain a holdee for the clay mines. Those are always needed. Holdees do not survive long at the mines."

"But you said he raped a girl. That should be a hanging offense."

"Ahhhh, but this is Kriiscon. Rape is not so serious—rutting causes no great harm."

"But . . . but . . ." the queen's man stammered. "It's the most horrible thing that can happen to a woman."

Meitra waved her hand in a dismissive gesture. "Is this the outlook of your weak Mainlander women? Do not be daft. It is but rutting without a woman's agreement—but still an activity in which all women indulge at one time." She stepped close and stared into his eyes. "I lost a daughter at eight seasons of age to a horrid accident. That is the worst thing that can happen to a woman. I would accept this rape, as you call it, a thousand times to reclaim my daughter."

She paused, took a deep breath, then pointed at the holdee. "His effrontery assaulting a woman, particularly a youngster, laying hands upon her of his volition, comprises a most grievous offense." Meitra grinned wickedly into Aarvan's unbelieving stare. "He is big and strong, will make a worker if he lives." She gestured to Locin. "Take the queen's man to the front, so he may watch the dogshit's face."

The guards propelled Aarvan to a position before the holdee.

The man's terrified eyes locked onto him. "They called you queen's man. Help me. Don't let them do this. Please, stop the . . ." His voice faded to incoherent babble.

Aarvan started to answer, but a guard clamped a hand over his mouth.

Locin explained. "You are queen's man. It is beneath your status to speak to a condemned holdee."

Aarvan's skin flushed hot. *Callous bitches. What kind of she-devils are they?* The holdee's life, his terror didn't seem to touch them. The man raped a girl, yet they didn't consider that his worst crime. That he touched her without assent brought upon him this ghastly punishment.

The voice in his head snarled, "*Attack! Escape!*" It started to explain how, to direct.

Too furious to listen, he lunged away from his guards.

The unexpected strength of that lean body, his speed so great, the guards were taken unaware. All but Locin lost their grips.

He kicked her feet from under her.

She held fast and they fell in a tangle.

The other guards piled on, grabbing hold of him any way they could.

The advantage of speed gone, Aarvan was no match for them. But he writhed, wiry and agile, slippery as a paaerta shoat. It required long moments to subdue him. Every one of the guards suffered for the effort. While their instructions restricted them from rough handling him, he tussled with no such qualms.

He landed some telling blows, employed elbows, knees and head butts to escape. Surprising himself, he pulled the power of the strikes. He didn't want to kill or seriously injure the women. He just wanted free of their grips.

Tressa locked an arm around his neck. "Be still or I choke," she hissed.

Both arms captive, the fourth guard's legs wrapped around his waist in a scissor grip, he went still. Chest heaving with exertion, ignoring stabs of agony, he glared at Locin.

The line leader said calmly, "You have managed to make a spectacle of yourself, Queen's Man." She looked at Meitra, who leaned on her strikepaddle, watching the fracas with a grin. "Please bring some rope and tie his feet. If he chooses to act an ass, we will so treat him."

Meitra brought a length of rope and leaned to grab his feet.

He scowled and flung a vicious kick at her head, missing but ruffling her hair in passing.

Tressa tightened her hold, and cut off his wind. The guard at his waist slid down his legs, pinned them. He tossed and jerked, fury still boiling. Unable to breathe, he finally collapsed.

Meitra tied his feet together, and Tressa loosened her grip.

While he lay gasping, the ugly punishment meter thrust her face close to his. "You missed, pretty little Queen's Man. Be assured, when you hang in my locchot, I will not."

He had no breath to answer.

The holdee's handlers grabbed Aarvan's arms, pulled them behind him and tied his hands. One looked at Locin and said, "Glad I do not have your function. We could trounce that wayscrape when he misbehaved."

Locin rose, grimacing, rapidly blinking her left eye. With two fingers she gently touched above it.

Patea, the guard of the scissors grip, rose too. She winced and rubbed her ribcage. "There are compensations," she said. "I slid my womancenter right down over that gorgeous keister of his—all in the service of my queen."

The women burst into laughter.

The holdee hung moaning, ignored.

A partial, ogling the queen's man admiringly, said, "I would wager that one proves a handful for the queen."

"It is his lack of obedience that causes him to be educated," Locin said.

Aarvan laid, stiff and quiet, as pain slammed through his head. The voice in his mind spoke. "*You didn't listen. You could have taken them.*" His impulsive attempt had been foolish, his only accomplishment his own misery. It would not happen again. Next time he would stand against them or take the required action to escape. *But how can I, one against many?* He opened his mind at last, listened to that voice, receptive to its chilling advice.

"Let us continue," Meitra barked, "now that the guards have subdued our guest of honor." She carried her paddle to stand before the holdee trapped in the locchot. Sercha did the same behind him.

The holdee took one look at Meitra's face and released a loud, lingering screech.

"Clamp jaw, dogshit," she grated. "In a moment, we will grant you reason to scream. Holdees who yell in anticipation disgust me."

Locin and Tressa grabbed Aarvan and pulled him to his feet.

Tied hand and foot, he couldn't resist. His head pounded, his knees wobbled, nausea clawed at his stomach. Cold sweat trickled down his cheeks and chest. He swallowed, feeling the push travel down his throat, determined not to vomit.

Locin noted his distress and said, "The whole of your misery falls to your sword point, Queen's Man. Now behave."

Meitra nodded to Sercha.

The assistant raised her strikepaddle. She extended it full length and swung hard. It crashed into the holdee's back.

He yelped and arched forward to escape the agony.

Meitra swung her paddle, meeting his forward-thrusting chest with a frightful thwack.

He screeched and jerked backward only to meet Sercha's paddle. His screaming filled the air as his body arched backward and forward, his only reward more brutal paddle blows.

After ten strokes, front and rear, Meitra nodded to Sercha. They paused.

While Sercha leaned nonchalantly on her paddle, Meitra walked to Aarvan, whose face was white, etched in pain as though he felt the paddle blows. "You look unwell, Queen's Man," she said. "We give this piece of dogshit a break, let him savor the pain and consider the lashes still to come. You will notice, we laced him ten strokes each, the holdee screams for mercy, and the paddles have thus far removed but skin. That is most skillful function."

"You're a sadistic shrew."

She caught his chin, tilted it so that their eyes met. "At this function, it is best to be."

Meitra returned to her victim. "Well, dogshit, still want to spit?" Getting no answer, she asked, "Ready for more?"

The holdee begged, moaning, voice piteous. "Please. I won't do it no more. I've had enough. Please. Please." He squawked as she lifted and swung the paddle.

The two women continued their attack on his body, and his movements grew increasingly disjointed, spastic. His screams hoarsened, sounding louder. Blood flowed in tiny rivulets down his arms. Bright red matted the rawhide beading and splattered as the strikepaddles landed. His bladder spilled. Urine ran down his legs and soaked the ground.

The cracking of the paddles continued, as sharp as the holdee's desperate screams.

The spastic twisting and screeching of the man in agony, the dreadful thwack of the paddles, the thumping of his own head, assaulted Aarvan until he lost the battle to retain his breakfast.

Locin felt him begin to heave. She signaled Tressa and they eased him to his knees as he retched.

He hung weakly in their grip.

Patea reached forward and wiped his mouth with a soft cloth.

The guards pulled him back to his feet, and a servant raced forward with a bucket and thin wooden scraper to dispose of the mess.

The second set ended. The holdee hung, moaning, his body trembling, twitching and jerking uncontrollably.

Meitra approached Aarvan. "Feel better now?" She glanced at the damp spot at his feet. "Just be glad that dogshit hangs there, not you. You will notice now his flesh shreds, in small, acutely painful hunks. We will finish the last set shortly, then you can go home, Queen's Man, with that smooth, pretty body intact—for today."

"If you give him ten more, you vulture, you'll kill him." Aarvan's voice dragged hoarsely.

She grinned, her deaths-head grimace. "Vulture, is it? I shall remember that when you hang in my locchot, pretty little Queen's Man. Hopefully he will not die, but if so, it is the will of LaSheena. So be it."

"You are one cold bitch."

She rubbed a hand across his belly, the tip of her finger barely sliding under his pants. "When the queen grows weary of your arrogance and places you at barter, I shall acquire you and allow you to determine that for yourself."

Chills of revulsion, laced with fear, chased each other up and down his spine, anchored in his bones. "I'll take that man's place first."

"I like a man who fights." She chucked him lightly under the chin with a bent finger, and returned to her chore. "Let us finish this dogshit," she called to Sercha, who immediately swung her paddle.

The beating continued. The blows landed loud and harsh.

The man's screams spiraled lower, more hoarse. His mouth flew wide open like an out-of-water fish gasping, seeking breaths it couldn't find, but emitted little sound. His body no longer arched, but hung jerking, uncoordinated, ineffective objections against the horrific pain.

Aarvan stood, head lowered, eyes tight shut. His body twitching each time a paddle struck made his awareness obvious, so the guards did not force him to watch.

The sound of the paddles stopped.

The holdee's handlers unfastened him, and he sprawled face down in his own blood and urine, moaning. His body jerked spastically, uncontrolled nerve twitches.

The women hauled him away by the arms. His toes and manhood dragged through the bloody dust, mutilated chest bumping over small rocks and uneven earth.

Meitra, a bit winded from effort, once more stood before Aarvan. “You can open your eyes, Queen’s Man. It is over. The holdee has paid for his crime. He will attack no more women. If he lives, he will be ready to castrate in a week.”

He lifted his head and stared at her, his limited vocabulary of curses and nasty names failing him. Finally, he said, “You’re repulsive. Get away from me.”

She handed her bloody strikepaddle to Sercha. “Be careful, Queen’s Man, you may visit me soon. I am very skilled.” Leaving him with that thought, she walked away.

“If you behave, Queen’s Man,” Locin said, “we will untie you. You may then walk with dignity to Alea’s home.”

“I’ll behave,” he said, voice low. He said nothing on the return, but walked flatly, the quick, lilting steps gone. At Alea’s house, he plodded to a soft chair and collapsed.

Locin spoke to Alea in Oldenspeak. “Check him closely. We unintentionally struck his head as we tussled. He lost his breakfast and appears unwell.”

When the door closed behind Locin, Aarvan asked, “Do you have something for a headache?”

“Come on.” Alea pulled him to his feet. She led him to a skindown room, gave him foul-tasting medicine.

He lay quietly as she examined his head.

Neither spoke.

He closed his eyes and relaxed, as she dropped the shades. The healer paused at the door, looked at him so still and pale. She sighed and shook her head sadly.

* * *

Late in the afternoon, Rejeena arrived at Alea’s home. The queen asked, “How is Aarvan? Locin said she left him unwell.”

“He has slept since he returned. He should be fine. You might allow him a day or two to recover.”

The queen shook her head. “No, his stubborn disobedience caused his suffering. He shall not reap reward for crass behavior. Bring him to my home tonight about skindown time. We may need you.”

“Will he refuse again, My Queen?”

Rejeena sat. "I hope not. Locin explained what occurred. She did not think the tour of the punishment room scared him, but the actual chastisement did. Meitra wore her evil face, to assure he would not wish to visit her again. He tried to flee and rough handled my guards. They found it needful to bind him."

"I warned you, My Queen, of a wildness in him."

"Clearly he grows wild when angry. Locin sports a nasty eye, and all the guards suffered cuts and bruises. It required all four to hold him. Meitra and the holdee's handlers bound him." Stern disapproval rang in the queen's voice.

"What happens if he does still refuse?"

The queen grimaced. "I have given that much thought. I came to acquire your opinion. I wish to be completed, and I must begin now. Even were he not so injured, due to the history between LaHeeka and my grandmother, I would be loath to visit heavy punishment on this queen's man. If he does refuse, would it greatly lower my queen's dignity to strike compromise?"

"No, My Queen, I think not. Compromise could be needful. He is exceptionally stubborn." Alea walked to her medicine chest. She handed the queen a measure of concoction. "Please take this with you. He will require it after the skindown romp."

Rejeena took the offered medicine and nodded. "See that he rests. It would be good if he can eat, also. We will see what happens tonight."

"Yes, My Queen." Alea saw her out.

* * *

When Aarvan awoke, he appeared rested but distant.

"Aarvan, you act most unfriendly tonight," Alea said as they ate a simple dinner.

He looked at her, eyes pensive. "I'm sorry, Alea. It's not your fault." He gave a tiny smile. "Still friends?"

"Yes, we are friends."

"Thank you."

"Aarvan, what will happen tonight?"

He stared at his plate, stabbed at a hapless vegetable with his fork. "I don't know." He arose and stood by a window, gazing into the gathering dusk. "After what I saw today, I want nothing to do with locchot and strikepaddles."

Alea's hopes soared. "I may presume then that you will stop behaving as a stubborn child and comply?"

He whirled. "A child? If refusing this concocted idea of bedding practice is childish, then I'll be a child." For a moment, he stared toward the darkened window. "I can't do as the queen requires." He struggled for words to express his thoughts. "It would make me less than I need to be." Standing beside her chair, Aarvan stared down. "You tell me, Alea, what's more important—saving your back today or hanging onto your sense of self for all the tomorrows?"

Alea looked into his dark eyes and saw resolve hardening. She sighed. "Go to the skindown room. Bathe, shave and dress. I will wait."

He nodded and walked into the hall.

* * *

Queen Rejeena perched cross-legged on her skindown when Alea and Aarvan arrived. They bowed and greeted her, then she bade them rise.

She stood and said, "You will enter the skindown now, Aarvan."

Alea interpreted.

Aarvan took a deep breath. "Tell my queen I will be honored to share her skindown, if she allows me to make love to her."

The queen walked to Aarvan, face to face, almost touching him. "Did the queen's man learn nothing today?"

"I learned I'm trapped in a cruel society, where those in power use fear and pain to rule. I learned my queen will try to scare me into submission to her will." He stood motionless, apparently relaxed, betraying no emotion.

Their eyes locked. They talked directly to each other, leaving Alea scrambling to interpret.

"Since you have so learned, then comply. Do you desire punishment?"

"Punishment is for those who commit crimes, My Queen."

"I would be patient with you, Aarvan, but you test me severely. As queen's man you are to obey."

"So I've been told."

"Then why do you defy me?"

"My Queen, we both want to join in skindown. You want to rut like a . . . an animal then roll over and forget it. I wish to engage in the euphoria, give and take pleasure from each other as man and woman were meant to do." He forced quiet words past a clenching jaw as he urgently checked his male reaction to her nearness. "If you will remove all your clothing, I will remove mine. Then I will show you—"

"How dare you." The queen snapped to full height, eyes blazing. "No man has ever gazed upon my upper body unclothed and no man ever will."

His black brows dipped. "I don't pretend to understand your aversion about your upper body, My Queen, or your attachment to tradition. When you don't include the whole body in touching and fondling before the completion act, you miss much of the pleasure of making love."

"I do not intend to engage in this touching and fondling; it is not needed to produce a daughter. Nor will your queen perform this *make love*. You are my queen's man. You will climb into my skindown, and complete me as you have been instructed. You will do it now."

"No, My Queen, I will not."

Alea winced, and awaited the explosion. Holding her temper was not Rejeena's strength.

The queen narrowed her eyes, voice glacial. "Then I assume, My Queen's Man, you wish to taste of locchot?"

"No."

Rejeena, standing so close to him, staring into those deep blue eyes, realized she faced resolve. *This then is the inner power LaHeeka felt.* No mere man should possess such strength, be so calm in the face of dire threat, so sure of his rightness. Men should be acquiescent, yield to their mistress and comply with all edicts. *Why have I been cursed with the one who will not, must hold himself to be different, willing to confront a queen?*

His scent filled her nostrils, a clean, heady aroma. She longed to bury her nose in his chest, breathe that scent and infuse her senses with it. Her mouth went dry, limbs flushed, skin burned with an intriguing, teasing excitement that sent tingles racing to her fingers and toes. Unfamiliar longing engulfed her, longing she could not identify but which set her aching to fulfill some obscure need. Her head floated, as though she stood on the far side of the wine cask. Never before had the queen experienced such chaotic urges. Through the headiness of all these feelings, only one thing remained certain in her confused thoughts—she wanted this man in her skindown, tonight.

If his observations in the punishment room today had not cured him of obstinacy and it obviously had not, on this subject he would not be swayed. She would have to compromise. Her stomach roiled. *I am queen. I will concede only so much. I should not have to concede at all. Blast him.*

Aarvan knew he pushed the queen's tolerance limit. Her eyes showed fury, but a deeper emotion lay beneath—she wanted him. He recognized the want. He had seen it before, too often, from more women than suited his taste. He experienced both relief and delight to detect it in Rejeena's green eyes, both for his safety and because the queen set carnal, exotic lust pushing at him, a wanton heat pulsing in unruly waves from his chest—and lower down—to his skin.

He wanted this woman, as deeply as she appeared to want him, but not her way. His manhood bulged against his pants so hard it grew painful. He steeled his mind and body to restrain his need. If the queen did not yield, his lust wouldn't be satisfied tonight; if she did, it would require some time on his part. To keep him away from locchot, strikepaddles and that repulsive punishment meter, their first intimate coupling must be done just right.

Aarvan felt the queen to be a passionate woman, likely to respond well to bedding intimacy. *She just doesn't know it yet.* Considering Alea's description of her past bedding practices, he could see why. His chore, and his pleasure, was to search for that passion, corral it, and coax it to life.

Rejeena turned, walked away from that magnetic body, those hypnotic eyes, far enough to think straight. With distance between them, she recalled her queenly hauteur. She had planned strategy earlier—in case. She stood with her back to him, long enough for fear and anxiety to rule, to terrify him. Then she turned.

He stood as before, appearing relaxed, calm.

Damn this man.

She spoke slowly, to allow Alea accurate interpretation. "The queen's man has lost the opportunity to cooperate with his queen without punishment. He has now but one choice, since he seems absorbed beyond reason with this creating euphoria and since the queen wishes completion now. The queen will allow him to make this love below her waist. He will not touch her above. In conjunction, the queen's man will understand, when he fully recovers, because of this disobedience, he will receive fifteen lashes with the kit paddle. The queen waits." She crossed her arms and glared at him, chin high, mouth tightly set.

After Alea interpreted, Aarvan said, "My queen leaves me little maneuvering room."

"It hangs to your sword point, for being such an ass," Alea said. "Take her offer. You will get no better. She is most lenient."

"Lenient? You call fifteen lashes lenient?"

"Fifteen lashes are not so many."

"Easy to say for someone not taking the lashes."

"Give the queen an answer. She grows impatient."

Aarvan stepped close to the queen, staring into her cold green eyes. "I accept my queen's offer. It will be worth the lashes to join my queen in love making, to complete her, and by doing so make her happy."

The queen's eyes narrowed. She deliberately concealed her feelings, but her heart quailed at his words. *Perhaps his motivation is my pleasure. But no! His disobedience stands paramount. He may not see his effect upon me.* She lifted her chin higher. "If my queen's man does not please me more than any other, he will receive five extra lashes for arrogance."

Aarvan's stomach lurched and he gulped in a deep breath. *I possess bedding skills, but better than any other? I've no way to assess the competition. I'll have to light the queen's fire and keep it burning. With only half of her to work with.* His mind raced. He closed his eyes for a moment, shutting out all else. As had happened before when he stood in dire need, the solidity of that wall to his memories leaked.

Sensuous, erotic thoughts escaped from behind it. Those thoughts surrounded another bed and another woman, who had taught him, slowly and meticulously over many nights, what a man needed to know about a woman's body. His uncooperative, conniving mind disallowed him access to her face or name, but he recovered what they did and how they did it. *I can blasted well give it a try.* He opened his eyes and smiled. "Then my queen will allow me to lead the love making?"

"The queen has so stated."

"Then I accept."

Alea looked from one to the other. "Well, it seems you have found agreement. If you will need me no more, My Queen . . ."

The queen waved her away.

Alea curtsied out the door.

*   *   *

Rejeena gazed at Aarvan. She needed simply to reach out to touch that solid-muscled chest. Her fingers itched to glide over the smooth skin, remove that obstructive vest. Oh, to unbutton his pants, savor with her palms those trim hips and enticing keister. She did not quite dare. She had never fondled a man. Touching him before had proved easier when he laid unconscious or sleeping, when those intense dark blue eyes did not stare.

She wanted to clasp him to her, fall onto the skindown and rut fiercely until his offspring shot released inside her. But she was queen. She would not betray eagerness, not grant him even a small vestige of power.

She jerked off her skirt, under which she wore nothing, and flung it down. "I wish to begin, Aarvan!"

She stalked to the skindown, sat, grabbed her jar of ointment and lifted the lid.

Two strong hands caught and held hers gently. He took the jar. "My Queen, if you need that, I'll have the extra lashes coming."

She looked up, straight into those wondrous blue eyes. Between his fumbled Oldenspeak and the gesture of taking the jar, she understood.

He replaced the jar lid, set it aside, then straightened and walked into the bathing room.

She waited impatiently, not sure of his intent. She had promised, though, to let him lead.

He returned, carrying a large hand basin of water, and set it on the floor. She watched as he removed his boots and vest, placing them neatly. With teasing slowness, he unbuttoned his pants and peeled them off, standing naked, obviously male, visibly interested.

He released a quick breath of relief. *Thank god, I can shed those pants before they put a permanent crease in my pecker.*

She reached for him, but he shook his head.

He knelt and took her feet, one at a time, gently with both hands, and placed them in the heated water.

She sighed. That water felt so good. *I did not even realize the tiredness of my feet.* The delicious wet warmth soothed them.

His hands rubbed those tired feet with gentle relaxing strokes.

She leaned forward, hands dropping to his shoulders, head almost touching his dark hair as he leaned down, immersed in his efforts. How she wished she dared fondle him. Her scrutiny caressed where her hands feared to venture, admired the lean, defined musculature of his body. His manhood—that vital portion, the instrument that would produce for her daughters—stood erect, looked efficient, handily declaring his enthusiasm. She licked her lips, gaze avidly upon it, hands itching. *I wish too grasp it. I cannot . . . I cannot. I have never . . .*

His hands kneaded her feet, thumbs smoothing through the arches. Fingers massaged the foot bones. He palmed the balls of her feet, stroking. Touch so gentle. Warmth so lulling.

She rested her cheek against his hair.

He delicately tugged at her toes, fingers tenderly probing between them, hands languorous, touch light, water warm. For long minutes he repeated these ministrations, gentle, soothing, calming.

The queen lay back on the skindown. She breathed deeply, allowing tension and anger to drain away. Her muscles slackened. Lassitude eased through her limbs. So wonderful. *When last have I felt so peaceful?*

He lifted one foot and eased his tongue along the arch. Warm tingles and soft pleasure entwined to travel through her ankles, up her legs. Teeth nibbled her toes, lightly nipping. He drew the tips into his mouth, tugged with his lips, ever so gently stretching them. His tongue probed between them, massaging those tender spots.

Relaxation pervaded Rejeena as her mind drifted, calm and peaceful.

His palms smoothed the contours of her lower legs, teasing her skin. That warm mouth, with gentle loops and sucks, paced up the inside, as fingertips tenderly stroked the delicate skin behind her knees.

Her skin tingled. She held her breath for a bit, concentrating on the pleasure of his touch. Warmth and relaxation turned to soft excitement. The temperature rose and quickened her breathing.

Queenly impatience invaded her mind. This was all most enjoyable, but unnecessary. He wasted time. Why will he not just get on with it? Perform his function. Drain his seed into her body, that most important act, his entire purpose. She sighed. *I did promise him control, but how can he, a mere man, understand the absolute necessity of daughters and the horrific ignominy of having none?*

The heat surging, flaming hotter, jerked her thoughts back to his arousing efforts, drowned her impatience in the rising impact of the moment.

Fingertips stroked her thighs, thumbs dragging, lips grazing along the inner sides. Lips and tongue led the way, quick flicks that skimmed and excited. The feather-light touches sent small bursts of fire racing up her veins, gathering in her belly, surrounding her most womanly part.

The spurts coalesced until a steady stream of sweltering heat poured up the sinews of her legs, swirled in a fiery whirlpool at their joining—at her womancenter.

Oh, my great LaSheena. Excitement squeezed her heart, stole her breath. She moaned gasping sounds, clasped his head between her hands, then released it.

Talented lips caressed the velvety spots between her thighs and womancenter, licking, sucking, kissing.

Of its own volition, her body squirmed, pressed into his touch, demanding more, demanding less, demanding—a mass of confused wanting. Unsure what she wanted, she could only wait for him to give it. Oh, to feel this fire burn forever. But what exquisite relief to have it quenched.

His lips glided over her belly, granted amorous attention to every inch of skin, kissed, sucked, laved, a relentless tortoise, a supple, fluid touch. One hand cupped her womancenter, stroking, creating another and newer rush of desire.

She dragged in a breath and thrust against the hand. Her legs clasped his arm. She must have more—must have release—must have him.

His fingers slipped inside her hot, moist, welcoming body, seeking. When she gasped, a single fingertip circled that spot gently.

Ecstasy pulsed from that spot, filling empty places in her heart, her inner woman. Awareness centered on that probing finger, sensual waves deluged her, rendered her helpless. Her bones melted in her limbs. She moaned his name and other sounds of raw desire.

Waves of heat rolled through her body and crashed into each other like ocean swells, flaming out of control when they met. She moaned and thrashed, thrust her hips, seeking some great pleasure she sensed in his hands. Had never felt—did not know how to find. But wanted desperately, more than air to breathe.

The lips skimmed to her womancenter, tongue flicking, probing the edges of her opening, grazed, touched, added new tremors to her pleasure. The tongue replaced the finger, a live thing inside her, hotly probing, lightly sucking, delicate, dancing everywhere, returning always to the mound where rapture and womanhood entwined.

He grasped her hips, lifted them. His shoulders pushed against her legs. He buried that roving, demanding tongue deep inside her.

The fiery pleasure between her legs, hot probing tongue, warm hands captivated her whole being. She arched and thrust her hips. *Oh LaSheena, what wonderful torture.* She wanted it to continue, but to end, surge to something greater. She hungered for more. A higher wonder poised just outside her reach. *More, please more. Please, please, more.*

Frenzy lifted her to the verge. Raging desire—sheet lightning from the clouds, raced through her to the far reaches. Turned and flowed back, rolling ceaseless waves of pleasure, beyond heat, unbearable but not to be missed. She clung to his shoulders, helpless, charged to explosion, drowning in ecstasy.

The tongue plunged, circled and tugged.

She exploded into a mass of white-hot flame, fully consumed. She flew through uncharted space, body twisting and turning in a current of exquisite passion, high, hot, wild.

Body bent in a tight arch, head whipping on her pillows, Rejeena screamed aloud in release and relief.

She collapsed—languid, satiated, fulfilled—preening with this newfound wonder.

He stilled, giving her respite.

Momentarily quiet, Aarvan desperately clenched his fists, set his jaw, jerking breaths in and out. He held himself in check, very nearly biting his tongue. He burned to drive into her, finish it and gain his satisfaction. *But I have to be as she said—better than any other. Even if it kills me. And it could. My pecker may explode.*

He slid upward, bringing them belly to belly. His manhood rubbed against her, hard and ready.

Her fires stoked again quickly, rising passion inundated satiation, craving burst out of control. She cried out eagerly, spread her legs wide. She must have more. She braced for the hard thrusting entry and wild ride to his fulfillment.

He did not oblige. He lightly grazed with his hard tip, barely entering before retreating. He delved to tease her mound then withdrew.

Oh, it was wonderful. Exquisite. Hot, grueling, agonized. It was unbearable, torturous ecstasy. The targeethan teased. He plundered, would not give her what she needed. Her womancenter throbbed and ached to be filled.

She grabbed, clutched his rear, a cheek in each hand and tugged him downward. Jerked, lunged to encase him.

His solid, powerful muscles resisted. He held her, strong hands on her thighs. He slid further into her, shaft rubbing her mound.

Those delicious waves radiated through her. *Oh, the hunger. The need. Please, please, fill me. Fill me! Please give me relief. Relief!*

Around her flaming desire, she managed to choke out, "Stop it, Aarvan. I want you now."

"Patience, My Queen. We've . . . the whole night." He grated between gasps for air.

"No!" Her voice shrieked and entreated. Her body shook with need. She dug with her nails, pulling at him. "I want you now!"

He pushed back. His breath puffed into her ear. "Good things come . . . to those who wait."

"Aarvan, I will kill you. I swear I will kill you!" She screeched. "Give me what I want."

He retreated again, then eased slowly into her, stroked, titillated, unhurried, his shaft a loving weapon.

She bucked beneath him, reared up in agony, ecstasy, anger, desire—feral desperation. She pulled at him with her groin muscles.

He resisted and titillated, finally relented, expelled a loud groan, then thrust deeply.

She rose eagerly to meet him, and they plunged together, wild, abandoned, in the age-old sexual dance. Their bodies rocked, melding together, wanting more. Super-heated tendrils pushed through them, between, around them in undulating waves, binding together and crushing beneath its weight. Panting, sweating, they shoved their bodies together, seeking completion of shared passion. They came together in a crashing climax, and waves of sensational, concluding relief washed over both.

She clasped him for long minutes, listening to his raspy breathing return to normal. Her hands traced his sweaty back, liking the feel of him on her and still in her.

Finally he rolled off and collapsed in exhaustion. Both still caught in the stupor from their passionate mating, they drifted to sleep.

* * *

Rejeena awoke, floating from sleep, warm, replete. Remembering why, she lay quiet, eyes closed, concentrating on and enjoying the feel of her body beneath the cover. That body would never be the same. It burst to life this night, passions she never suspected flared within. Knowing the feeling silly, she sensed a daughter growing within her.

Daughters. That is the purpose of this man. She frowned. She allowed herself to lose sight of that, engulfed in passion. Unbelievable. How inappropriate. She, Queen Rejeena, her queenship stripped away, reduced to mindless pleasure seeking. *That will not occur again.*

The queen looked at her body, almost felt the fire rekindle, and smiled slowly. *Then again, maybe it will.* It had been wonderful. Why could she not have both passion and completion? Why should she not share skindown as she pleased with her queen's man? *Who can deny me?* She had, after all, she remembered, feeling the release of his offspring shot, by instinct alone, clamped her legs tight around his trim waist and hips to catch it all.

The pleasure—she ran her hands down her thighs, over her belly, tried to ignite the sparks, recreate that ecstasy; but she felt no magic. *His hands, his fingertips, his manhood—oh, LaSheena, his tongue—held the magic.* She had heard rumors, while she allowed only tradition, of such skindown activities as he performed upon her. She giggled, remembering her disgust at the thought. When one became involved, the disgust dissolved before the delight.

She looked at him, asleep, facing her, naked, lean frame seductively outlined by the faint light of the brazier. Watching him breathe, she thought about their liaison. In one long, fiery session, he changed her entire outlook on the coupling of man and woman. The traditional method seemed so tame, could never again satisfy her. She had neither believed that a man could create such passion, nor that a woman could feel such.

Indeed, she had threatened that if he did not please her more than any other, he could expect extra lashes. She nearly laughed aloud at her foolishness. Please her? He melted her as candle wax in a hot fire, sent her exploding in a fireball of white heat, took all her beliefs about skindown indulgence and destroyed them—replaced them with new, exquisite, exciting ones.

How silly to ask Alea if he were a meithateran. Compared to him, the queen, who had conceived six offspring, stood the meithatera.

She thought about the fifteen lashes she assigned him for disobedience. Had he not been disobedient, she would not have discovered the wonder of his lovemaking. Unbearable. He would never feel the bite of those lashes.

Her gaze roved that superb male body, and she breathed in a faint aroma suggesting the aftermath of writhing bodies, dried sweat and . . . euphoria. *Can one smell spent euphoria?* Tiny, banked embers of desire burst to flame within her just looking at him. She had to have him again.

She traced that fascinating mouth with a finger.

Waking, eyes still closed, he captured it lightly between his teeth, tongue sliding provocatively along it.

Delicious anticipation fired through her chest and belly to her groin.

His eyes opened. "Were you pleased, My Queen?"

"I was pleased. Can you do it again?"

The tiniest of smiles tilted his lips. "If you can refrain from killing me, we'll find out." He pulled her to him.

* * *

Rejeena woke and stretched, mentally preening. She visualized a peacock she had once seen, strutting serenely, tail fanned, the circles and blues and greens displaying its magnificence to all. The queen felt like that peacock from the double jolts of passionate pleasure she had received from her queen's man. She lay still for a bit, muscles slack, mind languid, enjoying the sensation, then reached to touch him.

Her seeking hand found only empty skindown. She jerked upright. Where could he be? Had he escaped in the night? Surely, LaSheena would not so allow. *I cannot have found him, gripped him between my thighs, only to lose him.*

A soft gagging sounded from her bathing room.

She arose, slipped into a robe and walked to the door.

He slumped on the floor, leaning against the bathtub. The open night toilet rested before him, and the sour smell of vomit hung in the air. He sat motionless, a wet towel clamped to his head.

How magnificent he looked naked, even sick on the floor. "Aarvan?"

He started and looked around the towel. "My Queen." His voice sounded hoarse. All she could understand of his Oldenspeak was, "to skindown . . . your sleep."

She knelt beside him. "Come, Aarvan." She tugged lightly at his arm.

He spoke again, none of which she understood.

"Aarvan, come." She pulled the towel from his hand and gestured for him to follow.

He frowned, struggled to his feet, then followed her and sat on the skindown.

"Stay there." She motioned and gave him the towel.

Leaning forward, he pressed it to his head.

She mixed Alea's concoction with water. "Drink it, Aarvan." He drank, scrunching his face. She set the mug aside and motioned him to lie down. He lay on his side, curling his knees into a loose ball. She covered him and rang the servants' bell.

A servant arrived quickly.

The queen motioned her toward the bathing room. The servant would know what to do.

Rejeena arose and took the towel, soaked it with cold water and returned. When Aarvan reached for the towel, she caught his arm and tucked it under the cover. She sat beside him, in the curve formed by his belly and knees, and held the rag on his head.

He glanced up, sighed, closed his eyes and lay still.

"Go to sleep, Aarvan," she said softly. Alea made powerful concoctions, and the queen waited as his tense muscles relaxed.

He suffered serious pain. Still weak and ill, he gave her everything, held nothing back. He surely recognized the price he would pay, but he granted her every possible ounce of pleasure. She remembered, with a niggling nip of shame, fighting and threatening him, while he strove to maximize her euphoric experience. Women did not expect this selfless generosity from a man.

The servant came from the bathing room, carrying away his mess. She shot the queen a quick, startled stare, then curtsied from the room.

Rejeena smiled. She would be the topic of gossip in the servants' quarters tomorrow. Queens do not tend sick queen's men. Healers do that. However, she wanted to tend him, sit close against that lean body, listen to him breathe, sense his muscles slackening as the medicine took effect. This experience gave her pleasure, and she jealously kept it for herself. She wanted it, and as queen, she would have it.

When he succumbed to sleep, Rejeena lifted the rag and looked at him.

He lay relaxed, curled around her, face tranquil. Muscular body inert, expressive blue eyes shuttered by sleep, he appeared so innocent, defenseless as a child. The words, which LaHeeka used to describe him—strong, powerful, dangerous—seemed ludicrous.

She gently stroked the damp hair from his forehead and murmured, "You cannot fool me with that innocent face, Aarvan. I looked into those eyes when they would not yield, when they expressed lust to kill." She shivered with delicious, remembered pleasure, shunting away the frightening memory. "I have savored you between my thighs, inside me." She traced his lips with a fingertip. "I have been set ablaze." Thinking and touching spread warmth through her, a desire that could not be satisfied again tonight. She puffed a short, sorrowful breath, rose and went to dispose of the towel.

The queen returned, slid into skindown, turned her back to him and tried to sleep. Thoughts teased her mind, his giving, the tender touch of his fingertips, that hot tongue dancing inside her, his thick, swollen manhood exciting her nerve endings, sending her leaping into that incredible, alien realm, a place of dreams and fantasy. Unable to ignore him, she rolled over, ran a hand over his ribcage, feeling his hard, smooth body. The touch pleased and comforted her, and she slept with a hand resting on him.

* * *

When she awoke, Rejeena still touched him beneath the covers.

Aarvan had not moved.

She rose, rang for the servants, then drank coffee, bathed and dressed, performed her usual morning routine as the servants efficiently provided her needs.

Servants' curious glances slid over Aarvan's covered figure. They knew he was queen's man, but seeing a man asleep in the queen's skindown provided a novel experience.

Aarvan slept through it all.

Leaving the room, Rejeena tenderly touched his face. Outside the door, she told the guards, "The queen's man sleeps. None may disturb him. When he wakes, see that he receives befitting care. I want Alea to—"

Alea rose from a chair and curtsied. "You want me to check Aarvan since he became ill and suffered pain. Am I right, My Queen?"

"Yes. How did you know?"

"I am his healer. He is yet unwell, had a rough day yesterday, and"—she grinned—"likely partook of a wild ride last night. I made it my concern to be here."

The queen ignored the remark about the wild ride. "You are right, Alea. I gave him your draught. He has slept since. Please check him."

"Of course, and I will have healers sit with him until he wakes." Alea moved to the door of the skindown room and paused. "I need not ask how things progressed last night, My Queen. You positively glow this morning."

The queen glared at the guards, who hastily straightened faces and averted eyes. "Your imagination takes flight, Alea."

"Do not play coy, My Queen. I have known you too long. I have seen you look pleased after a night with a man, but this morning you gleam with inner light. You have, in the vernacular of allway women, been roundly rammed and rutted."

The queen's face flushed; she frowned and glared. Then she sighed, her eyes softening. "Is it so obvious?"

"I am afraid so, My Queen. All women will know at a glance."

The queen burst into laughter. "Well then, let them all dream upon the inner woman. He is queen's man—mine alone." She departed with jaunty steps, followed by her grinning guards.

Alea, with a wide smile, went to check her patient.

* * *

Aarvan awoke, sunk into softness in a shuttered room. Disoriented, he jerked to a sitting position. "Where am I?" he asked of Wecan, who smiled at him from a chair.

"Where else? In the queen's skindown." She gestured. "Careful, Aarvan, you display more of the queen's goods than circumstances justify."

Blinking, he yanked the covers around his bare hips.

She rose and opened the shutters, allowing light to stream into the room.

"Why are you here?"

"Tending you. Alea held concern as you tossed your dinner in the queen's bathing room last night."

"I did do that, didn't I? Is the queen upset?"

"No. The queen floats on air, smiling, treating women with unusual kindness. It is most disconcerting. You must perform with fervor in skindown."

He flushed.

"A servant will draw your bath."

"Bath? I'm hungry. How about some breakfast?"

"The queen bathes daily. You will, also. You may eat afterwards."

"Well then, I can draw my bath."

"You are queen's man. You do not draw your bath. While you bathe, the servants will ready your clothing. Then they will set a meal on the rockcaste." She flung open the doors to the garden revealing a large flat area made of rocks laid closely together. "You have missed breakfast and lunch. The queen will want you to dine with her, but she eats late. A light meal now will sustain you. Then Lateean will arrive for your language class."

"I see you have my day well laid out." He scooted to the edge of the skindown, covers tucked around him. "How do I move about the room with servants underfoot without revealing more of the queen's goods than circumstances justify?"

She lifted a robe from a wall peg and tossed it to him.

He caught it and stared at her.

She laughed and turned her back while he slipped into it.

Aarvan looked at the robe, which covered him only to mid-thigh. "Kinda short, isn't it?" He fingered the cloth. "Surely this isn't made on Kriiscon?"

"It is of Mainland cotton."

"I thought the queen is completely traditional. She allows Mainland cotton?"

"The queen stands for tradition, not stupidity. Mainland cotton is finer, more comfortable than the local cloth. She allows it within her home." Wecan rang for servants.

A servant entered; she curtsied to Aarvan but turned to Wecan, who said, "The queen's man wishes to bathe, dress and eat. Please see to it."

"Yes, Mistress." The servant vanished into the bathing room.

"This is ridiculous, Wecan. I can draw my bath and get out my clothes. I feel like a fool, having this girl bowing and doing things I can do."

"Her curtsey is but a courtesy shown a queen's man until they determine your outlook."

"My outlook?"

"Yes, whether you will be an arrogant queen's man who holds himself above servants or will treat them with civility."

He frowned. "I can't imagine why I would treat them other than with civility. You have a strange society, Wecan."

"Only to you. As for their serving you, have a heart. They reside in pleasant quarters in the queen's home, eat excellent meals, wear fine clothing, receive respectable barterek, and enjoy high status as queen's servants among their social stratum. They will feel distressed and insulted if you disallow them their function."

"I certainly don't want to distress and insult anyone. What is barterek?"

"It is payment for their function."

"Function?"

"Function is, ummm . . . that which you do for a living."

"Oh." He grinned. "Will they bathe me, too?"

"If you so desire. You are queen's man. In this house, your wishes are less important only than the queen's. They will bathe you, shave you, give you massages, hand feed you, anything you wish."

"I thought only the queen and healers could see a queen's man naked. I do bathe unclothed."

"Certain exceptions can be made."

"I'll pass on all those, thank you."

"While the servants are present, Aarvan, do not lean over." She flicked the bottom of his short robe, and exited.

* * *

The next four days followed a pattern. Aarvan and the queen dined together, conversing little due to his limited grasp of Oldenspeak, but conversation seemed unnecessary.

When they retired to skindown, Rejeena transformed from a haughty queen to a woman possessed, who, almost starved and now presented with a banquet, could not consume enough. Greedy, insatiable, desire seeming to devour her, she wanted to rush, grasp the moment.

By pure strength, Aarvan held her at bay, made her wait, titillated and tortured her until she reached orgasm. When he allowed himself release, they would come together in stunning climaxes that left them both sated and exhausted.

Her passionate explosions, while rocking her to the depths of her person, carried him to stunning heights of pleasure, knowing what he had done for her. She seemed to possess no sense of pleasing him, no knowledge that she should, certainly no clue of how to do so. For the time being, he would have to be satisfied with this partisan amorous play.

She demanded appeasement from him, until, in his weakened condition, exhaustion overcame him. Though he didn't again become ill, his head would pound, neck and shoulders ache so severely he would take Alea's concoction. Then he would fall asleep until late, long after the queen had arisen.

Aarvan spent his afternoons with Lateaan, his language coach, learning Oldenspeak, and with Alea, absorbing rules and rites of acceptable behavior. Each day he felt better, woke earlier. The fifth day, suffering from acute boredom, he needed change.

After class, with free time, he strolled to the guards' area.

Five guards gathered, playing muskee. At sight of him, they paused and waited attentively.

Locin rose to her feet, her left eye surrounded by shades of yellow and green.

Aarvan stopped and looked at it. "Did I do that?"

The huge guard said, "It happened in our tussle."

He grimaced. "Sorry about that. I didn't intend to hurt anyone. I just wanted to get away from you."

She crossed her arms over her chest. "Your escape, Queen's Man, was precisely that which we strove to prevent." She gestured to her eye. "I have been hurt worse. Though, for your savaging of guards, were you not queen's man, I would turn you over my knee and paddle you."

He flashed an impudent grin. "In that case, I'm lucky I'm queen's man."

"Arrogant little pup."

"I can afford to be. Women tell me I'm boss when the queen's not home."

"That is true, Queen's Man—to a point." She stared sternly.

"And where would that point be, Shiira Guardswoman?"

"You tell me what you want and I will tell you when you reach that point."

"Actually, I'd like to get out of this house. Except for that repellent tour of the punishment room, I've been trapped in this place. The walls are closing in."

"With guards, Queen's Man, you may roam about. The queen placed no restrictions."

"I'd like to see the towne."

"You will behave, not act rashly as you did the other day?"

"I'll be a perfect gentleman unless you make me watch some poor slob beaten senseless, Shiira Guardswoman."

"Today you may watch what pleases you, you arrogant pup. Stop calling me that. My name is Locin."

"If you'll stop calling me arrogant pup."

"You are an arrogant pup."

"And you are shiira and a guardswoman."

"Then we both go clothed with new titles," she said, turned to hide her grin and motioned two guards to follow. She picked up her weapons and helmet. "Come, I will give you a pleasant tour."

They walked into the warm sunlight side by side.

Locin indicated the rock-cobbled passage. "This is a sideway with residences only. To the right lies Mainway, the barter area. You will find that more interesting."

Aarvan stopped, breathing deeply of the clean, sweet air, perfumed from the flowering trees lining the sideway. He touched a huge blossom, which dwarfed his hand, sheer white with yellow center against the dark olive backdrop of the leaves. "What are these trees? They're not familiar."

"They are called shirtera, and bloom in early spring. Many women plant them for the fragrance."

He looked around. The residences, large, sturdy structures of wood and stone, sat back from the sideway, many surrounded by stonewalls with guarded entrances. Some retained small lawns and well-tended landscaping between the sideway and the wall. "This looks like the rich section of towne."

"It is. Seegarpt alone have means for such homes."

They strolled along the sideway.

Aarvan asked questions. "Who lives in that house? What does this woman do for a living? Why do houses have different height fences? Where does that sideway lead? Why does that house have so many guards?"

Locin did her best to answer, surprised by his sincere interest and relentless curiosity.

When they reached the Mainway and barter area, he stopped.

Open-air markets belonging to vendors lined the Mainway both directions until obscured by distance and obstructions. Women peddled varied wares for barter—plaited sitting mats, cushions, baskets, earthenware pottery, handmade jewelry, and paintings on hunks of tree bark. For those needing raiment, a variety of leather foot thongs, shoes and boots, hats, clothing of various materials lay stacked or hung in inviting displays. Cakes and breads, fresh fish and enticing early season vegetables filled baskets. Smoked and salted shanks of meat competed for hanging space with strings of dried fruit and flowers. Live animals and birds stirred in cages.

Noise abounded. The vendors hawking cries to prospective customers and the ensuing haggle to seal barter formed a continuous, undulating wall of sound. Wagon wheels rumbled over the cobblestones accompanied by the clop of horses' hooves. Dogs barked. Laughter sang in the air, as daughters shrieked in their high, trilling voices and raced about.

Holdees trailed mistresses, who hurried in every direction. All busy with their daily lives, they filled the Mainway, creating a spectacular sight.

The aroma of searing meat, baking bread, brewing coffee and roasting vegetables wafted in varied strengths on the air currents, pricking appetites, inducing memories of culinary delights and tempting women to partake.

For a short while, Aarvan stood and looked.

The guards waited.

"Whew." He grinned. "Where do we go first?"

Locin waved a hand about. "Pick a direction, Queen's Man. What you may not gaze upon today will be there tomorrow and the days following."

He shrugged and turned right, sauntered along and absorbed the ambience. He stopped and listened to a heated barter session between a well-dressed woman and a vendor. The woman bargained for a group of matched sitting mats, an attractive mix of skin and Mainland cloth. The vendor, waving her arms, demanded a price. The argument grew loud and boisterous. After much shouting, finger pointing and name calling, they settled upon a value. The buyer gave the vendor a skin bag and a piece of tree bark, upon which she scribbled quickly. Another squabble ensued as they adjusted the wording of the bark to mutual satisfaction.

The buyer's two holdees loaded her purchase on a handcart and she swaggered down the Mainway.

The vendor looked after her with a satisfied smile.

"What did she use for payment?" Aarvan asked Locin. "After all the yelling, that woman just gave the vendor a bag and a piece of wood."

"The bag held kruets, our coins. The wood is sparlin bark. Women dry and flatten the bark, which then can be used as writing surface or for paintings."

"Of what value is the piece of bark?"

"That is bark of terms, promise of payment. Within the agreed time, the woman must deliver the denoted barter goods."

"What do you barter?"

"Anything of value that a woman will give or accept, usually horses, cattle, other animals or skins. Sometimes coffee or tobacco"—she lifted her lip in a smirk, rolled her eyes sideways at him—"even holdees."

He lifted his lip in return. "What if the woman doesn't fulfill the terms of delivery?"

"Then they dispute in Queen's Hearing. Queen Rejeena looks unkindly upon women who do not satisfy their fair debts. All women of Rejeena's Towne know this."

"What if they're not of Rejeena's Towne?"

"Then a wise vendor would hold her goods until payment delivery."

"What besides kruets did that woman barter?"

She glared, hands on hips. "Not only do you stand an arrogant pup, but also a prying pup. Their bartering is their concern."

"Well, excuse me, Shiira Guardswoman, but it sounded like a public shouting match." He pointed toward a display of huge cats and kittens. "What are those?"

"Pesson cats. Some women keep them as pets. The pesson cat's fame lies not with its good temper or loyalty. If you place your hand in the cage with that black taatcat, he will explain it."

"Taatcat? I thought you said pesson cat."

The line leader heaved a sigh. "Alea warned me you are full of questions. Taatcat simply means the male of the species."

Aarvan knelt by the cage, but did not insert his hand.

The cat, as big as a large child, lay on its side staring with narrowed green eyes, a soft rumble issuing from its chest.

"Why do I feel it's not purring?" Aarvan asked.

Locin chuckled.

The vendor, a hefty woman wearing multi-colored, loose-fitting raiment, leaned on the cage. She spoke Universal, boldly ogling Aarvan. "Perhaps the queen's man would care to barter a kitten. We have great variety, all ages and colors."

Aarvan looked up, smiling. "I've never seen tame cats so big. These are pets?"

"Of course, Queen's Man," she said. "Come, look at the kittens."

He rose and followed her to a cage of mewing, hefty balls of fur. She plucked an armful, soft gray, and handed it to Aarvan.

"This is a kitten?"

"Just weaned, Queen's Man." The vendor fondly stroked it.

"This thing is heavy, huge for a weanling." He handed it back.

"If the gray does not please, perhaps another color." She reached for more kittens.

He stepped back. "Honestly, Shiira, I was just curious. I doubt a pesson kitten would please the queen. Besides, I have no goods to barter."

The vendor's eyes gleamed, and her gaze dropped to his trim hips, snugly encased in double-button pants. "Were you not queen's man, you would have much to barter."

Aarvan's face flushed bright red. He stepped back again, bumping into Locin.

The guard laughed, caught his shoulders and gently propelled him down the Mainway.

Safely away from the vendor, he paused. "I wish women wouldn't do that."

"Queen's Man, you will experience much of it. Women are expected to admire a queen's man. Some exhibit more grace than others. Mainway vendors do not hold to decorum."

"You're supposed to protect me."

"Not from embarrassment. If you color every time a woman makes a lewd comment, as fetching as you are, you may turn red permanently."

"You're not much help, Shiira Guardswoman."

"That was not my intent, Arrogant Pup."

He glared and continued down the Mainway.

Locin grinned and followed.

Aarvan stopped at a display of leather boots. He lifted a pair, ran a finger over them, inspecting.

"You will find no fault with my crafting, Queen's Man," the vendor said. She touched the boot, showing the detail as she spoke. "See those side stitches. Those are all of an exact size. Around the sole, triple stitching. These boots will fall from your feet of wear before those stitches give. That pair is too big for you, but I have another like them that should fit."

Locin interpreted, as the vendor used Oldenspeak.

He smiled. "Thank you, Shiira, but I need no boots today. Your craftwork is superb. When I do need a pair, I'll come to you."

The vendor beamed.

"Smooth when you choose to be," Locin said as they moved away.

He grinned.

Locin noticed women grew aware the queen's man trod the Mainway. All women of Rejeena's Towne knew the queen had taken a queen's man, rumored to be very expensive, extremely handsome. Few had seen him, and curiosity had mounted. The green armskin and guards branded him, but his male beauty alone would handily draw attention. Heads turned; curious eyes, both bold and surreptitious, followed their progress. The queen's man seemed unaware of the attention.

Locin studied him from the corner of her eye. Wearing that dark crown of hair, midnight blue eyes sharp and inquisitive, he seemed fascinated by the sights, smells and sounds surrounding him. His face appeared molded to perfection, as though sculpted by the hand of LaSheena, masculine but also curiously vulnerable, mouth curved in a smile. That lithe, funneled body, firm musculature, bulge in the right place, all rode feet which did not appear to touch the ground, but skimmed above it with fluid, panther-like grace. Altogether, he presented a picture assured to please the eye and fire the imagination. Locin felt proud to display him for her queen.

An elderly vendor hobbled from a jewelry exhibit straight to Aarvan. Short and stocky, dressed in clean but well-worn raiment, she smiled. Pattering a stream of Oldenspeak, the aged woman grasped his arm and tugged him toward her open-front trade hut.

When Aarvan hesitated, Locin said, "Here we respect age, Queen's Man. Go with her. She is aseberda."

"Aseberda?"

"A term of respect for the elderly." Locin pointed. "Go."

He followed the vendor.

Gripping him, the old woman fumbled under her display rack. She withdrew a skin bag and shook out an exquisite silver chain of entwined loops. She motioned Aarvan to lower his head. When he complied, she slipped the chain around his neck and smoothed it on his chest. Wrinkled face split into a wide grin, her eyes flitted between the chain and his face.

Aarvan looked at Locin. "Explain I can't barter for this, please."

The vendor next door growled in Universal, "She offers you a gift, Queen's Man. If you insult the old woman, you will find need of those guards."

Startled, Aarvan turned.

She wasn't tall, a thin wisp of woman, middle-aged, dark-skinned with brown hair and eyes. A flour-spattered apron partially obscured her long skirt of earth-toned doeskin and over shirt of bright blue Mainland cloth. She glared.

"I mean no insult, Shiira," he said. "The piece looks expensive. I couldn't possibly accept it."

"You dare not accept?" the vendor snapped. Her eyes flared, mouth tightened and she stepped toward him.

He stared. *What did I do?* As she neared him, Aarvan whiffed a riveting scent mix of coffee, sweetness and strong spices.

Locin spoke rapidly in Oldenspeak.

The old woman smiled, patted the chain as it lay against Aarvan's chest.

The second vendor relaxed. "Well, that is different, of course." Her gaze raked Aarvan, interest replacing anger.

"What did you tell them?" Aarvan asked.

"I told them, as you are a new queen's man, you do not yet know all the fine points of behavior. They needs show you patience."

"What rules don't I know?"

The middle-aged vendor answered. "A queen's man will be offered gifts by women. If he refuses, he thus indicates the presenter falls beneath his notice. Unless you wish to insult the giver, accept the gift, smile and thank her."

"This queen's man thing is complicated," Aarvan muttered.

"It is more than merely rutting the queen." The seller of goods grinned and watched, as Aarvan turned pink.

The elderly trader laid her hands on Aarvan's waist above his pants. She spoke, smiling, eyes performing a pagan jig.

Women chuckled.

"What did she say?" Aarvan asked.

"You do not want to know, Queen's Man," Locin said.

"Yes, I do."

"She said you have nice trim hips, made to fit perfectly between a woman's thighs. You surely give the queen a glorious ride."

Aarvan flushed deep red. "Don't you women think of anything but skindown?"

Everyone laughed—the guards, the vendors and a small knot of curious women who had gathered.

The other merchant answered. "The look of you, Queen's Man, inspires such thoughts. I am Balstra. Please accept my hospitality for coffee and cake." She gestured to her small shop, which included a snug room inside and a group of tiny tables and chairs on the Mainway.

When Aarvan hesitated, she said, "Please, take my offer as apology for my threats and your embarrassment. It will be my gift, Queen's Man."

"All right, in a moment." He took the old vendor's hand, lifted it to his lips and lightly kissed it. In a mixture of Universal and Oldenspeak, he touched the chain and said in that cloud-soft voice, "Thank you, Aseberda, for the gift. I accept with honor."

The old woman beamed.

Aarvan gently released her, followed Balstra and took a seat.

A flustered servess asked, "What do you wish, Q-Queen's Man?"

He smiled apologetically. "I don't know what you have." The familiar, inviting odor of fresh brewed coffee swirled from inside the shop. "But I'll take some of that coffee."

"Give the queen's man honey cake, too," Balstra said. "Bring me coffee. May I join you, Queen's Man?"

"Of course." The servess quickly brought his order, and he took a sip of coffee but looked skeptically at the honey cake. He picked it up and gazed at all sides. "This honey smells so strong, I expect a bee to come buzzing out of it."

Balstra chuckled and said, "You will like it, Queen's Man. Our local bees make exceptionally strong, sweet honey, but we balance it with spices in the cake."

He took a bite. "You're right; it's delicious."

Locin sat at the table also. The other two guards took stations at each side of the outdoor area.

"Queen's Man," Balstra smiled, "you must understand our ways. You are both gorgeous and queen's man. A woman of the allways can but look and wish. Being unattainable makes you even more desirable. Perverse, to be sure, but that is the way of it. Women will make remarks to you and about you. It is all they can do. You can only prevent it by hiding in the queen's house. That would quickly become most boring."

His lips twitched. "Am I that transparent?"

"Reading your discomfort does not require a scholar."

"No, I guess not." He toyed with his coffee caster.

"We will speak of other things." Balstra touched his hand. "How do you like Rejeena's Towne?"

His eyes lifted. "What I've seen is interesting. I'd like to see all of it."

"That will take a while," Locin said.

Aarvan shrugged. "It looks like I'm here for a while."

"Feel welcome at my cafe anytime, Queen's Man," Balstra said. "If your guards will permit, I can help show you the towne."

"The queen placed no restraints," Locin said. "He may go where and with whom he wishes."

"We have many fine sites in Rejeena's Towne," the vendor said.

He grinned. "I like old places, the older the better. You have any?"

"Oh yes, we do, some with frightening reputations."

"I want to see them all."

"We shall make it occur," Balstra said. "Do you wish to be always called queen's man, or do you have a name?"

Aarvan glanced sideways at Locin.

She laughed. "The queen's man holds no memory, so he does not know his name. The queen granted him a name that he finds embarrassing."

Balstra leaned forward onto her elbows. "I will not laugh, Queen's Man."

Aarvan heaved a sigh.

"Go on, Queen's Man," Locin said. "Tell her. You needs learn to look women right in the eye and speak it."

His lip twitched. "Aarvan."

Balstra, to her credit, did not laugh, though snickers sounded from other tables.

"It is a charming name," Balstra said. "The sound is clean, virile, matches that wonderful open expression of your eyes. You move with the grace and smoothness of a great stag. Wear the name with pride, Queen's Man."

"You almost make me like it." Aarvan gave her a weak smile.

The old woman from next door appeared at Aarvan's side. She prattled rapidly. Aarvan understood enough to know she asked about his name.

"Aseberda, my name is Aarvan," he stated in Oldenspeak.

The old vendor gaped for a moment then threw her arms around his shoulders, hugged him close, her shriveled cheek pressed against his. She pattered excitedly, too fast for Aarvan's limited grasp of the language.

"You have made a conquest, Queen's Man," Balstra said. "She finds you enthralling because you used Oldenspeak, you are so handsome, you called her aseberda, and you are queen's man. She thinks you are wonderful."

Aarvan grinned, only slightly embarrassed. "Locin said aseberda is a term of respect for the elderly."

"It is, Aarvan, but seldom does a queen's man waste such grandiose terms on a Mainway vendor."

"Maybe they should," he said. He turned to Locin. "I'd ask Aseberda if she'd join us, but I'm not sure of the rules. Would I be expected to buy? I have no kruets."

"Queen's Man," Balstra said, "you may invite anyone you wish to the table. I will absorb the expense."

"I couldn't do that. You're trying to make a living here."

Balstra looked at Locin. "Is he genuine, or a trick the queen plays on us?"

"He is genuine, every bit as ignorant as he acts," Locin chuckled.

Aarvan bristled. "Now, wait a minute . . ."

Balstra touched his arm. "Look behind you."

He swung and looked.

Women packed every table and more stood, all with cakes and coffee. The servess scurried about with orders.

He turned back. "You're busy. So?"

"When you arrived, Aarvan, my tables sat devoid of guests. You are the new, handsome queen's man. All women abound with curiosity. So long as you stay, I will enjoy much commerce. I can well afford to indulge you."

"So you're just using me, huh?"

Locin lightly slapped an open hand on the table. "See, Balstra, he is slow but he can learn."

Balstra chuckled and called the old woman to join them. When the elderly vendor understood it was Aarvan who invited her, she fluttered, prattled and hugged him. Finally, when she settled with coffee and cake, Balstra said, "Her name is Alaestrea, Queen's Man."

He tried to repeat it, jumbling the twisting syllables. Everyone laughed, including Aarvan and Alaestrea.

Aarvan glanced around. "Why is it that everyone is so fond of coffee? No matter where I am at any time of day, someone serves coffee."

"It is new to Kriiscon," Balstra said, "bartered from Mainland dealers through wander women. That which is new stands always in heavy demand."

Aarvan nodded. "Makes sense."

Locin said, "Queen's Man, if you wish to make barter, I have barks and marking prickle." She patted the skin bag at her waist. "The queen will honor your barks."

He looked at her, eyes flaring wide. "No thanks. Even if I had the nerve to barter the queen's goods, which I don't, I wouldn't know what she has to barter."

"No woman will refuse kruets."

"Sorry, no. I'm not that brave."

Locin leaned back and gave him a long, calculating stare. "You have a peculiar concept of the word brave, Queen's Man." She said no more, but thought about him and the queen. Though lacking details, all guards stood aware that he forced the queen to negotiate him into her skindown. Queen Rejeena had neither a negotiating nature nor much patience. *Vexing the queen with this negotiation had been an act of rare bravery—stupid, but brave.*

A pair of hands gripped Aarvan's shoulders from behind. A composed female voice spoke Universal over his head. "He really is a new queen's man, is he not? Most will barter a bundle of their queen's goods without blinking. For the economy of Rejeena's Towne, we needs train this one."

Locin looked up and said dryly, "I fear you hold more concern for your economy than the towne's. If I allowed you to train him, the queen would sear me with a full measure of grief."

"You malign me, guard. I offer a commerce like any other."

Locin snorted. "Queen's Man, the targeetha with her hands on you is Tatia. Do not ever allow her a tighter grip."

Aarvan twisted in his chair. "Tatia." He offered his hand.

She shook it, fastening him with her pale, almost colorless, bold eyes. Her gaze traveled leisurely over him. "The queen has chosen well."

"What's your commerce that Locin is so against?"

She leaned close and whispered into his ear, "I am a local pariah, Queen's Man, not held to good woman status by all."

Aarvan caught a trace of her tangy, intriguing aroma, both wispy as her colorless eyes and substantive as her grip on his shoulder. *Ummmmm.* He drew its aromatic caress deep into his lungs.

She raised her voice. "I run a genial gaming concern, needful to the relaxation of many. Though I offer only fair, honest games, the law forces ever peer over my shoulder, endlessly hopeful of catching me amiss. You are welcome anytime. For you, we would make special accommodation."

"Only beyond the reach of my sword point," Locin growled.

"A queen's man does not require his guard's permission," Tatia said.

"This one does," Locin said. "He's on ordeal."

"Ordeal?" Aarvan frowned.

Locin explained, "A period of trial to see if you will learn to behave."

"I'm on ordeal?"

"You are now."

"Perhaps you needs teach this guard her place, Queen's Man." Tatia's fingers kneaded his shoulders.

"I can't," Aarvan said. "I'm on ordeal. Besides, she's bigger than I am."

Locin granted Tatia a snide smile.

Tatia shrugged, accepting her defeat. "We will meet again, I do not doubt." Then she said softly, "You are one fine piece of skindown goods. Misfortunate Queen Rejeena saw you first." She released his shoulders and walked away.

"Stay away from that one, Aarvan," Balstra said. "She is indeed a pariah, not fitting company for a queen's man."

Aarvan raised a hand, palm outward. "She'd waste little time on me. I've nothing to gamble."

Balstra barked a hollow laugh. "Did you not see her eyes? You have that for which she would game."

"She would not dare." Locin snapped bolt upright. "He is queen's man."

Balstra shrugged. "That would not daunt Tatia. She defies law every day. You should descend from that misty mountain surrounding the queen occasionally, guard. Spend time on the allways. Both she and her games are crooked."

"She will not play games with the queen's man." Locin scowled.

"Locin," Aarvan said, "it requires two to play."

"If I thought she would even try . . ." Locin's voice and glare faded under Aarvan's steady, calm gaze.

A large woman crowded close, and thrust a hunk of cured meat, smelling of salt and ham, into Aarvan's hands. He also caught her stench, an unpleasant mixture of sweat, stale cooking and tobacco smoke, overlaid by unwashed body. Clearly, not all women bathed daily.

"I am Maata, Queen's Man," she smiled, displaying a mouth with missing teeth. "Come to my shop anytime." She waved vaguely down the Mainway. "I slaughter my own hogs and cure the meat. I will always have a spare ham for such a handsome man."

"Thank you, Shiira." He returned the smile, with no intention of eating her ham or seeking more. Her lack of cleanliness did not invite him to share her self-cured meats.

One of the guards shouldered Maata away, using the pretext of gathering his gifts and placing them in a bag. He didn't see the malodorous woman again.

More women arrived, and Aarvan rose to chat with them. They laughed and joked, trying to understand each other around the language barrier. Several women touched him, but only in allowable ways. Locin sat and watched.

Chatting, shaking hands and shuffling his attention from one woman to another, Aarvan had moved a small distance from the guards. Two persons, a scowling holdee and a girl of perhaps fourteen, appeared before him at the same time, from different directions.

The holdee, with a rude thrust of his arm, pushed in front of the girl. Several women frowned, but did not move. The girl looked at the man, showing more surprise than anger.

The holdee shoved a handcrafted, dark leather belt at Aarvan. "Here, Queen's Man." He stared with a hard-mouthed sneer and gestured down the Mainway. "My mistress wants you to have it as her gift."

Aarvan looked. Several vendors down, a woman, busy with customers, smiled and gave him a friendly waggle of fingers. He returned the smile and gesture.

The holdee leaned close and whispered. "I'm Palstan, Coastal Strip fellow. I'd like to loop that belt around your pompous queen's man neck and throttle you." He smiled to disguise his words.

Aarvan pulled back, stared for a moment, then said, "Good afternoon to you, Palstan."

The holdee turned abruptly and walked away.

The young girl stepped forward. "You should call your guards, Queen's Man," she said. "He acted most rude."

Aarvan shrugged. "What is a Coastal Strip fellow?"

"Fellows are loose men. Coastal Strip would indicate his group before he became a holdee," the girl explained. "I have brought you a gift." She smiled shyly and handed him several hanging strips of dried flowers. The strips entwined flowers and leaves, using both color and texture to vary and beautify. A faint but pleasant bouquet clung to the flowers that Aarvan didn't recognize.

"Thank you, Shiira," Aarvan said. "They're beautiful." He reached for them.

Before he grasped the strips, a large hand snatched them away. A bulky, frowning woman stood beside the girl. She snapped, "Get back to your function, Whanaara. Give away my profits indeed. Since you seem to so disrespect kruets, I will grant you no function stipend for this suntrek."

Whanaara stepped back and tears sprang to her eyes. "I just wanted to give the queen's man a gift, as others do, Maman."

The woman slapped the girl. "Get back to your function. I, not you, will decide upon gifts."

Whanaara whirled and dashed across the Mainway toward their vending booth, fists swiping at her eyes.

Aarvan scowled. "That was unnecessary and mean, Shiira. The girl was just being nice."

Locin, already on her feet and walking toward them, sped to a trot.

The woman turned. "When I require advice on the disciplining of my daughter from the queen's skindown dalliance, I will ask. If you wish to acquire the hangings to present to the queen to enhance your status, you may barter for them as any other."

Aarvan sucked in his breath and thrust out an arm to deter Locin's forward charge. "Believe me, Shiira, if I wanted the flower strips, you are the last vendor I'd barter with. I don't buy from shrews."

The woman's eyes flared, lip lifted. She stepped forward. "You arrogant . . . man. You cannot so speak to a woman."

"I just did," Aarvan said, eyes challenging with their straightforward stare.

Locin pushed his arm aside and stepped before him. "Go back to your area, vendor. You may not so speak to the queen's man."

The woman looked into stony gray eyes and retreated, grumbling.

Locin turned to Aarvan and gestured toward Balstra's area. "Go back and interact with good women."

Aarvan glared after the vendor then followed the guard's instructions.

More and more women, observing the handsome queen's man to be pleasant and approachable, gathered and encircled them for introductions. Several presented small gifts—a bark pouch, sitting mat and a large clay tankard. They badgered and mocked Aarvan in friendly ways, complimenting his male assets with bawdy and lewd admiration. He took it all in fun, turning red but smiling, taunting the women in his turn.

Aarvan tried to pronounce their names, using Oldenspeak. His efforts, however inept, caused teasing as well as appreciative laughter and approval. Aarvan enjoyed himself. The women appeared to have a good time. Locin sat and smiled. When the sun started to drop, the line leader suggested they return.

Aarvan rose immediately, thanked Balstra, bussed Alaestrea's cheek and said his good-byes to all women. He and his guards returned in silence to the queen's home.

Though physically tired, Aarvan felt exhilarated, warmed by the rowdy but pleasant human contact with the allway women.

At the door to the queen's private suite, Aarvan paused. "Thank you for the tour, Locin. I enjoyed it."

"You are welcome, Queen's Man," she said. "You performed well today, harmonizing graciously with the queen's subjects. She will be pleased."

"Praise the saints . . . a compliment from the shiira guardswoman?"

"Arrogant pup." She backhanded him across the belly.

"Ouch, that stings."

"As intended. Be on your way." She gestured to the door, a smile softening the sharp words.

* * *

He opened the door, rubbing his belly and passed into the queen's quarters.

Rejeena sat on a sofa.

Aarvan bowed. "My Queen, you're early." He used Oldenspeak, short phrases which lay within his grasp.

"You, My Queen's Man, are late," she said.

"I'm sorry, My Queen. I didn't know"—he floundered for words—"you were early."

She smiled. "It is no concern. We must attend a dinner. Wear these." She held up a set of short pants, vest and leather boots, dyed dark blue. "The color will enhance you as it matches your eyes."

"Yes, My Queen." Since she waited, he hurried.

She looked him over when he was ready and tilted her head. "Your queen stands corrected; your eyes enhance the clothing.

LaSheena surely granted you a generous portion of manly beauty." She touched his silver chain.

"It's a gift, My Queen, from an aseberda on the Mainway."

She nodded, turned and led the way.

Trailed by guards, they walked a short distance on the sideway and turned in at an imposing house.

Aarvan felt the impact of many gazes as they entered a large dining area.

The dinner party awaited the queen. Everyone, well-dressed women and one young man, turned and bowed, women heads up, holdee head lowered.

The queen stood regally, allowing the homage to stretch.

Aarvan shifted his weight, unsure of his expected role.

The queen placed a hand flat against the small of his back, rooting him to the spot.

"Rise please." The queen smiled about the room. "This is my queen's man, Aarvan."

No one laughed.

The queen whispered, "All here are mistress or below." Aarvan hoped he understood.

Women advanced for introductions, according to their status, the first a tall, cadaverous woman. She stopped before Aarvan, dark eyes glittering like those of a crow, neither benevolent nor hostile. A long, soft robe of brown cloth draped her, swaying with her movement, alternately revealing and concealing her thin frame. Curved bone pins held a short matching shawl pushed back at the shoulders. Her eyes met his, but her focus fixed behind him, as though she looked straight through his head.

"Aarvan," the queen said, hand light against his back, "this is Krysiild, our talented conjurah."

Krysiild offered her hand. Aarvan took it, lifted it to his lips and inclined his head. "Mistress Conjurah, I am proud to meet you."

The queen's hand circled slowly on his back.

The conjurah's eyes flashed, focus halting at his eyes. "You are most smooth, Queen's Man," she said and moved on. She used Oldenspeak, but Aarvan understood.

The next woman stood short, a bit pudgy with brown hair and brown eyes, barely rising to Aarvan's chin. She wore simple raiment of gray skin. Her hawk-sharp stare and indigo land leader's sash, cutting from left shoulder to right waist, contrasted sharply with her nondescript appearance.

The male holdee walked behind her.

"This is Parria, Aarvan, land leader of this packet."

Aarvan took her hand and raised it to his lips. "Mistress, I am pleased to know you." Raising his eyes, Aarvan started. The holdee glared at him, lip curled, eyes baleful, accusative.

Do I know this man? This was the second man he'd met and both seemed to hate him on sight. Why? What's wrong with this island? *Or what's wrong with me?* Aarvan's memory offered nothing.

Parria smiled, speaking Universal. "What a captivating gesture, Aarvan. Is that a Mainland greeting?"

Aarvan's mind twisted, confused. "It must be, Mistress. It seems natural."

"It is most charming." Parria clung to his hand. Her scrutiny raked him. "You have a most attractive queen's man, My Queen. When you tire of him, there will be a ready market."

The stroke of the queen's hand on Aarvan's back felt like the emotive equivalent of a cat's purr.

"This," Parria said, with a dismissive wave of her hand, "is my favored holdee, Billy. Sometimes I let him call himself land leader's man."

Billy scowled.

Aarvan nodded, thrust out his hand and said softly, "How do you do, Billy?"

The holdee made no move to shake the offered hand, so Aarvan dropped it back to his side.

The land leader, with another quick ogle of Aarvan's manly figure, moved on. Billy followed, giving Aarvan a flinty glare.

Focused on the retreating holdee and his inexplicable hostility, Aarvan wasn't immediately aware of the next woman who stepped before him. His gaze returning, he recognized her and recoiled against the queen's hand.

The hand rubbed with long, soothing strokes.

Aarvan stared into the penetrating, amused eyes of Meitra.

"We meet again, pretty Queen's Man," the rusty hinge creaked. "You appear surprised to see me."

"I am."

Meitra smirked. "Chief punishment meter is near the top of the towne and quarter hierarchy."

"A strange hierarchy."

"Aarvan," the queen said, "you must call her mistress."

"Mistress, My Queen? I must call *her* mistress?"

"Yes, Aarvan, you must." The queen's hand stroked his tense back muscles.

Aarvan took a deep breath, said, "Mistress," and inclined his head.

Meitra's eyes glinted. "What, Aarvan, no hand kiss such as you granted others? How ungracious."

Aarvan growled, "Mistress, I—"

The queen's hand stilled against his back, lifted slightly.

"As you wish, Mistress." He raised Meitra's hand to his lips, released it and forced a twisted smile.

Meitra laughed. "You do not disappoint, Aarvan."

The queen's thumb smoothed up and down his spine.

There followed a procession of women—commerce and religious leaders of Rejeena's Towne, members of the queen's council, names and faces too numerous to remember. Unsure of some women's status, Aarvan called them all mistress, kissed all their hands and granted each a gracious word.

The queen's lightly rubbing hand indicated her approval.

Gently extracting his hand from the grip of an elderly banquer, Aarvan felt the queen's palm freeze against his back, fingers curling.

He looked up. Tatia stood before him. She and the queen stared at each other with matching haughty frowns.

The queen said, "This is Tatia, Aarvan. She performs low-caste commerce. You need not address her as mistress."

"We meet again, Queen's Man." Tatia turned her pale eyes on him and smiled.

Aarvan reached for Tatia's hand, and the queen pinched him, hard, under his vest. He winced and shook Tatia's hand but didn't lift it to his lips, a slight likely obvious to all women.

Tatia's eyes narrowed, flicked to the queen; anger flashed then vanished.

The queen's hand rubbed, contact firm. "You have met?"

"Today, My Queen, on Mainway," Aarvan said. "We spoke briefly." He caught a drifting hint of Tatia's intoxicating perfume and breathed deep.

"Too briefly," Tatia said. "You have a most provocative queen's man, My Queen." The perusal of her pale eyes again traveled a bold circuit of Aarvan. "Were I you, I would not allow such a handsome man to wander. His beauty could incite the unsavory elements about towne."

The queen's hand tightened. "My guards will protect my queen's man. Spare us your concern."

"Yes, do spare us, Tatia," the next woman said. "My guards stand well able to meet any challenge." Shouldering Tatia aside, this big, husky woman took her place. She wore the black trousers and tunic of the guards, a scarlet sash of Mainland silk slicing from shoulder to waist. Her voice rang flat, cool. She offered her hand. "I am Shabet, Queen's Man, captain of the queen's guards. You may have seen me about. I am shiira not mistress, and do not kiss my hand. Such a gesture will not impress *me*."

"As you wish, Shiira," Aarvan said and shook her hand.

The queen's fingertips smoothed his spine. "You have met all women, Aarvan. There will be social time before dinner. A queen's man is expected to circulate and charm."

A servant appeared at the queen's elbow with a tray of steaming goblets.

The queen selected one.

The servant turned to Aarvan. "Queen's Man?" A strong odor, both sour and fruity, assaulted his nostrils from the tray. He didn't find it a cordial fragrance.

"Try the hot shaarberry wine, Queen's Man," Parria said as Aarvan hesitated. She stood beside him, Billy behind her. "One full glass will set you soaring, two will generate wild sport for the queen tonight, three and the queen shall have no sport."

Laughter rippled.

Even the queen smiled, eyes warm and possessive as she watched Aarvan through the steam from her goblet.

Aarvan's color rose, but he took a glass and smiled. "In that case, Mistress, perhaps I'll have just the two."

The laughter rolled louder, and someone behind Aarvan said, "Good spirit, Queen's Man."

The queen touched his arm. "I needs speak with a woman in private. I will return. Stay and enjoy yourself."

Aarvan dipped into a half bow, as the queen walked away.

The curious leaders of Rejeena's Towne crowded around, talking and laughing, competing amicably for the attention of the handsome queen's man.

They laughed and joked, and hands trailed over his body—arm, shoulder, back, belly and ribcage under his vest. Certain women found a way to fasten their palms to his skin as leeches cling to their prey. Thumbs trailed, as if by accident, across his nipples. Each hand, every touch silently implied wishful possession. *What do they do, practice for the day they get to grapple a queen's man?* Someone thrust a finger just under the rear waistband of his pants. He spun, but several women stood behind him, all appearing innocent.

Three women converged on him. He remembered one to be a banquer, another owned farms, the third was a clothier. They chattered at him, part of which he understood. He smiled and answered as best he could. Each woman seemed to have doused herself with her most cloying perfume. The odors, pleasant if whiffed alone, when joined created an unpleasant stench that nearly caused him to gag. He choked back the reaction, but escaped as quickly as he could, allowing another woman to claim his attention. Older women hugged him, a privilege seemingly reserved for advanced age. Except for the one, no hand touched him inappropriately, according to their rules.

Aarvan twisted away from some touches, camouflaging the act as movement toward the next woman demanding his notice. He despised but tolerated this hands-on approach. His wellbeing still depended upon the queen's goodwill, and this society accepted and expected the touching.

I'm like some exotic pet that every woman wants but can't have.

He strove to be gracious, struggling with the language. Some women spoke Universal, some Oldenspeak, some both. Most of the conversation he understood and answered using his mixture of Oldenspeak and Universal. The company he found borderline tolerable, but not the hot wine. While hot it tasted unpleasant, cooling it became foul, the sour portion he had detected in its odor dominating the fruit. Since everyone else seemed to enjoy the fermented juice, he sipped politely.

The group changed, flowed and eddied, until for a few moments Aarvan stood alone. He glared with distaste at his wine flagon.

"It is an acquired taste," the familiar rusty hinge squeaked.

He glanced in that direction.

Meitra leaned against the wall in a small alcove, a cryptic smile tilting her lips.

Aarvan turned away.

The punishment meter stepped in front of him, thrusting a hand flat against his chest. "Do not flee, pretty Queen's Man. I carry no strikepaddle."

"What is it you want, Mistress?" Her touch outside the punishment room, without her evil aura and sardonic grin, or a threatening locchot looming in the background, felt like any other, unwelcome but bearable. She was just an unattractive woman, his knowledge of her function plunging her attraction to below zero.

"I wish only to acquaint myself with you, as do all women. Women fantasize about the queen's man, the more handsome, the wilder the fantasy. And, Queen's Man, you are most handsome."

Aarvan felt his color rising.

Parria, appearing with fresh wine, saved him from a reply. She took his wine and replaced it with a steaming one. "That stuff tastes repulsive when it cools, Aarvan. You must drink fast."

"Mistress, you warned me not to drink three."

"Queen's problem, not mine," the land leader laughed.

Billy stood behind her and glowered. A young man, Billy appeared well formed, starting to soften, good living slackening his muscles. He wore grey pants of soft Mainland cloth, tight, emphasizing the bulge between his legs but revealing a small roll of extra weight around the waist. Hair light brown, eyes pale blue, lips full and pouty, he was a good-looking man in a soft, boyish way.

Aarvan asked quietly, "Do we have a problem, Billy?

Billy started, eyes skittering sideways to Parria. "I don't know what you mean, Queen's Man."

"You've been glaring at me like I'm poison."

"It's your imagination, Queen's Man." Billy watched Parria, who frowned.

"I know a glare when I see one."

Billy shuffled his feet, gaze flicked to Parria and back.

The land leader crossed her arms, her chin rose, eyes squinted. "Well, Billy?"

Billy gulped and swallowed. "I apologize for any wrong impression, Queen's Man. I didn't mean to glare. I'm sorry."

"All right, Billy, apology accepted," Aarvan said. He didn't believe a word of that apology, but he didn't press the issue.

Parria spoke. "It is time for dinner. I must check arrangements. Come, Billy." She hurried away.

Billy followed, avoiding Aarvan's eyes.

Meitra spoke. "He glares, Aarvan, because he is a spoiled, sniveling wayscrape. He has been the only male with status about towne, the zenith of the holdee heap. Your arrival lowered his importance. He carries resentment."

"When someone stares murder at me," Aarvan said, "I like to know the reason."

"Who will murder you, My Queen's Man?" the queen's husky voice asked.

"My Queen." He turned and smiled, glad of her arrival, rescuing him from Meitra.

"It is time for dinner, Aarvan." The queen gently pressured him toward the table.

"Mistress." He inclined his head to Meitra, whose lips curved into her sardonic grin.

The guests stood waiting. A servant pulled out the chair at the head of the table as the queen approached. Rejeena stepped to her place and allowed the servant to seat her.

"Aarvan, you will sit there." Parria indicated the chair to the queen's left around the corner of the table. Aarvan walked to his chair, unsure of the etiquette of seating.

Four servants advanced and simultaneously seated the conjurah, the queen's man, the land leader and chief punishment meter. The remaining guests seated themselves.

Aarvan sat beside Parria. Directly across the table, to the queen's right, was Krysiild, beside her Meitra. Billy, relegated to the far end of the table among the lowest-ranked women, glared. When Aarvan glanced at him, the holdee's eyes flicked away, face smoothing to blandness.

The servants carried in huge platters of meats, hot and cold vegetable dishes, gravies and sauces, bread plates, cheeses and fruit—a stunning array of food.

Aarvan gently puffed out his breath. The sight and stimulating whiffs of seared meat, spicy vegetables and fresh, yeasty bread sent his appetite into frenzy. He resisted the temptation to forget his manners and start grabbing.

The servant assigned to fill his plate waited.

Parria, the hostess, inquired, "Difficulty, Aarvan?"

"This food all looks delicious, Mistress. I can't decide what to choose."

Parria told the servant, "Give the queen's man a small portion of everything." To Aarvan she said, "Eat only what pleases you. My feelings are not attached to food choices."

"Thank you, Mistress."

The food tasted as delicious as the sight and smell promised. Aarvan ate with enthusiasm. He forgot about being tired, the dinner reviving him. Polite conversation flowed, some of which he could follow. When a woman addressed him, he answered politely but didn't pursue conversation.

He observed the queen. Here in her element, among her community and council leaders, she sat animated, eyes flashing, seeming to revel in being queen, the one to whom everyone deferred. Her verbal skills, having a good grasp of the process of argument and using it, matched any woman in the room. A powerful woman, surrounded by her hierarchy, the queen appeared to enjoy her power without abusing it.

The women began a discussion on the merits of taxation. Aarvan understood tariffs to be the subject discussed, but couldn't follow the subtleties. He focused on his dinner.

Parria addressed him. "What do you think, Queen's Man? We need a man's opinion."

"About what, Mistress?"

"Tariff, Aarvan," the land leader said. "Since you are the only male of value at our disposal, perhaps you will give us the male perspective." Her eyes flicked to Billy, who flushed, lips pushing together. "A male opinion has not before been offered at this table." She leaned forward, eyes boring into his. "Grant us a boon."

Aarvan glanced around the table. Every gaze rested on him, most amused. Billy's lips curled in a sneer. The queen watched him with a speculative, tolerantly bemused scrutiny. The conjurah's brows drew down in disdain. Surprisingly, Meitra alone appeared interested and attentive.

The land leader set for him a test, which everyone including the queen expected him to fail because he was a man. A wave of irritation flooded him. With it came words from behind the barrier to his memory—words he had heard spoken but didn't know where, when or by whom.

He smiled at Parria and answered in Universal. "I'll try, Mistress, since you desire a male perspective." He paused a moment for effect, then said, "In order for a society to be organized, it must be governed. The only way the governing body can be supported and serve the governed is through taxation. The governed must understand the necessity of taxation and demand the most benefit from each baagar . . . kruet. The amount, frequency and usage of taxation should be mutually decided between the governed and governing."

Meitra repeated Aarvan's words in Oldenspeak.

Silence reigned, faces rearranging from amused to amazed. Whatever they had expected, Aarvan's short speech was not it. The queen studied him, no longer bemused but still speculative. Billy's mouth hung open.

"An excellent answer, Queen's Man," Parria said. "It is most surprising coming from a male. Did the queen rehearse that speech with you before you came to dinner so you could deliver it perfectly?"

Aarvan said, "It must be a shock, Mistress, a man saying something intelligent. Kind of like the dog sitting up and talking."

Parria stared, eyes narrowing, frown forming.

A smiling Meitra softly interpreted.

"Aarvan," the queen said, "that was not respectful."

Aarvan faced the queen, brows knit.

Meitra continued to interpret.

"Thank you, Mistress," Aarvan said to Meitra. "Please tell my queen that respect was not considered. The land leader set me up to look stupid. We played a game of one-upmanship and I won."

"I do not understand this one-upmanship," the queen said.

"It is a game of mind and words in which two persons try to outdo one another," Aarvan explained.

"Tell my queen's man it is not his place to play one-upmanship with the land leader."

"Please tell my queen that I won't play if the land leader doesn't introduce the game."

Around the circumference of the table, gasps, frowns and eyes rolling upward followed this remark.

The queen's eyes flashed and her voice carried an edge. "Aarvan, you act an ass. I will hear no more. You embarrass your queen."

He understood without Meitra's help. Green eyes and dark blue clashed across the corner of the table. "Yes, My Queen," he said after a moment.

Aarvan lapsed into silence, picked up his hot wine and sipped.

Conversations began anew.

He lifted his eyes, and met Meitra's across the table.

Meitra grinned and winked.

Aarvan returned the grin; after all, she had interpreted for him.

Through the remainder of the meal, the women ignored Aarvan. He ate quietly, listened to the flow of conversation, what he could understand, but made no effort to join.

Over dessert, a verbal altercation erupted at the other end of the table. Sepa, a young merchant who specialized in cooking paraphernalia, and Billy, both appearing to have enjoyed too much wine, argued.

"Well, I want my own," Billy whined.

"You are but a holdee," Sepa said. "It is not fitting."

"I am land leader's man."

"Mistress Parria allows you to so call yourself. It is not a true station. Do not trade upon it."

"If queens have queen's men, land leaders should have land leader's men. Then it'd be a true station, and I could have my own."

"Your own what?" Hestera, an older tradeswoman of fine furs, snapped. "What has you whining, Billy?"

"I'm not whining," Billy whined. "I want a kruet box at the new banque."

Sepa glowered. "Holdees have not such privilege. Do not be daft."

"I'm land leader's man. I should have privileges." He stabbed a finger at Aarvan. "You said *he* could have one."

"He is queen's man," Hestera said. "He may have that which the queen allows. As a holdee, all you have is your ass, Billy, and not even that if your mistress wants it. There is no such title as *land leader's man.*"

"Well, there should be." Billy slammed his fist on the table, making mugs dance.

Parria snapped, "Billy, cease now! You stand on the far side of the wine cask. Drunkenness does not excuse arrogance."

"Yes, Mistress," Billy whined.

"Aarvan, what do you think?" Parria asked. "Should land leader's man be an accepted station?"

Aarvan glued his gaze to his wine chalice. "I've no opinion, Mistress."

"Oh come now. You have much to say otherwise. A land leader is second only to the queen. Should not the man she chooses have privileged status?"

"I'm sorry, Mistress, I have no opinion."

"The question has been asked of you, Aarvan, by a woman of high status." Parria's voice flowed rabbitt-fur soft spiced by a sly undertone. "It would be arrogant and disrespectful not to answer."

Aarvan glanced at Queen Rejeena, who watched him, green eyes inscrutable. He looked at Parria. "Why are you baiting me, Mistress?"

"Baiting you?" Parria leaned back, quirking a brow.

"Yes, baiting, as in trying to hook a snapfish."

"I merely asked your opinion, Queen's Man."

"An opinion which I am not allowed to give, Mistress."

"None have disallowed you."

"Mistress, my outlook on that subject would not be allowed."

"Now I truly wish to hear your view, Queen's Man."

Aarvan looked at the queen. "Do you want me to answer, My Queen?"

She smiled. "It would be most impolite not to do so."

"Then please tell me my opinion and I will pass it to the land leader."

Unbelieving gasps filled the silence.

"Aarvan!"

Aarvan leaned forward onto his elbows, gazing directly into the queen's eyes. "My Queen, the land leader is baiting me. I've tried to extract myself. You say I must answer. Falsehood being a punishable crime, I am bound to tell the truth. If I give you my honest view, you'll be angry and tell me I'm being an ass. What do you want me to do?"

"If I tell you to answer?"

"I will do so."

"Honestly?"

"Yes, My Queen."

The queen leaned back and gave him a beatific smile. "Speak then, Aarvan, because I too desire to hear your opinion."

"As you wish, My Queen." He turned to Parria. "The whole question is irrelevant, Mistress."

Meitra continued to interpret for the queen and the benefit of all women who did not speak Universal. As well, she changed Oldenspeak so Aarvan could understand. It made for slow, awkward conversation, but it worked.

"Irrelevant, Aarvan? I think it not irrelevant. Do you disparage the status of land leader? Of status privilege?" Parria's eyes blazed.

"Mistress, the question of privilege, accepted title, whether Billy is holdee or land leader's man is irrelevant because there should be none of either. One person shouldn't own another. All persons should be allowed to do their own choosing. Your enholding men, retaining them against their will, is a travesty of decent behavior, fairness and justice."

"Well, Queen's Man," the land leader said slowly, "you certainly make your opinion clear. Yet you are queen's man. You obey your queen."

"I enjoy breathing and wasn't presented a choice."

"If you had a choice, Aarvan?" the queen asked.

He looked her square in the eye. "I would not choose enholdment, My Queen."

"As queen's man you have many privileges," Tanalet, a banquer, said. "Your queen is rich and you enjoy unlimited kruets. You may come and go nearly as you please. I do not comprehend your outlook, Queen's Man."

"While you count my blessings, Mistress, consider that the queen can have me whipped, beaten, dragged through the ways or killed at her whim. No woman would lift a hand to stop her. In a truly civil society, there are laws to protect the lives and fates of every person, not just some."

Hestera leaned forward, eyes snapping. "So you think we should turn all holdees loose to flee to the Mainland or worse, to the fellows of loose men in the hills to kill women and plunder."

Any second Aarvan expected the queen to pounce on him, call him an ass and demand his silence. *I tried to avoid this conversation. Now, since they insisted, I'll have my say.* "Precisely, Mistress. Maybe if you stopped killing and plundering loose men, they'd stop killing and plundering you."

Hestera said, "Queen's Man, you blather nonsense. Women have ruled this island, this society, for hundreds of season turnings without your twisted outlook."

"Has it improved, Mistress?"

"You go too far." Parria leaped to her feet. "You are but a mere man, a privileged holdee. How may you determine what we do wrong on our island? Has LaSheena whispered truths to you alone? What makes you so right?"

"It works on the Mainland."

"This is not the Mainland," Tanalet said.

"No, it isn't, Mistress; but if you could observe how society there works, you might see there's a better way."

"A better way?" Parria said. "We have heard of Mainland measures. How men treat women, hold them to low status, disparage them."

"Only a few places, Mistress. In most countries men and women are equal, as it should be." Engrossed in the conversation, Aarvan failed to realize his answers came from scattered bits of memory.

"We will have none of that here."

"So instead you hold men to low status, disparage them."

"Yes. Men, not fettered," the land leader growled, "grow aggressive, untrustworthy, arrogant. Become bold, try to wrest control. Countless hundreds of seasons past men ruled here, disparaged women, considered them the lesser. LaSheena changed all that. We shall not allow the situation to revert."

"Mistress, eventually enholdment, such as you practice, will destroy everyone involved, especially the enholder." Aarvan frowned. "Slavery hasn't stood the test of time in any society."

Tanalet leaped to her feet. "You arrogant targeethan. Were you not queen's man, I would have you in locchot until you plead for the privilege of being but a low-caste, fettered holdee."

"There, Mistress, is the problem," Aarvan said. "You don't like what I'm saying, so your first reaction is 'send me to locchot.' How is your society going to improve if you won't even listen to different ideas?"

"Women," grated the rusty hinge of Meitra, "before you begin to heave wine flagons and eating utensils at the queen's man, you attack him for daring to give his opinion, which you required. If you did not wish to hear it, you should not have demanded it."

In the silence that ensued, Aarvan stared at Meitra. *The punishment meter defends me?*

"You agree with him?" Tanalet choked.

"No, I do not. I defend not his words, but his situation. You demanded his opinion. Now you would send him to locchot for stating it."

"I would send him to locchot for unbearable rudeness," Tanalet grumbled. "Tell us what we do wrong, indeed. Daft man. Asshole." She flopped into her seat, glaring.

"You do act an ass, Aarvan," the queen said.

He smiled. "You did ask, My Queen, and you suffered me acting an ass longer than I thought you would."

"You just finished," she said. "You will be silent. When you speak, you embarrass your queen. I shall be embarrassed no more tonight."

Aarvan started to reply then, looking into the queen's eyes, clamped his jaw. "Yes, My Queen."

Servants bustled about, refilling coffee mugs and hot wine glasses.

Aarvan lifted his eyes.

Meitra grinned at him.

He couldn't fathom what linked him tonight to this big, squat woman, but he responded in kind to her infectious grin. Then he made the mistake of looking at Krysiild. Under the conjurah's intense stare of disapproval, he dropped his gaze. He didn't look at the queen.

Everyone relaxed and the conversation grew genial. Though women's eyes flashed anger or disapproval when they flicked to Aarvan, with him quiet under order of silence, they paid him little heed. Some women arose and milled about the room. A few had made polite excuses and departed.

That strange, inner voice boomed in Aarvan's head. "*Move!*" He shoved sideways. Heat seared by his face. He leaped up and spun to face the source.

Billy stood near, staring at the hot wine flagon in his hand. The wine lay splattered on the table. Billy's face twisted in chagrin.

Parria jumped to her feet. "What are you about, you clumsy fool? You nearly burned the queen's man."

Billy shuffled his feet, head hung, swaying slightly. "Sorry, Mistress. Didn't mean to. I tripped." He pointed at the smooth floor.

"Well, return to your place. You disgrace your mistress. Repetition of such action, intended or accidental, will merit punishment."

For one fleeting second, Billy's eyes met Aarvan's. They shone sly, malicious, as well as drunk. Mumbling, Billy lurched away to his seat.

Parria called a servant to wipe away the wine. The land leader fussed over Aarvan, apologizing, hands needlessly touching.

Billy hunched in his chair, glowering.

* * *

Later at the queen's home, Rejeena disappeared into the bathing room.

Aarvan sank into a deep chair, closed his eyes, body slumped. Weariness descended like a heavy blanket.

"You look tired, Aarvan." The queen stood before him. "I hope not too much so."

"Would it make any difference?"

She looked perplexed, but he didn't explain. He grasped her skirt and tugged; she came readily. He loosened the ties holding the garment and let it slide to the floor.

He placed his hands on her waist. Slowly, fingers splayed, touch gentle, thumbs trailing over her belly, he slid both hands down her hips, stopping at the widest part.

The queen trembled.

He looked into her eyes, which had glazed, just short of lighting with passion. "You have wide, beautiful hips, My Queen, made for cradling offspring," he whispered.

The queen's face softened into a warm smile. "Do you think so?" She appeared to have understood.

"Yes, I do." He pulled her to him and, feather-light, nuzzled her belly.

She gasped and her hands gripped his shoulders. Her husky voice deepened. "Perhaps my queen's man can fill the cradle."

"Perhaps." He nuzzled lower. She quivered, her hands clenching.

He slid to his knees, lips and fingers gliding over her smooth skin.

The queen shook with delicious anticipation, her knees turning to rubber, leg muscles going liquid. She clutched him for support and moaned, "Oh, my beautiful queen's man, what you do to me. A man should not hold such power in his palm."

He paused, lifted his eyes. "I don't understand, My Queen."

She grasped his head between her hands, gazed into his eyes. "It is just as well, Aarvan."

* * *

That night Locin ruled the contingent of guards assigned in the queen's home. Six gathered outside the queen's skindown room, playing muskee, chatting and sipping coffee. Deep in the morning, a loud, hoarse yell from the skindown room startled them. All six rushed into the room, swords in hand.

The queen's man crouched in the middle of the room, naked, yelling in a strange language. He poised on the balls of his feet, knees bent. His hands forged a defensive position, open, fingers rigid.

Queen Rejeena sat in the skindown, eyes wide, staring at him.

Locin could discern no threat in the room. She sheathed her sword, grabbed the first thing at hand, the queen's skirt, and leaped to cover him.

She did not see him move. Suddenly he faced her. She did see the eyes. Frigid, remorseless, feral beast's eyes stared at her—promised her death. She skidded to a halt.

A tiny heart skip of time—then the eyes changed. They softened with recognition. The feral beast vanished. He stood stiffly. "Locin?" His voice grated hoarse, questioning, as if filtering through a long, cloudy distance.

"Queen's Man," Locin coaxed, "let me clothe you. You stand naked."

His gaze scoured the room, brow wrinkled, chest heaving.

Locin whipped the queen's skirt around him and tied it in place.

The queen asked, "Aarvan, are you unwell?"

He did not answer, stood looking perplexed at the room.

Locin caught him by the shoulders and guided him to the skindown.

He yielded, sank onto the edge, shaking, face buried in his hands, body slick with cold sweat.

The queen slid next to him and gently rubbed his back.

Locin used hand signals to send the other guards back to their posts.

The queen leaned close. "Aarvan, what plagues you?"

He lifted his head, gulped a deep breath. His glance flicked around the room again in a search pattern. "I'm sorry, My Queen. I had a nightmare. I'll be all right."

"It must have been fierce, Queen's Man, to cause you such travail," Locin said.

"It was." He sounded dazed. He lifted his eyes to meet hers.

The ferocious beast that meant to kill her only a long minute ago no longer resided in those blue depths. Now Locin saw only the confused, innocent eyes of the queen's man.

"What was it, Aarvan," Rejeena asked, "to have upset you so?"

He straightened his spine, blew his breath out hard between tight lips, causing his cheeks to puff. "It was just a nightmare. It will go away."

"I wish to know."

He looked at her and swallowed visibly. "I saw cats, a lot of cats, at first little house cats. My memories. I chased them, tried to catch them, catch my memories. They ran fast, twisted, spun, leaped . . . too agile. I couldn't catch a single one." He shook once as though casting off a chill. "Then they started to grow, became huge. They had gaping mouths filled with these impossibly massive teeth and yellow, wild eyes glaring like something that . . . that rose up from Hell. They turned and started to chase me. Dozens of them."

He stopped and took a steadying breath. "We raced across this long, dark, flat place. I knew if they caught me, they would tear me to pieces. I tried to run, but I sank to my ankles in deep dust at every step. The cats skimmed across the top. The slower I ran, the faster they came." His chest heaved as though he suppressed a shudder. "Then they rolled into each other, combined and became one gigantic cat. It caught me, reached out with a paw and knocked me tumbling head over heels the way it would a mouse."

His eyes filled with an agonized anger. "The worst part was that the cat could kill me, but I couldn't fight back, couldn't kill it because it was a memory, not real." He dropped his head back into his hands, sucked air into his lungs in long, ragged breaths. "I woke up standing in the middle of the room."

The queen stroked his back again. "Aarvan, it was indeed merely a nightmare." She waved around the room and smiled. "See, no cats, not a single one."

"I know, but it seemed so real. It came out of the back of my mind where all those memories are locked away. I wish I could go there, awake . . . without any blasted cats."

Locin controlled a cold tremor, which rippled through her. *I think I met your cat—your beast—and it was you. Those eyes were, anyway.*

"Locin, have the servants bring us warm milk," the queen said. "Aarvan could use some."

"Yes, My Queen." Locin used the servants' bell. *I shall not step from this room until certain of my queen's safety.*

Later, the queen and queen's man sat against pillows, sipping milk. Locin waited.

Aarvan appeared to calm and relax. Finally, he put his empty mug aside, reached under the covers, and pulled out the queen's skirt. "You look much better in this, My Queen," he said with a feeble attempt to grin.

Locin arose, gathered the mugs. "I will go now, My Queen, if nothing more is needed."

The queen dismissed her with a quick nod.

Locin returned to her guard station, satisfied the feral beast was gone.

* * *

Aarvan arose, feeling rested despite his difficult evening at the dinner, coupling with the queen and the mind-shattering nightmare.

During his breakfast on the rockcaste, Alea arrived.

"You have arisen early," she said, accepted coffee and joined him.

He smiled. "I'm getting better."

"Do not hurry. You have fifteen lashes coming when you are well for being a hardheaded ass about skindown."

He grimaced. "I'd managed to put that out of my mind, but I'll take the lashes to feel like myself again."

She leaned back. "How does that feel?"

"I think normally I'm energetic and I don't sleep so much." He patted his flat stomach. "I need work to keep this body in shape. What can I do here that's useful and demanding?"

Alea grinned. "By the appearance of our queen these days, you are most useful."

"I need work besides that."

"There remains time. When you are well, we may then approach the queen. Speaking of the queen, what imbecilic stunt did you perform last night?"

"What stunt?"

"I speak of the dinner, where you told many seegarpt of Rejeena's Towne that they lack civility. Additionally, that their ways, which have functioned well for hundreds of season turnings, stand completely wrongful."

"Oh that." His impudent grin flickered. "They did ask."

"Aarvan, you cannot so plague seegarpt. Those are leaders, commerce and councilwomen, the governing body of this packet, this quarter. I understand that you acted publicly rude to the queen."

"Gossip sure travels fast in this towne. I wasn't rude to the queen. I just disagreed with her outlook."

"Aarvan, I . . . I swear . . . Really . . . Aarvan, you may not seize such privilege. Have you learned nothing? You are absolutely the most hardheaded, exasperating man ever to be chosen by a queen. After such antics, I wonder the queen did not have you in locchot this morning."

"Maybe the queen's embarrassment at my dinner antics is less than her appreciation of my skindown antics."

Alea glared. "I fear you will never learn to be a proper queen's man."

"I would hope not."

"Oh, Aarvan," she sighed, "I do not know what is to become of you."

He waved away the servant who appeared to refill his empty caster. "Hopefully," he said, "I'll complete my queen, find useful work and regain my memory. Then I can reconsider."

"You will still belong to the queen."

He smiled, paused for a moment then asked, "Where do I find Meitra?"

"Meitra? What possible purpose could you have with Meitra? Most men wish to maintain great distance from her."

"I'm curious about last night. Where would I find her?"

"Likely at the punishment room. That is her function. What about last night?"

He rose. "Walk with me and find out."

"As long as you do not go for punishment. That I cannot watch."

"As far as I know, I'm not."

Two guards followed them.

They strolled down Mainway and entered the punishment room.

Meitra, busy polishing the head of a strikepaddle, turned. She stopped and stared, then walked to meet them.

"Alea," she greeted. "Pretty Queen's Man, are you lost or did the queen send you to learn regret for your boorish behavior?"

"Good morning, Mistress. This is an informal visit."

"Well, I must say, Aarvan, I receive few visitors in the punishment room. I certainly did not expect the queen's man." Meitra hung the strikepaddle, wiped her hands and motioned to a viewing bench. She featured her favorite sardonic grin. "Had you informed me of your visit, I could have offered coffee and cakes. Since you did not, you will find no comforts. What can I do for you, Queen's Man?"

Alea stood, while Aarvan sat on the end of a bleacher. "I want to thank you for last night," he said.

"For what?"

"For rescuing me when those women seemed prepared to jump on me en masse with cudgels and unkind intentions."

"I feared they would throw things, and I would be struck."

"Liar."

Meitra shrugged. "As I said, they put you to sword point, insisted you answer, then attacked you for doing so."

"Careful," he grinned, "you may convince me you hide a heart."

"There is much you do not know about me, pretty Queen's Man."

"The other thing, Meitra . . . excuse me, Mistress, I wanted to thank you for interpreting."

"You may drop the mistress, except before seegarpt. As for interpreting, do not be too quick to thank me. All those cranky old bariits now know everything you said. That is not necessarily to your favor."

Aarvan shrugged. "I only have to please the queen."

"Last night you pleased the queen?" Alea snorted.

Aarvan flicked her a grin, then said to Meitra, "There's something that bothers me. Maybe you can explain since you were there."

"What bothers you?"

"Did I commit some social blunder? At first, the land leader seemed friendly. Then at dinner she started to bait me, trying to cause trouble. I can't figure the woman."

Meitra leaned on a high bleacher seat, chin in hand, and stared into his eyes, hers narrow black slits. "Is he truly so ignorant, Alea?"

"I fear so."

"What am I missing now?" Aarvan asked.

Meitra stood upright and lightly gripped his arm. "Come, I will show you."

She led him into her function room.

Alea followed.

His guards stayed sitting on the bleachers, looking discomfited but unsure of their precise role at this point.

Behind a door, Meitra disclosed a full-length mirror. She spun Aarvan to face it, peering over his shoulder, lightly gripping, her face so close their cheeks almost touched.

Alea stood watching.

"That is a mirror," Meitra said. "You should be familiar with them, as they come from the Mainland. What do you see?"

"Me?"

"Yes, but let us be more detailed. You see one gorgeous queen's man, handsome face with blue eyes that could melt rock, dark hair, perfect features—"

"Meitra, this is embarrassing." He tried to turn.

Her huge hands tightened on his shoulders. "Clamp jaw. You asked a question. I answer."

He shrugged but stood.

"Look at you, Queen's Man—all the right muscles, lean and graceful, no extra weight, nice wide shoulders, trim hips, interesting bulge in the correct place and a fantastic ass. You are, by the length of a glaalet's stride, the best-looking piece of skindown goods in Rejeena's Towne, maybe even on the island." Releasing him, Meitra settled back.

He turned, face slightly flushed. "To save argument, let's grant all that. So?"

"You still do not understand the game?" Meitra crossed her arms and studied him.

"I guess not."

"Every woman who views you wants that gorgeous keister in her skindown. But you are queen's man. None may touch you unless the queen loses interest and places you at barter."

His blue eyes widened as comprehension dawned. "No one would deliberately create a rift between the queen and queen's man . . . would they?"

"Some would."

"Surely not the land leader?"

"She did not grasp the land leader position by acting placid and reticent. She grows bored with Billy but has found nothing better. Think of your image in the mirror and compare it to Billy. Parria has now seen that which is better. Many of those women concocted much of the anger and outrage displayed concerning your statements strictly for the queen's benefit."

"The queen's not stupid. Surely she knows that."

"Of course, it is a game. Last night she let you talk, then silenced you, claiming embarrassment to allow them hope. After dinner she took your fetching keister home to her skindown. She departed to function this morning leaving you with no threat of locchot. She thus declared these women have the same chance as a broken-winged bird in a windstorm. The queen knows how to play the game."

"Politics," he muttered. "I hate politics."

"Why do you hate politics?" Alea asked, seeking to jog his memory.

"I don't know, but I hate politics."

Meitra leaned forward, tapping him on the chest with a forefinger. "You watch your step with Billy."

"Billy? He's no threat."

"Not directly. Face to face, he poses no risk, lacking courage. Make no mistake, Queen's Man; Billy is a sneaking, conniving targeethan who displays jealousy. He cannot be trusted. He enjoys his position and status. The insidious rogue invented the hot wine incident last evening. Naught existed on that floor to trip Billy. He aimed for your face, intended to burn you. Had he done so, he would surely have tasted locchot, if not worse. I believe he does not make rational decisions when he has indulged of shaarberry wine, and he indulges much. He views you as a threat, and will not lose without a fight."

"Why are you telling me all this?"

"I want you around, pretty Queen's Man, so when the queen tires of you, I may barter well."

Aarvan leaned close and said softly, "You ever hear of the impossible dream, Meitra?"

Meitra laughed. "Oh, pretty Queen's Man, I do like a man who fights."

Sercha interrupted, arriving with a set of rolled whips. "Ready for practice, Meitra?" She spied Alea and Aarvan. "I did not know you had visitors."

"That's all right," Aarvan said. "We were just leaving."

"Do not rush away," Meitra purred in that rusty hinge voice, which made for a distinctly bizarre sound. Her hand fell on his shoulder. "I will show you the function of this." She flipped one whip free, making it writhe over the floor like a live snake.

"No thanks." He eyed the long whip, his face scrunching as he leaned backward.

"Stay, Queen's Man," Sercha said. "Observe. She possesses much skill."

"I'm sure, but . . ."

"Watch, Aarvan," Alea said. "She can snap a fly from a horse's back without touching the horse."

"I'm not to be the target, am I?"

Meitra laughed. "Of course not, this is for fun."

"Is anything alive going to be the target?"

"No, nothing alive."

"All right then. I'll watch."

They walked to an enclosed area behind the punishment room. Wooden riggings filled a corner, with surfaces set at every conceivable angle. Sercha placed small, colored knobs in holes in the riggings, so that only a tiny portion of each showed.

Meitra snapped the whip. She looked at Aarvan. "Pick a knob."

"The blue one on top." He pointed. The whip cracked and the knob vanished.

"Give me difficulty."

He pointed to a red one canted at a barely accessible angle. The whip sang and the red knob disappeared.

"Not bad," he said.

"Step back, and watch." Meitra waved Alea and Aarvan away from her.

"First the blue, then the red," Sercha called.

The great whip snapped and sang in a steady rhythm, flicked, slashed. At each strike, a knob flew from its hole. Meitra's arm flashed overhead, underhand, backhand, sideways, low to the ground. From every angle, her aim proved perfect.

When she finished, Aarvan stared in awe. He walked to the wooden riggings, running his finger over the soft wood where the knobs had been. No mark marred the surface; the knobs had simply vanished.

Meitra said, "Impressed, Queen's Man?"

"Yes, I am."

"Let us discern how impressed. Take a knob, hold it between your lips and I will pluck it out."

"I'm not that impressed."

Sercha walked to the riggings, picked a green knob, placed it between her lips and turned sideways to Meitra.

"You don't have to—"

The whip snapped and the green knob vanished. Sercha walked to Aarvan. "See, Queen's Man, no damage. I would ask you to so perform, but all women know men possess no courage." She stalked away, head high.

"So it's a woman versus man thing?" Aarvan growled.

"Hold no concern, Queen's Man," Sercha grinned. "We understand."

Aarvan spun abruptly toward the riggings.

"Aarvan, do not dare!" Alea squalled. "Should she sever half that handsome face, all of us would likely die in locchot." When Aarvan ignored her and picked a yellow knob, she yelled, "Meitra!"

"She speaks well, Aarvan," Meitra said. "Replace the knob."

"You women issued the challenge. Now live up to it."

Meitra frowned and received a cocked eyebrow in response. The punishment meter sighed. "Very well, hold it in your thumb and forefinger as far from your body as you can reach."

"Now who lacks courage? Price too high?"

"The skill of the whip hand is but half; the nerve of the target is the other."

"One way to find out." He placed the knob in his lips, and presented her a target.

"Aarvan!" Alea shrieked. "Meitra, do not dare!"

"Shhhh," Meitra said, "you will break my concentration." She readied the whip, her eyes steady on the yellow knob. "Do not move, Aarvan." The long whip flashed.

The door in Aarvan's mind slammed open. That rage exploded through it, enveloped him and formed a new entity. Possessed strength, power and unflinching nerve. Watched the whip slice the air. Tracked its course. Gauged speed and trajectory. Knew it would take the knob. Not touch him. Permitted it to come, unmolested. He almost laughed aloud. *I could dodge the whip. I could grab it. I am faster than the whip—faster than the hand behind the whip.* He felt the knob leave his lips. Heard the whip crack. The entity dissolved, the rage retreated, leaving Aarvan standing alone.

He stood stunned by this revelation. *What sort of man am I? I must recover those memories, find the person I've lost.* He yearned for that superbly fast, supremely confident entity he had been for one split second. *What a creature to be. What a way to feel, to live.*

"Queen's Man, you can move now," Meitra said.

He covered his lapse with a saucy grin. "Just wanted to be sure you were finished."

"Aarvan," Alea cried, "this is absurdity. The queen will not approve your daring of a whip."

"I wasn't planning to tell her."

"And you." Alea rounded on Meitra. "How dare you endanger the queen's man?"

"He suffered no danger so long as he did not move," Meitra said.

I wasn't in any danger at all. What is lurking in my head? What is that thing? Aarvan shivered slightly—that rage, the presence both uplifted and terrified him. What sort of monstrous life had he lived, to have need of such?

"It is time to go, Aarvan," Alea said, standing stiffly. She scolded him all the way to the queen's house.

The guards followed, smiling at Alea's fury.

He turned in at the gate and looked at her, eyes dancing. "Yes, Mother."

She whacked him on the back with her open hand and marched off.

Aarvan walked through the door.

* * *

A large hand fell on Aarvan's shoulder as he entered the queen's house. It was Locin, frowning, her gray eyes squinted, feet planted wide. "We must talk, Queen's Man."

"Of course, Locin, what is it?"

She motioned him to follow and led the way to the garden.

"I am not sure how to say what I must," Locin said.

"Straight out is a good way."

The huge guard stood tall. "I have come to like you, Queen's Man, a ridiculous emotion to waste on a mere man, but I do. It would displease me to see you suffer harm. But my allegiance belongs my queen, my function to protect her. She will always come first."

His brow wrinkled but he nodded, waiting.

"Last night you suffered that nightmare," she said.

Aarvan flushed, remembering all six guards, while performing their duty, had seen him nude.

Locin ignored his discomfort. "When I tried to clothe you, you turned on me. Your eyes harbored a vicious beast. I read in them a powerful intent to kill me." She paused.

He stared. "A beast?"

"That is what I saw."

"Beast? What sort of beast? I didn't touch you."

"No. As you awoke, you recognized me, and the beast retreated."

"I was the one in danger, not you."

"In your nightmare. My concern is for my queen."

"The queen?" He leaned forward, arms spread. "What do you mean?"

"You spend nights alone with her. Her safety concerns me."

"I wouldn't harm the queen. What are you saying? I don't even understand this conversation. What beast? What are we talking about?"

Locin moved close, glaring. "Do not think to palter or deny. I know what I saw. There lies within you a danger and for my queen's sake, I must ferret it out."

"You're imagining things, Locin. There's nothing to ferret."

She grabbed his vest front and shoved him against a tree. "Death dwelt in your eyes, Queen's Man. You stand capable of killing. You will tell me of this beast."

"There's nothing to tell." He didn't attempt to wrest free, but his mouth twisted. "What's wrong, guardswoman? Afraid of a mere man? We're nothing. Have you forgotten? How could a man pose danger?"

She shoved harder, wringing from him a grunt. "Do not taunt me. I will know of this."

He wilted in her grip, muscles slackened, arms at his side. "I can't tell you what I don't know, Locin."

She frowned. He indeed lacked memory. Perhaps he did stand unaware. She thought of how much happier the queen seemed since his arrival. He appeared gentle, pliable. She released him and motioned to a stone bench. "Sit down, Queen's Man."

"I don't want to sit down. I want to know what we're talking about."

"Then I will sit down." Locin sat. "I do not believe you intend harm. If I did, I would slice you as a melon. LaHeeka required the queen take you. Surely she would not have done so if you pose a hazard. It is the beast which frightens me for my queen." She raised a hand, forestalling his comment. "Think deeply of your past. Your memory could help us understand this beast."

"What beast?"

"The one inside you."

"I don't remember anything of my past, Locin. I wish to God I did!"

"There is that which makes you different from your customary demeanor. You know of no change which happens in you?"

His gaze wavered and a dark shadow flickered in his eyes.

Locin pounced. "You do know something, Queen's Man. I saw it in your eyes. Do not fling falsehood."

He walked away, stopped at a short distance with his back to her. His shoulder muscles rippled, head dropped then returned to its normal position.

Locin waited until he heaved a deep sigh and turned.

He joined her on the bench. The dark blue eyes, calm and guileless, lifted and met hers.

"I'm going to trust you, Locin," he said. "I don't know why. You're a woman of this island with that blasted superiority precept. But I believe you do want only what's best for the queen. There is . . . something, but I don't see it as a beast." He told her about the door in his mind, the voice that talked to him, some of the things it said, the exultant feeling of having total power even as a whip slashed at his face. "I don't know where this presence comes from, what it is, its purpose or use in my former life. But Locin, it's not a beast and I control it. I'd never hurt the queen."

Locin studied his eyes, which met hers without evasion, calm, unruffled as a deep lake on a still day. *How hard it surely is for him to admit these things, how much trust he offers me in the telling.* "This presence inferred you could best six queen's guards?"

A grin flickered. "Yes, and another time four, you being one."

"Your presence must be most unwise, Queen's Man."

"That I can't say. I only told you because I want you to understand, that at no time did any threat include the queen."

"I will accept your words. But should you ever—you or your beast—harm the queen, I will carve your heart out slowly with a dull knife."

"Should that happen, I'd stand and let you do it."

"Then we have understanding, Queen's Man?"

"Yes." His gaze dropped. "Will you tell the queen?"

"No," she said. "You have made my queen happy. I would not take that away."

"Thank you."

She rose and stared down at him for a moment. "Now, Arrogant Pup, you need a haircut. You look a bit shaggy."

Aarvan ran a hand through his dark hair. "I do need a cut. Do you have places to do that?"

"Of course. We are civilized."

"The word *civilized* coming from a woman who's going to carve my heart out slowly with a dull knife?"

"Only should you harm my queen. Will you come or sit making rude remarks?"

"With what do I pay, Shiira Guardswoman? I've no kruets." He flung his arms wide. "No barter goods." That impudent grin flashed. "The only thing I have to barter in this towne, the queen insists upon keeping for herself."

"I told you, the queen will honor your barks."

"I told you, I won't barter my queen's goods."

"I will pay then. I have kruets."

"Thanks, but no thanks. Wouldn't that enhance the queen's image with all women, her guard having to buy the queen's man a haircut?"

"What do you suggest?"

"I'll wait until my queen notices I need a haircut, then I'll beg a few kruets."

"You most certainly will not. It is the function of guards and servants to notice these things. The queen cannot be bothered with trifles."

"I'll get a job then."

"A job?"

"Yes, you know, you do work, someone pays you kruets. A job."

"Oh, function. A queen's man does not take function. You have function."

"I do?"

"Rutting the queen."

"Not exactly my idea of a jo . . . function. Besides, it hasn't produced any kruets. Where I come from people go to jail for taking baagars . . . kruets for rutting."

The huge guard leaned down, placed a hand on either side of him against the back of the bench, nose almost touching his. "You no longer reside in that place. You are here. Here, Queen's Man, rutting the queen stands honor and privilege. Most holdees would gladly grant ten seasons of life to become queen's man. I do not believe you truly appreciate your station."

"Well, pardon me, Shiira Guardswoman, but I wasn't consulted about whether I wanted this station."

"Your wants are not important. You were chosen."

"Then don't blame me if I'm not thrilled by it."

Locin stood upright and glared. "Alea is right; you are an infuriating man."

"Locin, I know it is considered an honor and privilege to be queen's man."

"Then you needs show you are honored."

"How?"

"Get a haircut. The queen favors short hair on men."

"Which circles us straight back to my lack of kruets."

Locin stared, eyes hard, hands planted on hips.

He stared back.

She released an exasperated sigh. "Come with me, Queen's Man." She turned and walked toward the house.

"Where are we going?" he demanded, striding after her.

"You will know when we get there."

"If you drag me to some haircut place with no kruets, Locin, I'm going to embarrass you."

"They are called shingly shops, not haircut places."

"Shingly? What's that mean?"

"It has to do with the top. I do not know for certainty, nor do I concern myself. In any case, that is not our destination. For once, you arrogant pup, follow in silence."

He shrugged and followed. At the outside door, she motioned two guards to join them.

They walked a labyrinth of sideways and backways and emerged onto the Mainway, at an area Aarvan didn't recognize. They stood beside a large, imposing building with heavily armed guards at the entrances—every woman bedecked with swords, large shields, hand crossbows and quivers of bolts. Locin motioned him forward and walked through a side door. The guards stood aside and let them pass.

The line leader led down a corridor into a large reception area. "Sit," she said and pointed to a chair.

He sank onto it.

Women filled the room, one sat behind a flat desk beside another door. Certain persons appeared to be waiting, both sitting and standing. Armed guards watched alertly.

Locin passed through the inner door. She returned after a few minutes and motioned for him.

He rose and followed, smiling at the woman by the door.

He stepped into another reception area, with more guards and a woman behind a flat desk beside a door. He stopped abruptly. "Locin, where are we?" At her broad smile, his eyes narrowed. "Are we where I think we are?"

"Yes, but your wisdom has found you too late. The queen expects you." She swept her arm toward the closed door.

He hesitated.

The woman behind the desk rose and opened the door. "The queen cannot be kept waiting, Queen's Man."

He speared Locin with a poisonous glare and walked through the opening.

The queen sat behind a huge desk at the end of the room.

Aarvan bowed, rose and approached at her gesture.

Rejeena smiled. "Locin tells me you suffer a lack of kruets, Aarvan."

"I'm embarrassed, My Queen. Locin didn't have the right—"

She stilled his protest with a raised hand. "You need not feel embarrassment. I have been remiss not providing you with kruets." She rose and walked to a wall, lifted from a peg a large leather pouch attached to a belt. The queen strode to him and fastened the belt about his waist. "This pouch contains kruets enough for many purchases, also barks and marking prickle."

"My Queen, I don't require much."

"You are queen's man and will have means to barter. I would expect to be consulted, of course, before you buy a house or tracher of land." Her wide mouth curved in a smile.

"I'll remember that, My Queen." He grimaced weakly, having no idea what a tracher of land might be.

She waved him toward the door. "Go and enjoy yourself, Aarvan." Her eyes flashed, and she shook her finger. "Do not approach the gaming house of that trollop, Tatia."

"No, My Queen."

As he departed, she said, "Aarvan, while you jaunt upon Mainway, get a haircut."

"Yes, My Queen." Pleasantly surprised that he and the queen understood one another, he snapped the door shut. He stalked to Locin, who leaned against the wall. "I ought to wring you neck."

"Why? I solved your problem. I was glad to be of assistance."

"That was embarrassing."

"Queen's Man, everything embarrasses you."

Aarvan glanced around the room. All the women watched them. He raised both hands palm out before his chest. "All right, Shiira Guardswoman, you win one."

Locin said, "Now we must get you a haircut."

Aarvan spent several hours on Mainway, trailed by his patient guards.

Locin took him to Lesta's Shingly—Trimming the Top, Our Specialty.

Lesta, the owner, appeared delighted. Upon his questioning, she explained that shingly had to do with roofs, the reference to hair concerning the roof of a person, she supposed. She and her assistants fussed, brought coffee, assured the comfort of the chair and trimmed the cut just right. She shaved Aarvan, though he didn't need it. Lesta tried to refuse payment, but with determination and tact he pressed the kruets on her. When they left, women poured into the shop. The shingly owner would enjoy much commerce, relating the pleasures of serving the queen's man.

Aarvan wandered around, ending at Balstra's cake and coffee shop.

Balstra greeted then seated and served him.

Alaestrea arrived from next door, hugged him and prattled.

Aarvan laughed and joked with women who appeared as if by magic, filling the shop to capacity and beyond. He suffered embarrassment more than once; but time with the friendly, boisterous allway women passed pleasantly, relaxed, untouched by politics or the need to constantly guard his tongue against offense.

Balstra ran interference, fended off some of the worst, most bawdy remarks.

He stayed until time for his language class.

Locin sat beaming, a partridge hen with but one hatchling.

* * *

After dinner, as the queen and Aarvan relaxed with coffee, Alea entered. She sat beside Aarvan, facing the queen.

Aarvan grinned at the healer and asked in Universal, "Did you come to rat on me about the whip, Alea?"

"No, I come at the queen's invitation."

"What had you to do with a whip, Aarvan?" the queen asked in Oldenspeak.

Aarvan's brows arched. "I'll have to be more careful. My queen is learning Universal."

"Some, Aarvan," she said smugly. "Now tell me of this whip?"

He grimaced, his dark blue eyes flicked between Alea and the queen. He told her about the whip incident, a barebones account not including mention of the presence. The small amount of interpretation needed from Alea pleasantly surprised him.

The queen said, "That was most unwise. You could have been seriously injured, causing grave consequences for you, your queen and those who allowed you. In future refrain from similar acts."

Aarvan bristled at the word *allowed*, but held his tongue. "It was stupid."

"Yes, it was," Alea said.

"Yes, Mother," Aarvan muttered.

Alea punched him on the shoulder.

"Ouch." He rubbed the spot. "You can't wallop me before my queen."

"She is your healer. If she deems a solid clout the required medicine, so be it," Rejeena said.

"If you're going to gang up on me . . ." Aarvan threw his hands upward.

The queen leaned back, eyes serious. "Aarvan, I asked Alea to coffee so you may understand all my words. Much will happen in the next few weeks.

"In five days," the queen said, "I must depart to Queens' Council. Three queens and many land leaders will attend. Our quarter and those neighboring to the west and southwest encompass the Alvastrea Mountains. These three quarters encounter constantly increasing outlaw activity. We must take council and decide how to defeat them. Parria, two neighboring land leaders, and I will journey together.

"Since I must leave for council, Queen's Hearing will begin tomorrow and continue for four days. Tomorrow evening we will hold a meeting concerning life surety for the journey.

"As you are queen's man, and healing well"—a smile flickered—"able to face whistling whips with impunity, you will accompany your queen to these functions."

"Do I have a purpose at these functions?"

"Your purpose is to impress all women with the fine choice your queen has made for queen's man. Do you think you can so achieve, without embarrassing your queen?"

"I believe so. I don't intentionally embarrass my queen. I'll try to restrain myself."

"Most wise, Aarvan." The queen's eyes held his in an intense stare, full of naked desire. She reached across the table, and her fingertips grazed his wrist.

Her stare caused his groin muscles to tighten, and her touch sent hot sparks racing up his arm. The air between them sizzled.

Alea rose. "I will depart, My Queen. I see you are ready . . . for skindown." Neither paid any attention as she curtsied from the room.

The queen rose and held out her hand.

Aarvan allowed her to lead him into the skindown room.

He reached to remove his vest.

She caught his hand. "I have wanted to do this, Aarvan," she whispered. "I have lacked courage."

"Do what, My Queen?"

"Unclothe your body with my own hands."

Aarvan smiled. The queen, except for performing the completion act in the traditional manner, still showed herself to be inexperienced in the skindown arena. Removing his clothing would indeed be adventure for her, part courage and part pleasure. A warm tenderness squeezed at his heart. He invited her with a sensual stare.

She slid both hands upward from his belly and slipped the vest from his shoulders. Mesmerized, eyes following hands, palms pressed against his skin, she caressed his upper body, slowly, studiously, as a queenly chore. Her hands circled to his back, and she leaned close, cheek pressed to his chest. She murmured, "You are so beautiful, my Aarvan. Your skin is silk stretched over iron. I can never touch you enough. The feel of you pleases me." She sighed. "You have so changed your queen."

"How is that?" he whispered.

"You brought to my skindown great pleasure. You taught your queen passion."

"No, My Queen, I didn't."

She pulled back to look at him. "How can you so state? Before you, I had not skindown passion, but mild pleasure only."

"No one can teach another passion, My Queen. You are an ardent woman and the passion lies within you. You denied yourself because of tradition. I awakened it in you, but I didn't teach it. Neither man nor woman can find what doesn't exist."

She cocked her head slightly. "I do not know if I believe that, Aarvan. But it is hardly significant. Whether awakened or taught, your queen now knows passion. She wants you and shall have you." She pulled him close again, hands roaming his back.

He didn't answer, just enjoyed her fondling, which stoked the fire she lit at dinner.

Her hands dropped to his pants buttons. "I do not know how to proceed, My Queen's Man."

"Let your urges guide you. There is no wrong way between a man and a woman. You did well when you woke me the first time we met."

A smile tugged at her wide mouth. She opened the buttons, slid her hands deeper. Fingertips teased his groin muscles, which quivered at her touch.

"I like that." The queen's husky whisper heightened his growing arousal. "When I make you vibrate so, I feel most powerful." She explored this new experience, like a child fired with anticipation.

"Your touch, My Queen, is powerful," he whispered. He didn't move, sensing she wanted to do it all.

The buttons open, she splayed her fingers, slid her hands to cup his taut rear, massaging. Leaning against him, she caressed, stroked, explored. She played, using him like a new toy; and he stood, the willing toy.

She smoothed her hands to his hipbones and pushed his pants down.

They fell to his ankles and he kicked them aside. His manhood, already hardening, stood partially erect.

She grasped it in both hands, rubbed, squeezed and stroked its full length. Her fingertips glided along the sensitive line at the bottom.

It grew, swelled swiftly in her hands. Spears of heat lanced his body. When need closed upon agony, he caught her hands in his. "My Queen," he moaned, "if you continue, I'll not be able to wait until you're ready."

Her throaty laugh was a sultry caress. "Aarvan, I have been ready since you tempted me with those skindown eyes at coffee. I swelter so, I wonder my skirt is not afire."

"We'd best remove it then. We don't want to scorch a good skirt." He suited action to words. Her skirt slipped to the floor.

She grasped his manhood again.

"My Queen."

She leaned close. "Do you know what I want?"

"Tell me."

"Rut me fast and hard like the great stag whose name you carry."

"My Queen, gentleness—"

"You may be gentle later. Right now, I want you to rut me, hard, wild, like a mad creature."

He caught her around the waist, lifted her, dropped her on the skindown and fulfilled her wish.

* * *

"Aarvan, it is time to rise." The queen's husky voice invaded his sleep.

"It can't be," he groaned, and burrowed under the covers.

She laughed, pulled the covers off and slapped him lightly on the bare rear. "It is, Aarvan. Arise."

He peered at her with sleep-shrouded eyes. "Are you sure?"

"Yes, I am sure." She smiled, hand warm on his back. "Your bath is ready, your clothing laid out. Following breakfast, I must conduct hearing, and you must attend."

He twisted into a sitting position and muttered, "I should have gotten more sleep."

"It is your own fault. I did not wake you. You woke me."

"Just serving my queen to the best of my ability."

"Your ability stands most gratifying, My Queen's Man, but you must still perform other duties."

"You're merciless."

"Yes, I am. Now go." She pointed.

He rose and padded away.

Energized and refreshed by breakfast and coffee, Aarvan felt alert and interested by the time he and the queen arrived at the great Hearing Hall. As instructed, he entered between guards and queen's council, stood by his cubicle, bowed as the queen entered, then sat following the seating of council.

"Very nice, Aarvan," the queen whispered. "You performed most smoothly."

"Thank you, My Queen."

The first case was a complicated, serious land dispute between two wealthy women from the Packet of Tameera's Towne, part of Quarter Seven. The queen listened to their presentations, then referred the case to her council, as resolution of the convoluted claims would require study of the ancient laws and past decisions.

A short lull followed while the reader and heralda settled an apparent disagreement about the next case.

Queen Rejeena did not soundly upbraid them for not being ready, as she would have done in the immediate past. Her failure to do so shocked many women to include the two involved officials.

Instead the queen leaned toward her handsome queen's man, placed a hand on his shoulder and spoke to him. The queen's man answered with a mischievous grin and a remark. The queen laughed and spoke again. He answered and both smiled.

A shock wave rolled through the hall. Most of her subjects, who saw her only in hearing or occasionally on the Mainway, had not for a long time seen the queen smile, certainly not laugh. They had heard through rumor, by LaHeeka's declaration, the new queen's man would complete the queen, sire for her Queen's Line, reinstating the queenly joy of living. He seemed to have made a good start.

The reader called the next dispute. "Areva disputes Carrasea, lack of good faith bartering."

A hissing and rustling ran around the hall. Queen Rejeena abhorred violations concerning the making of promised payments. She demanded of all women good faith bartering.

Two women advanced. One was plainly dressed and alone. The other dressed in expensive fabric, head high, step jaunty, glancing around at the crowd with an air of disdain. A servant and two holdees accompanied her. The holdees carried bundles.

Both women and attendants halted at disputants' place then bowed. The women arose; the holdees remained, heads lowered.

Aarvan recognized the vendor and wealthy purchaser he and Locin observed bartering on Mainway two days ago. The women spoke Oldenspeak, but by listening carefully and applying what he knew of the situation, he understood.

"Good morning, My Queen," the well-dressed woman said.

"Good morning, Carrasea."

Aarvan noted the alert, unhappy look of the vendor Areva, finding the queen and her opponent apparently well acquainted.

"What a wonderfully attractive queen's man, My Queen," Carrasea cooed.

Aarvan thought her smile phony.

"Thank you, Carrasea," the queen said, voice neutral. "What is the complaint?"

The wealthy woman frowned. "My Queen, this vendor practices knavery. I can so prove by my word and that of my servant and holdees."

Areva cried, "My Queen—"

The heralda jumped forward. "The queen will hear both sides of the dispute . . . one at a time."

Areva fell silent but glared at her disputer.

"Continue," the queen said.

Carrasea cast Areva a triumphant smirk. "Two days ago, My Queen, I bartered these sitting mats from this vendor. May my holdees rise, in order to perform my bidding?"

"Of course."

The holdees rose and opened the packages. A set of sitting mats lay revealed, beautifully crafted, but marred by a greasy, black stain.

"The mats I saw, My Queen," Carrasea said, "were beautiful as these once were. Packaging covered the set she sold me. When I arrived at my home, this is what I found." She gestured with a dramatic flourish at the ruined mats.

Aarvan frowned, but didn't speak.

"What you say can be verified?" the queen asked.

"Yes, My Queen. My servant, Ittal, and these two holdees accompanied me. They can verify my words."

Areva spluttered, "My Queen, this is falsehood."

"Vendor," the heralda snapped, "you will have your turn. Your disputer speaks. Stand silent."

Areva stood shifting her feet, glowering.

Aarvan leaned forward. *The woman, Carrasea, does lie.*

"Is this fact, Ittal?" the queen asked.

Ittal curtsied. "Yes, My Queen, as my mistress stated."

The queen turned a stern stare upon the two men. "The word of holdees carries small value, but I will inquire. Holdees, note that the truth must always be told to the queen. Do you verify your mistress's statement?"

One holdee answered immediately. "It is true, O Queen, as my mistress said." The other's gaze skittered to his left, to his mistress then the floor. "It's all true, O Queen," he mumbled.

Aarvan, unsure of his hearing privileges, remained silent.

The queen said, "Where lies the problem, Carrasea? You return the set, the vendor replaces them or returns your barter goods."

"The vendor, My Queen, refuses the exchange."

"Vendor, what have you to say?"

Areva's voice quivered. "My Queen, Carrasea and her minions fling falsehood. That is not what occurred."

The queen arched a brow, waiting.

Areva took a deep breath. "My Queen, I indeed bartered the mat set to this woman. When she departed my shop, they were perfect. She purchased my only set, the display. The holdees piled the set, not packaged, into a handcart and withdrew along Mainway. No servant accompanied her. The ruining of the mats happened later. I am not responsible. As any honest vendor, I accept losses in trading, but not this heavy loss for a targeetha who will fling falsehood."

Confine your name calling to outside the Hearing Hall, vendor," the heralda said.

"I apologize," Areva said. "Their falsehoods anger me."

"Have you a woman who can verify your word?" the queen asked.

"No, My Queen. I was alone at my shop. Women moved about Mainway, but none I can call for verification."

"What of the vendors next to you?"

"One lay ill that day, My Queen. The other was busy and cannot say. I have asked."

The queen's voice hardened. "You realize, vendor, stiff penalties apply to relating fabrications in hearing."

"Yes, My Queen. I know the penalties." Areva's voice rose. "It is they"—she stabbed a finger at her disputers—"who mouth untruths."

"One of you assuredly lies," the queen said. "Carrasea has presented verification; you have not. If you have other information to present in your behalf, do so now. Otherwise, I shall be required to rule in her favor."

The vendor, sensing defeat, stretched tall to face the queen's verdict. "My Queen, I have only my word."

Into the following moment of silence, Aarvan said, "My Queen, may I speak?"

Everyone stared at him.

"Wait until after this hearing, Aarvan," the queen said sharply.

"It concerns this hearing, My Queen."

"You hold knowledge of this dispute?"

"Yes, My Queen. On Mainway two days ago, I watched this barter."

Carrasea's eyes narrowed, and Ittal's widened. Both holdees' glances darted to their mistress. Areva's gaze fastened on the queen's man.

The queen shifted in her chair. "What did you see?"

The reader moved nearer to interpret.

"Areva stated the facts, My Queen." Aarvan chose his words carefully. "This vendor and purchaser did come to agreement. Bark and kruets changed hands. The goods, carried off by the holdees, were open, not packaged and no servant accompanied them. Mistress Carrasea perhaps confuses this barter with another."

"My Queen—" Carrasea cried.

The queen quieted her with a lifted hand. "You stand certain, Aarvan?"

"Yes, My Queen."

"You could not be erroneous as to vendor or purchaser?"

"No, they are the ones."

Areva smiled. The wealthy woman glared.

"You have heard the words of the queen's man, Carrasea," Rejeena said. "Have you anything to add?"

"No, My Queen, I do not. Your queen's man mouths fantasy—and I do not *confuse* barters. I hold position as a prominent woman, have presented truth, and my servant and holdees have so verified. That stands solidly against the word of one man, even with status."

Queen Rejeena leaned back, looked at Aarvan, Carrasea, Areva, Ittal and the holdees in turn. Her cool green eyes gauged each.

"My Queen," Aarvan said, "Line Leader Locin was with me. We discussed the purchase. I'm sure she would remember."

"Bring Locin," the queen said.

A paiga departed at a run.

The heralda motioned to the disputants. "Stand aside until the guard can be located, so hearing may continue."

Aarvan watched Carrasea huddle with her servant and holdees. The woman leaned forward, shook a finger at them, face set in harsh lines. The servant appeared near panic, arms wrapped around herself, shifting from foot to foot. The holdees stood sullen, heads hung.

The reader called, "Faseeta disputes Maagia, ownership of a lamb."

Two young girls, no more than ten seasons, came hesitantly forward, leading a fluffy white lamb.

The queen's hand rose to her chest, fingers splayed. She looked at her council members, cocking her head sideways.

Several shrugged, looking as perplexed as she felt.

Titters sounded through the hall.

The girls bowed together at disputants' place. "My Queen," they chimed in unison.

The queen, lips crinkled at the corners, turned her attention to them. "What is the difficulty, disputants?"

One girl stood tall, serious. "My Queen, I am Faseeta. This lamb is Bektill. My lamb. My mother bought her for me at weaning. I love my lamb. I like Maagia, too; but she wants my lamb."

The queen asked, voice low and warm, "If the lamb is Faseeta's, Maagia, what is your claim?"

Maagia swiped at tears, eyes round, staring at the queen. "My Queen, Faseeta and her mother lived next door. They moved away. She left Bektill with me. We were choicest friends. I cried when she left. My mother said she would not return. I thought Bektill was mine. Then she came back with her mother. Now she wants Bektill, but I love Bektill, too."

"And you are friends?" The queen addressed Maagia.

"Yes, My Queen, we were . . ." More tears spilled. "I want her as my friend, but she would take my lamb."

"Your mothers could not resolve this dispute?"

"No, My Queen," Faseeta said. "They told us, since we could not agree, we would needs attend Queen's Hearing."

The queen leaned back, took a deep breath and regarded the girls silently for a moment. "You now live near each other?"

"Yes, My Queen, next door."

"As you have both housed Bektill, you must have a means of restraint."

"Yes, My Queen, our mothers both built fences."

"I would suggest you open your yards to form one, making a large area for Bektill, and you share both the lamb and your friendship equally." The queen smiled.

Maagia turned shyly to Faseeta, who nodded eagerly. The girls hugged.

Faseeta's mouth pursed. "Suppose our mothers do not wish to combine the yards, My Queen?"

"Remind your mothers that they sent you to Queen's Hearing, and it is the resolution of the queen."

"Yes, My Queen." Faseeta beamed. "We will do it. Now we can be choicest friends and both have Bektill." She frowned. "Except, what happens when we grow older and move away?"

"I think by then concerns other than your lamb will captivate you."

"Yes, My Queen."

"Then your difficulty is resolved?"

"Yes, My Queen. Thank you, My Queen." The girls spoke together, curtsied and left the hall, arms around each other, leading a cavorting Bektill.

Rejeena glanced at Aarvan. He smiled, displaying warm, approving eyes. Unexpected pleasure surged through her. *He approves.* She shook her head to clear the thought. *Why should a queen care about the approval of a mere queen's man?*

Locin entered the hall. "My Queen, you called for me?"

The heralda gestured for Carrasea and Areva to retake disputants' place.

The queen asked Locin, "Two days ago you guarded the queen's man on Mainway?"

"Yes, My Queen."

"Do you remember these women?" Rejeena pointed.

Locin's brow lowered. "They do appear familiar, My Queen, but . . ." She looked at the merchandise. "Of course, one is a vendor." Her gray eyes flicked twice to the wealthy woman. "Mistress Carrasea bartered this mat set."

"You beheld this exchange?"

"Yes, My Queen, their loud bartering claimed our attention."

"I wish to know if the purchased mat set was open or packaged, and how many persons comprised the purchaser's party. Be most accurate, Locin."

Locin thought. "The mat set was open, My Queen. The holdees loaded it upon a cart and pulled it away. The purchaser's party consisted of herself and two holdees."

"You are quite certain, Locin? You make no mistake?"

"No mistake, My Queen. The queen's man showed interest in our system of barter. We watched, discussing the exchange as they walked away."

"Very well, Locin. That is all."

Locin curtsied and joined other guards along the wall.

The queen turned and speared Carrasea with icy eyes. "You have heard the words of the queen's man and guard. Have you anything you wish to say?"

Ittal stood, face tight, eyes flared. Both holdees fidgeted.

Carrasea stretched to full height. "My Queen, your queen's man and guard describe that which did not occur. They are wrong. My servant and holdees have verified my words."

"Your servant and holdees might, upon your direction, tell less than the truth." The queen's voice stung as the prick of a wasp. "My queen's man and my guard hold no reason to speak untruth. Unless you can offer some other explanation, I must conclude you passed falsehood in hearing to your queen."

"My Queen, I have spoken truth and my words are verified. The vendor flings falsehood for gain." The wealthy disputer matched the queen's hauteur. "The motivation of your queen's man"—she glared at Aarvan—"and your guard"—she transferred her glare to Locin—"are not known to me. I stand a prominent woman in this towne, enjoying friends and favor, good woman status. I expect to be believed over a wayscrape Mainway vendor, a guard and a *man*."

"Before I pass judgment, I will confer with council." The queen rose, strolled the needed few steps and huddled with her advisors.

The disputants stood in place.

Locin walked to Aarvan. She asked in a low voice, "What have you drawn me into, you arrogant pup?"

"I told the queen you observed this exchange." His voice turned tart. "My word didn't seem to carry much weight."

"It cannot, you being but a man," Locin said with a quick smile. "Do you know of Carrasea?"

"No. Should I?"

"I recognized her upon second glance; she is seegarpt of upper hierarchy, though rumor holds her a skillfully concealed miscreant. She holds much wealth and will not make a good enemy."

"She shouldn't have lied to cheat that vendor."

"Queen's Man, the vendor is of Mainway and could have weathered the queen's anger. Her punishment would have been mild. Utter honesty is not expected of Mainway vendors. Carrasea's flinging falsehood at the queen stands most serious. Such cannot be tolerated from prominent women. Tradition demands they show the path of correctness and honesty for those less favored of LaSheena. The queen will needs severely punish her. Carrasea will carry a disagreeable feeling toward us."

Aarvan shrugged. "The vendor did no wrong."

Locin looked into his guileless eyes. "My queen would saddle me with a queen's man who possesses a conscience." She squeezed his shoulder, turned and took her place by the wall. The queen appeared ready to resume hearing.

Rejeena returned to her cathedra seat. "The council and I have considered. It is obvious that you, Carrasea, passed falsehood to your queen in hearing. You therefore, through influence, induced your servant and holdees to do so. It is misfortunate, for they must share your punishment."

Ittal fell to her knees, hands clasped, eyes rolling. She wailed, "Please, My Queen, she forced me. Threatened to loose me. Please."

The heralda jerked the young woman to her feet. "Silence! The queen speaks."

The girl stood trembling and pale.

The queen continued, "You, Carrasea, will pay the vendor three times the agreed value of the barter goods, as restitution for her time and embarrassment. You will also pay the sum of three hundred kruets as fine."

Carrasea glared at Aarvan.

He met her eyes without expression.

As the queen changed her focus, offering no more punishment, Carrasea's braced shoulders dropped. She took a small backward step, and her eyes displayed a crafty glint.

"I am aware," the queen said, "that holdees stand with few options, but this is a most serious offense. Each holdee will receive three lashes by strife paddle to be administered immediately." She looked at Ittal. "You had options. Your mistress is not responsible for your behavior. As well, you and Carrasea are unfit to be servant and mistress. You stand by queen's decree, loosed with rancor, without commend. You will needs search long and hard to find further function in Rejeena's Towne. You will receive four lashes with the strife paddle to be administered immediately."

The queen turned her cold eyes back to Carrasea.

The rich disputer froze and her smug look faded.

The queen clasped her hands before her. “Your actions, Carrasea, stand particularly reprehensible. As a prominent woman, favored seegarpt, you must hold yourself above petty, malicious behavior. You disgrace yourself, your lineage, the towne and your queen. In addition to the fines, you will receive eight lashes from the strife paddle to be administered immediately.”

Carrasea’s face turned red then deepened to purple. Her hands clenched, mouth moved without sound. Finally she sputtered, “How dare you? You cannot send me to locchot. I am of seegarpt, enjoy influence with many prominent women.”

The queen simply stared.

The guards closed on Carrasea. She appeared dangerously close to injudicious action.

Ittal stood weeping. The holdees waited with drooped shoulders for their punishment.

The guards grasped Carrasea, but she stood steady. “I demand proxy,” she screeched. “One of these holdees can stand as proxy.”

Rejeena’s voice dripped acid. “There will be no proxy. You must personally taste the bite of locchot to assure you learn the needed lesson.”

As the guards propelled her toward the entrance, headed for the punishment room, Carrasea screamed, “One day, Queen Rejeena, you will suffer for this. You will.”

The queen called, “Two added lashes for threatening the queen.”

Despite the guards, Carrasea lurched to a halt, eyes flaming, jaw jerking open and closed.

The queen arched a brow. “Did you wish to earn more lashes?”

Carrasea clamped her mouth and allowed the guards to lead her away. Passing Locin, she speared the line leader with a glare of pure hatred. Other guards ushered the servant and holdees after her.

Glancing at Aarvan, who stared at her, the queen said, “Yes, Aarvan, we do send women to locchot, too.”

The queen turned to Areva. “Your queen regrets, vendor, the inconvenience of this misfortunate incident. I trust the judgment will compensate for loss of commerce.”

"Thank you, My Queen," Areva said, "for your wise decision. The compensation is adequate." She looked at Aarvan. "And I would thank your queen's man. Few men of such status would expend concern for the fate of a Mainway vendor. He is obviously as beautiful within as without."

"Thank you, vendor." The queen's thumb massaged Aarvan's collarbone. "You are dismissed."

* * *

A voice rang from the crowd. "Request pause in hearing, My Queen."

"Pause in hearing granted, Tameera," the queen said. "Come forward."

A lovely, petite woman with a delicate pixie-like aura, flowing blonde hair and bright blue eyes, rose gracefully. She wore a long, simple dress of dark doeskin with a land leader sash resting across her chest. Though appearing young for her position, she strode forward, steps long, chin high, shoulders back. Her eyes probed the queen's.

She bowed, then arose and smiled. "My Queen, by all accounts you bartered many of your subjects' tariff kruets for this handsome queen's man. You display him in hearing, but you have not yet acknowledged him. Your subjects request acknowledgment here, today, so they may judge if their kruets were well spent."

"If that is the wish of my subjects, it will be done." Rejeena spoke to the mass of women. "Do you so wish?"

An affirmative roar filled the air.

The queen grinned. "I must acknowledge you, Aarvan. It will be an interesting experience. Come." She stood and held out her hand.

He took the hand and arose, hesitant.

She led him to a central position before the crowd, announcing, "Queen Rejeena acknowledges her queen's man, Aarvan."

Cackles and snickers circulated the hall.

"Aarvan comes with commend by LaHeeka," Rejeena continued. "LaHeeka states this queen's man possesses the strength to overcome the curse which plagues your queen. From his seed, your queen will produce daughters who shall survive, continuing the Queen's Line of Quarter Seven. He has shared your queen's skindown only a short time, but his efforts in that regard stand more than excellent."

"My Queen!" Aarvan coughed and backed a step.

The queen smiled, eyes warm, voice soft. "I believe my queen's man shall know success."

The women rose and cheered, continuing for several minutes, hurling lewd, suggestive remarks at the queen's man. Each comment more lurid and bawdy than the last, the women seemed to try to outdo one another.

"Queen's Man, drop those drawers so all women may view this magical phallus."

"Indeed, all women needs cast sight upon our new Queen's Line."

"Even if it is not yet Queen's Line?"

"Yes, best time to view."

"View it? We funded it. We should grasp it, inspect it closely."

All this came from a group standing together on the left.

Aarvan squirmed, shoved his free hand in his pocket, grimacing and shuffling his feet.

Not to be outdone, those on the right chimed in.

"With that ass, the queen likely thinks she rides a bucking steed. More likely, the whole skindown bucks."

Uproarious laughter drowned several more remarks.

The queen held Aarvan's hand tightly. It appeared he might bolt if allowed the opportunity.

His clear discomfort spurred the women to greater efforts.

From near the center of the room, hidden, a voice bellowed, "Let me grasp it, ride it. Perhaps I, too, may hurtle out Queen's Line."

Another yelled, "You are too old, would hurtle from the height and batter your brain out."

Laughter rolled.

Aarvan's face now flamed deep red. He backed two more steps, as far as the queen's grasp would allow, glancing around as though seeking an escape route.

"Women, you have discerned incorrectly," a woman at the fringe of the crowd yelled. "Observe him. Clearly the queen's man is as a rabbitt, likely with a woodypiece to match. Our poor queen probably has to search for it."

"On the contrary," another disputed, "sometimes the rabbitts are best, display schlongs like glaalets, and hop all over a woman in skindown."

Again laughter, whistles and wordless screeches drowned all other sound.

"He can hop all over me anytime," someone hooted.

Finally, Rejeena raised her hand and silence descended. "As you can see," the queen said, "my queen's man is shy, and all women have enjoyed your fun at his expense. Your queen asks you to be kind to him on acknowledgment round."

More lascivious calls sounded. Way in the back, hidden from the queen's view, a woman shouted, "Let him near enough for me to grasp that ass, and I shall show him the meaning of acknowledgment."

Laughter roared from the group.

"Acknowledgment round?" Aarvan asked.

"You must walk among your queen's subjects so they may touch and observe you, Aarvan."

He twitched, eyes flared, and he tugged against the queen's grasp. "No! No, My Queen. I'm not doing that. They'll . . . they'll . . ." He frantically searched his limited vocabulary. "I'm not doing that."

"You must, Aarvan," the queen said, firm but sympathetic. "It is part of the acknowledgment ceremony. You are queen's man. They will not harm you."

"Did you hear them? They're . . . they're perverts . . . or worse. I don't want them clutching me."

Locin's hands fell onto his shoulders. "I will accompany him, My Queen," the guard said. "He harbors the nature of a mouse."

"Thank you, Locin." The queen released his hand.

Locin urged Aarvan forward.

He rooted himself to the spot. "My Queen, please."

"Aarvan, you must."

He twisted his face, pushed his breath out, but allowed Locin to propel him toward the eagerly waiting crowd.

Aarvan's imagination proved the worst of the adventure. Facing the huge, overpowering bulk of Locin, having already expressed their wanton brand of fun, the women acted reasonably respectful and polite. Suggestive comments and lewd compliments rated no worse than Aarvan's visits to Mainway. Young daughters danced around him, impeding his progress, singing, "Queeeen's Man. Queeeen's Man." Hands touched, sliding over his body. Seated women reached to stroke and caress his legs.

He pasted a shaky smile on his face—*what disgusting traditions these women have, all embarrassing to the man involved. If they favor embarrassment so much, why don't they embarrass themselves for a change*—shook hands, received hugs from old women and accepted gifts.

A paiga, following him for just that purpose, took the gifts, so as not to burden Aarvan.

Locin guided him around several large groups.

He deferred to her judgment, until one woman, almost as big as Locin, departed a cluster and stood firmly before him. "In acknowledgment round, Queen's Man, it is traditional to speak to all women. My group," she said, gesturing toward them, "desires acknowledgment." She spoke Universal. Her brown eyes, like hard little marbles, bored into his.

Locin said, "The queen's man does not acknowledge wayscrape. Move from his path." Her hand fell to sword hilt.

The woman's eyes squinted and her hand dropped to sword.

Aarvan frowned. *Why cause disruption in hearing? I'm not afraid of these women, just hate all this repulsive touching.* He said, "Locin, they too are the queen's subjects, aren't they?"

"Yes, Queen's Man, but—"

"No buts. It would be rude not to acknowledge all who wish it." He motioned toward the small knot, slightly separated from those around them. "Please, Shiira, lead on."

The woman flicked Locin a snide grimace, grasped Aarvan's upper arm and led him away.

Locin followed, eyes narrow, back rigid.

The woman led Aarvan to her group. They closed in a circle behind him, cutting off Locin.

The line leader stood, watching them. She signaled other guards, and five gathered like hovering hawks.

"I am Tarees, Queen's Man," the woman said. She introduced each woman in the group ending with, "This is Alossia, our leader," pointing to a slender woman sitting cross-legged on a mat.

Alossia lifted her tawny-colored eyes slowly, gaze traveling up Aarvan to his face. She rose gracefully straight up, like a long-stemmed flower springing from the earth. "Thank you, Queen's Man, for acknowledging our group." Voice warm, handshake firm, she said, "A wise queen's man would follow his guard's advice. Are you brave or daft?"

"I plead ignorance, Shiira. I know no reason I shouldn't acknowledge you."

She crossed her arms, and studied his forthright eyes. "You have not been warned about unruly women who inhabit the backways of the towne?"

"Is that what you are?"

"We stand among the worst. A queen's man is unsafe in our grasp."

"I doubt you would attack in Queen's Hearing."

"You guess rightly, Queen's Man." Her voice dropped low. "Listen to your guards. Under other circumstances, that gorgeous keister would be unbearable temptation."

"So I've been told," he muttered.

Locin's sharp call interrupted. "The queen's man has acknowledged you. Others wait."

"Your sentinel grows restive. Go." The wall of women parted.

He backed away. "Good day, Shiira. Women."

Locin grabbed him roughly by the shoulder. "You do that again, Queen's Man, and I will—"

"You'd have preferred a sword fight in Queen's Hearing?"

"I could have contained her."

"I contained her better, Shiira Guardswoman."

"Arrogant Pup."

"What is wayscrape?"

"An insult. Forget you heard it."

Aarvan continued his trek, then rejoined the queen. "Am I finished?"

"One more thing, Aarvan." The queen caught his hand. She led him before the hall and spoke to the crowd. "Your queen acknowledged her queen's man and he performed acknowledgment round. Those who approve so indicate."

A great roar rose from the crowd.

"Those who do not?"

Not a sound issued from the hall.

"Then you consider your tariff kruets well spent?"

Again the throng roared.

"It appears all women sanction the queen's man. Is acknowledgment satisfactory, Tameera?"

The land leader rose from her sitting mat and curtsied. "Most satisfactory, My Queen."

"Then let hearing proceed."

The reader called the next dispute. "Pierta disputes Jessaan, ownership of holdees."

A woman rose and advanced to disputants' place.

Another entered the hall, with three women handlers and two clothed holdees. Among them, they hustled along five holdees, shackled, naked for viewing. Three of the naked men, large, muscular fellows, strolled along, apparently unembarrassed. One, who had been castrated, trod heavily, gaze downcast, shoulders slumped. The fifth holdee was young, slim and attractive. His eyes darted about, and his hands sought to cover his maleness. The partials and clothed holdees jerked his hands away with the bonds, laughing, making remarks. "Show your wares, pretty boy. Do not be shy. Mistress desires a good barter for your weighted woodypiece." They pulled him forward.

The group gained disputants' place, all bowing. The young holdee grasped his mistress's skirt. "Please, Mistress," he pleaded in Universal, "may I have my pants? I can't stand all these eyes."

"Excuse me, My Queen," the woman said. "One moment."

The queen nodded.

The woman drew her truchon, turned, and smacked the young man so hard his head snapped sideways. "Silence, holdee, you appear before the queen."

The young man moaned and dropped his head.

Rejeena glanced at Aarvan. He stared at the woman, brow wrinkled. He turned to the queen, mouth forming words.

She cut him off. "No, Aarvan, you may not speak."

For a moment, it appeared he might defy her. Then he clamped his jaw and dropped back in his seat.

The holdees' mistress spoke. "My Queen, I am Pierta. I offered these holdees for barter. Jessaan promised to buy. Bark of terms was written. When I attempted to deliver, requesting payment, she refused, demanding a trial period for the young one."

"Upon what did you agree?"

"Only for payment, My Queen. I do not grant trial periods. The young one rates at seventy. Should he show reluctance, he can be forced to perform."

"Yes, of course," the queen said. "Jessaan, what have you to say?"

"My Queen," Jessaan said, "I agreed to purchase these holdees, the young one for skindown. But he is expensive, new and untried, so I demanded a trial period. I do not favor beating holdees, so I must assure cooperation before I buy."

"Where is bark of terms?" the queen asked.

Pierta produced the bark and gave it to the heralda, who passed it to the queen. The queen read it, had it passed to Jessaan, then asked, "Is this the correct bark of terms?"

"Yes, My Queen."

"The bark does not mention a trial period."

"No, My Queen. Pierta said a verbal agreement would suffice, that she merely wished the barter goods noted."

"Have you anyone to confirm your word?"

"No, My Queen, Pierta and I were alone."

The queen turned to Pierta. "Did you voice a verbal agreement for trial period with Jessaan concerning the young holdee?"

Pierta smiled slyly. "No, My Queen, I did not."

"Jessaan," the queen said, "I believe you thought you agreed upon a trial period. However, bark of terms does not so state. You must honor the bark as written. Henceforth, I suggest you ascertain that all agreements are noted on the bark."

"Yes, My Queen." Jessaan sighed. "I will honor the bark." She gave Pierta a baleful glare.

"In addition, in accord with law," the queen said, "you must pay Pierta twenty kruets for her time and a fine of fifty kruets to the hearing council for deciding a case you should have known you could not win."

"Only twenty kruets, My Queen?" Pierta said. "I have lost much barter time. It is not sufficient."

The queen's eyes hardened. "Silence. This is not your first appearance in hearing concerning your sharp commerce practices. Your queen is not pleased."

Pierta grimaced, face losing its smug look.

"You are dismissed." The queen called for lunch break, rose and left the hall.

Aarvan followed.

In her break area, the queen seated and lunch served, Aarvan asked, "My Queen, may I speak now?"

"Yes, Aarvan, you may."

"We might need an interpreter, My Queen."

The queen signaled a guard. "Have Locin join us."

Locin entered, bowed, sat and accepted coffee.

"My Queen, why were those holdees brought to hearing naked before all women?" Aarvan asked.

"I can answer that, My Queen," Locin said. "The holdees stand in sale status. When displayed for viewing, holdees always appear naked. Women must be able to see that which they purchase."

Aarvan nearly choked. "Holdees parade around naked until they're bought?"

"When displayed for viewing, yes. When not, they wear clothing." Locin grinned wickedly. "Does that cause you concern, Queen's Man?"

"Yes, as a matter of fact, it does. How do you think men feel, My Queen, standing naked before countless women?"

Rejeena accepted a coffee refill from a servant. "It is not a matter of relevance. Holdees must be displayed so women may fully view them. It is our way. It works."

"Works for whom, My Queen? It wasn't working for that young fellow dying of embarrassment."

"He is likely newly acquired. In time, he will learn the way of things."

"My Queen, that's"—he searched for a word—"barbaric. Cruel. No one should be treated like that."

The queen washed down a bite of lunch with her coffee, studying him. "Aarvan, I understand your sentiment. Your concern for less fortunate holdees is most charming. However, our way works with efficiency. It has functioned for Kriisconian women long before you and I first viewed the light of a suntrek. It will continue long after we dance on the four winds."

Aarvan said softly, "My Queen, imagine the roles reversed. Suppose men held power and you were the holdee. How would you like to be displayed naked before men?"

"It would be unpleasant. However, I am queen. They are holdees."

Aarvan leaned forward and stared into her eyes. "*With your top off,* My Queen, before *countless* men."

Something flickered deep in the green eyes. "That would be most unpleasant, but I am still queen, men still holdees."

"Which means misfortunate for men." Aarvan leaned back.

"Yes, Aarvan."

His cocked his head sideways with eyes squinted. "When you bought me, My Queen, was I on view naked?'

"Of course."

"So I was just laid out like a piece of meat on a slab?"

"Yes, Queen's Man, and a pretty piece you were." Locin grinned.

"You saw me?"

"I accompanied my queen when she viewed you."

Spots of red brightened below his flaming blue eyes. "I was lying there naked for dozens of women to march by and look at?"

"You were in a tent. Only certain women were allowed to view you."

"So it was more like a handful?"

"Yes, more like that."

He snarled in that language only he knew, rose and stalked away. He stood staring at the wall, arms clasped in front of him, muscles tense. A vague memory flickered, of waking, feeling the rage, seeing the angel that he now knew to be his queen, being naked—*yes, I was naked*—and then the blackness again. He wasn't sure if he should be more furious or embarrassed. Either emotion wouldn't change anything at this point.

The queen's eyes met Locin's. They both smiled.

Aarvan turned around. "Why did that woman hit the young holdee?"

"He spoke in hearing without permission," the queen said. "That is unacceptable behavior."

"She about took his head off. It shouldn't be allowed."

"It is her right and duty to exert discipline. I do not regulate the actions of women toward their holdees."

"And if she stabbed him in the heart, that too would be permissible?"

"The woman owns him. If she wishes to kill him, it is her loss."

"So holdees have no rights, no protection at all under your law? They're lower than worms crawling from the earth?"

The queen met the fiery blue eyes, her mouth curved into a tiny smile. "It could be so termed, Aarvan."

He dropped his eyes. When he lifted them, a veil obscured any emotion. "My Queen, men are persons, too. When you hit a man, it hurts. When you stick him, he bleeds. Men know fear, anger, and pain, just like women. Men too need protection under law."

"There exists protection for holdees—their value." Rejeena waved a hand dismissively. "Holdees cost barter goods. A woman would be daft to needlessly obliterate valuable property. Many women, especially in the farming areas, count their riches in holdees. To kill holdees is to destroy wealth."

"My Queen, a great gulf lies between fair treatment and killing. Every society contains individuals who enjoy performing cruelty against the powerless. Your lack of protective laws is an open invitation for those women to indulge in brutality. Seeing men as you do, important only for work and skindown, encourages all women, otherwise normal individuals, to practice cruelty because it's accepted, even expected and carries no penalty."

"What you say may be true, Aarvan, but your queen perceives no significance. Ours laws have withstood the test of hundreds of season turnings. I do not think we will change them because my queen's man finds offense."

Aarvan's lips compressed as he stared at the queen. "Of all the cruelty inflicted on holdees, My Queen, the worst is castration. I'd dared hope, when women spoke of castration, it was just for scare. But one of those holdees was castrated."

"It happens. If a holdee is big and strong, useful for work but carries no weight between his legs, castration makes him easier to control."

"You sound like you're discussing cattle."

"That is a fair comparison."

Fire flashed in his eyes, was quenched.

Locin watched him intently, alert for the beast.

"My Queen," he said, "when you castrate a man, you take away his identity as a man. You . . . remove his . . . his sense of self."

"Yes, Aarvan. By removing his identity, we create a docile workhorse. That is the intent."

He swallowed, mouth tight, eyes narrowed. "I can't see how that happens. Castrating a full-grown man? It seems more likely the man would be furious, want to kill—definitely not turn docile."

Locin smirked. "Many do at first, Queen's Man. However, we have convincing methods of returning them to the path of rightness."

"Path of rightness?"

"Yes, our path, the path women choose."

"I see."

"Aarvan, finish your lunch," the queen said. "We must shortly return to hearing."

Aarvan glared with distaste at the remainder of his meal. "I have no appetite. May I take a walk?"

"If you wish. Do not stay long, and do not leave the hearing complex without guards."

He left the room.

Rejeena looked at Locin. "Aarvan has much to learn. He displays outrage, but the stage will pass. He will learn to accept our ways."

"Yes, My Queen. He is newly acquired. He has time."

The queen smiled. "You like the queen's man, do you not?"

"Yes, My Queen. I like his sassy nature, his charm. He is refreshing."

The queen arched a brow. "How well do you like him, Locin?"

Locin's voice tightened. "My Queen, I have functioned as a queen's guard for seven seasons. I protect the queen's man. There exists no space in my life for inappropriate behavior."

The queen blinked. "I did not intend to insult you, Locin. Such beauty as the queen's man possesses causes angst."

"Then do not waste your angst, My Queen. No mere male beauty can tempt me from my path of rightness. I like your queen's man, but he belongs to my queen. I do not view him in a skindown way."

The queen smiled. "Then you may guard the queen's man well. You like him, speak Universal and do not desire him. Your queen feels blessed of LaSheena to have such an excellent guard."

"It is the way of it, My Queen. If you no longer need me, I will check guard placing for hearing to resume."

The queen dismissed her.

Rejeena sipped coffee. Aarvan's remark about her standing before men with no top set her thinking. She visualized herself before countless men, shackled, naked, her breasts—her most personal part—uncovered for all to view. The queen imagined men grasping her, feeling, checking to see if she were firm, well formed, muscular. She shuddered—perhaps thrusting fingers into her womancenter. Such indignity could not be borne. Swallowing to clear a lump forming in her throat, Rejeena set her mug on the serving table. She scrubbed both palms up and down her thighs.

A vision of the young man in hearing flitted through her mind. His maleness had been exposed; he had been forced to bear this unbearable indignity. She clamped off the thought quickly. *It is not the same. Men need not know dignity.* To her disgust, the idea did not properly expire. It burrowed into a quiet corner of her mind and sat—tiny, unfocused, a bare but living seed.

Aarvan stood outside. He ground his teeth, visions of castration strokes and heavy truchon blows falling on men filled his mind. He raised his head, pulled air into his chest, puffed it out. He clenched his eyes shut and reopened them. How callous these women. They considered cruelty and vindictiveness to men, who were mere chattel, normal. But they learned it in infancy, grew with it, absorbed and expected it.

It would be no easy chore to change that . . . *Change? Why should I bother?* He could simply wait until he recovered, then flee. *Because I care.* This island, these women, needed changing. The queen needed changing. He heaved a deep sigh. *Why do I care about changing her? I'm not sure, but I do . . . a lot. What have I gotten myself into?*

Aarvan returned to the lunchroom. Except for a bow and short greeting, he and the queen did not speak. As they stood waiting to reenter the Hearing Hall, the queen's hand slipped under his vest, paused, barely touching. He pressed lightly backward against it. The hand stroked, the smooth motion an unseen smile.

* * *

Hearing had resumed when a soldier, wearing the rank insignia of a linaar, leader of a line of ten women, raced into the Hearing Hall. She ran to the queen and performed a bare dip of a bow. "My Queen," she cried, "we captured the outlaw, Saradan, and three of her band."

"Indeed Saradan?"

"Yes, My Queen. We encountered outlaws and chased them into a blind draw. We killed four, took Saradan and the others captive."

"Did you suffer losses?"

"Six wounded, My Queen, none seriously."

"Excellent. Are the outlaws here?"

"Our column escorts them along Mainway."

The queen sat back. "Bring them quickly."

The soldier curtsied and dashed away.

The queen looked at Aarvan, who watched her, inquiry in his eyes. Rejeena explained. "Saradan is a leader of outlaws, who have terrorized this quarter for many seasons. Capturing her comprises a great feat."

"What happens to her now, My Queen?"

"I shall assign her public execution. Her shameful death will discourage others who would take to outlaw ways."

"She won't have a trial?"

"She has had trials, been sentenced to death for crimes against the quarter. Her fate is assured. The others will likely be convicted and die with her. Outlaw activity often carries a death sentence."

He nodded.

"You do not object?"

"No, My Queen, why should I?"

"You object to so many things."

"Only what's unfair. Executing outlaws seems fair."

"I am glad some of our ways meet your approval, My Queen's Man."

The soldier column arrived. Ten shepherded the shackled prisoners forward. Arsen, with uniform insignia indicating her to be a trarysaar, leader of two hundred women, walked before the group.

Two outlaws, coarse, scruffy-appearing women, hung back, requiring their escorts to prod them forward. Soldiers assisted another outlaw, who dragged a leg, her thigh swathed in bandages.

The last, tall, well groomed for a woman who had recently engaged in battle, marched between spectators, head high, chin thrust forward. She wore short brown hair and her frosty hazel eyes locked with those of the queen, unwavering. She halted at disputants' place, and planted her feet wide.

"On your knees, outlaw," the heralda said. "You stand before the queen."

"I stand before an impostor, a bogus queen. I bow to no such."

"Put her on her knees," the heralda said.

Two soldiers with truchons slammed the outlaw in the back of her knees, drove her down.

Though kneeling, the woman called, loud and clear, "I state before all women, I was forced into this position. I do not bow to Rejeena."

"Your insolence is noted, Saradan," the queen said. "I regret that I can execute you but once."

"You have not the authority to execute me, impostor."

"We will not discuss that old argument. It is long settled."

"Perhaps for you, but not for me or the true queen, Ishtabarra."

"Ishtabarra stands a condemned outlaw. She will swing from the gallows, as will you."

Saradan sneered. "You shall not live to see it. Your impostor feet will dance upon the four winds before Queens' Council convenes."

"You outlaws grow bold. Now you believe you can defeat queen's guards?"

"We have made our plans, Rejeena. Grant my words credence; you will not live to attend Queens' Council."

"My guards can easily double their forces."

"You could triple them, and you would not prevent our actions."

"Your confidence is misplaced. My guards know their function. Let us discuss you, Saradan. You will instruct us where to find Ishtabarra's stronghold."

"When glaalets overrun LaSheena's Forest."

"It can be as hard or easy as you choose. After you tell all, you will be hanged in the public market before all women."

Saradan spat at the queen.

Patea, guard on the queen's left, flipped up her shield and caught the spittle. The guard rammed the sharp-spiked shield into the outlaw's face, ripped her cheek open, and knocked her backwards. Patea then wiped the spittle on Saradan's tunic.

Saradan righted herself, blood flowing down her face. Her eyes fixed on Patea. "I shall remember you, guard."

Patea grinned. "You may—but not for long."

"What of this rabble that accompanies her?" the queen asked. She gestured at the other outlaws.

"Mecaa, My Queen," Arsen said, indicating the wounded woman, "another condemned one. The others are naught but banal wayscrape. However, they fought beside Saradan."

The queen's scrutiny raked them. She pointed. "Take them away and confine them. Have a healer see to Mecaa. I wish her to live long enough to hang."

Soldiers hustled them away.

"Arsen." The queen gestured to the traryse leader.

"Yes, My Queen."

"You have lost good soldiers killed by Ishtabarra's outlaws, I believe."

"We have, My Queen."

"Then you will enjoy the chore of questioning Saradan and eliciting from her the location of the stronghold."

Arsen smiled. "Oh yes, My Queen. My women and I would be most appreciative."

"Then consider the function yours." The queen turned to the outlaw. "You may save yourself much suffering, Saradan, by relating of your volition the information we seek."

"Rut you!"

"Then the information will be wrung from you as Trarysaar Arsen chooses." To the soldier leader the queen said, "Remember to leave enough to hang publicly." She glanced at Aarvan who stared at her, eyes full of questions. "Do not ask, Aarvan," she said.

At Rejeena's gentle, warm tone, Saradan's sharp, hazel eyes locked on him. Her gaze swept his trim form then met the midnight blue eyes.

"So, Rejeena, this is the whelp whose weighted schlong LaHeeka declares will break your curse. Let me compliment your taste. He seems exceedingly well-suited to the function." Her eyes dropped to Aarvan's crotch.

Aarvan, sitting with one toe tucked behind his other knee, started, dropped his foot to the floor and slid back, gaze flicking away from the outlaw.

Saradan leered. "Shy, is he not? He will neither finish his function nor beget for you daughters. After we kill you, all our women will sample your potent-peckered whelp. Then we shall slice from him his manly portions and hang them in your favorite display place, the public market. All women may thus view the remains of your Queen's Line."

No one made a sound for a long moment.

Queen Rejeena rose and stood before the outlaw, eyes ablaze.

Guards hovered. The two soldiers nearest Saradan grabbed her, though she was bound.

Without a word, the queen held out her hand to Arsen, who slapped a truchon into it.

The queen smashed the truchon against the outlaw's face, snapping her head sideways. Rejeena hit her on the other side and repeated both blows.

The outlaw lowered her head and gulped air. Blood from her mouth and nose flowed to join that from the slash on her cheek.

The queen spoke. "It is understandable, Saradan, that you abhor and threaten me. We share a mean history. Even your public contempt and refusal to recognize your queen, considering who and what you are, can be ignored. You will be executed anyway. Your vile threat to the queen's man cannot be excused. He has rendered you no harm. For this iniquity you will taste of the public locchot, beaten with the grand paddle until you die."

A gasp circulated, in response to this worst possible punishment, an excruciating death.

"May I speak, My Queen?" Aarvan's soft voice filled the silence.

The queen turned. "What is it, Aarvan?"

He sat forward in his cubicle, as though ready to push upright. "My Queen, I don't want to interfere with your punishment. That's for you to decide. You intended to hang this outlaw. Since she threatened me, you choose to execute her by locchot. Please do not destroy her in this way . . . not in my name." The blue eyes met hers. "I don't want this woman's locchot death on my head."

Women throughout the Hearing Hall held their breath, awaited the queen's reaction. Such a request had never before been made in hearing.

Rejeena faced the outlaw. "My queen's man shows more mercy than you deserve, but he makes a fair request. You will be hanged. However, if you voice another threat to the queen's man, you will die in locchot despite his wishes."

The outlaw, past her pain, sneered. Her cold, hard eyes raked the queen's man, with speculation.

Aarvan relaxed and dropped backward in his cubicle, releasing his breath in a rush.

The queen said to Arsen, "I tire of this outlaw. Take her to a secure cell. Allow her tonight to think upon what will come. Tomorrow you may begin persuasion."

"Yes, My Queen." Arsen motioned to the soldiers, who jerked Saradan to her feet and hustled her away.

Saradan tossed over her shoulder, tiny droplets of blood spraying as she spoke, "Enjoy the short time left to you, Rejeena. You needs tie on your dancing shoes—the four winds beckon."

The queen called for a break.

Seated in the lunchroom, Aarvan said, "I don't think that outlaw likes you, My Queen."

"It is mutual, Aarvan."

"Would it be too forward to ask why she calls you an impostor?"

"No, it is not." She paused. "You become adept in Oldenspeak, to follow the conversation with Saradan."

"Lateean is a good teacher. If I know most of the words, I can fill in the rest. I can't always follow."

"Perhaps I should call Locin to be sure you understand."

"If it pleases my queen."

Waiting for Locin, Aarvan asked, "Saradan used an expression, something about glaalets and LaSheena's Forest. What does that mean?"

Locin joined them, interpreting as needed.

"A glaalet is a mythical creature, huge and hairy. In legend, it inhabits mountainous areas. According to old tales, in ancient times glaalets and women stood united during the battles between LaSheena and Goosran. Then, for unknown reasons, they grew vicious, became enemies, killed women and retreated into mountain fortresses. If ever they truly existed, they do no longer. The outlaw's words are an expression, indicating a particular thing is not possible, will never happen.

"As for my being an impostor, there exists a curse on my Queen's Line." Rejeena ignored the amused disbelief that filled his eyes. "I will not paint details as it would require too much time. Accept that my Queen's Line is to expire. Thus far, it has proved so. I have conceived six offspring, all useless males or daughters who died at birth or during infancy."

Her voice coarsened, but she continued. "When my grandmother, then queen, died and a new queen was to be staffed, I stood the obvious staff scion. Ishtabarra, related through my grandmother's sister, greatly desired to be queen. She claimed the curse as a reason not to staff me. She avowed, not without some merit, that a doomed Queen's Line should be replaced. She garnered followers, and there ensued a grand battle of words and opinions at Great Queen's Council. Ishtabarra lost. With the support of LaHeeka, I won.

"After my staffing, as I returned to Rejeena's Towne, Ishtabarra and her followers attacked and tried to kill me. She almost succeeded. Only quick thought and action by then Line Leader Shabet elicited her failure."

Rejeena frowned. "Ishtabarra felt if I were dead, she would be staffed queen. Instead, she earned outlaw status and a death sentence. She strives continually to send me dancing on the four winds. Saradan is her chief outlaw leader. Her loss will be a great blow to Ishtabarra."

Aarvan lifted his eyes, somber and thoughtful. His voice changed, alive with an intense timbre. "How serious, My Queen, are Saradan's threats on your life?"

"Oh, their intent is most serious, their ability doubtful."

"Doubtful?" Aarvan's spine snapped straight, eyes squinted, voice rose slightly. "When it comes to the life of my queen, doubtful doesn't even fall within the realm of consideration. We have to be sure."

Rejeena smiled. "Are you concerned for me, Aarvan?"

"Yes, My Queen." He paused for a beat. "Do we know the outlaws' strength? What proportionate ratio of guards will you take for travel? How will we—?"

"Hold, Aarvan, hold. Tonight at the meeting, all protective measures for the trip will be discussed. Your questions will then be answered. My guard force is most efficient."

"Yes, My Queen," he said and studied his caster. When he connected the outlaw's threats with the queen's trip to council, he realized he held a great store of knowledge of security provisions, of life surety. The source remained obscured by his impenetrable memory loss, but the information resided in his mind. He could contribute. At the queen's suggestion, he put it away for later.

The queen's gaze traveled over Aarvan. "LaHeeka believes you possess the strength to break the curse on my Queen's Line, to seed your queen with daughters who will live. The outlaws cannot be pleased with your presence."

"Me?" A grin flickered. "I never imagined myself a breaker of curses."

"LaHeeka was very specific."

"Why would she say that?"

"LaHeeka possesses knowing that others do not. She is never wrong. That is why your queen bartered much wealth to acquire your skindown services."

"You and the ancient conjurah place a great burden on my shoulder—breaking curses to create live daughters." That skeptical grin flickered again.

"I think it not too great a burden."

He tilted his head. "Dancing on the four winds. What is that exactly?"

"Those who please LaSheena in life dance on the four winds after death before being invited to LaSheena's Forest Glen by LaSheena's Forcewoman." At his questioning look, she explained, "The forest glen is LaSheena's abode. The forcewoman guards the gates. Those who have pleased our goddess may dance long. A long dance is much desired."

"And those who do not please her?"

"Queens are never included in that group." She studied him, a tiny smile quirking her mouth. "Locin, I would like to be alone with the queen's man. Assure that we are not disturbed."

"Yes, My Queen." Locin rose, curtsied, flicked Aarvan a lewd wink and left.

Rejeena rose and motioned Aarvan to join her. She watched as he flowed to his feet, smooth as silk from a roll. She stood nose to nose. Unbuttoning his pants, she whispered, "You should not sit as you do in Queen's Hearing."

"Why is that?"

"You incite in your queen lustful thoughts when her mind should be on function."

"Should I stay away from hearing then?"

She uttered a sultry laugh. Her hands slid inside his pants.

Aarvan's gaze fixed on her wide mouth with the full lips. His fingers itched to take her face in his hands and kiss her until she melted. He didn't quite dare. Instead he cupped her buttocks and pulled her against him.

"We have not much time, Aarvan." Her whisper trembled. "How quickly can you satisfy your queen?"

"How lustful is my queen?"

"Most lustful."

"Most quickly." He pulled the tie to her skirt, letting it slither to the floor.

* * *

After dinner, the queen and Aarvan attended the life surety meeting to review protection for the queen and land leaders during the three-day journey to Queens' Council.

Aarvan sat alone while the queen spoke in privacy with a land leader. Mind on the upcoming meeting, he paid scant attention when Locin, Patea, Tressa and Tenraan, a guard he had met only briefly, all wearing wicked smiles, surrounded his chair.

Locin leaned close. "Queen's Man, you should not so rattle the queen during hearing."

"What?"

"Rut her during break."

"What makes you think . . .?" He choked, voice fading.

"You two spent much time returning to hearing, and the queen wore a most satisfied smile. She adjudged so kindly after break that the protests of unfair treatment from earlier disputants will require three hearing sessions to appease."

Patea said, "You needs be fair, Queen's Man. Either rut only of evenings or during every break and lunch. All disputants may thus receive equal treatment."

The guards roared.

Aarvan said, "Get away from me, you . . . you perverts."

"Queen's Man, we mind our guard duty," Tressa said. "You appear the pervert. Or is it the queen?"

Locin linked her hands behind her back, leaned forward. "It must be the queen. She tore the clothing from him, threw him down and forced him."

"Queen's Man, you needs resist with vigor," Tressa said.

"As you did in the punishment room when you near cracked my ribs," Patea added.

"Next time, Patea, it'll be your head," he growled. "Get away from me, all of you. You have no idea what you're talking about."

"Surely you jest," Patea grinned. "When you have rutted the queen, she glows as though stuffed with firebugs."

Tressa said, "Or screams."

"Screams? What . . ." Aarvan almost yelled, rising.

Locin shoved him back into his chair.

Tressa leaned down, nose inches from his. "Yes, screams. Our queen is noisy in skindown, or were you too captivated to notice? She screams in the night—a joyous refrain, not requiring guard interference. Being right outside the door, we cannot help but hear."

Face crimson, Aarvan flashed his impudent grin. "What's the matter, women, jealous? Don't you have a man who can make you scream?"

"You arrogant pup," Locin said, "I may take you over my knee even if you are queen's man."

"Try it, you big lummox. I'll leave pieces of you scattered up and down Mainway."

"Oh, women, hear the pup." Locin rolled her eyes. She poked him on the shoulder with a hard finger. "Do not allow your—"

"Women, the queen," Tenraan whispered.

The wicked grins vanished; the guards slipped behind Aarvan's chair.

He rose and half-bowed.

Rejeena looked at the guards' bland faces and Aarvan's flush. "What has turned the queen's man red?"

"My Queen, it requires little to turn the queen's man red," Locin said.

Aarvan stood silent.

Parria stopped to ask a question, claiming the queen's attention. The guards used the distraction to fade away with haste. Rejeena turned, smiling. "Come, Aarvan, I want you to meet the women who comprise the meeting. As queen's man, in this company, you needs call only the land leaders mistress."

He followed her toward a knot of women gathered near the clay coffee urn.

"Women," the queen called. Everyone swung to face them. Rejeena's hand slid onto Aarvan's back. "This is Aarvan, my queen's man." A few snickers erupted. The queen glared. The snickers ceased.

Tameera, the land leader, stepped forward, followed by a huge, swarthy man with black hair and brown eyes. His imposing bulk presented a pleasing appearance in a dark, heavy-muscled way.

Aarvan accepted Tameera's small hand, and lifted it to his lips.

She smiled. "I hope you will not hold me in anger, Queen's Man, for calling for your acknowledgment. It clearly embarrassed you."

The queen answered. "The queen's man embarrasses often. Hopefully, he will grow into his role."

"My queen is right, Mistress," Aarvan said. "I won't hold you in anger."

"Good." Tameera pulled the huge man closer. "This is Richard, my favored holdee."

Richard, a smile as big as the man stretching his face, gripped Aarvan's offered hand. The smile vaulted from the holdee's eyes, meeting Aarvan's with a warm, friendly aura. "My mistress calls me Richard, Queen's Man," he rumbled from the depths of his great chest, "but I kinda like to be called Dick." He bent forward, still holding the handshake. "That's, a'course, if bein' queen's man, you can be bothered with a mere holdee."

"I'll bother with pleasure, Dick," Aarvan grinned, delighted to meet a friendly male.

"Great," Dick said, slapping Aarvan's shoulder so hard the queen's man quick stepped sideways to regain balance. Dick leaned close and muttered, "Careful o' Tuuman."

Puzzled, Aarvan nodded.

"Come, Richard," Tameera said, "let us depart before the queen thrashes you for striking her queen's man and whispering secrets." She led him away.

Aarvan looked after them. "What a mismatched pair."

"No wonder she remains so tiny with all that weight atop her," the queen said.

"My Queen . . ."

Aarvan met the remaining land leader, Barsa, a thin, unattractive woman with scraggly, mud-blonde hair and doleful eyes. She waved to the man beside her. "This is Tuuman, my favored holdee."

Aarvan cautiously eyed the holdee, who shouldered his mistress aside and stepped in front of the queen's man.

Barsa did not seem to mind his boorish act.

The queen frowned and her hand stilled against Aarvan's back.

Tuuman was a big man, handsome with sharp features, dark hair and brazen eyes. A string-thin mustache adorned his upper lip.

Aarvan's mouth twitched. The women forbade facial hair. Yet a land leader's holdee stood before the queen with a mustache. The queen's man smiled and offered his hand. "How do you do, Tuuman?" He remained alert, remembering Dick's remark. From the corner of his eye, he noted Tameera and Dick watching intently, as did other women about the room.

Tuuman's smile did not reflect in his eyes. He wrapped a big hand around Aarvan's. His grip, while not painful, held tight. The favored holdee studied the queen's man with an insolent lift of lip.

"Queen's Man, eh? I'm Tuuman." He poked his chest with a large thumb. "I'm of good stock, Northern Mountain fellows. Don't kiss no hands, don't wear no fancy double buttons. Don't need to. Hain't no weak-kneed, weak-hearted *Mainlander.*" His hand tightened in a crushing grip on Aarvan's, bending it backward and down.

The rage exploded. *"Kill!"* Aarvan lunged. *No. Just stop him.* He drove stiffened fingers into Tuuman's throat.

Tuuman's grip slackened. He dropped. On his knees, he retched. Clutched his throat. No more interest in the contest.

Aarvan stared at the downed man. Elation pounded in his veins and behind his eyes. In an immeasurable flick of time, the deadly rage had claimed him again, formed the entity—part killer, part man. *What in the name of God am I?* The strength and instinct of the killer vied with the intellect and mercy of the man. *"Kill him. Finish it."* No, *he's down. There's no need.*

Silence reigned as Aarvan stepped back. The killer slid away to hidden recesses in his mind. That raging presence, himself, they were one, belonged together, worked together, could kill together. He still didn't truly understand its origin or purpose, but it hovered behind that door—ready, waiting.

The queen's hand flattened against Aarvan's spine. *My Great LaSheena, what did I just see? What dangerous quirk resides within my queen's man? But LaHeeka said it poses no danger to me.*

Barsa stooped beside her holdee. Assured he would live, she screeched, "You idiot. You are before the queen. You cannot play your inane games with the queen's man. I told you that. I warned you." She looked up. "My Queen, I apologize for my holdee. He can be incurably daft."

Rejeena recovered her aplomb and her icy voice whipped. "Teach that holdee proper manners, Barsa. Had not Aarvan already trounced him, he would taste locchot."

"Yes, My Queen." Barsa helped Tuuman to his feet.

"If I see facial hair again, you may both taste locchot. If you cannot control your holdee, barter him to someone who can."

"Yes, My Queen." Barsa, red-faced, shoulders slumping, turned Tuuman over to her guards and crept away from the queen's sight.

"You surprise me, My Queen's Man," Rejeena said.

"My Queen?"

"I did not know you are so adept at defending yourself."

"Neither did I."

Locin stared at the queen's man. She had just watched his beast attack. LaSheena, he struck fast! She hardly saw him move. And efficient. He disabled big Tuuman with one blow. *If the beast turns on the queen, I will require more than a dull knife.*

A smiling woman, wearing a full red sash across her chest, appeared before the queen. "My Queen, I would shake the hand of your queen's man. Nothing could have pleased me more than to see Tuuman on his knees." She laughed aloud.

Aarvan extended his hand.

She shook it. "I am Latere, captain of Mistress Barsa's guards."

"Shiira."

Another woman, clad in a captain's uniform, said, "I am Reesan, captain of Mistress Tameera's guard." She grinned as Aarvan took her hand. "Your action pleased all women, Queen's Man. Tuuman has deserved that for some time."

"He left me little choice, Shiira."

The remainder of the leaders Aarvan knew—Parria, Shabet and Henna, captain of Parria's guards. Billy accompanied Parria but avoided Aarvan. The various under leaders were not introduced.

Women began to choose refreshment and take places around a long table.

Accepting a caster of coffee from a servant, Aarvan felt a viselike grip clamp his shoulder. He turned to face Dick.

Dick's face split into a grin. "Queen's Man, I'd give a lot to see you put that bully on his knees ag'in."

"Lucky jab."

"Lucky my ass," the big man rumbled. "You coulda killed him. You pulled that blow. Shoulda gone ahead and done it, made ever'body happy."

"I doubt it would have made Mistress Barsa happy."

"Who cares? Woman ain't got no sense. Man's a bully. Does that to every man he meets."

"You?"

Dick flushed. "Yeah. Took me by surprise. Won't get another chance." His grin revived. "Mebbe he'll think twice now 'fore he grabs holda someone." His gaze traveled Aarvan's compact frame. "Never seen a man move that fast. What are you, part snattsnake?"

"Maybe just part," Aarvan said, assuming a snattsnake to be fast. He frowned. "Why does Tuuman keep doing it? I'd think he'd have been in locchot before this."

"Never done it b'fore to a queen's man. Mistress Barsa protected him from women the same or lower rank." Dick laughed. "She shoulda protected him today from you." The big man's face took a serious mien. "If it won't offend you, Queen's Man, I'd like to be your friend."

"I'd like that, Dick."

"Man needs a friend."

"My name's Aarvan."

"As a holdee, I gotta call you queen's man. I'd not wanna slip up in front of the queen. Woman's got a wicked eye."

"Fair enough."

"You'd best be joinin' her. She's lookin' this way, and she ain't smilin'."

"So she is." Aarvan shook Dick's hand. "Until later, friend."

Aarvan took an indicated seat to the left of the queen, who sat at the table head. Land leaders and guard captains took chairs on both sides, with lesser-ranked guards toward the far end. Each land leader's holdee sat to the left of his respective mistress. Dick sprawled comfortably, sipping wine. Billy scowled, gulping wine. Tuuman, mustache gone, glowered and avoided meeting Aarvan's eyes.

A lively discourse circled the table as the women discussed, discarded and accepted methods to guarantee the safety of the queen and land leaders during their journey. Queens' Council would take place in Rhotha's Towne, which lay in Quarter Eight.

As queen's guard captain, Shabet dominated, demanding the final word on all arrangements. She contradicted, jeered, scolded and verbally brutalized all who dared oppose her. Only to the queen, who said very little, did Shabet remain polite. Even the land leaders did not escape the lash of her sharp tongue. She appeared to hold her knowledge and experience as the ultimate authority.

Shabet stifled the opposition, women relenting. She had been captain of the queen's guard for many season turnings, manipulating the queen's survival through determined attempts on her life. Women yielded both out of respect for the captain's impressive record and fear of her caustic tongue.

Aarvan concentrated to follow the conversation. He found life surety intensely interesting, especially since it concerned the queen. Hunks of knowledge forced their way through the wall to his memory like water streaming through a broken dike. The extent of his comprehension and perception in this area astonished him. Some of the women's arrangements sounded adequate; some he felt required improvement. He sat quietly, knowing his input wouldn't be appreciated, the women holding men in contempt as they did, until one provision goaded him into action.

He asked, "May I speak, My Queen?"

"You wish to offer a contribution, Aarvan?"

Irritation boiled in him at the incredulity on women's faces. He pushed it down. "Yes, My Queen, I believe I do."

Shabet smirked, lip curling. "Well, Queen's Man, pray let us hear your profound contribution."

Aarvan studied the woman he felt would be an adversary. Shabet stood tall, stocky, the crimson captain's sash gleaming against black leather. Her sandy hair hung short, slicked tight to her head. Her gray-green eyes swept the room, jolting, torching the confidence of any woman they touched. Her face pulled long and lean, small mouth pursed, nose thin, cheeks slightly sunken. A smile would have uplifted her features, but the perpetual frown fit her persona. A disagreeable woman, her sense of superiority buoyed her as the wind conveys aloft the soaring hawk.

Shabet stood before a large bark spread on the table, showing the camp and guard positions. She did not welcome suggestions, not even from her life surety women. Comments from a man would receive scant consideration.

The life of the queen hung in the balance. Her life was well worth fighting for, risking the fury of the captain, possibly the anger of the queen. He would first try tact, stroke a little fur. He took a slow, deep breath and spoke. "Captain, your boundary arrangements appear excellent. Your guard perimeters are well-defined and placed, the outer line disallowing a group access, the inner perimeter containing penetration by even an individual."

Shabet planted fists to hips. "I shall sleep well this night knowing I have garnered your approval, Queen's Man."

Snickers erupted around the table.

Aarvan steeled his mind to ignore both Shabet's derision and the snickering.

Locin stepped behind him to interpret if needed.

He leaned forward and tapped the bark, which sketched the tent arrangement. The queen's large tent would be placed back to back with the three land leader's tents. "This tent arrangement is good, allowing you to cover all tents with fewest guards. There is one thing that concerns me, Captain."

Shabet leaned over the table, hands flat, intense eyes boring into Aarvan's. "Well, Queen's Man, do explain. LaSheena forbid something should be allowed to bother you. Enlighten us as to exactly how you, whose best quality is a shapely ass, can improve upon tenting arrangements which have functioned for many season turnings. We breathlessly await your wisdom."

"You have guards at the entrances, Captain, but none between or inside the tents."

Shabet sneered. "No guards are within, since women prefer private time with their holdees. Perhaps being so fast as to promptly strike down one worthless holdee, you rut so swiftly my queen barely notices your efforts. Others require more time."

Aarvan warmed to his subject, that confident timbre filling his voice. He leaned forward, engrossed, touching the sketch as he spoke, discounting Shabet's scorn. "The area between the tents at night will be pitch-black. None of the guards at the entrances can see the side areas, particularly of the queen's larger tent. Should enemies enter the camp in spite of precautions, they could gain access, slip between the tents, enter from the rear and kill the occupants."

"You are truly ignorant. No enemy can penetrate my defenses. My perimeter stands completely secure."

"What harm could there be, Captain, in posting guards between tents?"

"It is not needed, wastes womanpower, Queen's . . . Twiddle. You needs clamp jaw and hold to your skindown duties. We women, who possess knowledge and reason, will concern ourselves with the safety of the queen."

"Your perimeter is excellent, Captain, but is your confidence worth betting the life of your queen?"

Women at the table, having been lashed by Shabet's contemptuous tongue, smiled or ducked their heads, gaze flicking to each other. This queen's man, besides being an enticing piece of skindown goods, proved entertaining. He did not retreat from Shabet's scorn. While not taking him seriously—after all, what could a mere man know—they found his verbal duel with the scornful, mean-mouthed guard captain satisfying. He did what they wished they could.

The queen sat, sipped coffee and watched the exchange with unreadable green eyes.

"You question my concern for my queen's safety?" Shabet's voice hardened. "For nine seasons, my measures have functioned without change. I do not require advice from any double-buttoned, glorified schlong. You will—"

"In nine seasons defenses do require change. Complacency could kill your queen." Tact wouldn't work with this woman . . . maybe logic with a touch of agitation? Make her think?

"You arrogant targeethan. How dare you presume to tell me my function?"

"In order to remain effective, life surety measures must be constantly questioned and upgraded. A determined, wily enemy will find a way to breach the best of plans."

"What do you know of it, Queen's Twiddle? You are but a useless man. Go play with your little woodypiece until my queen calls for your favors."

Voice gentle but intense, he said, "There are three ways, Captain, that I could breach your perimeter defenses."

Silence hung like a shroud. Of one thing all women were certain—Shabet's perimeter could not be breached.

Shabet crossed her arms and glared. "You are demented, Queen's Twiddle. Do share your great knowledge with us lesser beings."

Aarvan leaned back, glanced at the queen who sat expressionless, and said, "Let's presume I am a woman and wish to assassinate the queen. My first chosen avenue of penetration would be the kitchen. Your kitchen operation is huge, with women from each of the townes. They can't possibly all know each other. You depend on armskins to identify the kitchen workers. From what I understand of the conversation around this table, those armskins are dispensed rather carelessly. I'd get one of those and try to plant a woman ahead of time. I'm sure all your hiring practices are not so careful, especially the land leaders whose life surety hasn't the same urgency as the queen's." He paused, glancing at each land leader.

Tameera, with an apologetic grimace, said, "It is so. We hired a kitchen servant only five days ago who will make this trip."

Aarvan continued. "With a woman established inside, acquiring another armskin and access to the camp would be easy. Once inside your defenses, I simply slip between the tents and—"

"You buffoon," Shabet barked, "the tents sit in the open with fires burning. The guards would see you skulking about."

"I wouldn't skulk. I'd wait outside the light until the area cleared except for guards. Then I'd boldly march past those at the entrance to the queen's tent, wishing them a pleasant evening. Since I'm a woman inside your perimeter, wearing an armskin, they'd pay me scant attention. Out of their sight, I'd slip between the tents. The guards for the land leaders' tents wouldn't yet be able to see me. I'd have open access to the rear of the queen's tent."

"That is absurd, you fool."

Aarvan leaned forward, blue eyes intense. "If I wasn't able to acquire an armskin, I'd use your garbage routine."

"Garbage?"

"Your kitchen help takes the garbage beyond the perimeter and dumps it, washes the containers and leaves them to dry. Two women return, well after dark, to collect the containers. I simply wait with a companion and jump them, kill them, take their armskins and return the containers. A more risky method, but workable. The guards, expecting to see us, will offer only a cursory challenge. We avoid anyone near the kitchen, and we have access."

"That is daft. It could not work. You could not penetrate either perimeter. You meddle. You know nothing."

"Captain, we are all persons, subject to fallacies. A perimeter which can't be penetrated does not exist. A relentless assassin will find a way."

"My perimeter has never been breached," she snarled. "Your demented ravings do not impress."

"I could just walk through the front entrance."

Reesan said, "The front entrance, Queen's Man?"

"Yes, I understand you intend to use the same password all three days. The password should be changed frequently. Too many women in your extended group know it. It would be impossible to secure against a determined enemy for three days. Even from outside the camp, using one of several devious methods, I would have your password in one day."

"You blather idiocy. No woman would grant you access to the password." Shabet glowered.

He gave her a snide smile—*nothing else is working, time for verbal assault.* "I could shake my shapely ass at her and promise a romp with my glorified schlong."

Snickers erupted around the table.

Shabet exploded. "That is enough. I have heard all the drivel I can stomach. Stupid. Arrogant. Unthinkable. My Queen, please silence your queen's man so we may continue the meeting."

"Aarvan," the queen said, "you unduly irritate Captain Shabet. I am sure your intentions are worthy, but it is not your concern. We do need to continue the meeting."

Aarvan turned. "My Queen, today Saradan said you wouldn't live to attend Queens' Council. I don't think she mouthed idle threats."

"Aarvan, the outlaws always threaten the queen. Thus far they have not achieved success."

He frowned. "Saradan spoke as though she held the goddess cull in muskee, which as you know, almost always wins the game. She mentioned your demise before Queen's Council. As well, when she harassed me, she said all her women would sample me after they kill you. These outlaws specifically intend to attack during the first part of your journey. All defensive angles must be covered for your safety."

"I have complete confidence in Shabet's grasp of my life surety."

"Nobody can think of everything. Captain Shabet is overlooking small accesses that can give an assassin a chance at you."

"You indulge in flights of fancy," Shabet growled. "Such escapades have never been tried."

Aarvan's fists clenched under the table, his hard held temper fraying. *What will it take to open this woman's closed mind?* He choked back an acidic reply. "Precisely, Captain. If they had been, you'd guard against them. To stop an assassin, you have to think ahead of him . . . or her. Behind is too late."

Shabet, face twisted in fury, leaned across the table. "Queen's Twiddle, clamp jaw. I, and I alone, rule my queen's life surety. The point stands, you discuss what is beyond your male understanding, which does not concern you and of which you know naught."

His temper snapped and he rose, leaned to meet her, their blazing eyes inches apart. "The point is, Shiira, you seem more interested in your pride and controlling everyone than the safety of your queen."

"Aarvan, enough," Queen Rejeena snapped. "Sit down!"

He sucked in a deep breath, jaw clenched; but he sat, hands balled into fists.

"Aarvan, must you be an ass every time we appear in public?" the queen asked.

Staring at Shabet, he said, "Only when I must deal with other asses."

A collective gasp raced down the table. Women ducked behind casters and chalices to hide their grins.

Standing behind Aarvan, Locin barely contained a shout of laughter. She had never truly liked the captain, but functioned for her out of respect for her many seasons of success and Locin's need to serve her queen.

"That will be all, Aarvan," the queen said. "Shabet decides my life surety. One more word and you will regret it." Again, the dark blue and green eyes clashed across the corner of a table.

Again, Aarvan conceded. "Yes, My Queen."

"Shabet," the queen's voice softened to a mild scold, "do not call the queen's man by that name."

"No, My Queen." Shabet's triumphant gaze traveled the table, paused at each significant woman and came to rest on the queen's man.

"I think it time for a break," the queen said. "Tempers need to cool. Aarvan, come with me." She walked to a small, outside courtyard.

Aarvan followed.

The queen stared at the wall before turning to face him. "Why must you constantly try my patience? When I strive to display you, you embarrass me. Why can you not act as a proper queen's man?"

"Exactly how, My Queen, would you have me act?" Aarvan still tightly balled his fists, fingers digging into palms, the force diffusing some of his rampant frustration.

The queen walked close, placed her hands on his hips. Her green eyes held his. "A queen's man is to please his queen in skindown and complete her." A smile tickled her mouth. "At that you excel. A queen's man is to be charming and gracious, make his queen proud. You do that well much of the time. A queen's man is to sit quietly and look handsome. The handsome part, Aarvan, you cannot help but fulfill. It is the quiet part where you fail your queen. You seem determined to argue with everyone about everything."

Flame flashed in his eyes. "I do not argue with everyone about everything, My Queen. I argued with your land leader when goaded. Today I argued with Shabet . . . because I feel the life of my queen worth fighting for." His words started hard and angry, ended softly intense.

Her voice gentled. "Aarvan, you are but a man. You cannot possibly know of life surety. Men do not."

"Men do not? I understand on the Mainland men run things. Somehow they seem to muddle through."

"I do not know of Mainland practices, nor do I care. Here men know naught. Accept it. Shabet has guarded me successfully for many seasons. How could you be wiser?"

He broke eye contact and stared over her right shoulder. A deep sigh, almost a shudder, wracked his body. His gaze sharpened with the intensity of a raptor seeking prey, and returned to hers. "I don't know about wisdom. I know that I have this knowledge, and I need to share it for the safety of my queen."

Hearing the intense confidence of his voice, Rejeena almost granted his words credence. She reminded herself what men were and were not. The moment passed.

"Aarvan, you must accept your place. You are a man, queen's man. Concern yourself only with pleasing your queen, not with life surety. It is most arrogant of you to presume you can teach Captain Shabet."

He ground his teeth, then spoke. "I cannot sit quietly through a meeting in which my queen is not receiving the best service from her life surety forces. My Queen, I beg you not to dismiss what I've said. Shabet allows holes in your defenses that are open invitations to the outlaws. If I can see the holes, surely they can. Please have her close them. Two guards at the sides of the tent would prevent someone from slipping between—a very simple solution."

"Shabet has granted your queen safety for many seasons. I have not interfered, and will not do so now."

"The tent arrangement—"

"Aarvan, I will hear no more." The queen placed a hand flat against his chest. "Shabet is life surety. If she sees no merit in your words, then so be it. You may not quarrel with her."

"Does that mean I can't speak?"

"It means you will be polite. If Shabet so demands, you will be silent without insulting her and embarrassing your queen."

"Yes, My Queen." He again stared over her right shoulder. His body was present, but his mind nowhere near.

She stood, hands touching him, studying those perfect, chiseled features. "What is it you see, when you peer into the distance?"

"Nothing, My Queen. That's the problem. I see nothing."

"Perhaps your memory will return in time."

"Perhaps."

They reentered the meeting room, and Aarvan went for coffee, seething but out of arguments for the moment.

Dick joined him. "You got guts, boy, but you got no smarts," he said in a low rumble.

"How so?"

"How many times you think you can safely rile the queen?"

Aarvan shrugged. "As many as needed."

"Better get some hot wine, boy. You need cheered up."

"I don't need cheered up. I need to be taken seriously," Aarvan groused. "These women think our brains run out through our peckers."

Dick guffawed. "That's the truth. I been with my mistress two season turnin's, on the island three. I'm usta it."

"Season turnings?" Aarvan frowned. "Can't you say years like normal people? You even talk like them."

"You are mad, aren't you?"

"I'm sorry, Dick, I shouldn't snap at you. It's not your fault."

"Better you snap at me than the queen. Ain't that what friends are for? Speakin' of the queen, she's takin' her seat. You best scat."

Aarvan watched as Shabet, a map of the route laid out, outlined her travel plans. With apparent disdain she assumed the outlaws would not develop different approaches. He drummed his fingers on his knee and shifted positions in his chair. *If the woman is so good at life surety, how can she be so blind?* Nothing bothered him enough to risk the queen's disapproval until near the end of the trip.

The map showed the queen's convoy moving through a narrow pass with mountains rising on each side. The majority of guards would ride through well ahead of the coaches. A large group would follow, to the rear. Only eight guards would escort the coaches along the road. It seemed to him an odd arrangement, but not objectionable since the walls rose so steep and high that attack appeared virtually impossible. But a trail, cutting through side mountains all the way from the flat land beyond, joined the main road midway through the pass. Shabet's plan showed no precautions against the trail.

Hoping there might be a reason for Shabet's lack of concern but unable to restrain his need to know, Aarvan approached the subject gingerly. "My Queen, may I ask a question?"

"If Shabet wishes to answer."

He looked at the captain.

Shabet frowned but said, "By all means, ask, Queen's T . . . Man."

He pointed. "This trail, Captain, appears to run from the pass to open country. I see no provisions against attack through it as the queen passes with only eight guards. Am I missing something?" He forced a smile.

"Your ignorance is appalling, even for a man." Shabet pointed to a wide spot in the trail marked with red. "Here, Queen's Man, stands a most holy shrine of LaSheena; the trail is thus called LaSheena's Corridor. No woman may tread this corridor except in the presence of an exalted holy woman. The queen will be perfectly safe."

Warning bells chimed in Aarvan's mind. Shabet's smug, unshakable faith that the outlaws lacked the imagination to find new solutions to old problems struck him as gross incompetence. Saradan's confidence had been equally smug as she threatened the queen's life during this journey. He needed to convince this obstinate guard captain, without angering her, that she endangered the queen. Once she demanded his silence, he would be finished.

"Captain, I admit ignorance of your ways. How can you be certain the outlaws won't use this corridor? If I wished to assassinate the queen, I'd do exactly what you believe I wouldn't."

"You know nothing. No woman of Kriiscon would risk the wrath of LaSheena. It is not done."

"Which makes it the perfect line of attack. These women are outlaws, risk their lives daily against law forces." He kept his voice soft, conciliatory, inquiring. "They scorn the wrath of even the great queen. How much bigger a step is it to scorn the wrath of LaSheena?"

"Queen's Man," Reesan said, "the wrath of LaSheena rises far above the level of queens. The goddess's power knows no bounds. No woman would enter that corridor unless accompanied by an exalted holy woman. Even outlaws would not dare."

"An exalted holy woman?"

"It is the highest rank of holy woman, Aarvan," the queen explained. "There are but ten on Kriiscon, one in each quarter, two with the great queen."

"The outlaws couldn't have one, My Queen?"

"No, there are just the ten, ordained by the great queen through LaSheena. They are all most holy, filled with reverence of the goddess. An exalted holy woman spends her days within her holy house, teaching learners to be righteous, kind and reverent. She basks always in the good will of LaSheena. None would stray from that sanctified path to commune with outlaws."

"Could the outlaws mask their presence through the corridor?" Aarvan glanced around the table. He received negative headshakes and blank looks. The queen's eyes held amused indulgence; Shabet's showed scorn. Both caused his anger to boil. He squelched it.

Aarvan verbalized his way carefully. The women, to include the queen, believed not only in the goddess but also in her protected corridor—to him, a logical avenue of attack. He doubted LaSheena, presuming she existed, would concern her goddess self with a bunch of outlaws riding a particular trail. He didn't want to infuriate the women, but he needed to know the basis of their belief—how solid the supporting facts. "If the outlaws did use the corridor without an exalted holy woman, what would be the consequences?"

Tameera answered. "Over the seasons, Queen's Man, foolish women have occasionally flaunted the rules. None survived. One group was found outside the corridor hacked to pieces, another small bunch inside, dead of arrows from the bows of LaSheena's forest guards. A lone woman tried to walk the corridor. She entered and never emerged. Surely you can see no woman would dare."

"So the price is death?"

"Yes, immediate death," Latere said. "Even were the outlaws willing to sacrifice their lives, they could not survive long enough to harm the queen. The effort would be futile."

"What about unbelievers? On the Mainland, we have gods, too. Some people simply don't believe. Are there women among the outlaws who don't believe in LaSheena?"

Shabet sneered. "Unbelievers are shunned. A force large enough to perform the function could not be mustered. In any case, lack of belief would not save them. They too would die."

"Could the outlaws align with loose men? Could men pass through the corridor alive?"

"No," Shabet snapped. "It is LaSheena's Corridor. What she will not tolerate from women, she certainly will not tolerate from dogshit men."

"I see." Aarvan searched his mind without success for an argument to circumvent or shake their convictions. "What would be the harm, Captain, just for assurance, of sending a larger force of guards with the queen?" He gestured with one hand, palm up. "You have a very large group in front. Why couldn't some of them—?"

"Enough inanity." Shabet scorched Aarvan with a caustic glare. "The harm, Queen's Man, would be guards I need elsewhere to counter true threats. I have shown patience for the sake of my queen. No outlaw force will tread the corridor. This discussion is finished."

"Yes, Captain." Aarvan sat back. He did not again risk speaking.

The women concluded the meeting, Shabet berating the others into silence.

The triple specters of the tent arrangement, LaSheena's Corridor and Saradan's certainty of the queen's death haunted Aarvan. The opportunities so clear to him, surely the outlaws could see them. With Shabet's callous dismissal of the possibilities and the queen's trust in her, Aarvan feared for the queen's life.

* * *

"My Queen! My Queen!" a guard yelled, awakening the queen and Aarvan in the morning. Six guards stood inside the door, shifting feet, hands fluttering.

"What is it, Tressa?" The queen sat, wrenching her sleepy mind awake.

Aarvan jerked to a sitting position.

"My Queen, the prisoners have escaped."

"Prisoners?"

"The outlaws, My Queen. They are gone."

Understanding dawned. Rejeena snapped awake and leaped from skindown. She snatched her skirt, and flung Aarvan his pants.

He wriggled into them beneath the covers, then grabbed his boots and vest.

The queen fired questions. "How did they escape? How could they?"

"We do not yet know, My Queen. Soldiers secured them in the large cave cell. They fled through seven guards and three locked doors. The guards in the cave complex say that did not occur. Yet the outlaws vanished."

"Impossible! Has Shabet been called?"

"Yes, My Queen."

"Then let us go. Aarvan?"

"Ready, My Queen."

Damp coolness and breaking dawn greeted them as they hurried outside. Six more guards joined them, hovering, watchful, hands near sword hilts. With the outlaws free, they would take no chances.

The queen strode swiftly toward the combined Hearing Hall and cave complex, a deep frown marring her face.

Locin appeared beside Aarvan.

They entered a side door into the rear complex of rooms, which led to the queen's lunchroom and Hearing Hall. They turned left, passed through a locked door with two armed guards. Most of the queen's guards halted. Locin stayed with Aarvan.

The dirt floor led swiftly downward beneath their feet, and shortly they walked on sloping solid rock.

"What is this place?" Aarvan asked Locin.

"It is a prison. Caves and fissures teem within the mountain. This one boasts but one access, having several areas below. With doors and locks fastened inside, it functions well for confining criminals and other miscreants."

"Yet the outlaws escaped."

"It would so appear."

"Through seven guards and three locked doors?"

"Clamp jaw, Arrogant Pup, so we may learn how this occurred."

They arrived at the second door. "We?"

"We as in women." Locin smirked.

"Has Shabet arrived?" the queen asked as the guards tried to curtsey and unlock the door.

"Yes, My Queen, she is within."

"Good." The queen swept through.

Locin and Aarvan followed.

The third door led to the room from which the outlaws disappeared. Women bustled about inside.

Shabet turned as the queen entered, the captain's eyes pits of fury. "My Queen," she said, "we will discern what happened. They could not have escaped without aid. When I determine those responsible, the gallows will claim guests."

"What you have discovered thus far, Shabet?"

"Arsen's women confined the four outlaws together, gave all food, pallets and blankets. A healer tended the wounded one, granting her a potion to dull the pain of her wound. Once locked in, they were to be ignored until morning.

"The guards state they did not open the door until they entered to arouse the prisoners this morning. They discovered Saradan and two others gone." The captain gestured to a still form on a pallet. "The wounded one lies dead. They could not take her, so they killed her to still her tongue.

"The only escape route, My Queen, is through those doors and up the passageway. Yesterday I would have staked my life on the loyalty of Line Leader Batear. She ruled six excellent guards." Shabet pointed toward seven guards standing to one side. "Now I do not know. All are loosed until I have answers."

Locin observed the queen's man, who stopped inside the entrance. He again exuded that aura of confidence, his gaze traveling over the room, the floor, walls and ceiling. His perusal stopped three times, at a large crack in the wall, a small hole in the ceiling and the placid pool of water covering part of the floor.

He walked to the dead woman, lifted the cover. The shaft of a knife protruded from her ribcage. "They made it quick," he said to Locin. Raising his voice, looking at the woman's body, he asked, "Captain Shabet, where do you suppose this knife came from? Surely the outlaws had no knives when confined."

Shabet turned and glared. "Are you not just the wise one to so discern? Obviously, the guards who helped them furnished the knife."

"This is a rather fancy knife." He indicated the carved handle. "Guards all carry a smooth-handled knife."

"They would hardly use their guard's knife, Queen's Man."

Ignoring her sarcasm, he pointed to the crack in the wall. "Has that crack ever been thoroughly checked, Captain, to be sure it's not more than it appears?"

"Yes, long ago, before we confined a prisoner." Shabet gestured to one of her guard chiefs. "Pamma, heed the queen's man and his inane questions. I cannot be disturbed by his insipid disruptions." She turned her back.

Pamma, a short, muscular woman with warm brown eyes, said, "Sorry, Queen's Man, losing the prisoners is failure. Captain Shabet does not bear failure well. When upset she can be rude."

Aarvan grinned. "Only when she's upset?"

Pamma grimaced.

Aarvan pointed to the hole in the ceiling. "Has that hole ever been checked?"

"Checked, Queen's Man?" Pamma stared at him.

"Yes, checked. Has anyone ever made sure it's surrounded by solid rock, that there's nothing tricky about it?"

Pamma arched a brow at Locin, who shrugged and said, "I guard him. I do not explain him."

"Queen's Man," Pamma said, "it is but a hole, perhaps big enough for a rat. The room consists of solid rock. What is your intent?"

"I'm trying to find an exit other than the doors."

"The doors are the only exit. Forget the hole in the ceiling."

"Where does the hole lead?"

"When we used braziers in this cell, the heat rose to a storage room above. But it is still just a rat hole. No one could escape through it."

"Yet someone did escape from your inescapable room. There has to be a way."

"Through the doors, Queen's Man."

Aarvan glanced at the seven guards, who looked shamed, miserable and confused. He shook his head. "I don't think so, not through three locked doors and seven trusted guards. There is another answer. We need to find it."

"Well, it is not through that rat hole," Pamma said.

"How will you know until you look?" Aarvan again studied the hole. "If heat can rise to that storage room, we might be able to lower a rope through into this cell. Then we could climb the rope and see."

Pamma laughed. "You do possess a most active imagination. If it restrains you from irritating the captain, when this furor settles, I will take guards and do that."

Aarvan looked at her. "I'd appreciate that very much."

"Consider it done. Do you harbor other concerns with this room?"

"Yes." He turned to the pond. "Where's this water come from?"

The queen called, "Aarvan, I am ready." She and Shabet stood by the door.

"My Queen, I'd like to stay a while," Aarvan said. "I'm trying to figure this out."

The queen frowned.

Shabet said, "Let him stay, My Queen. If he stirs about down here, he will not badger us with worthless questions."

"Very well, Aarvan. Locin, return him in time for hearing."

"Yes, My Queen."

The queen spun and left.

"Thank you, My Queen," Aarvan called to her back. Then he growled softly to the air around him, "You should pay a pile of baagars for this."

"What did you say?" Locin asked, she and Pamma the only ones to hear.

"I said she should pay a pile of baagars for this," he repeated.

"What does that mean?"

"I'm not sure. I remembered something, but not enough."

"What did you remember?"

"That I am talented at finding rat holes that don't exist. Someone somewhere has paid a lot of baagars for my service, but I don't know who or where."

"What is a baagar?"

"A form of currency."

"You think you are good at this, Queen's Man?" Pamma stood, arms crossed.

He displayed a slow, self-assured smile that spoke more than a volume of words.

Locin read intense confidence, far beyond any he showed before. He had pulled from his shadowed memories something that pleased him, buoyed his spirit. She felt glad for him.

"Back to the water," he said. "Where's it come from?"

"From an underground river beneath the mountain," Pamma said. "Most of these lower rooms flood in spring and some retain water all year long."

He stood by the small pond and surveyed the surface. "When did someone last look for an exit through here?"

The guard chief puffed out her breath. "Queen's Man, no woman ever has. It would be suicide. The underground river is strong."

"Then how do you know what's down there?"

"A woman once swam down for a jest. Her body appeared days later where the river surfaces. Nothing resides down that water but certain death."

"Shiira, last night this room held three outlaws, but this morning they're gone. The guards say they didn't exit through the doors. I believe that. Which begs another question. If the outlaws left through the doors, why did they kill their companion?" He pointed to the dead woman. "If the guards cooperated, there seems small reason to kill her. She could have gone with them."

"I cannot explain the actions of outlaws," Pamma muttered. "They of necessity traversed the passageway."

He shook his head. "The prisoners found a means of escape. If they found it, we can find it. This pond seems the most likely possibility. It needs to be explored. If you women are afraid, I'll do it."

"You will do no such thing, Queen's Man," Locin said. "The queen would not so allow."

"Who mentioned asking her?"

"You will certainly not do so without her permission."

He flashed a grin. "Don't I need to get ready for Queen's Hearing?"

"Yes. You will do that and forget this foolishness."

He turned to Pamma. "Thank you for answering my questions, Shiira. I appreciate it. Don't forget, you have that rat hole to check."

"You are welcome," she said. "I will check your rat hole. But forget the water. No woman will go down there."

He turned to leave.

"Do you need another guard, Locin?" Pamma asked.

"No. I have only to return him to the queen's house alive. If I must tolerate that arrogant smile one more time, I may kill him myself." Locin followed Aarvan.

Between the locked doors, Aarvan spoke. "I intend to search that water. I could use your help."

"Queen's Man, I will not even discuss this. You will not search that water, and I certainly will not aid you."

He stopped and looked at her, blue eyes hard as dark mirrors. "I need to know what's down there. You can help me or I can do it alone. If you won't help, it will be more dangerous."

"You will go nowhere and do nothing unless the queen approves."

He continued up the rock slope. "I'll have to do it myself then."

She laughed, close behind him. "You would needs elude the home guards. That will not happen."

They reached the last gate, and both remained silent until well away from the other guards.

"I know four ways to get by the home guards," Aarvan said.

Locin snorted. "And they are?"

"For me to know and you to wish you did."

"Queen's Man, you are packed with mertan's rot. Even if you could elude the home guards, which you cannot, the queen would have you in locchot."

He shrugged. "Everyone keeps threatening me with locchot anyway. Might as well be for a good cause."

"Do not even consider this harebrained scheme. You have no idea how much grief you can reap in Rejeena's Towne without protection."

"The whole problem could be avoided if you'd help me."

"I will not, Queen's Man. Forget that water."

He shrugged and said no more.

* * *

All women of Rejeena's Towne soon grew aware of the outlaws' escape and that Queen's Hearing would not be pleasant that morning. Queen Rejeena sat, toe tapping, hands clenched on her chair arms, mouth pursed tight. Though she strove to make fair decisions, she spoke curtly to disputants and showed little civility.

Aarvan thought hard, to develop a way of eluding his guards, in order to search the cave pond without his absence being discovered. It would be no easy chore. Evading the queen for the needed amount of time presented a giant obstacle.

Nearing lunchtime, the reader's call interrupted his contemplation. "Tarkan requests queen's punishment, holdee strikes mistress, fifth offense."

Aarvan snapped to attention.

The queen glared as she noted the large woman and her emaciated holdee approach disputants' place.

Tarkan bowed and rose as the holdee fell to his knee, head down.

"Have we not solved this before, Tarkan?"

"My Queen, the holdee learned nothing."

"Then why do you not cut his throat and get another?"

Frowning, Aarvan stared at Rejeena.

"My Queen, I have not great means. This holdee must suffice."

The queen sighed audibly. "Refresh my mind on your problem with this holdee."

"He is a proper holdee, My Queen, except when I wake him from sleep. When I do, he strikes out and frequently hits me. It is intolerable. I have tried every punishment, even to the lashes at hearing last time. Nothing stops him. I request severe queen's punishment."

The queen considered. This woman claimed to lack kruets to replace her holdee, yet requested severe queen's punishment, which added to the lashes received before, could kill such a gaunt man.

Tarkan had to know that. A doubt, not quite glimpsed, niggled at Rejeena's mind, but she shoved it down. *Punishment for crime, not the woman's motive, is my concern.* She noticed, from the corner of her eye, Aarvan leaning forward, face intense, brows knit.

"Holdee, look at me."

The skinny holdee lifted his eyes and met the queen's. Resignation had replaced terror in his.

"Why do you persist, holdee, in this behavior when you know it requires punishment?"

"O Queen, I suffer from a problem I can't control. Discussing it will change nothing. I would not waste the queen's time."

"I wish to hear, holdee."

The man inclined his head. "Yes, O Queen. I can't help myself. My actions on waking aren't under my control. I wake fighting and strike out. If someone is too close, she will be struck. It has always been so with me, even as a child. If I could stop, O Queen, I would. These punishments are terrible. I have no desire to strike my mistress. I do all I can to make her happy. This one thing I can't do. No punishment will change it. I have tried, O Queen, staying awake at night, waking before my mistress, but she disallows me. She says she has tried everything. This, O Queen, is not entirely true."

He ducked his head and glanced sideways at Tarkan, who reached for her truchon.

The queen raised her hand. "Allow the holdee to speak. If he verbalizes offense, I will consider that in his punishment."

Tarkan scowled but desisted.

The holdee continued. "I have begged my mistress, O Queen, to hit me with a stick, throw a pillow, anything. She insists upon touching me in my sleep. All she need do is awaken me otherwise. She would not be struck—and would have no need to punish me.

"O Queen, it isn't in my power to change this behavior." The holdee's chin thrust upward. "It isn't! When you punish me, O Queen, I ask only that you make it permanent. I can't bear living like this anymore."

The holdee ceased talking, dropped his head and awaited his fate.

Silence hung over the hall. A holdee had never before made such a request—to die instead of continuing as a holdee. This was new, interesting entertainment.

The queen sat back, and regarded the man. That tiny, formless niggle in her mind whispered, give the holdee to someone else and send Tarkan to locchot. A ridiculous thought. She squelched it.

"Tarkan," the queen said, "this holdee earlier received ten lashes with the strife paddle front and rear. That should have cured his behavior. He cannot yet have healed from those. If I add to that punishment, as I must, the extra lashes may kill him. Is that what you wish?"

"My Queen, I wish his behavior changed."

"Have you tried awakening him as he requested?"

"My Queen, I will not be ruled by a holdee. He can and will change his behavior. I wish queen's punishment."

"Very well. The holdee will receive—"

"My Queen, may I speak?" Aarvan's soft voice interrupted.

Gasps circulated through the hall. Tarkan, the holdee, the queen, even the heralda stared at Aarvan.

"Aarvan," the queen said with studied patience, "you may not interrupt your queen when she speaks."

"I apologize sincerely, My Queen, but I had to interrupt before you pronounced punishment."

"This is not your affair, Aarvan. You may not speak."

"I must insist, My Queen."

"Insist? You are queen's man. You do not insist. You will be silent!"

Aarvan's eyes locked with the queen's. They clashed for a long beat of time.

Every woman in the hall held her breath. No one argued with the queen in hearing. Certainly no man. This was most unexpected entertainment.

"No, My Queen, on this subject I won't be silent."

The queen stared into those calm, determined midnight blue eyes. She rose in one fluid motion, face set, spine rigid. "Heralda, pipe lunch. Tarkan, you will return after lunch to finish this hearing. Aarvan, come!" She stalked toward the door of her lunchroom.

Aarvan rose and walked behind her, face calm.

"At least she does not send him straight to the punishment room," Locin whispered to Patea as they followed.

"He goes too far," Patea said.

The queen halted halfway across the lunchroom and stood.

Aarvan stopped and waited.

Eight guards entered. At Locin's signals, four formed a semi-circle behind the queen's man. Four, including Patea and her, took positions to leap between the queen and queen's man if needed. Locin had not forgotten the beast.

The queen turned.

Aarvan stood relaxed, eyes and face revealing nothing.

Damn the man. How can he be so calm? What will break that composure, make him show proper respect for his queen? Fury seethed in Rejeena as a kettle boils. "I could not credit my ears in hearing. Do you not fear locchot, Aarvan?"

"I'd be a fool not to, My Queen."

"Then why do you strive to taste of it?"

"My efforts are toward fairness for that holdee."

"You are queen's man. Our fairness, laws, punishments are not your concern." The fury frothed wildly as heat waves pushed one another toward the surface of her skin. The queen's face flushed, her teeth clenched and a vein pulsed at her temple.

"Fairness must concern everyone, My Queen."

The queen walked close and struck him sharply on the chest with the heel of her hand.

He absorbed the blow, motionless, hands at his sides, eyes locked with hers.

Locin stepped forward, hand on sword hilt. *The queen stands so close and he is so fast. Oh LaSheena, keep that beast quiet.*

The queen's voice cracked as the snap of a bullwhip. "Aarvan, I have been more than patient with you, considered your condition. But you constantly try me. Today you interrupted your queen in hearing. No one may do so. I stood willing to excuse that, since your training is not complete. Then you flouted me, in public, in hearing, before my subjects. Deliberately, Aarvan. That cannot be mistaken. It is intolerable. I can no longer dismiss or overlook your blatant defiance and disobedience." The queen paused, sucking in deep breaths, eyes blazing.

Aarvan said softly, "My Queen, I regret that what passed between us was in public. I had to interrupt to gain your attention. I had to defy you in order to speak. A man's life could depend upon it."

"I have told you, this is not your concern. I will not hear your words."

"I've made it my concern, My Queen."

"You continue to defy me?"

"I'll do what's necessary to make you listen."

As a lidded pot, the fury bubbling in Rejeena's heart boiled over. Her voice quivered, hand thumped his chest again and again. She yelled, "You have just earned locchot, Aarvan. I am willing to wait until you are well and able to withstand it. But I swear by LaSheena, if you say one more word about this, you will taste of locchot today." She crossed her arms, chest heaving, green eyes skewering him.

Aarvan took a slow, deep breath, and considered his options. It didn't require much time. He seemed fated for locchot. *The queen and the law are so callously contemptuous of the simplest rights, the very life of the holdee. Who are these despotic women to decide men have no value? Rut them!* "I don't accept your order of silence. I'm a man, not a dog. I will be heard."

The queen glared.

Guards rolled their eyes at each other. The queen's man had leaped from the precipice.

Head back, chin lifted, the queen said, "Very well, Aarvan, say what you wish. Your queen will listen, then tell you the cost of your words."

He paused for a second. "My Queen, that woman is a targeetha. Her holdee has a problem he can't control. He offered her a simple solution, but she refuses to use it. She states she can't afford another holdee, then demands severe queen's punishment, which will likely kill him. The woman lies. She enjoys torturing him. Her problem has nothing to do with kruets. She doesn't want another holdee until she has completely destroyed this one."

His words echoed Rejeena's thoughts during hearing, but she held her face implacable.

He continued. "My Queen, that holdee tries to please his mistress. She can't . . . she won't be pleased. You saw his condition, beaten into submission and skinny as a wharf rat. She's made his life intolerable misery. He even asked you to put him to death to end her hold. That's the request of a man who has lost all hope, definitely not a man who could solve his problem. That woman doesn't want his problem solved. She wants to torture him under the guise of punishment until he dies. Then she'll seek another holdee that she can find excuse to punish."

"Is that it, Aarvan? You have said nothing I did not know."

A frown marred his features, his mouth tightened. "Then consider this, My Queen. I've accused your society of being merciless, unreasonable on certain subjects. But I've never felt that your actions and laws were based on cruelty without function. Each thing you do, each law, has a value, a purpose. It's a means to an end, necessary to maintain your society as you wish it.

"What this woman does to her holdee is not discipline or punishment. It's pure, unadulterated torture for her perverted pleasure. If you recognize this, My Queen, and you just said that you do, and you lend your queen's power to her brutal game—then you're no better than she is." He stood quiet.

Her green eyes and his midnight blue remained locked.

Aarvan waited. He realized he tested Queen Rejeena, tested her worthiness. *Worthiness for what?* He wasn't sure what he wanted from her. His mind remained cloudy, confused about his motives and expectations. *If only I could remember.*

"Is that all, Aarvan?"

"Yes, My Queen, that's all."

"Was voicing it worth the price?"

"You have not yet revealed the price."

"You will receive fifteen strokes with the kit paddle to be administered immediately."

Locin watched his muscles twitch and tighten. She drew her sword. *His beast spoke to him. The queen stood so close.*

Aarvan's stomach lurched and his muscles tightened. The queen acted as could be expected. The idea, now a reality, of being punished for simply speaking his mind sent conflicting hot and cold bursts rampaging through his chest. He thought of what he had seen of locchot. The skin flayed from the body, outraging those very sensitive nerves, the agony. *Can I bear it in silence?* The holdee had been unable to do so. *Does she think I'll be quiet, sink into the background if beaten? Who does she think she is? Who do they all think they are? To think they can punish me like a disobedient dog.*

The presence whispered. "*Attack. You can take them. Don't allow this.*" It told him exactly the actions he would be required to perform to defeat eight guards. As it explained, knowledge, memory but not quite memory, flowed into his conscious mind. He believed the voice, believed he could best eight guards—if his head injury didn't interfere. He understood finally the mayhem this rage, which lived within him, could create. The man in him answered. *I know we could, but I won't. There are eight; we'd have to kill. It's Locin, Patea, Tressa, guards simply doing their duty. I like them. I won't—I can't kill them. This time we have to do it my way.*

He had been apprised of the law, and chose to defy the queen, knowing the consequences. He would have to face those consequences, deal with his offended senses as best he could. For the sake of the holdee, he hoped his argument impressed the queen, though her frigid eyes and imperious stance didn't offer encouragement. *Will she pass my test?*

He sighed, looked at Locin with her drawn sword. "You won't need that, sharp or dull," he said.

Their eyes met and Locin sheathed the sword.

He inclined his head. "As you wish, My Queen."

"You will go now, Aarvan."

"Yes, My Queen." He turned and a guard reached for him. He growled, "Don't touch me. I know the way."

The guard dropped her arm.

All eight guards, at a signal from Locin, followed him. He had assured her he wouldn't harm the queen, but made no promises about guards.

He stopped and looked at the queen, who stood unmoving. "My queen will not watch?"

Her chin snapped higher. "Your queen chooses not to do so."

"So, my queen can find the anger to send me to locchot . . . but not the courage to watch?"

The green eyes blazed anew. "Very well, Aarvan, I will watch. You will receive five extra lashes for arrogance."

He stared at her for a tiny beat of time—*not exactly an angel*—then he half-bowed and exited.

* * *

Aarvan and the guards entered the punishment room.

Meitra glanced up from polishing the locchot. Her mouth quirked, then jerked into a comprehending grimace. There could be no mistake, as the queen's man arrived surrounded by guards, all grim and silent. Her countenance cleared to blandness and she faced Locin.

"Twenty with the kit," Locin said. "Rear only, of course."

Meitra walked to a cabinet, extracted an item and returned to the locchot. She had not been mocking, during his earlier, unpleasant visit to the punishment room, about padding the wrist holders so the metal would not tear his wrists. She smoothed padding around them.

Frigidity like a plunge into ice water flooded Aarvan's chest. Perhaps he should have visited a bathing room. He fervently hoped he wouldn't lose his bladder contents as the holdee had.

What am I doing here? Why should I allow this? It's wrong. I'm a man. I can speak my mind.

The presence responded, the rage roiling and swirling like a maelstrom held captive by his ribcage. "*It's not too late. You don't have to stay.*"

He quieted it. Nothing had changed, as guards still surrounded him. Choosing not to kill, he would have to stand and suffer the penalty. He closed his eyes and looked within. Strength and courage flowed from a hidden wellspring in his inaccessible past, not to the dangerous entity, but to the man.

Meitra turned, square, ugly face closed. No hint showed of the woman who teased him, explained things and shared grins. She stood a punishment meter, ready for function.

Patea reached for him. He said, "We wait for the queen."

The guard said in a gentle voice, "Queen's Man, you needs remove the vest and neck chain. I will hold them for you."

He shrugged from his vest, lifted the chain from his neck and handed them to her without a word. With these simple acts, preparing to receive a vicious beating, a hard mass rose in his throat almost choking him. The deadly rage clamored. "*Release me. Release me. I'll handle it.*" In his mind, from the dark halls where it prowled, it shoved, thrust, howled. For a moment, one heart skip of time—pulsing fear, scalding fury and bitter resentment pushing at him—he nearly capitulated; the rage nearly won. *No! We can't always kill.* He squelched that lethal side, clenching his fists tightly, shoulders bunching. His set face didn't reveal how closely disaster brushed.

Locin watched him intently. Though his face revealed no emotion, he clenched his fists. She remembered the ferocious beast that had stared at her, the speed of his downing strike on Tuuman. *Are eight guards enough? Is the queen having him punished—or is he allowing it?* Silly thought. No one man, even with his beast, could best eight queen's guards.

The queen strode into the room.

Without a word, before a guard could touch him, Aarvan walked to the locchot and dropped to his knees across the buried bar. Meitra fastened his legs. He raised his arms, placed his wrists in the holders. Guards locked him in.

From across the room, he clinched the queen's eyes in a fiery blue grip. He lifted the veil, allowed her to glimpse outrage, fury and resentment. *Let her know how I feel.* But he denied her any glimpse of the fear freezing his bones.

The queen walked closer, held eye contact. Hers remained veiled. She did not speak.

The guards wound the pulley handles, stretched his body. When he felt he could stretch no more, they stretched him more. He understood then why the holdee screamed. The over stretching agonized, but the knowledge of its purpose, more than the immediate physical pain, spiraled terror through his gut like a sardonic worm. He clenched his fists again and breathed in jerks. The presence lay quiet; but with his body securely fastened in the locchot, it couldn't help him now.

Aarvan sensed movement behind him and guessed Sercha handed Meitra the kit paddle. Bile and debilitating terror roiled in his belly. *If I yell for mercy, beg, will she stop the pain before it starts? No! She has no right to start the pain. Damn her to hell, I won't yell. I won't beg. Not even if they kill me.*

Meitra spoke. "Do you wish a respite in the middle, Queen's Man?"

His voice surprised him by its strength and coldness. "No, Mistress, just get it done."

He heard the swish of the paddle before it struck. He never imagined such pain. A thousand hornets drove their stingers into him. Despite his efforts, his muscles recoiled forward. He clamped his teeth tight to stop a bellow. Desperately he held eye lock with the queen. He would give her no satisfaction.

The second blow struck, too quickly, much worse. A white-hot iron branded him, flamed, drove the air from his lungs. His body arched. A gasp escaped as he snapped his teeth closed, contained a yell. He held tight to his eye lock with the queen. His head warned with its first stab; sharp darts raced up into his brain and down his back.

The third blow fell. It came too fast, white hot, stabbing. He grunted as it hit. His lungs froze in his chest, an indrawn breath slamming to a hurtful halt. Fiery shards lanced up his neck and down his spine. The shock to his system, being unable to move, more than his efforts, allowed him to hold the queen's eyes.

She stared at him, face rigid.

The fourth blow struck. It was easier to absorb, to manage. No more surprise, the intense agony expected. His mind control had adjusted. The paddle still tore at his skin with scalding teeth. He couldn't breathe. His head wanted to explode through his ears. He made no more sounds. He held the queen's green eyes, unwavering, without appeal, showing her only what he wanted her to see.

He lost track of the count. Blow after blow crashed onto his back. Each impact scorched as dragon's breath. The blows fell fast and hard. His head howled, a morass of screaming agony. His spine weakened, muscles trembled. He couldn't draw a single breath. His chest burned, lungs crying for air, but none came. Someone poured boiling oil down his back. They wouldn't stop.

Cold sweat trickled down him. *Why won't the sweat put out the fire?* The blows kept slamming. He had to hold the queen's eyes. He couldn't yell. His body jerked and lurched. Arm muscles and tendons stretched in ways they weren't meant to stretch, tearing. He still couldn't breathe.

The strokes fell like a rain of fire. The heat flaming from his back should have incinerated the building. His head blazed. It exploded off his neck. His spine twisted and sagged, useless, a long fiery, jellied rope. His muscles collapsed.

New agony spread through his chest. A fluttering, squeezing struggle. *My heart? No wonder, it had no air.* His chest heaved, trying to gulp air but couldn't. No breath, struggling heart, cold sweat—he wondered if he would die from twenty lashes. *Did they stop at twenty?* He had no idea. *It will serve her right if I die. All those kruets. Bitch. I hope she isn't completed.*

Strange, he couldn't decide which set of spinning queen's eyes to hold. He willed them be still but they kept spinning. Darkness closed over him, then lifted. He silently cursed his weakness. *I can't lose eye contact now. If I could just get one breath. It has to be almost over. Not now. Hang on. Breathe, please breathe.* His head shredded from his body. That boiling oil branded him, a stigma of uncommitted crime. His skin seared. The queen's eyes spun. His mind spun with them. Dizziness clouded his brain. *Hang on. Hold still. It has to be almost . . .* Blackness descended.

* * *

Rejeena watched Aarvan leave for the punishment room upon her edict, her face a set, cold mask, lips pressed together. Nausea churned behind her breastbone. Her beautiful queen's man, going to locchot. *Damn the man. He refuses to learn.* Why could he not be like other queen's men, follow the rules? Why did he so concern himself with the fate of some luckless holdee? What churned about in that head of his? *Why does he fight me, defy me at every turn?* He was so gorgeous, wonderful in skindown. He could make her so proud and happy. Why would he not so limit himself? Blast him. He manipulated her into watching him beaten in locchot. The ass. Sending him had been agony enough; she did not wish to watch. *But I am queen. I will show no weakness. Blast and damn him.*

His words haunted her . . . "if you lend your queen's power to her brutal game, then you're no better than she is." They rankled, because they rang true. *How many times have I been guilty? Is he right?* Tradition and her policy dictated she not interfere with her subjects and their holdees. *Blast him for forcing my thoughts against tradition. Blast him for an interfering ass. Blast him.*

A memory of killer eyes flickered. *Did I actually stand there and pound him on the chest*? Suppose he had reacted? He just stood there, absorbing her blows and her yelling. Had she actually seen those eyes? Were they real or a figment of imagination? If only LaHeeka were here so she could ask. LaHeeka would know. She clenched her eyes shut and shoved the thoughts away. *I am queen.*

She steeled her mind and walked to the door, said to a guard, "Have Alea prepare to treat the queen's man."

"Yes, My Queen." The guard curtsied out.

Rejeena hurried along Mainway and entered the punishment room.

Aarvan walked to the locchot and placed himself in it.

The targeethan. Even here he has to be an ass. That is not the way of it. A man does not go calmly to locchot. Always, guards must drag him.

His eyes lifted and locked with hers. He allowed her to see his seething emotions. She recognized fury, bitter resentment. What she did not see was fear. *He is a person. He must be terrified.* He watched the holdee suffer locchot. Surely, he could appreciate the force of pain about to descend upon him. If he felt fear, it did not show. He would fight her even now.

The queen walked closer, holding eye contact, hers cold, emotionless. *He will not have the satisfaction of seeing my conflict. He punishes me even as I punish him. He will not know how deeply it cleaves.*

Were twenty lashes too many? She applied the last five in anger. Twenty lashes would be solid punishment for a well man, but Aarvan was weak, head injury not healed. Should she remove the five? No, she would not, but would hold open the possibility. She could decide as the lashing proceeded. *When he submits, yields, I may then show mercy.*

Meitra spoke. "Do you wish a respite in the middle, Queen's Man?"

His voice rang strong, not a tremor. His eyes did not waver. "No, Mistress, just get it done."

Meitra, even as she swung her paddle, motioned to Sercha to grab another. They would go double on him, coordinating the strikes, each woman landing half the blows. He asked them to get it done, and Meitra would do just that.

Rejeena watched him closely as the first blow struck. His face twisted, jaw tightened, body lurched. He held eye contact, uttered no sound. *Blast him.*

The second blow struck and his body arched. She thought she heard a gasp. Those angry, resentful eyes remained steadfast.

At the third blow, his eye contact wavered, then reasserted. She heard him grunt. *Good. As the pain worsens, he will weaken, yield. Then I can stop it.*

He made no more sounds. The eye contact locked and stayed. His body and face reacted as the paddle blows rained, but he remained stubbornly silent.

No one else in the room made a sound. Normally, at punishments, women hurled catcalls, verbally tormented the punished, laughed and jeered. In contrast, the silence with this queen's man in locchot crackled with eeriness. Rejeena wanted to shiver. The only sounds heard—the swish of the paddles and the thud as they slammed into his back.

Would the stress of locchot affect his head? Could it seriously harm him? The blows continued to fall, and he continued to stare into her eyes. *Oh LaSheena, Aarvan show fear. Cry out. Yield. Give me a reason to stop it. I cannot unless you do. I am queen.* She could not show mercy—no, not mercy—weakness. She could not show weakness.

But he just absorbed the blows and held her eyes in their locked embrace.

Sweat popped out on his forehead, upper lip, trickled down his chest. Droplets of blood flew, splattered in grotesque patterns, chasing the swinging paddles as the beading flayed his skin. *Please, Aarvan, beg, even just ask and I will end it.* She recalled Alea's warning. How weak was he from the head injury? How vulnerable? How much could his body endure? What if he died in locchot? How could she explain to LaHeeka? She thought of cold, lonely nights in her skindown. *What if I am not completed?* She thought of never having daughters because she lost her temper with the queen's man LaSheena granted her. She thought of the horrific pain he silently suffered. Surely neither LaSheena nor LaHeeka would expect her to tolerate his disobedience and disrespect. *If only he will yield, just a little . . .*

She had not counted the blows, but they had passed fifteen. His eyes wavered, as though he sought to maintain contact but could not. Then his eyes blanked. He was not behind them anymore, not breathing. *Does he die right before my eyes?*

Three things happened simultaneously—she raised her hand to stop the beating, he slumped, the last paddle blow struck.

For an elongated second no one moved. Then Meitra slammed her paddle into the dirt, and fell to her knees beside the man she had beaten. She screamed, "Crank him down. Bring cooler. Grab a blanket. Move!"

Women moved.

The guards released him, and Meitra caught his limp body in her long, powerful arms. She held him above the dirt.

A guard flipped a blanket onto the ground. Meitra lowered him face down. Sercha raced to them with the cooler, wet and smelling of the natural vegetal, pain-killing secretions, which made it so effective. The punishment meters placed the thick, heavy wrap on his raw and bleeding back and gently turned him. Sercha fastened the ties and Meitra checked him. His heart beat, weak, erratic. His lungs, still, no breath. Meitra struck him a sharp blow just below the breastbone. The stored air burst from his lungs. He gulped and began to breathe, fast and shallow, but he breathed.

Two guards came running with a skin litter. They lifted him onto it and covered him.

"Take him to Alea quickly," Meitra said.

The guards, Locin leading, rushed out carrying the collapsed queen's man.

Meitra said, "Your queen's man suffered a perilous state, My Queen. I trust my actions were proper."

"You did exactly right, Meitra. I sent word ahead. Alea will expect him."

The queen jerked in several deep breaths, trying to loosen the tight thickness in the back of her throat. Her heart pounded in her chest, hands twisted her skirt material, arms muscles tight. She desperately yearned to run after him, enfold him in her arms, tell him how sorry she was, beg his forgiveness . . . *Great Goddess LaSheena . . .*

stop it, Rejeena, you are queen. He is but a man, just another damned man. How has he brought me to this juncture?

She motioned to Krystera, a young training guard, who appeared on the verge of tears. "Run . . ." Rejeena paused and coughed to clear her throat. "Go after Locin. Tell her to send word of his condition, as she is able. I must return to hearing. There is much to finish before I leave for Queens' Council."

"Yes, My Queen." Krystera curtsied out.

Queen Rejeena returned to hearing.

When she entered alone, gasps and sighs sounded in the hall. Though expected, and certainly the rightful duty of the queen, the thought of that gorgeous queen's man bearing the misery of locchot saddened many women. The queen had so recently, happily acknowledged him. He earned the punishment, though. No woman could deny that.

Dick, who sat with Tameera, moaned, "Oh, God."

Tameera squeezed his hand.

Tarkan strode forward, smiling as her eyes locked onto the empty cubicle of the queen's man.

The queen stared. This woman indeed stood a targeetha, disgraceful, practiced cruelty for its own sake, unfitted for good woman status. To lend her use of the queen's power was to share with her. Queen Rejeena would not share with such a one.

Tarkan curtsied and smiled. Her holdee dropped to his knee, head lowered.

"Tarkan," the queen said, "I will make no decision today. Return the day after tomorrow for another hearing time. Meanwhile, since queen's punishment has been requested, you may not punish this holdee for the offense presented at hearing. Is this understood?"

"Yes, My Queen." Tarkan looked perplexed and disappointed, but yielded with fair grace, curtsied and retreated with her holdee.

* * *

Locin stayed with the queen's man while Alea and Wecan treated him. They placed him on his belly, raised his feet, covered him and monitored his heart and breathing. The cooler would numb the agony on his back, thus lessening the life stress to his system.

Time passed without change, but finally his heart began to beat stronger, more regular. His shallow breathing deepened.

Locin sent Krystera to the queen to inform her.

Aarvan drifted in and out of consciousness, though never fully aware, for hours. Once Alea roused him enough to give him painkiller for his head. His condition improved. Again, Locin sent Krystera with word to the queen.

Late in the day, vastly improved, he drifted into a deep sleep.

"Good," Alea smiled at Locin, "he rests. It is what he needs. You may tell the queen he has passed immediate danger."

* * *

Rejeena arrived at the healer's home after hearing. "How is he, Alea?"

"He rests, My Queen. We will not know until he awakes if he suffers head damage."

"Surely not, he rests so well."

"You took a big chance, My Queen. You let temper override good sense."

"Yes, and of that I am not proud." Rejeena sank into a chair. "The outlaws' escape infuriated me. My queen's man paid the price. Women would not dare speak to me as he does. He picked the wrong day to be an ass."

She leaped to her feet, moving restlessly around the room. "He will not learn his place. He is maddening. He deserved it. He argued with me in hearing, in public, before my subjects. He refused to be silent. He was arrogant and disobedient beyond belief. I had to apply discipline, Alea."

"No doubt, My Queen." Alea's voice gentled. "You do have other options besides locchot. With his head injury, twenty . . . any lashes, were too many."

"I know that now. I would gladly have stopped the lashing if he had submitted. He would not, just stared at me with angry eyes." Rejeena plopped into a chair.

Alea glanced at her sideways. "Had the lashing not begun, there would have been no need to stop it."

Rejeena sighed. She stared without seeing out a window, lips pursed. "LaHeeka warned me Aarvan would be a trial, and he is so."

"Perhaps you needs find a path to tolerance with him."

"I cannot. He may not argue with me in public. I will not have it. He must learn to accede to his queen's wishes."

"I fear Aarvan is not the only one who holds stubborn above wisdom."

"I am queen."

"If you kill this man, you will remain a lonely queen, without daughters."

Rejeena rose, walked to Aarvan's still form and knelt beside him. She gently touched the side of his face. Her heart lurched against her ribs. His face was ghostly pale. He looked so ill. *Oh LaSheena, what if the beating caused more damage to his head? What if he should wake witless or not at all?* His head injury had caused the collapse. Twenty lashes would not threaten the life a well man.

She looked up at Alea. "I sincerely wish I could muster more patience, stand less quick to jump to the punishment option."

"Patience can be learned, My Queen."

Rejeena arched a brow. "You do not sound sympathetic, Alea."

Alea stared at the queen. "We have known each other, been friends for many seasons, My Queen. Since childhood. You know that I love you as I do my mother and daughters. But just now I do not think I like you much."

Rejeena looked away, fingers plucking at her raiment. She murmured, "At this moment, nor do I."

The queen retook her chair and they sat in silence for a bit. Then Rejeena, voice once more brisk, asked, "Alea, do you truly believe he bears more injury?"

"I honestly cannot say. The cooler and medicine have removed his pain. His heartbeat and breathing have returned to normal. He sleeps deeply and well. His recuperative powers amaze me."

Alea's words gave the queen a great surge of hope. Things would be all right. She lowered her head and gritted her teeth. She must be queen, first and last, strong, unyielding. She could show no weakness, and concern for the queen's man would be weakness. Her heart breaking with the pain that Aarvan would experience and that she would cause herself, she rose. "Alea, I must insist my next edict be followed."

"And that is, My Queen?"

"As soon as danger to life has passed, you will remove cooler and give him medicine only to sustain life."

"My Queen, he is queen's man. It is proper and traditional for him to remain in cooler after locchot. His recovery will be much more pleasant."

"He acted with extreme disobedience and disrespect."

"And you punished him."

"He remained unrepentant and stubborn until he passed out. When he will admit he acted wrongfully and apologize to his queen, he may wear cooler. Until then, he will suffer all the pain locchot has to offer."

"Oh, My Queen, I plead with you—"

"Alea, do it. It will not endanger him, and he will learn."

"Yes, My Queen."

Rejeena walked to the door. "I trust arrangements have been made for his care during the night?"

"Of course. He will have two healers with him and Locin arranged for guards."

Rejeena returned to her home, shoved dinner around her plate and retired. She lay on her skindown, back turned to his side. It did not help. The empty space yawned as though she could see it. It had to be imagination, but she shivered with a biting cold. She reached to touch his space, trying to recall his warmth. She wanted him to make love to her, work that mind-bending magic on her body. Even more, she wanted his trim, muscular body beside her. *Oh LaSheena, what is he doing to me? I am Queen Rejeena, a Queen of Kriiscon. This cannot be allowed.*

She leaped from skindown and paced the floor, willing him from her mind. The targeethan had shared her life and skindown for less than half a moonchange. How had he acquired such a hold on her?

She dressed and went to her home function room, tried to work and glared at any guard or servant who cracked a knowing smile. Concentration eluded her. Fiery midnight blue eyes glared from her desktop. His weakened body collapsing under the agony of locchot, his face so still and pale, haunted her. She squeezed her eyes shut, imagined the damage locchot might have rendered to his head. Her body flushed, heat pushing against her skin from inside. She thought about the pain he would suffer from her newest edict. *He must submit. I cannot bear his anguish. The instant he yields, I will send him cooler.*

She arose, went outside and sat on a cold stone bench for a long while. Finally she returned to her skindown and fell into an exhausted sleep.

* * *

Aarvan awoke slowly, disoriented. He lay on his stomach, left side propped up, holding him from lying face first in the pillow. His head ached, dull, steady and his back stung like nettle burn. He moved his left arm and every muscle and tendon from wrist to shoulder protested.

Gorsa's face appeared over him. "Alea, his eyes are open." She smiled. "Good morning, Aarvan."

"Morning," he croaked past a dry throat. He remembered locchot.

Alea's worried face peered over Gorsa's shoulder. "How do you feel?"

"Badly mistreated."

Gorsa grinned. "He makes gibes. He is better."

Alea asked, "Are you in pain?"

"Just all over."

"It will grow worse. The queen denied you cooler and the strong pain medicine. As the present medicine ebbs, your pain will increase greatly."

"Thank you for telling me that," he said dryly. "What's a cooler?"

Alea sat in front of him. "It is something you should know. When the pain increases, you will not be surprised. Cooler is a pad filled with dried herbs. Wetted and placed on your back, it numbs the pain of locchot and disallows your wounds to turn septic."

He displayed a twisted grin. "That's what the queen denied me?" At her nod, he asked, "Did she give a reason?"

"You needs ask the queen."

"Suppose I turn septic? She could lose her investment."

"You wear a back pad saturated with secretions to prevent that, but it kills no pain." She sighed. "I warned you. You do not listen . . ."

"Alea, please don't scold me. I think that's been done."

"You are right." She helped him drink water. "Are you hungry?"

His contorted face gave her answer enough.

"Then you must rest."

He closed his eyes, relaxed, tried to ignore the pain. He needed to rest while he could. He dozed fitfully.

That voice like a rusty hinge, speaking to Alea, jolted him awake.

He looked up. "Come to check on your handiwork, Meitra?"

"I am most pleased to hear you sound so saucy," she chuckled. "Clearly, we did you no great harm. And pretty Queen's Man, I need not check on my handiwork. I can describe to you how and where each blow landed."

"Please don't." He yielded with a waggle of fingers. "I felt them. That's enough, thank you."

Meitra sat before him. "If it is of any comfort, I derived no pleasure from introducing you to locchot."

He slanted an eyebrow. "I truly regret causing you to lose pleasure in your function. I know what joy it gives you."

"Your sarcasm is noted. Perhaps next time I will enjoy myself."

Alea leaned over him. "Aarvan, you should not so plague Meitra. She is credited with saving your life. You stopped breathing. Meitra had wits enough to strike you and start you breathing again."

"Oh great," he growled, "she beats the breath out of me, then smacks me to save the queen's investment. And I'm supposed to say thank you?"

Meitra laughed. "Pretty Queen's Man, if you badger the queen as you do others, I wonder she waited this long to have you visit me."

"I don't badger the queen."

"Oh? Then why did she send you to locchot?"

"My queen and I don't always see eye to eye."

"You had best then change the perspective of *your* eye."

"You're starting to sound like Alea."

"Is that bad?"

Alea said, "He does not credit the voice of reason."

"Stop tormenting the queen's man," Gorsa said from behind him. "He suffers pain."

Meitra rose. "I will torment him no more. I am satisfied, contrary as he acts, he will be fine."

Alea saw Meitra to the door.

The punishment meter left, and Locin and Patea entered.

Locin stood with arms crossed and stared down at Aarvan from her full height. "You truly made a spectacle of yourself this time, Arrogant Pup."

"It appears to be my special skill."

"You needs curb your tongue. Whatever inspired you to speak so to the queen?"

"Where I come from, men speak their minds."

Locin dropped to her knees, pushed a finger against the tip of his nose. "Listen to me carefully. Perhaps my words may penetrate that hard head. You are now on Kriiscon. You may not argue with, defy and challenge the queen."

"Did I do all that?"

"Yes, and you well know it."

"I had good reason."

"And your good reason acquired for you locchot. Was it enjoyable?"

"No."

"Then, Queen's Man, cease acting an ass. Be respectful and obey the queen."

"You ask too much—and she asks too much."

"I fear he is hopeless, Locin," Alea said. "His head is thick as a centenary tree trunk, and he strives to have his way, no matter the cost."

"Undoubtedly you are right." Locin rose. "We brought you a gift, Queen's Man."

"A cooler, I hope."

"That is between you and the queen. We brought these." She took from Patea a clay pot, from which grew a spindly green plant sagging with huge purple flowers.

Aarvan blinked. *Flowers*? Then noting how pleased she looked, he said, "They're beautiful. Thank you."

"They are more than flowers, Queen's Man." Patea peered around Locin. "Their fragrance induces sleep. It will not lessen the pain, but will encourage rest despite the hurt."

He winked. "All this time, Patea, I thought you didn't care."

"Ass." She grinned.

"Locin," he said, as she placed the flowers near his head, "what did the queen decide about the holdee?"

"What holdee?"

"You know very well what holdee. The one that belongs to that targeetha, Tarkan."

"Oh, that holdee. You best ask the queen."

"It's hardly a secret, is it? She decides in open hearing."

"The queen punished you in connection with that decision. I cannot possibly guess what she does or does not want you to know about it."

"What harm is there in telling? She hasn't told you not to, has she?"

"I will not anger my queen and follow you in locchot. You stand arrogant, hardheaded and think yourself wiser than the queen, consider your willfulness worth the pain of locchot. I do not agree. Even without threat of locchot, I would not tell you. I do not displease my queen."

"Well then, could you go in the corner and discuss it with Alea. I'll pretend I'm sleeping."

"No, I will not. Since you will act an ass, we shall leave. I hope those flowers render you ill."

"You're an unkind woman," he said as she and Patea walked away. When she reached the door, he called softly, "Locin?"

She turned. "Yes, Queen's Man."

"Did you bring your dull knife, Shiira Guardswoman?"

Locin returned, and glared at his prickly grin. She planted fists on hips. "If so, Arrogant Pup, I should be tempted to use it."

"That would hardly please the queen."

The line leader dropped to one knee, poked his arm with a finger. "When you have recovered, I will indeed take you over my knee."

"Which attempt will still end with pieces of you scattered up and down Mainway."

"It would require ten times your scrawny self for the function." She gently cupped his chin in one hand, gray eyes growing warm. "I hope the flowers help, Queen's Man. It was all we could do."

His eyes warmed in return. "Thank you."

"Now get some rest." She reverted to her usual half-command, half-banter voice as she arose. "The queen will likely visit during lunch. If you behave properly, she may allow you cooler."

"It's not lunch yet?"

"No, Queen's Man."

He groaned and closed his eyes.

The guards departed.

"Aarvan, where did you learn that word?" Alea asked.

"What word?"

"Targeetha."

"I just picked it up."

"It is not appropriate for a man to so call a woman. The queen could become angry."

"I used it yesterday in front of her."

"And consider what she did to you yesterday. I suggest you use it no more."

"Aarvan," Gorsa said, "the term targeetha roughly converts to bitch in Universal."

"That pretty well describes Tarkan."

"Aarvan!" Alea heaved a sigh. "Oh, go to sleep."

Aarvan closed his eyes and relaxed. The purple flowers reeked with a piquant, almost peppery aroma, stimulating his senses but causing a general torpor to steal over him at the same time. *What an odd sensation, what peculiar flowers. If there is something strange to be found, these women will.* Though the pain in his back and head increased, he dozed, drifting in and out of sleep.

* * *

Voices lifted in anger roused Aarvan from slumber. He recognized Alea's.

"I am his healer and I say you will not disturb the queen's man. I do not know that he would wish to see you."

"Nor do you know that he does not, healer," a voice snapped back, one he should recognize but for the fog swirling in his head.

"The queen's man sleeps. I will not awaken him for allway women."

"So that is it? We are but allway women. We are queen's subjects as well as you."

The fog cleared. "Balstra?"

"Yes, Aarvan. Tell this obscenity of a healer to let us pass."

"It's all right, Alea," Aarvan called. "She's a friend."

"You have strange friends, Aarvan." Alea stepped aside.

Balstra, wearing a grin, walked into sight. Areva followed her, carrying another pot of the large purple flowers.

Two guards followed closely.

He smiled at Balstra and Areva but spoke to the guards. "If seegarpt, like Mistress Meitra and guards are allowed unescorted, so will be allway women. Get out of here."

The chastened guards backed away, but remained in sight.

"What are you doing here," he asked the vendors, "lowering your standards?"

Balstra sat before him. "Yes, well, Aarvan, sometimes we must do so when our friends consort with queens and whatnot."

Areva, holding the flowers, said, "We thought we brought you something special, Queen's Man, but it appears others did as well."

"Thank you. I appreciate the thought. Put it with the other. Maybe together they'll knock me out for a few days."

Balstra lowered her voice. "When we heard the queen denied you cooler, we thought you might need them."

Aarvan blinked. "Does everyone know the queen's concerns?"

"Few secrets exist in Rejeena's Towne." Areva placed the flowerpot and dropped beside Balstra.

"We slipped away when Alaestrea did not see," Balstra chuckled. "She boiled with outrage when she heard the queen sent you to locchot. We nearly had to bind her to her bench." The vendor lowered her voice. "She proposed to visit hearing and severely upbraid, and I use her verbiage—that silly, ignoramus, upstart of a queen."

Aarvan laughed, then groaned. "Oh, Balstra, don't make me laugh. I can picture Alaestrea doing that, but if she talks as fast as usual, the queen wouldn't understand a word."

All three laughed, Aarvan's collapsing into a groan.

Balstra's eyes narrowed. "Where is your neck chain?"

He waved a hand. "I had to take it off. It's around here somewhere."

"If a guard did not slicker it. That piece is valuable."

A guard said, "Queen's guards do not slicker things, vendor. We leave such to allway women. The healer has the chain."

"It best find its way back to his neck. That was a gift to the queen's man."

"Balstra," Aarvan said, "no one will take the chain. Queen's guards don't slicker things."

"If you say so." She glowered at the guards. "We must not stay long. You need to rest. We wanted to bring you the flowers and remind you that you have friends on Mainway."

"Thank you for coming. You've made my day brighter. Please give Alaestrea a hug for me. Tell her to stay away from the queen. I'll heal."

"Restrain yourself, Aarvan, so the queen need punish you no more," Balstra said. "It grieves me to see you thus."

"I'll be fine. The queen can't afford to kill me. I cost too much."

The two women departed.

"Honestly, Aarvan, the friends you have," Alea said.

"What's wrong with them?"

"They are allway vendors. It is not fitting for a queen's man to be so friendly with such."

"Hogwash."

"I am surprised Locin allows you such company."

"Locin doesn't object to my friendships, nor does the queen," Aarvan said. "In any case, I won't be told who to have as friends. I didn't realize you're such a snob."

Alea dropped to her knees before him. "I am sorry, Aarvan, but I worry about you. You are so handsome, and allway women can be vicious."

He looked at her sideways from those deep blue eyes. "Alea, it's not my allway friends who give me problems. I wasn't sent to, escorted to, or beaten in locchot by allway women. No allway vendor has tormented me at dinner to make my queen furious with me. Nor have they called me an idiot and told me to go back to the queen's skindown where I belong. My times with them have been more pleasant than with my upper-crust associates. So if you don't mind, I don't care to discuss it further."

"I am sorry, Aarvan."

His eyelids drooped.

Alea arose, allowing him to sleep.

Gorsa looked at Alea and said, "I think you have been censured."

"It would appear so."

* * *

Aarvan woke to the queen's husky voice. He couldn't see her, but caught part of Alea's answer.

". . . is better, My Queen. He has been flippant with his visitors. He recovers well, as usual faster than I expected, but suffers pain."

"Visitors?"

"Yes, a cavalcade. Your queen's man is favored of many," Alea said. "Meitra visited to inquire after his health."

"Meitra?" The queen chuckled. "Most surprising. Who else?"

"Some of your guards."

"Locin, of course."

"And Patea. The last were allway women he declared friends."

"I see my queen's man garners a following. I suppose it should not surprise me. He is intensely attractive."

"Yes, My Queen, though his attraction cleaves deeper than outward appearance. Were I not his healer, I would have been among his visitors."

"Now it is my turn," the queen said. She stopped and looked at the purple flowers. "Maascan blooms? I see women try to circumvent the full force of punishment."

"Your guards and the allway women," Alea admitted.

Aarvan heard the rustle of skirts. They entered his sight. He lifted his eyes and met the queen's. "I'm not sure of the rules, My Queen. Am I to rise and bow?"

"I think that will not be necessary, Aarvan."

"Thank you."

She flipped her large green skirt and sat before him.

Alea vanished.

The queen studied him.

He returned her gaze, waiting, feeling foolish lying with his face half buried in the pillows. He had tried moving though, and found the experience agonizing.

"You do not display anger, Aarvan."

"Should I, My Queen?"

"Usually those who have tasted of locchot are angry."

"Would anger solve the difficulties between us?"

"No, it would not." She heaved a sigh and her eyes flickered. "I did not enjoy having you punished."

"I hadn't thought that you did." *Was that regret I detected just now? Maybe . . . maybe not.*

"Your actions were intolerable. You allowed me no choice."

"Sometimes, My Queen, having a choice is a matter of choice."

She lifted an eyebrow. "You speak riddles."

"I know that you do as your laws and traditions require, as you perceive to be correct. Sometimes I have to do what I feel is correct, even when our outlooks are opposite. On Kriiscon, I don't have the power to enforce my will. You do. As for choices, My Queen, you may always choose to try to see my point of view."

"Your point of view was not the problem, Aarvan. Your interrupting your queen in hearing, arguing in public and refusing to be silent, comprised the problems."

"My Queen, you reduced my choices to nothing. You make your decisions and proclaim them immediately. I chose to interrupt you, trying to save a holdee who didn't deserve punishment and death."

"When I told you it was not your affair, to be silent?"

"I still had the same choice."

"You made your choice."

"Yes, My Queen, I did. Now I suffer for it."

"But you are not angry?"

"I am angry. I'm furious about your laws and traditions, the way they allow no rights to holdees, strip men of their dignity and . . . and standing as persons."

"You are not angry with your queen for punishing you?"

"I've been told of your laws and traditions. I violated them. Rather than hold anger, I'd seek compromise."

Rejeena sat straighter, clasped her hands in her lap. "Queens do not compromise with men. It is neither necessary nor desired." She smiled, a sly grimace. "You were angry in locchot."

"Mostly I was offended."

"Offended, Aarvan?"

"Yes, offended. I am a grown man. I have opinions, needs and I believe myself to have certain . . . privileges as a person . . . rights. I am not a child to be punished upon the whim of another, not even my queen. Certainly not for simply speaking my mind."

"As you so stated, Aarvan, we have laws and traditions. You must learn to live by them."

"My Queen, I can't always do that. If you intend to send me to locchot every time I speak my mind, you'd best have Meitra engrave my name on the handle of one of her paddles."

"I would think that after tasting of locchot, you would be most cautious about speaking your mind."

He stared at her for a moment in silence. "There is worse pain than locchot."

She cocked her head. "For instance?"

"Kowtowing, living in fear, allowing wrongs without objection . . . being a coward, not a man. That would be far worse."

"The purpose of locchot, Aarvan, is to convince you to deny thoughts such as you just expressed. I fear you have learned nothing."

"Certainly not what you wished me to learn, My Queen."

"It would so appear." Rejeena studied him for a moment. "You seem to be using Oldenspeak very well."

"Lateean is relentless."

The queen took a deep breath and unclasped her hands. "I offer you the opportunity of redemption, My Queen's Man. We have much to accomplish in the upcoming days. You will join me in hearing tomorrow. Afterwards we must attend a dinner. You will also share skindown with your queen. In two days we begin the journey to Queens' Council. It is my desire to have you in cooler. Your activities will be much more comfortable. With or without cooler, you will perform these functions. Your level of comfort stands as your next choice."

"What must I do for redemption?"

"You will admit you stand entirely wrong, your words and deeds completely inappropriate and askew, apologize to your queen, and assure your queen that you will neither interrupt nor argue with her again."

Aarvan dropped his gaze to the soft doeskin on which he lay. The queen needn't see what he feared might show in his eyes. *Definitely not an angel. Damn her. Damn her to Hell.* The dragon's breath on his back steadily burned hotter. Oh, to have that cooler quench it, to be able to lie here and truly sleep.

That skinny holdee's only crime had been to be born male. What was wrong with these women—with the queen? Some of the women were raving bitches. The others supported them. All practiced harsh cruelty as though it were normal. Slavery? Most of the world had abandoned it. For good reason. It twisted the souls of all, slaves and slaveholders alike. Why couldn't they see how wrong it was? *Blast it, why can't she see?*

He risked a glance at the queen. She sat quiet, awaiting his answer. Either she must change her outlook or, when able to do so, he would change his abode. He couldn't stay here watching silently while men suffered, and he wouldn't be beaten every time he objected. The presence surged within him, and a certainty pervaded his mind. He didn't have to stay nor tolerate beatings. With a healed body and intact mind, he and the rage could cut through Shabet's defenses like a fresh-honed scythe through soft summer grass.

He looked at the queen's green skirt, a small foot and shapely ankle showing. A giant hand gently squeezed his heart. Molten fire that was no part of anger flashed through him. If he could, he'd rise, flip that skirt over her head and rut her until she screamed surrender.

Damn her. She will make me do all those activities. Without the cooler, it'll be ceaseless agony. She knows that, is depending upon it to bring me to heel. She and her blasted locchot can both go rot in the darkest hole.

He lifted his eyes. Voice soft, without anger, he said, "I apologize to my queen for any embarrassment or discomfort my actions may have caused her. However, my thoughts and actions were not wrong, not inappropriate nor askew. I won't say that they were. I can't promise it won't happen again, because it likely will, and such a promise would be dishonest."

The queen's hands clenched again in her lap. "I am most sorry to hear that, Aarvan. I dared hope you would be sensible. As the day progresses, you may wish to reconsider. Until you walk into hearing, you may change your mind. If you do, Alea will so inform me. If you continue with this stubborn stance, once hearing begins, you have doomed yourself to recover in misery. Is that clear?"

"Yes, My Queen, quite clear."

"Very well. I must return to hearing. You need not rise as I leave. However, after this you will accord your queen proper respect."

"Yes, My Queen. May I ask a question?"

"Of course," she said, as she rose.

"What punishment did you give Tarkan's holdee?"

She looked at him speculatively. "I do not believe you need to know that just yet. Your decision must not be affected by that knowledge."

"I made my decision. I took a beating over yours. I feel I have the right to know."

"We will see if you hold to your path. You will be told my decision when I deem you should know." The queen departed.

* * *

The afternoon droned along on sloth claws. The dragon breathing on Aarvan's tortured back continuously stoked its fire. As time dragged, the fiendish dragon breathed hotter and hotter. When necessary body functions or aching joints forced movement, the dragon fanned the flame to scorching intensity. As though in sympathy, his head ached dully then sprang to sharp pounding with movement. When he lay still again, each time the headache took longer to return to its former dullness. Unable to even doze through most of the afternoon, despite the double pots of maascan blooms, Aarvan lay there in misery.

A shift of position to relieve pressure on an aching hip caused the fire like molten wax to pour onto his back, staying and searing. He snapped his teeth together. Cymbals clanged between his ears. The combined agony of head and back was unbearable. His lungs stilled and for a few moments he couldn't breathe. He lifted a hand to call Alea, then dropped it as he dragged in a small gulp of air. He breathed in short, sharp gasps until his mind could function again.

Why didn't he call for the cooler, quench that fire? Ask for the pain draught, quiet the cymbals? Sink into blessed oblivion. Sleep. Why be so stubborn? Whatever the queen decided about the holdee, it was done. His lying here like an idiot in pain wouldn't change that.

The holdee . . . neither he nor Aarvan had done wrong. They suffered, not for crimes, but because they were cursed with the wrong gender at birth. Giving in, submitting would validate the women's wrongful laws and traditions. *Blasted if I'll be guilty of that!* He clenched his fists, causing more pain, but focusing his resolve. *I will call for no cooler.*

Deep in the afternoon a rumbling voice said, "Well, ain't you just a purty sight. Like I said, Queen's Man, all guts, no brains."

"Dick?"

"Yeah, boy, it's me." Dick sat in front of Aarvan, lips twisted in sympathy. He placed a third pot of maascan flowers. "Tammy sent them. How you doin'?"

"I hurt."

"Yeah, I know. Been there."

"You have?"

"Yeah, had a bad mistress onct." The big man shrugged. "Whyn't you give in, make the queen happy, get the cooler?"

"I can't do that."

"Stubborn. What's the deal anyways?"

Aarvan sighed. "I have until tomorrow morning to refute my entire view of life and my manhood, subject myself to her total domination. If I do that, she'll let me wear the cooler."

Dick grumbled, "Don't seem hardly worth it."

"It's not."

"Pretty sneaky, that queen."

"How's that?"

"Givin' you 'til mornin'. I'm gonna tell you what these women won't. I bin there. Know how it works. You're gonna suffer the miseries of Nether this afternoon and tonight. 'Bout tomorrow mornin' it'll start to taper off. Tomorrow'll be better'n today. Each day it'll be better, and in about a week you'll be in fair shape. Don't get me wrong." Dick waggled a finger. "You're in for a few miser'ble days, but it'll get better." He chuckled. "Queen figures if you think you're gonna keep sufferin' miser'ble like this, you'll give in."

Aarvan grinned despite his pain. "Thanks for the tip, Dick. It makes a big difference. What is the miseries of Nether?"

"Nether is Kriiscon for Hell, I guess. Way they use it anyways. Figured the tip would help. We can't let these bossy women have all the advantages, now can we?"

"Absolutely not. I'm glad we met."

"So'm I. There's too many like Tuuman and Billy. Path don't cross much with reg'lar holdees. When it does, found 'em not real friendly, 'round Tameera's Towne anyways. Can get pretty lonely. Knowin' you got a buddy, even if he lives a ways off, helps."

"No doubt you're right."

"Listen, boy, don't wanna sit here yakkin' if it's gonna make you more miser'ble." Dick peered at Aarvan. "I can go."

"No. Talking to you helps. I can't sleep. You give me something to think about besides how much I hurt."

"Good." The big man relaxed. "Gotta question. Tell me, while you're layin' there burnin', if the same thin' happened, would you do it again?"

Aarvan squeezed his eyes shut, thought, opened them and said, "Yeah."

A great laugh rolled from Dick's chest. "Figured that'd be your answer." He cocked his head. "Worth it, huh?"

"I'm not sure." Aarvan frowned. "No one will tell me what the queen decided."

"Ask the queen?"

"Yes, but she won't say, and she won't let anyone else tell me."

"Our queen is sneaky." Dick chuckled.

"How so?"

Dick leaned close, whispering. "If them women find out who told you, I'll be on a pallet beside you. Can you keep it hushed?"

"Yes. I just want to know."

"Queen didn't make no decision. She told Tarkan to return tomorrow, and not to be doin' no punishment 'til then."

"What's she up to?"

"Don't know."

Aarvan's dark brows lowered. "I'll be at hearing tomorrow. Is she giving me another chance to earn locchot?"

"Don't know. Was you, wouldn't rise to the bait." Dick's face scrunched. "She makin' you 'tend hearin' tomorrow?"

"Yes, dinner and skindown, too." Aarvan gave him a lopsided grin.

Dick winced. "Woman knows no mercy. With us traveling in two days, you'd think she'd let you rest. You're goin', ain't you?"

"Oh yes. My queen will make the next few days as pleasant as possible for me."

"Skindown, huh?" Dick grimaced. "Way you feel, think you can get it up?"

"Did you?"

"Wasn't asked to. Can't help there."

"Well, I'd best be able to. If not, the queen will probably have the guards strap sticks to the side of it." Both men laughed, Aarvan's face twisting.

The queen's man frowned. "Suppose the queen waits to see what I do before she decides about the holdee. If I don't give in, it shows I'm serious, so she lets the holdee off lightly. If I do give in, I was being an ass, so she punishes the holdee." His eyes widened as they met Dick's. "Worse yet, suppose it's the other way around. If I give in, she shows the holdee mercy. If I don't, she punishes me again by punishing him. Blast, what if she makes me watch." He groaned aloud.

Dick contemplated the possibilities. "Think I'm sorry I told you."

"I think I'm sorry I know."

"You listen to me, boy." Dick gently poked Aarvan's arm. "You can't second-guess the queen. You did your best for that holdee. Now do what's right for you."

Aarvan heaved a weary sigh. "I guess it's all I can do."

"Healer's givin' me a dirty look," Dick said. "I'd best go."

Despite the jab from protesting tendons, Aarvan grabbed the big man's wrist as he rose. "Dick . . . thanks. You're a good friend."

"I'm the one ahead for it."

Aarvan released him and he left.

Alea appeared. "Do you plan more visitors, Aarvan, or will you rest?"

"I'm not resting much anyway."

"I wish I could do more for you." She knelt and stroked his face; her gaze flicked away and back again. "You could help yourself."

"The price is too high."

"Oh, Aarvan, you are so stubborn." She pinched the centers of the purple flowers.

He gave her a questioning look.

"It releases more of the sedative effect."

"You're a soft-hearted thing, Alea."

"I am a healer. It is my function."

He smiled and closed his eyes. His task now was to endure. From the back of his mind, thoughts flowed. *It's only pain. It hurts but it will go away. I've endured before; I can again.*

As Dick promised, the pain deepened steadily through the afternoon and into the evening. The healers came and went, changed shifts, one always within easy call. He vaguely noted as Locin and Patea replaced the pots of purple flowers with fresh ones. They didn't bother him and he didn't speak. Once he heard the queen's husky voice, but she didn't speak to him either. He ignored them all, lying quietly, bearing the grinding, incessant pain.

Late into the evening, the fire reached a plateau. It didn't cool but it flamed no hotter. His dragon had done its worst. As long as he lay motionless, his shoulders and arms just ached. The pounding in his head leveled to a steady throb.

A flood of triumphant, savage glee engulfed him. *I will endure. You won't win, My Queen . . . my not quite an angel.* The rest of the night seemed easier.

* * *

Gorsa's voice pulled Aarvan to wakefulness. He opened his eyes and stared blearily at her and Wecan. *Did I actually sleep?*

"Aarvan, I am sorry, but you needs rise. We must prepare you for hearing."

He grimaced.

"We will do all," Gorsa said firmly, "bathe you, change your back pad, shave you, comb your hair. You will not argue. We promise not to tease. If Wecan so much as grins lewdly, I will throw her out and call another."

"I'll not argue, Gorsa, except I'll bathe myself." Slowly, carefully he rose to a sitting position, to knees, then feet, walking stiffly. Dick had stated fact. The pain, though great, was not debilitating. Yesterday, he hadn't been able to visualize surviving a day involving movement. Today he knew he could, but the pain would render him miserable. *The queen uses strategy. I just have to counter her.*

Gorsa and Wecan proved true to their word. They allowed him privacy to bathe his manly parts, helped him dress, shave, comb his hair, and replaced his back pad. Neither teased nor made remarks. They produced a large vest, which covered the back pad and most of the straps. Still, anyone could see he had been to locchot. They found his silver chain and placed it around his neck.

"Thanks," he said. "I wouldn't dare be seen without it. Alaestrea would start a riot."

Gorsa laughed. "You possess too much charm, Aarvan."

"Then tell me how to work it on the queen."

"That you will have to determine. Are you hungry? We have breakfast coming."

He made a face, but ate breakfast and felt better. It didn't help the pain, but it strengthened his quaking knees.

Locin appeared with three guards. "We come to collect you, Queen's Man. I brought enough help so, if you faint, we can carry you."

"You're so kind, but I'll not put you to all that trouble." He carefully rose.

Locin walked around him. "You do not look bad, Arrogant Pup, having tasted of locchot with no cooler—pale, pinched around the eyes but not bad."

"Thank you for the assessment, Shiira Guardswoman."

"You are welcome. After you." She motioned him forward.

They entered the queen's lunchroom. Women gathered about, a few sitting but most on their feet—the queen, Shabet, Parria, Tameera, Barsa and several others. Billy, Dick and Tuuman stood to one side.

Everyone turned as Aarvan entered. Shabet smirked. Tuuman and Billy wore matching smug smiles.

"Good morning, Aarvan." The queen smiled as he bowed stiffly.

"Good morning, My Queen." He didn't smile.

She drew him aside. "It is time for hearing, Aarvan. I need your decision."

He met her eyes, squeezing the words past the plug of bitter bile caught in his throat. *God have mercy on the holdee and me.* "My answer remains the same as yesterday, My Queen."

The queen's mouth tightened. "Very well, Aarvan. Take your place to enter hearing."

"Yes, My Queen." As he moved between the guards and queen's councilors, Dick's gaze questioned. He winked assurance at the big man.

By the time he entered the Hearing Hall, performed the public bowing and took his seat, Aarvan's body screamed with pain. Unable to relax and lean against the rear of the cubicle, he had to sit upright. As the morning progressed, if he moved, pain slashed. When he sat perfectly still, it grew grievously uncomfortable. He could see no recourse. The pain remained just tolerable, as Dick had warned him. He suffered, as well, the thumping head. The more his body hurt, the more his head pounded in commiseration.

He paid scant heed to the first group of hearings. Dealing with his agony took all his attention.

Late in the morning the reader called, "Tarkan for queen's punishment. Holdee strikes mistress, fifth offense. Return to hearing from day two." A loud murmur ran through the hall.

Aarvan glanced at the queen to find her looking at him.

She spoke low, firm. "Aarvan, you will not speak concerning this hearing. If you choose to defy me, I will have the guards tie you hand and foot, restrain your mouth, and you will remain so for the rest of the day before the entire Hearing Hall. Is that clear?"

"Yes, My Queen, very clear."

"Good." The queen turned to disputants' place.

Aarvan's chest tightened until he had to force breathing. He clenched his hands, sending sharp stabs of pain up his sore tendons. *Blast.* If the queen were unfair, he would speak up. No doubt, she would do exactly as she said. *How in utter miseries have I managed to get into this mess? What am I doing on this crazy island? If only I could remember.*

Tarkan gained disputants' place, curtsied and stared at the silent queen's man, a sly, malicious smile twitching her lips.

Her holdee bowed.

The queen said, "Tarkan, let us review your complaint quickly. Correct me if I err. Your holdee strikes you when you wake him, and he has done so for a fifth time. He claims he cannot help himself. You claim he can. Your holdee wants you to wake him with other than your hand, but you choose not to do so. He received ten lashes front and rear recently. You cannot afford a new holdee so you keep this one. You have demanded severe queen's punishment and are aware this could kill him. Is this accurate, Tarkan?"

"Yes, My Queen, most accurate."

The queen said, "Holdee, look at me."

He lifted his head and waited, eyes flat, devoid of feeling.

"Holdee, you struck your mistress. Regardless of the reason, this requires the pain of locchot. However, you will not taste of locchot this day. The queen's man received punishment, and his pain embodies sufficient for both."

A collective gasp made its round among the listeners.

Aarvan looked up sharply.

The holdee gaped first at the queen then at Aarvan.

Tarkan jerked as though she had been struck and frowned.

The queen's eyes and voice comprised a frigid, matched set. "Tarkan, I conclude that your purpose is not to discipline your holdee. You choose to torture him for your perverted enjoyment. Though not specifically excluded by law, your conduct stands disgraceful. The queen's power will not be used to support your cruelty.

"Take your holdee home. From this moment forward, you will wake him in the manner he suggests. Should you ever reappear in Queen's Hearing or should I ever hear of you punishing this holdee for this offense, as LaSheena stands witness to my words, you will receive queen's punishment and it will be harsh. And, Tarkan, feed this man; he appears starved as a backway cur."

"My Queen," Tarkan cried, "this is not right. I come to you for assistance. You blame me."

The queen raised her hand to quiet the heralda. "Tarkan, I will tolerate no argument. I have made my decision."

"It is a most strange decision, My Queen. You encamp with the holdee." Tarkan's eyes narrowed, flame glowed in their depths.

"When there is not clear law or tradition, it is the queen's duty to determine that which is justified. My decision stands. I will hear no more."

The woman sneered. "Will you place upon me the blame, My Queen, that you needs sent your unruly skindown piece to locchot, then craved, without fulfillment, his lusty attentions?"

In the following moment of silence, Patea looked at Tressa, mouth pulling sideways with knowing disgust. Together they levered from the wall and closed on Tarkan. Experienced guards, they already guessed the queen's reaction.

"Three lashes with the strife paddle," the queen said, "to be administered immediately. Two for arguing with the queen, one for being a disgrace."

The guards grabbed Tarkan and hustled her toward the punishment room.

The holdee followed his mistress, nodding at Aarvan as he passed.

Aarvan stared at the queen. The queen looked at Aarvan. He dropped his eyes and turned away.

She frowned. Her decision should have pleased him. A smile would be appropriate, even a warm flash of eyes. *He looks away, ignores me. Rut him.* She expected his approval and he granted only cold withdrawal.

The queen's decision took Aarvan by surprise. He had hoped for light punishment for the holdee. However, no punishment for the man, with Tarkan going to locchot instead, made him want to stand up and shout for joy. *Why did the queen so radically change her mind?* Due to her threat, he wouldn't ask. He could imagine the agony of being rough handled by the guards, bound and gagged. To sit before the crowded Hearing Hall in that state would be too humiliating.

He averted his eyes from the queen through the remainder of the morning.

When the queen called for lunch, Aarvan was ready. Sitting there, still and upright, tolerating the ceaseless pain, exhausted him. Fatigue crushed him like a giant hand. He couldn't remember ever having been so incredibly tired. He thought wryly, I can't remember much of anything.

He followed the queen to the lunchroom. It seemed she deliberately flaunted her ability to flip her long, green skirt and sit with swift grace on the sitting cushions. Conversely, he sat slowly, tentative with small, stiff movements.

The servants poured coffee and served a lunch of pan-fried fish, vegetables, hunks of wheat bread and berry tart. It tasted delicious and, to his surprise, Aarvan ate it all. He sat silent, not looking at the queen.

Rejeena, coffee caster in hand, leaned against the wall. "You have said nothing, My Queen's Man, about the hearing decision."

He lifted his gaze, keenly aware of his inability to lean back and relax as she did. "You forbade me, My Queen."

"If you always took my warnings so direly, you would not so suffer now."

"The promised consequences today far outweighed the incentive to defy you."

"And two days ago?"

He gave a slight shrug, which he regretted. "The incentive justified the consequences."

"Sometimes, Aarvan, I find you hard to comprehend. Why are you so concerned, enough to go to locchot, about a holdee you do not even know?"

"My Queen, that holdee is a man—like me. You were going to send him for severe punishment simply because he displeased his mistress. That is, from my viewpoint, unjust. Justice doesn't exist here for holdees."

She studied him, head cocked. "This includes justice for you?"

"Yes, My Queen."

"You feel you have been unjustly treated?"

He didn't answer right away, eyes on his coffee, weighing his words. "Yes, My Queen, I have been unjustly treated."

"You said you understand my motives."

"It's possible to understand your motives while disagreeing with your purpose."

She nodded, eyes squinted, steady on his face. "You still have not asked about the decision concerning the holdee."

"Am I allowed to ask?"

"Yes, Aarvan."

"I'm curious to know why you decided as you did, My Queen, and why you waited until today to make your decision."

"I became convinced that Tarkan's motives were based upon an obscene desire to torture rather than discipline." She smiled. "The eloquent plea of a compassionate queen's man convinced me. As well, the queen felt it to be a wrongful situation. I waited until today for two reasons. My decision departed from tradition. A queen, with responsibilities to an entire quarter, should grant much thought to such a great change. Also, I wanted to observe your reaction."

"Then you must have been disappointed."

"I was indeed. So tell me, what is your reaction?"

He again chose his words with care. "I am gratified for the holdee and for all men. And greatly pleased to know you recognized that woman's vicious game and withdrew the use of your power." His eyes warmed and he smiled. "I'm proud of my queen for her perception and willingness to oppose tradition." His smile turned to a smirk. "I'm delighted that woman got what she earned."

Inside his chest a geyser of warmth lifted, trilling as a bird in springtime courts his mate. At an elemental level of his being, obscured from true understanding by his memory loss, he recognized Rejeena passed the test he set for her. *All right, so maybe she is sort of an angel. My queen is worthy. Worthy of what*? He didn't know, but this knowledge greatly diminished the irritating bane of *belonging* to her. Belonging would keep him close, close enough to . . . Close enough to what? He didn't know that either, but it was vitally important.

The queen sipped coffee. She studied her shoes before meeting his eyes. "I have missed you in skindown these past two nights."

"It was not my choice to be elsewhere."

She grinned. "Sometimes having a choice is a matter of choice."

He smiled at her quick rejoinder. "I did make choices, but so did you. Maybe it's only fitting we both suffer."

The queen rose. "The queen is not to suffer. It is your learning experience."

"Life sometimes teaches us lessons we hadn't anticipated learning. I spent two nights of misery, but you had to do without my skindown services."

She leaned over him, hands planted on hips. "You think much of the quality of your skindown services, do you not, My Queen's Man?"

"As do you, My Queen."

"I will let you have the last word this time, Aarvan," she laughed. "Come, we must return to hearing."

Hearing progressed through the afternoon. It blurred into indistinct sights and sounds to Aarvan. The fiery pain clawed relentlessly at his back. His head throbbed until his eyes pushed out, wanting to pop from their sockets. The louder, sharper sounds accosted his eardrums with hurtful vibrations, making him wince. Fatigue pushed down on his shoulders, a suffocating burden, rendering the simple act of sitting almost more than bone and muscle could endure. Nausea shoved upward into his throat. He choked it down. *I will not throw up in hearing.* Just when he knew he could no longer hold out, the queen called a break. He rose, the movement both agonizing and welcome relief. He followed her to the lunchroom.

The queen faced him. "Aarvan, I must hold a short meeting with Shabet and others. Do you wish to attend?"

He could barely keep his knees from buckling. "I'd prefer to rest, My Queen."

"If that is what you wish."

"Thank you, My Queen." His half-bow became a collapse onto the sitting cushions.

The queen exited.

He arranged cushions, rolled onto his stomach and passed out.

* * *

That was how Rejeena found him upon return from her meeting.

Locin, who accompanied her, knelt to wake him, but the whiteness of his face jolted her. She touched his forehead, covered with cold sweat, then held her hand for the queen to see.

The queen knelt. “He does not look good, does he?”

“No, My Queen.”

“Perhaps an entire day of hearing is too much.”

“It would appear so.”

With a tender smile, Rejeena gently pushed back a dark, damp lock of hair. “His head has no doubt been affected. We will let him rest. Stay with him, Locin.” The queen left.

Locin withdrew a light blanket from a cabinet and covered Aarvan, checked his pulse and breathing, finding them acceptable. She arranged some cushions, sat and looked at Patea, who had stayed for a moment. “I surprise myself,” Locin said. “I feel sympathy for the misery he suffers. It is an emotion sorely wasted on a man.”

Patea nodded. “He is different from other men. There is about him an aura which pleases and intrigues.” She grinned. “I surely enjoyed his vexing of Captain Shabet.”

“As did I,” Locin said. “The captain can be mean-mouthed. His temerity pleased many women. Unfortunately, he chose to vex the queen as well. I greatly fear it will not be the last time.”

Patea agreed and left.

Locin sighed and leaned against the wall, resigned to the boring but necessary function of keeping a close eye on the queen’s valuable piece of property.

Hours later Patea entered the room. “The queen closes hearing. You needs wake the queen’s man.”

Locin assessed her charge. He had not moved even a finger. His heart and breathing were solid and steady, skin dry, color in his face. She gently shook him.

His eyes snapped open. “Is it time to go back to hearing?”

Both guards laughed. “Queen’s Man, hearing is over.”

“Over?” He eased into a sitting position. “I just took a little nap.”

“It was more like you died. The queen took pity on you,” Patea said. From the corner of her eye, the guard saw the queen enter the room behind Aarvan.

“I wasn’t aware the queen possessed pity,” he said.

Both guards froze as the queen approached.

She dropped to one knee, hands resting on his shoulders. Her husky voice spoke almost in his ear. "With your back so sore, Aarvan, it is not wise to speak so of your queen, who is right behind you."

He started and shot an accusatory glance at Locin and Patea, then went very still. "No, My Queen, it isn't."

Feeling the pulse in his throat increase, Rejeena chuckled, rose and released him. "When you can rise from the floor, come home. We must prepare for dinner."

"Yes, My Queen," he said as she swept from the room. "Thanks for the warning, women," he grouched at Locin and Patea.

"The look on your face." Locin burst into laughter.

Patea winced. "Honestly, Queen's Man, there was no time."

Locin, stifling her mirth, walked behind him. "I will make amends. Sit still." She leaned down, reached with both hands and slid her thumbs under his pants on either side. Clenching her hands into the material, she gently eased him upward. "How is that?" she asked, settling him on his feet.

"Oh, Shiira Guardswoman," he sighed, "you're forgiven a thousand fold. Do that every time I have to get up."

She whacked him lightly on the rear. "I will not, you arrogant pup. If the queen saw that, she would grant me a fair measure of grief. You are to suffer."

He turned slowly. "If the queen saw you whack my butt, she'd take a truchon to you. I thought you never displeased your queen."

"Exceptions exist to all rules."

"Come on, Queen's Man." Patea motioned toward the door. He walked toward it. Locin and Patea matched his slow pace.

Aarvan dressed and shaved, with help from Wecan, who met him in the queen's skindown room. He felt much better after his rest, particularly his head. It had quieted to a mild, irritating throb. His back still burned steadily, with arms and shoulders protesting every movement. Though tired, he no longer felt the heavy, crushing exhaustion. He might survive the evening, though he winced at the thought of the upcoming skindown romp with the queen

* * *

The queen rushed into the room as Aarvan finished dressing. The servants had her clothes laid out.

Aarvan sat and waited.

Clean and dressed, the queen turned to him. "You look better, Aarvan."

"I feel better, My Queen." He rose to accompany her. "Thank you for letting me rest."

"It was apparent you needed it. My intent is to punish, not have you collapse in hearing. If you become so ill again, you have merely to so state. You can be excused."

"Then my queen is not totally without mercy?"

"Not totally, but do not think to take advantage."

"No, My Queen."

"It is good you will meet no one new at dinner tonight," the queen said as they exited.

"Why is that?"

"I cannot signal my desires with my hand on your back."

"Oh, My Queen, this situation seems to be absolutely replete with inconveniences for you."

"Are you being an ass?" she asked as they left the house.

"I'm afraid so."

"You take great chances for a man with a sore back."

"Would you be that cruel?"

"Perhaps not, but your wisdom is suspect."

"That appears to be my lot, My Queen."

They arrived at the home of Coltera, a towne banquer. The queen took a seat at the huge oval table, Aarvan to her left. The land leaders grouped nearest the queen.

Aarvan grinned at Dick but ignored Billy, who scowled and Tuuman, who glared. The queen's man had neither the strength nor energy to spar, verbally or otherwise, with the two hostile holdees.

Beside him that rusty hinge creaked, "Move your chair, Barsa. The queen's man does not want to sit so close to that sorry clod you call a holdee." Without apology, Meitra forced half the table to move so she could sit beside the queen's man.

Coltera frowned.

The queen ducked her head, a grin lifting the sides of her mouth.

Aarvan said, "What makes you think I want to sit beside you, Meit . . . Mistress?"

"Who asked you, pretty Queen's Man?"

"The land leader is higher ranking. She should sit closer to the queen."

"This is an informal dinner, rank not so important. If you persist in plaguing me, I will strike you soundly on the back." Meitra leered.

"I'm honored to have you, Mistress."

Meitra sat. "I thought you might see reason."

Aarvan scowled but quieted. Under the table, the queen gently rubbed his thigh.

"My Queen, there are details about guard positions which must be discussed tonight," Shabet called.

The queen waved her hand, permitting Shabet to continue.

A heated discussion ensued, mostly between Shabet and Reesan. They disagreed about the distance the rear column of guards should follow behind the traveling coaches. Shabet belittled and browbeat the younger captain. Reesan stood her ground. Finally, when nothing else worked, Shabet used her rank and declared her wishes final.

The queen did not join the discussion. She ate in silence.

With Reesan muzzled, beaten by length of sash and proximity to the queen, Shabet stood, chest puffed out, a sneering smile on her lips. She looked around the table, and her scrutiny stopped at Aarvan. "Queen's Man, perhaps you have some invaluable advice for our entertainment this night."

Aarvan stopped shoving vegetables around his dish and turned his head. Face bland, voice even, he said, "No, none."

"Surely you have some blighted kernel of knowledge to crack open before us."

"I have nothing to say, Captain."

"Nothing? You blathered and jabbered many idiotic ideas a few days ago. Does locchot give you lockjaw?" She sniggered at her own wit.

Billy and Tuuman joined her. Dick gave them an ugly scowl. Other women smiled at the gibe. The queen did not.

Aarvan's voice squeezed between clenched teeth. "I have nothing to say, Shiira."

"Truly, Queen's Man"—Shabet still snickered—"grant us some advice."

"I'll give you some advice. Stop badgering me before I get mad."

"That is your advice, Queen's Man?" Shabet's snicker turned to a full laugh. "Your little man mad should concern me?"

"If I get mad, Shabet, I might tell you the full truth about your inadequate life surety measures, complete lack of leadership, highly over-inflated opinion of yourself, your lousy disposition and—"

The queen's hand dropped lightly onto his arm and stopped his tirade. Her husky voice rang soft, "Aarvan." Her tone raised and hardened. "Shabet, you will not badger the queen's man. If he has naught to say, then leave it so."

Both Aarvan and Shabet stared at her.

The queen gazed calmly at Shabet until the guard captain lowered her eyes and sat.

The queen met Aarvan's blue eyes, hers softening. "Eat your dinner, Aarvan." Her hand stroked his thigh under the table.

Shabet glared at Aarvan for a while. When he refused to acknowledge her, she engaged in conversation elsewhere.

Through the meal, Rejeena watched her queen's man. He defied understanding. He should hate Meitra, be terrified of her. He sat, back still on fire from the beating she administered, amiably quarreling with the squat, ugly punishment meter concerning the taste comparison of two vegetable dishes. He embarrassed easily in public at mention of the completion act. Yet alone with his queen in skindown, he was knowledgeable, uninhibited, patient and committed to her pleasure. At times, he seemed quiet, easily molded and as pliable as new clay from the Legarne Plaine. The next minute he would strengthen, grow unbendable as Mainland steel.

When he committed to a goal, he dared all to achieve it. The threat—the actuality—of locchot, did not deter him. He embodied the essence of stubbornness. He could be in cooler, painless and comfortable. Instead, he suffered, refusing to admit he was wrong. *Hardheaded ass. LaSheena, is he gorgeous.* Every inch of that trim, wickedly enticing body was perfect in every detail. He had no physical flaws. *If only I could discover how to correct his mental flaws . . . Are they flaws?* She shook the thought from her mind, turning her attention to the table and conversation.

Dinner over, coffee and wine served, the women gathered in small groups around the room, chatting.

The queen wandered away from the table, talking with the land leaders.

Aarvan remained in his seat, uninterested in conversation with touchy, arrogant women. He had neither patience nor energy for verbal jousting, content to sit and sip coffee until the queen called him. He hurt, not as bad as earlier, but the pain jabbed, tedious and unrelenting.

Dick dropped into Meitra's abandoned chair. "If you feel like gettin' up, Queen's Man, could go outside and get some air. Too many women 'round in here."

Aarvan smiled. "That's the truth." He rose slowly and with Dick moved toward one of the doors to Coltera's garden.

Locin and two guards followed.

Billy and Tuuman observed Dick and Aarvan exit the room, then huddled together and left by another door.

Aarvan's mood lightened with fresh air, Dick's companionship and Coltera's charming garden. Enough of the fading light remained to see the riot of colorful flowers, tastefully laid stone walks and a large pond with golden fish swimming languidly. The pleasant aroma of shirtera blooms wafted on the air.

Aarvan smiled. "Thanks for dragging me out of there. I even hurt less."

"Thought that might work. It's peaceful, quiet, free of women." Dick jerked a thumb over his shoulder. "That is 'cept your guards. Can't seem to get away from 'em."

"They stick to me like pine gum."

Dick chuckled.

"How did you come to be a holdee, Dick?" Aarvan asked. "You're obviously a Mainlander."

"Yeah, from Guthaland," the big man rumbled. "Took to the sea when I was a young'un. Folks died. No one to look out for me. Signed on with a merchant ship. Sailed 'round with it fer quite a spell. Got shipwrecked. Cracked up in a storm off the coast of this island. Damn few made it to shore. Those o' us did were snatched up by women, like they was waitin'. Went through several mistresses 'fore Mistress Tameera saw me, liked my looks and"—he patted his crotch—"my weight. That was 'bout two years ago. Been with her since."

"Don't you want to return?"

"Naw, not really. Got no family, no friends. Don't even much miss the sea. Thought I would, but I don't." A tender smile lit Dick's darkly pleasant face. "Like that tiny li'l spitfire. A lot. Mostly I do what she says, don't irk her. I got food, clothin', servants caterin'. That li'l gal sizzles in skindown. Don't know what more a man could want.

"She already had one daughter by me." Dick beamed. "Can't see it yet, but she's completed agin."

"Been busy, haven't you?"

"Likely no busier'n you. Had longer to work on it."

Behind them, a sharp exclamation sounded. Tuuman staggered toward them, shoulder lowered, aimed squarely at Aarvan's back.

Dick threw his shoulder into the onrushing Tuuman's, deflecting him toward the fishpond.

Tuuman jerked to a halt, teetered on the edge of the pond, then regained his balance. He whirled. "What'd you think you're doing, you dogshit? You near knocked me in the pond."

"You 'bout ran into the queen's man. What'd you think you was doin'?"

"I stumbled over that rock." Tuuman pointed. "Nearly fell down. Didn't mean to hurt no one." He gave Aarvan a toothy wolf grin. "Of course, wouldn't felt good if I'd run into your back."

"No, I don't—" Aarvan began.

Locin's explosive arrival cut him off. Despite Tuuman's size, Locin slammed him against a tree trunk. "You sorry excuse for mertan's rot, I saw that fake stumble. I should slice you like a melon. Had the queen seen that, you would taste of locchot."

Tuuman's tone suddenly grew apologetic, conciliatory. "Honest, guard, I did stumble. I meant the queen's man no harm." He almost pleaded. "The queen doesn't need to hear of this."

"Let him go please, Locin," Aarvan said. "Just keep those two away from me." He waved toward Billy who skulked near the house.

The huge guard released Tuuman. "I will do as the queen's man wishes, but I will watch you. Do not come near him, either of you." She included Billy in her glare.

Tuuman and Billy scooted back into the house.

Locin crossed her arms and stared. "You are the only queen's man who requires rescue while standing in a garden."

"That's why I let you follow me about, Shiira Guardswoman."

"You do not let me do anything, Arrogant Pup. I perform my duty to the queen by keeping your scrawny self safe."

Aarvan nodded at Dick. "With a little help from my friends. What is mertan's rot?"

"What?"

"Mertan's rot. You called Tuuman mertan's rot."

Dick answered. "Mertan's a nasty little creature, kinda looks like a weasel, lives in old ground burrows. Meat eater, but likes it ripe. Drags things down its burrow, rots it some, 'fore eating it. Tellin' someone to rot in a mertan's burrow or callin' 'em mertan's rot is big insults."

"I'll keep that in mind when I need an insult. Thanks for redirecting Tuuman, Dick. Intended or not, that would have hurt."

"Glad to do it, Queen's Man. Best keep an eye on him. Don't think he much likes you."

Aarvan said, "That's fair. I don't like him either."

Tameera walked from the house. "There you are, Richard. I have been looking for you." She planted small fists on hips. "It is a shameful holdee who keeps his mistress waiting, you great lout." Her twinkling eyes belied the sharp words.

"My deepest apologies, Mistress. Was protectin' the queen's man, seein' as his guards ain't up to it."

Locin glared.

Tameera said, "Since you performed such important function, I can overlook it. We must leave. Morning will come early." She bestowed a warm smile on Aarvan. "Good evening, Queen's Man."

"Mistress."

Dick said, "See you later, Queen's Man."

Tameera and Dick stolled away, and his large hand dropped and cupped the land leader's shapely rear.

She swatted his hand away, but her laugh tinkled on the evening air.

Locin stared after them. "That land leader likes her holdee entirely too much."

"Is it possible to like someone too much?"

"If he is a holdee."

"Oh, I see. Don't like them too well, but send them to locchot if they misbehave."

"Exactly." She smiled wickedly. "You begin to understand. Perhaps locchot jolted your thinking."

"It's not me whose thinking needs jolted."

She sighed. "For a moment, Queen's Man, I held hope for you."

"You should know better. I suppose we'd better go back. I don't want to keep the queen waiting." He hustled toward the door. "Patience doesn't seem to be her strong point."

Locin chuckled and followed.

Later, as promised, the queen demanded Aarvan perform in skindown.

Rejeena thought, for a man who suffered intense pain, he performed magnificently. While not up to his usual standards, he attended to her pleasure, brought her to the height of passion, allowed his release and discharged his seed inside her. He then pushed away and collapsed onto his stomach.

His hoarse breathing sounded loud in the quiet room. She could not sleep, listening to him. *This is mean. I am mean.* She reached for the bell to summon the servants with a cooler. *No!* She jerked her hand back. *Sometimes meanness is required.* The man needed to learn. No matter how gorgeous, how great in skindown, he must accept her authority—her womanly superiority. Certain acts a queen could not tolerate. *Blast and boil his beautiful, cantankerous hide. Why can he not be a complacent queen's man—like others?*

Finally his breathing quieted and he fell asleep. She slept, too.

She awoke later. At sight of him stretched beside her, desire ignited. She wanted him. She fought it, telling herself to let the man rest, rutting causes him such pain. Her want grew even as she thought. She was queen, he, her queen's man, his function to complete her. His condition hung upon his sword point, let his suffering be on his head. She gently shook him. "Aarvan."

"Yes, My Queen?" he mumbled.

"I want you."

Even half asleep, he understood. "Yes, My Queen." His voice revealed no anger, no censure, just compliance.

He made long and passionate love to her, her body the elated, singing violin, his, the adroit and expertly fingered bow. He endured the pain long enough to bring her to climax, legs wrapped around him, as he allowed release and filled her again with his seed.

Languorous, satiated to her core, the queen was hardly aware as he pushed away and collapsed. She drifted tranquilly to sleep and did not hear his breath rasping in short, choppy groans.

Aarvan lay face down for a long time, trying to regulate his breathing, willing the pain to lessen. His back seared, arms and shoulders throbbed fiercely. Neck and spine stretched as one long rope of agony, head pounding fast and hard as a roofer threatened by an imminent rainstorm.

After a time he recovered enough to lift his head. The queen slept, lips curved in a satisfied smile. Shakily he eased from skindown and stumbled to the bathing room. He soaked a towel in cold water, slipped on his pants and shambled into the garden. Breathing the cool air, he sank onto a stone bench, leaned forward, eyes closed, towel clamped in place on his head.

Rejeena awoke and stretched languidly. *Had ever a queen owned such a wonderful queen's man?* Even enduring great pain, he could make her body sing, build her passion, bring her appeasement. Surely, such generosity deserved better than locchot misery. Indeed, it did.

She paused and scolded herself. Such inept thoughts of inappropriate mercy were unworthy of a queen. He had chosen his path; he needed to bear the consequences.

She turned. The empty skindown yawned. She leaped up, looked in the bathing room. He was not there.

Tenraan stepped into the room. "My Queen, he is in the garden, has been for a while."

Rejeena considered—his head injury, locchot. Everything had a limit, and for tonight his suffering need not continue. She could not justify calling for cooler, but other options existed. "Bring him in, Tenraan."

Aarvan entered, followed by the guard, and the queen met him with a small clay mug. "Drink this."

He looked at the mug, lip twisting. "What is this stuff, My Queen?" His voice dragged, low, listless.

"It is for your head. Your headache falls outside your punishment."

He sighed deeply, drank the mixture and walked into the bathing room.

Tenraan said, "My Queen, that looked like a strong potion. I suspect it will do more than squelch his headache."

Rejeena flashed a sly smile. "The queen's man may not fling falsehood to his queen, but the queen is not so hampered."

"Yes, My Queen." Tenraan grinned and curtsied from the room.

Aarvan returned.

The queen sat in skindown, eyes bright. A half-smile played at the corners of her mouth.

He stopped beside the skindown, his heart plummeted and his stomach roiled. "My Queen, I'm not able to make love with you again tonight."

Her smile widened. "I know that. Remove your pants and lie down."

His knees almost collapsed in relief. A great weight pressed on him. His mind reeled. He felt strange and his parts not weighted down seemed to float chaotically. Slipping from his pants, he dropped onto the skindown on his stomach. The pillow received him and greyness extinguished all else.

Rejeena snuggled down, pulled a cover over them and slept, one hand resting on his back.

In the morning, Rejeena left Aarvan sleeping, with strict instructions that he not be disturbed.

Alea came early and checked him, finding his vital signs in good order. She looked at him lying still and quiet under the Mainland coverlet. The thin blanket clung, outlining rather than concealing the contours of his trim body. That sight and the knowledge that he lay naked were almost unbearably erotic. She smiled. The queen deliberately flaunted his male beauty, knowing no one dared touch. She placed a heavier, less revealing cover over him.

Entering later, servants worked quietly around him, packing necessities for the upcoming trip, not knowing Alea cheated them of such a sight.

He slept through it all.

* * *

The Alvastrea Mountains towered majestically above the flatlands of Kriiscon, the peaks thrusting high, white-capped through all but the warmest season. Sheltered valleys nestled, green and inviting, between great walls of rock that leaped hundreds of feet into the air. Hillocks bound them together, sloping upward, offering grazing for goats and cattle. Great forests thrived on the lower slopes, changing at higher elevations to evergreen then scrub brush and finally bare rock. In the great geological upheaval that created them, the mountains formed pocked with cave systems. Lakes glittered where basins could hold water.

Many creatures found homes and shelter here, some shared with the Mainland, some never seen off Kriiscon. Numerous varieties of small wildlife flourished—rabbits, mice, birds, squirrels, grouse and wild turkeys. Larger herbivores—mountain goats, deer and herds of paaertae—thrived among the grazing lands and scrub. The combination of all these creatures created an abundance of fare for predators seeking prey—weasels, mertans, wild pesson cats, hawks and eagles, the gray-yellow tarag cat, brown bear, and the mountain glaalet.

The tarag cat and brown bear, related to the better-known varieties, copied the eating patterns and habits of the Mainland species. The tarag cats, larger and less shy than their puma cousin, found shelter and raised their kits in quiet caves on the less-accessible mountainsides. They ate meat, including human, if presented the opportunity. The brown bear was small, just slightly larger in weight than the tarag cat. Both herbivore and carnivore, it ate berries, plants, grubs and ants, leaves of scarner trees, or any small creature luckless enough to fall prey.

The mountain glaalet enjoyed a reputation more myth than reality, no one really certain it existed. Few women could say they had seen one and lived to tell of it. Those who did were amusedly disbelieved. According to the legends and tales of the glaalet, it was a huge, dark hairy creature, which moved both on all fours and upright. Some fables gave it a hairless face with great fangs and claws. Notoriously impossible to find, it supposedly lived in the deepest, darkest mountain caves. Legend indicated it thrived on meat, turning other predators into prey, human flesh not scorned in its diet.

The mountains also sheltered humans. Bands of loose men found sanctuary. Certain women, frequently anti-social, often rugged individualists, chose to reside in the rocky, bleak terrain. Groups formed small, protected townes in the valleys and lived off the abundant soil, farming and herding. Some valleys were so enclosed by the protecting mountains as to be almost inaccessible.

In these valleys and great cavern systems, the outlaws of Kriiscon flourished.

Ishtabarra, the self-proclaimed queen of Quarter Seven, and her band of followers had found a natural fortress. Their small, fertile valley nestled between great mountainsides. With a spring-fed lake for water, the valley supported horses, goats, cattle and crops. A narrow, defensible gorge served as main entrance. Adding to their security, comfort and portability, they enjoyed a direct route to the sea and a hidden entrance under the mountains. These routes remained carefully guarded secrets, even from many of their women. A cave system in the mountain had been explored and routes marked. Too small for a large force to effectively use, the cave routes would allow the leaders to escape should the need arise.

Ishtabarra was a tall, spare woman, prematurely gray hair peppering jet-black. Piercing gray-blue eyes, watchful, missing nothing, peered from beneath heavy dark brows. Bones prominent, her face stretched long and gaunt, striking for the bold symmetry of its planes and angles. She carried herself with the imperious aura of one already staffed. With her bold, queenly hauteur and her arresting face, Ishtabarra need only walk into a room for every person within to feel her presence.

She sat at a large, scarred wooden table, looking around at her outlaw leaders, Saradan among them.

Ishtabarra spoke, her voice a deep, rich sound, as arresting as her appearance. "Then we all know what we must do. This time we shall not fail. Rejeena will finally dance upon the four winds. The great queen will then needs staff me. No other woman even remotely related offers value as queen."

Ishtabarra rose and walked to a large bark hanging from pegs on the wall. The detailed, accurate depiction of the queen's camp would have furnished a revelation to Shabet. "I will once more enumerate the details of our plan, so each may understand her part and no mistakes will be made."

The outlaw leader tapped the bark with her finger. "Tierga, Laasa and Fiilat will penetrate the queen's camp using the password, which will be furnished us by the land leader's holdee, Tuuman."

"What does Tuuman derive from this, My Leiga?" an outlaw asked. "He is of loose man origin. Can he be trusted?"

Ishtabarra had heard the term leiga, a royal title in a Mainland language. She liked the sound and insisted her outlaws use it. It kept them at arm's length and, using the exalted title, prepared them for her queenship.

"He can be trusted, Lepka," Ishtabarra said. "Tuuman despises his mistress. With the kruets we pay, he can escape, return to his fellows and buy a leader position in his group. He will do as promised."

Lepka nodded, satisfied.

"Since none of the three chosen for the function are known members of our band," Ishtabarra continued, "they will not stand out in the camp. We have acquired kitchen armskins. So many women do kitchen function, no one will notice they do not belong." Her smile glittered. "Should the queen's blood splatter on them, it will seem natural on kitchen workers."

Answering grins flashed around the table, the widest on Saradan. "I wish I could go in Tierga's place, My Leiga. Slicing Rejeena's arrogant throat would be personal pleasure and triumph."

"You and I have the same problem," Ishtabarra sighed. "Every queen's guard knows our faces. We could not penetrate past the gates. We needs enjoy the deed from afar."

She turned to the bark representation of the queen's camp, tapping the tents. "Shabet, in her hidebound ignorance, places no guards except at the tent entrances. Our women will slip between and slice into the queen's tent from the rear. With Laasa's assistance, Tierga will cut the queen's throat. They will leave the same way.

Lepka will await them with horses in a designated spot outside the camp." She smiled at her appreciative audience. "I would give much to see Rejeena's eyes between her waking and dying." Ishtabarra flipped a dismissive hand, almost like an afterthought. "Fiilat will restrain the queen's man."

Saradan smirked. "The queen's man will present no difficulty. He is but a scared rabbitt. When I granted him my glower and mentioned his manly function in Queen's Hearing, he turned red and jumped, nearly wetting his pants. As well, the smuush pleaded with Rejeena not to beat me to death in locchot. I would judge him pleasing in skindown, but no danger to our women." She took a sip of shaarberry wine. "I do wish our women could bring him out. Rejeena chose well. That is the prettiest piece of skindown goods I have viewed in a long time. I would like to slide those double-button pants off and feel what he can do between my thighs."

The outlaw leaders laughed, the loudest from Gaanda, whose oddly offset eyes and protruding teeth gave her a dull and unattractive horse-like appearance.

Ishtabarra returned to her seat. "Unfortunately, it is too dangerous. Once Rejeena is dead, we may have a chance at him."

"Why not kill the queen's man with the queen, My Leiga?" asked a muscular woman with a scarred face and narrow-set eyes. "It would be safer for our women."

Ishtabarra's black brows knit. "Sookan, if the queen's man is all Saradan says and rated eighty-five, he is too valuable to destroy. A beautiful male with such a rate is rare indeed. Despite your hatred of them, men are necessary. Some can render great pleasure."

Sookan sneered.

Ishtabarra smiled. "LaHeeka declared this man the redemption of Rejeena. It would be most fitting for me to take him as queen's man when I am staffed. Would that acquisition not set that interfering old bariit to abiding distraught in her Lair of Serenity—Rejeena dead, me as queen, breeding daughters from the man she chose for my blighted cousin?"

All the women laughed, even Sookan.

"Does everyone now understand? And you, Gaanda?" Ishtabarra asked.

"Yes, My Leiga, I do indeed," Gaanda said. The other leaders answered or nodded affirmatively.

"Very well, then we adjourn and await Tierga's success." Ishtabarra rose and exited.

* * *

Aarvan awoke in the afternoon. The servants saw to his needs. With no duties—the queen had not called for him—he relaxed in the garden, remaining quiet to minimize his pain.

Hearing footsteps, he turned.

Pamma approached. "You appear much improved, Queen's Man."

"I am, thank you."

"I checked your rat hole, as I promised," the guard chief said. "It is merely that, a rat hole, surrounded by solid rock."

He jerked his mind back to business. The outlaws had escaped and the queen's forces needed to know how. "Thank you, Pamma. And the water?"

"Forget the water, Queen's Man. Shabet loosed and detained the seven guards involved. The outlaws could not have escaped without their cooperation. When the queen returns from Queens' Council, they will be tried."

"Loosed and detained, what does that mean?"

"Loosed is no longer held to function, and they will be confined until tried."

"Tried for what, the misfortune of having that particular assigned duty when the outlaws demonstrated more daring and imagination than the queen's guards?"

Pamma crossed her arms and glared. "There is a limit to what a queen's man may say. You needs learn to hold your tongue. The queen's guards stand more than equal to wayscrape outlaws."

"Then start showing it. Help me find that rat hole."

"There is no rat hole, Queen's Man. The loosed guards allowed the escape and will pay for their disloyalty. Freeing outlaws, who have sworn to kill your queen, carries a most dire penalty. If they evade dying in locchot, they will hang."

"Pamma, those seven women were trusted queen's guards, loyalty unquestioned. Shabet set them to guarding vital prisoners. Now they are traitors to be put to death? There is a rat hole; and, since it appears to be nowhere else, it's down that water. The queen will find it difficult to forgive herself if she executes loyal guards, then the rat hole is discovered after the next batch of prisoners escape."

"Queen's Man, you are the most argumentative man. How the queen bears you, I cannot imagine. No woman is going down that water to a sure death. That ends it." She turned and stalked away.

"Pamma," he called quietly after her, "if you were a disloyal guard, after allowing dangerous outlaws to escape from an inescapable prison cell, would you remain on duty to be caught, tried and executed by the queen?"

She stopped at the door, turned slowly, considering his implication and logic. "Nothing will happen to the loosed guards, Queen's Man, until the queen returns. I am to rule the towne guard force as Captain Shabet and the other guard chiefs accompany the queen. I will conduct all possible probing to discover another answer, will retain a clear mind and not assume the loosed guards guilty. But I shall send no woman into that water."

He smiled. "That's a beginning. I thank you, and those guards will thank you."

Pamma departed without further comment.

* * *

At dinner, Rejeena smiled and slid a clay mug across the table. "Drink this now, Aarvan, and your head will not hurt in skindown."

He pushed it away. "If I drink Alea's concoction, My Queen, I won't do anything in skindown."

She thrust it back. "It is only for headache. It will not affect you otherwise."

"That's what you said last night, just before it knocked me cold." He propelled the mug back toward her.

"Aarvan, you are most aggravating." She shoved the mug at him, medicine sloshing. "I show kindness, and you fight me even in that. Drink the medicine."

"Yes, My Queen," he murmured and drank it. His midnight blue eyes danced over the rim of the mug.

Her eyes narrowed. "You deliberately badger your queen."

"Yes."

"You must feel much better, to devise torment. I shall expect your skindown performance to so indicate."

"Somehow, My Queen, I think you expect that anyway. I didn't notice you complaining last night."

"You must make amends for lost nights." The queen dropped her eyes. "You did not use your . . . tongue. I have missed it."

He whispered, "The tongue, My Queen, becomes paralyzed during bouts of pain. It can't function if the body hurts."

She lifted her gaze to his face, her brows pulling down. Noting the frolicking eyes and wide grin, she smacked her hand onto the table. "You ass," she hissed like an agitated cat, causing the servant, entering with a meat platter, to start and almost drop it.

They sat silently until the servant placed the platter and left.

Rejeena smirked. "You will pay in skindown, Aarvan, for this badgering."

"I'll pay anyway, so I might as well get some fun out of it beforehand." His grin turned to a warm smile, ogled her seductively, voice soft, sultry. "Sharing euphoria with my queen has not been a great sacrifice, regardless of my condition."

She stared into those deep eyes, full of carnal fire, and desire surged like a hot bath from inside her. *He is so good to me. I am so mean to him.* She slammed her eyes closed, shutting his out. *I am queen. I cannot allow him to so influence me. I must remain strong, inflexible. He, not I, must relent. I will send for no cooler.*

That night he satisfied the queen, in every way, took her to the heights of passion, brought her to soul-shattering fulfillment, filled her with his seed.

Aarvan found the exercise painful but bearable. As she promised, his head remained quiet. Her soft animal moans, passionately grasping hands, begging with hungry thrusts of her body, their final melding and her wild climatic scream crowned the night. Passionately spent and physically exhausted, he slept despite his burning back. The queen lay collapsed beside him, bones jelly, sated. Neither woke the remainder of the night.

* * *

In the morning, Aarvan complained to Dick. "This is disgusting. You have to ride in the coach with Tuuman. Parria and Billy ride with the queen and me."

"Yeah," Dick growled. "Women're perverse. Coulda put us together."

"It'll not be a pleasant ride," Aarvan said, "with Billy hostile and Parria baiting me. I'll try to ignore them."

"Best thin' to do." Dick turned to leave as Tameera called him.

Aarvan walked with the queen toward the coach. He glanced around and tried to discern the guard arrangements. Darkness still hovered, obscuring most of the travel convoy. The surrounding noise suggested a multitude of wagons, horses and women ready to move.

"Good morning, Queen's Man." Alea stood beside him flanked by two pretty women of tender years.

"Good morning, Alea. Will you make this trip?"

"Of course. I accompany my queen on most long trips." She indicated the two youngsters. "This is Taera and Shaala, assistants who I am training. This will be their first function travel from Rejeena's Towne."

"With luck we won't need you, but it's good to know you're there." Aarvan nodded to the youngsters. "Taera. Shaala."

They giggled and dropped their eyes.

Alea laughed. "We must take our places, Aarvan."

He flashed a stone-melting smile and the girls dissolved into giggles as they followed Alea.

The queen settled comfortably in one corner of the coach. Aarvan climbed in, careful of his back. She motioned him to sit facing her. He sat, leaning forward, unable to find comfort. His back burned, arms and shoulders jabbing when he moved.

Parria and the queen spent the morning conferring about towne and packet concerns.

When the queen's attention diverted, Parria's eyes lingered with suggestive stares on the queen's man. She made sure Aarvan noticed and paid no heed to Billy.

Billy hunched in stony silence, lips waspishly clenched together, eyes seeming to study his feet. When sure the women didn't notice, he shot Aarvan venomous glances.

Aarvan sat hurting, wishing he were somewhere else. Billy's repressed hostility and Parria's unwelcome lustful scrutiny grated on his nerves, heaping mental irritation upon his physical pain.

The coach rolled, bounced, swayed and bumped over the rough track. Aarvan's pain steadily worsened. The forced unnatural position, forward and upright, grew miserably uncomfortable.

He sighed with relief when Shabet called for a lunch halt.

As Aarvan eased from the coach, Dick appeared, glowering. "Blasted women," he muttered, "not lettin' us ride in the same coach." Then he chuckled. "Tuuman's givin' me the cold shoulder after I ruined his game t'other day. If'n a glare could kill, Tammy'd be lookin' for a new skindown partner."

"Tammy?"

Dick flushed. "Ain't to be sayin' that in public, am I?"

"Not unless you want to join me."

They walked away from the coach.

Aarvan said, "You think you've got problems? The way Billy acts, he's no doubt plotting how to kill me in the most painful manner. Parria keeps inspecting me like a hungry lioness eyeing a hunk of raw meat."

Dick guffawed. "It's your own fault, you know."

"My fault?" Aarvan arched a brow. "How do you figure?"

"You got'em all droolin' over you. These women are hot for looks an' queen's men . . . all want what the queen's got. You got no chance atall, boy."

Aarvan grimaced and looked around. "Now that it's light, I want to see how Shabet has the queen's life surety forces arranged."

"You don't give up, do you?" Dick said. "Shabet leads the fore group, 'bout eighty guards. In the open country, fifty ride with the coaches. Rear guard's thirty women."

Aarvan nodded. "When they go through the trail past the corridor—just the regular eight?"

"Yep, just them stay with the coaches."

"How stupid," Aarvan snapped. "Who's in charge of the rear guard?"

"Locin. Shabet give her some sorta makeshift upgrade to guard chief, Patea to line leader. Patea'll lead the coach group through the pass."

"At least Shabet put some functional brains in leader positions," Aarvan said. "You're well informed."

The big man shrugged. "Figured you'd wanna know, so found out."

"Thanks. I appreciate it." Aarvan contemplated. "Locin is in charge of the rear group. That might ease things a bit."

"What you plottin'?"

"Keeping the queen alive."

"Boy, ain't you in enough trouble? Let life surety to Shabet and all them."

Aarvan looked at him, eyes calm, serious. "I admit to being ignorant about Kriiscon, these women, their habits and traditions. But I know about assassins, how they think. Saradan meant it when she said the queen wouldn't survive this trip. If the outlaws intended to use tactics that failed before, Saradan wouldn't have been so confident. They're going to spring something on Shabet that she won't see coming, and she refuses to even entertain the possibility. She's grown complacent from past success, and I don't want the queen to pay the price."

"What'cha plannin' to do?"

"I have to stay awake both nights we camp."

"How're you gonna do that?" The big man's brows knit. "Why're you gonna do that?"

"The how is by just doing it. I'll prop my eyes open with sticks if needed. That tent arrangement is wide open for an assassin attack from the rear. Someone has to stop it."

Dick tilted his head and looked Aarvan over. "What's one man with a banged head and sore back gonna do?"

"Stay awake and, when they come—and they will come—I'll have time to yell for the guards and get them into the tent before the assassins can complete their job."

"How's Locin an' the rear guard fit into this?"

"Oh, that's for the corridor—"

A guard called, "Queen's Man, the queen wants you to eat lunch."

"We been summoned," Dick said. "The dictators call."

Aarvan grinned and they went to join the queen and Tameera.

* * *

During the afternoon, the trail grew rougher, the constant jolting caused the flames to ignite on Aarvan's back. His head reacted, throbbing, then advanced to pounding. He endured the heightened misery, ignored Parria's hot-eyed ogling and avoided Billy's hostile stares. With these efforts and trying without success to find a comfortable way to sit, he thought things had grown as wretched as they could until the coach driver failed to avoid a large hole.

The coach tipped sideways, sending Parria and Billy crashing into Aarvan and the queen. The driver righted the coach almost immediately.

The passengers unscrambled, and Aarvan took a hard, solid blow on his sore back.

The next few minutes blurred through a haze of absolute agony. Guards yelled at the driver. The queen asked, tone worried, "Aarvan, are you injured?" Someone offered him water. Parria apologized profusely. Unable to respond, gritting his teeth to contain tortured bellows demanding release, he clamped his eyes shut, and shoved his head hard against an upright on the carriage. Clenching his fists, he gulped to breathe. He finally caught his breath, opened his eyes and met Billy's.

The holdee's eyes glittered, palms rubbing together, head nodding vigorously.

Fury flashed through Aarvan, overriding part of the pain. *Did Billy hit me? Or just enjoying the effects? No matter. I'll allow the bastard a minimum of pleasure.* He straightened his back, swallowed hard and pasted a shaky smile on his face. "I'm fine, My Queen."

"Are you sure, Aarvan? Did you hurt yourself?"

"No, My Queen." *It isn't exactly a lie. I didn't hurt myself.*

The rest of the afternoon's ride he suffered, barely able to refrain from yelling when the coach rocked over a bump. He ground his teeth and held his face impassive, gaining satisfaction from Billy's clear disappointment.

When the queen's eyes lit on him, he twisted his lips into a grimace meant to be a smile. *I'll give her no satisfaction either.*

Rejeena watched Aarvan through the afternoon following the incident. She had seen Billy's elbow slam into Aarvan's back, but if he felt the kind of pain he should, he didn't show it. *Perhaps I should have cooler brought for him.* Even before the elbow, he had borne great misery. After last night and the pleasure he gave her, how could she wish him ill? She was so utterly weary of his hurting and travail. He had to be, also. She wished to reward him, not continue punishment . . . *Drat him. He steadfastly refuses to yield. I cannot call for cooler except for an excellent reason. If the hardheaded ass would relent . . .*

She wondered if Billy's blow had been inadvertent, caused by the coach lurching, or an act of revenge, allowed by opportunity. Were she sure of his guilt, Billy would know the wrath of a queen. Due to the animosity between the men, she would ride with Tameera and Richard tomorrow. In retrospect she should have foreseen difficulty and done so today. Aarvan stood vulnerable.

Shabet called a halt for the night.

Aarvan stiffly slipped from the coach, wanting to sit on something that didn't move. While the women set camp, he picked a small tree, eased down and leaned sideways against it. He closed his eyes, ignoring the bustling activity around him.

Women organized the camp and set the perimeter. With the kitchen tent placed, the cooks hustled to prepare a meal. Servants arranged the tents for the queen and land leaders as specified by Shabet.

"Here drink this." Dick sat beside Aarvan and offered a caster of hot, greenish liquid. A pungent, woody odor wafted upward with the steam.

"What's that stuff?"

"It's a kind o' tea made from some sorta tree roots. Don't taste near as bad as it looks. Never seen as it does no good, nor no harm. Tam . . . my mistress swears by it. Says it'll cure whatever ails you. Make the li'l woman happy and drink it."

Aarvan grinned, considering Tameera's sending Dick to him with her ill-curing tea. He took the caster and sipped.

"Billy got you when that coach lurched, didn't he?"

"Something got into me. Billy certainly enjoyed it. I'm pretending I'm fine, don't want him to enjoy it too much."

"Blasted fool. If you let the queen know you're hurtin', she might let you have a cooler."

Aarvan snorted. "The only time the queen let me have a cooler was when she thought I might die and she'd lose her investment. My queen wants me to suffer, so suffer I will. But I'll be hanged if I'll let her know how much." He stared upward into the darkening evening sky. "To defeat her—I just have to outlast her."

Dick shook his head. "Stubborn bastard. Was me, I'd been on my knees beggin' a cooler long ago. Tell her what she wanted to hear. Promise anythin'."

"What about when you have to make a liar of yourself later?"

Dick shrugged. "Wouldn't. Ain't no use fussin' with these women. Gonna do what they wanna do."

"So you're telling me I'm an idiot?"

"Yeah," Dick grinned, "but I admire your guts, boy. Whole camp's talkin' 'bout how you're drivin' the queen ragged. Big wager goin' on how long before she barters you off, LaHeeka or no."

"I'm safe until she knows she's completed."

"Now you've had your back smashed, whatcha gonna do 'bout tonight?"

Aarvan shifted slightly against the tree. "Stay awake."

"Long hard night."

"Yeah."

"Listen, boy, anythin' I can do to help?"

"Take care of Mistress Tameera. There's been no threat directed at land leaders, but why take chances?"

"Hadn't thought of that." Dick frowned, brows beetling down. "Best not be messin' with that li'l gal. Mebbe I'll stay awake, too."

"I have a plan," Aarvan said. "As soon as the queen's tent is up, I'll ask to rest. I can get some sleep before our usual nightly entertainment. After that, I'll just have to stay awake."

"What about dinner?"

"If I looked at food right now, I'd throw up."

"What about when you gotta be awake?"

"She'll wake me when she comes to skindown."

"You sure?"

"That, my friend, is the one thing I am sure of."

Dick gestured. "Looks like my pint-sized dictator wants me. Gotta go. Drink that tea, all o' it. Somethin' warm in your stomach'll help."

Aarvan nodded.

When the queen's tent was in place, Aarvan strolled to where she sat by a wagon. "My Queen, may I be excused to retire?"

"What of your dinner, Aarvan?"

"I'm not hungry."

She studied him. "Are you in great pain?"

"I'm very tired, My Queen."

"Very well, as you wish. Dinner will be saved for you."

"Thank you." He retired to the sleeping pallet in the queen's tent. Determined to rest, he slipped from vest and boots, stretched out on his belly, deliberately one by one relaxed his muscles. Dick had called it—a long, hard night. Exhaustion overcame him and he slept.

* * *

When the queen joined Aarvan, he slept soundly. She brought him dinner. She stood and looked at him, convinced he had been hurt during the coaching mishap, but remained too stubborn to admit it. Rejeena experienced an unqueenly attack of kindness.

On the wrong night for his plans—staying awake to call for the guards—she put her desires aside and let him rest.

Handing the plate of food through the tent flap to a guard, she eased a light cover over Aarvan and slipped onto the pallet. So as not to wake him, she lay as far away as the pallet allowed. It had been a long, tiring day, and the queen slipped into slumber, her confidence in Shabet absolute.

* * *

After midnight, three figures, wearing the armskins of kitchen help, chatted and laughed as they strolled on a line past the queen's tent toward the tent and pallet area of the main travel group. They greeted the guards, expressing sympathy for their night vigil. The three implied that, having finished in the kitchen, they now sought their sleeping pallets.

The guards greeted and forgot them, as they disappeared around the end of the queen's tent. They were women with function about the camp.

Out of sight of the queen's sentinels, not yet in sight of the land leaders' guards, the three glanced around then ducked between the tents, blending with the darkness.

Fiilat had earlier helped set up the tents. She then worked in the kitchen preparing food. Though tired, she felt her part of this adventure not difficult. She need only restrain the queen's man, and Saradan said he was docile. A knife at his throat would keep him quiet. They would gag and tie him to grant them sufficient time to escape.

Fiilat located the seam in the rear of the queen's shelter, which she earlier noted, while helping pitch the tents. With barely a sound, they sliced it near the ground.

Tierga dropped prone and checked the interior. A small brazier held back the night chill and cast faint light. Except for the sleeping figures, the tent was empty. The queen's man slept on his stomach. The queen, as though placed for their convenience, lay on her back, arms at her sides under a light cover.

The pallet was of generous size, the two forms well separated. They might even perform their function without disturbing the queen's man.

The assassins finished the hole and slipped into the tent.

Fiilat knelt by the queen's man, dagger in hand.

Tierga dropped with a knee on either side of the queen's chest, pinning her with the cover.

Laasa clamped the queen's mouth with one hand. Grabbed her chin with the other. Exposed her throat.

Tierga's dagger flashed.

* * *

Rejeena awoke. Saw the knife. Recognized the game. Knew she was dead. She could not stop them. Ice crystals imploded in her chest. She would die here—without daughters. *Damn them to pin me so. Render me helpless. They give me no chance. Damn them!*

A blur of movement. Something hit the outlaw, hard. Flung her off. A distinct crack vibrated through the tent. The knife spun into the air. A great bird of prey crouched over the queen. Rejeena looked into blue eyes. Not the familiar queen's man. The raging killer of their first moment together. Eyes with no fear. Without pity. Soulless. The eyes of a snattsnake. Faster than a snattsnake. Faster than belief. He kicked the woman behind her. The hand jerked from the queen's mouth.

She screamed, "Guards!" She did not know which she feared most—the assassins or the ferine creature squatted over her.

* * *

"Danger! The queen!" The midnight blue eyes snapped open. Instinct drove him. No thought. No voice. Knowledge, power, speed seared. Protesting tendons ignored. He exploded from the pallet. Fiilat way too slow. He rose, fluid motion. Balanced on hands and left leg. The right foot drove sideways. Smashed sole first into Tierga. Kill strike, just below the jaw.

Her neck snapped, loud in the hush. The force flung her, dying, from the queen.

Right leg landed. Left flashed forward over the queen. Caught Laasa in the throat. Left her retching but alive.

Laasa flipped backwards. Released the queen.

The queen screamed, "Guards!"

Fiilat leaped to complete the function. Knife plunged for the queen's chest.

He drove his left hand into Fiilat's throat. Pounded his right fist over her heart. She crumpled. Fell.

Guards raced into the tent. The queen's man knelt over the screaming queen. He smashed down a woman. They attacked the queen's man. One flung her truchon.

He knocked it aside. Rolled away from the queen. Shot to his feet. Sprang sideways. Spun away from a sword thrust. Another swung her shield. He deflected it with his arm. Wrapped his fingers around the edge. Twisted down and away. Arm in the straps, she followed. He lifted a knee into her ribcage. She grunted. Hit the ground.

Two rushed at him. One from each side.

The queen gained her senses and screamed. "Stop! Guards. Leave the queen's man. Get the outlaws."

One stopped. The other, knife slashing, charged.

He stepped inside her arm. Grabbed. Twisted it back. Kicked her feet from under her. As she fell, he leaped away.

More guards raced into the tent. Swords drawn, crossbows cocked. Seeking a target. A crossbow bolt discharged. At Aarvan.

He swiveled. Twisted his body from its path. The bolt tore through the side of the tent.

"Stop it! Stop it! That is enough!"

The queen's words penetrated as more guards raced into the tent, swords drawn, ready for battle.

Fiilat, retching, crawled toward the hole.

Laasa just retched.

"Stop those women. They tried to kill your queen."

The guards finally understood. They grabbed Laasa, jerked Fiilat to her feet and verified that Tierga was dead.

Pandemonium reigned as more guards entered, bellowing questions. Others shouted answers. They roughly bound the live outlaws.

The queen yelled orders.

Aarvan stood quietly. The deadly presence faded behind its door. He killed a woman. *I've killed before. Who and why?* He felt no regret, neither for the woman tonight nor the others. The woman had placed herself in harm's way. He performed as needed to preserve his queen. His memory loss obscured the others' motives and his reasons to kill.

He started as a large hand wrapped around the back of his neck.

"What have you done, Queen's Man?" Locin whispered.

He looked at her, blue eyes guileless. "Me?"

"Yes, you. You are the creator of this bedlam, are you not?" She waved her hand about the tent.

"Only part."

"The beast emerged."

"Keep your dull knife sheathed. It wasn't after the queen."

"I see that. How is your back?"

He groaned. "It hurts like blazes, after all that jumping and rolling around."

She motioned to a chair. "You best sit. The queen busies herself screaming and yelling, but she will remember you in a bit."

"Don't see what difference that's going to make." Aarvan sat.

Shabet stormed into the tent. "What occurs here? What happened? This is outrage. My Queen, are you all right?"

"Yes, Shabet, I am fine," the queen said.

"What happened?" Shabet regarded at the queen, the dead outlaw, the live outlaws, the queen's man. Her sharp face pinched, thin lips tightened. Her eyes snapped and glared.

Tenraan, one of the first through the tent flaps, told her efficiently what had occurred.

The queen added details.

When she understood, the guard captain stared at the tent wall. She turned, face twisted. "He must hang, My Queen."

The queen stared. "What?"

"The queen's man must hang. He violated law."

"Shabet, what are you talking about?" Aarvan snapped.

"You killed a woman, injured two and assaulted guards."

He stared, eyes bewildered. "They were about to cut the queen's throat. What was I expected to do?"

"Call the guards."

"That would have been too late for the queen."

"No man is allowed to kill a woman."

"Not even in defense of his queen?"

She sneered. "Queen's men do not defend."

"Well pardon me, but my queen appeared to need assistance. And I didn't assault the guards. I restrained them from assaulting me."

The queen said, "Shabet, that will be quite enough. It is also law that the queen alone may chastise the queen's man. You forget your place."

Shabet's eyes clashed with the queen's. The captain's dropped. "Yes, My Queen." Stiffly, she walked to the queen's man, voice gritted tight. "I suppose I should thank you for saving my queen."

"Don't overstrain yourself. She is also my queen."

"Do not expect a change of life surety measures. Your correct guess stands merely a fluke."

"I expect nothing from you, Captain."

"That is good, for nothing is what you get." Confidence surged back into the captain's voice. She turned and walked away. "My Queen, we will take this vermin and determine how they entered the camp. I will post guards in your tent for the remainder of the night. You will be disturbed no more."

"Disturbed," Aarvan grumped to Locin. "The queen came within a hair's breadth of having her throat slashed, and Shabet says *disturbed*."

Locin chuckled. "Captain Shabet does not well receive others functioning better than she."

"Then maybe she should start functioning like she has good sense." He slumped backward in the chair, then jerked forward again.

Shabet and the guards left, taking the outlaws.

The queen walked to Aarvan, eyes warm. "You surprise me again, My Queen's Man."

He met her eyes. "My Queen?"

"It would appear, Aarvan, not only are you adept at defending yourself, but also your queen. It is most unexpected."

He dropped his gaze, making no comment. His shoulders sagged.

"Your actions required practice and much skill, that of a seasoned warrior. You dispatched those outlaws before your queen could move. Your speed is beyond comprehension, Aarvan. What kind of man are you?" Rejeena caught his chin gently, lifting it so she could meet his eyes.

"A tired one, My Queen." His personal dragon had found its flame igniter and spewed molten fire onto his back. Stretched tendons screamed, head pounded. The action over, adrenaline draining away, a deep weariness settled in his bones, and his muscles slackened. The slightest movement required a gigantic effort, left no energy to spar words with the queen or contemplate his past. He wanted to lie down, let the pain ebb and sleep.

She lightly touched his shoulder. "Were you injured?"

"No, My Queen."

"You are in pain?"

"Yes, and I'm completely bushed."

"Why did you not so state?"

"To what purpose?"

"Actions may be taken for your comfort."

He met her eyes again, anger flickering in his. "You wanted my healing in misery. You're getting your wish. I'll not crawl to you because I'm hurting—not now, not ever."

Rejeena looked into to those dark eyes. *Indeed he will not. This man will act only upon his own terms.* "Oh, Aarvan, you can be such a fool. You have kept your queen from being killed this night. I cannot now wish you pain." Her face softened, and her hand rose to stroke his cheek.

He puffed breath out, and weariness replaced the anger. "I can't read your mind, My Queen. I don't know when you change the rules."

The queen looked at Locin.

The huge guard shrugged. "Sometimes, My Queen, he thinks with absurdity. I do not believe the condition to be fatal."

The queen's lips twitched. He slumped, head lowered, eyes closed, breath labored. He appeared more the vanquished than the victor. She said, "Locin, have Alea bring the queen's man cooler and all required for his comfort."

"Yes, My Queen." Locin rushed to the tent flap and snapped orders to guards, then returned.

"I must see how Shabet progresses with the prisoners," the queen said. "We must learn how those outlaws entered the camp, and if there are more. Aarvan, I wish you to be in cooler, comfortable. Locin will see to it."

He didn't respond.

"Locin, until we know what occurs, stay with the queen's man. I do not want him alone. There may be other outlaws about."

"There won't be any, My Queen." For a moment Aarvan's voice strengthened. "That was their whole effort for now. They were confident it would work, and it nearly did. Precautions would be judicious, but they're done for tonight."

"I believe precautions would be most wise, Aarvan."

"Yes, My Queen."

The queen nodded and departed.

"Come, Queen's Man, sit up." Locin reached for the ties to his back pad. "We needs remove this." She frowned. "The queen has allowed you cooler. You could display enthusiasm."

He straightened and lifted his gaze. "Enthusiasm is not what I feel."

She read his eyes and said, "I would ask, but I do not believe I wish to know what you feel." She removed the pad from his back and winced at the sight of the healing lashes. "If you do not irritate your queen again, you need suffer no more."

"I seem to be extraordinarily gifted in the ability to irritate my queen."

"And to save her from sure death."

He grunted.

Alea bustled into the tent with her assistants, carrying an assortment of items. She rushed to Aarvan with a large, thick pad. "Oh, Aarvan, I am so glad the queen will put you in cooler." With Locin's assistance she placed it on him and fastened the ties.

To Aarvan the cooler touching his back seemed a phenomenal reprieve. Within seconds of the herbs and whatever magical potions it contained soaking into his slices and abrasions, right through the scabbing process, the pain faded away. The dratted dragon stopped spewing flame, and the burning agony simply ceased to exist. He sighed, closed his eyes, leaned against a tent pole and enjoyed the divine moments of relief, allowing no intruding thoughts or feelings.

"Locin, I heard outlaws entered the camp and tried to kill the queen. Is it true?" Alea asked.

In a few terse sentences, Locin enlightened her about Aarvan and the queen's midnight adventure.

"Aarvan saved the queen?"

Locin nodded. Then she grinned and gestured silently for Alea to observe Aarvan.

Alea looked.

He slowly straightened his back, stretched it carefully and wiggled his shoulders, a blissful expression on his face. Eyes closed, he whispered, "That blasted dragon is dead."

"Dragon?" Alea thrust two small mugs at him. "Drink these."

"Oh, no you don't," he griped. "I'm not taking that stuff. You're not knocking me out."

"These will not do that. One will relieve your headache, the other your arm pain." Alea squinted at him. "By the look of your eyes, once the pain is gone, we could not keep you awake."

"Suppose I guessed wrong and there are more outlaws about?"

"Suppose there are?" Locin said. "You are queen's man, to be protected. The guards will do so."

His gaze flicked at her. "As the guards did a little while ago?"

Locin contorted her face. "Speak of striking without compassion. We made a mistake. Captain Shabet corrected that. This tent is guarded, within and without. Besides which, you arrogant pup, I stay until morning personally. I will not step foot outside this tent except upon edict of my queen."

The ghost of his impudent grin flickered. "That settles it. With the shiira guardswoman on duty, I can sleep without concern."

"If you do not, I shall knock you out myself." She shook a large fist.

"Before you trounce my patient, Locin," Alea said, "I would have him drink these potions."

Aarvan drank the concoctions, making such a horrific face that Shaala and Taera burst into giggles.

Alea held a long round roll of skin. "Put your arm into this."

"What's that thing?"

"It is a petuur wrap," Alea explained. "It contains petuur, an herb which produces a pleasant heat. Your arms will feel better until the potion takes effect. In a while we will remove them. Now put your arm in this."

Eyeing the wrap with suspicion, Aarvan complied.

Alea placed one on him.

Her assistants, amid giggles and unnecessary hand contact with his upper body, managed the other. Taera and Shaala made a production of tying the straps, giggling and touching and giggling.

Aarvan treated the youngsters to his irresistible smile. "If giggling could help, I'd be a well man."

The girls dissolved into helpless giggles.

Alea viewed her work. "When your head quits hurting, you should be quite comfortable."

The wraps covered him from wrists to shoulders, leaving his hands free. "I feel like a trussed-up turkey."

"You look like a trussed-up arrogant pup," Locin said. She pointed to the sleeping pallet. "Go rest."

"Can I trust you to hold back the outlaws, Shiira Guardswoman?"

Locin turned to Alea. "We should have left him without cooler. He displays a more amenable disposition when miserable." She pointed to his pallet. "Get!"

He retreated to the pallet, and stretched luxuriously. Not having to lie on his face was a treat.

Alea laid a blanket over him. "Go to sleep, Aarvan."

He eyelids closed.

* * *

The captured outlaws, subjected to Shabet's interrogation, revealed useful information. Neither the queen nor Shabet believed the outlaws spoke the full truth, but were convinced the camp harbored no more would-be assassins.

Fiilat readily revealed they received the password from Tuuman.

Women sent for him found him gone.

Barsa, half-drunk when awakened, lay alone in her tent.

The captives assured them, with some painful persuasion, that Ishtabarra had been confident of the success of this assassination attempt. The outlaws added explicit, ugly descriptions of the queen's man for having thwarted it and of his ancestors for having aborned him.

With the immediate danger past and need for rest, the outlaws received light treatment. Shabet assured the queen they would learn more when they reached Rhotha's Towne.

Rejeena returned to her tent. "How is Aarvan?" the queen asked Locin. Three other guards blended into the shadows around the tent walls.

"He sleeps, My Queen."

"Did he enjoy cooler?"

"My Queen, he appeared to have died, trod the four winds and awakened in LaSheena's Forest Glen."

Rejeena nodded. "He has suffered enough. The service which he rendered his queen this night more than compensates for his misdeeds." The queen frowned. "I had heard rumors of what you call a beast residing in my queen's man." The queen still did not reveal that she had seen it, also, before today. "This night I glimpsed it"—she gulped, remembering those lethal eyes—"watched him conquer outlaws and rough handle armed queen's guards. Such is not expected of a man."

"He is, My Queen, unique."

The queen stared at the dark wall of the tent. "Yes, Locin, he is that. I must retire now."

* * *

Cringing, Locin watched the queen. Though she did not rule the guard force, their failure filled her with shame. Her queen faced an imminent, life-threatening situation that Shabet could have—no, should have—anticipated and prevented. The guard shuddered. Their queen watched that knife slash, helpless to save her own life. The queen's man and his deadly beast did what the guards could not. He told them what might happen. No woman believed him or took him seriously, the consensus even now that he made a lucky guess.

Locin wondered. She considered his beast that appeared when needed. What had been his former function to require such? Why and how did this beast sprout and grow inside him? He seemed so confident when he discussed life surety. He moved with incredible speed, faster than the eye, faster even than she could rightfully credit. His actions in the queen's tent opened the mind's eye, called for new reflections on the capabilities of men—of this particular man. Who was he? What was he? What information lay hidden in his lost memories? She wondered.

* * *

Rejeena, shivering on her pallet, pulled a cover over her. It did not help, as she had known it would not. In the quiet, semi-dark she could think. She had been terrified of dying tonight. Death was not a state to be sought, but stood the inevitable end of life for all. A queen should not be so terrified—lesser women maybe, but not a queen.

Death had brushed her before. In her younger days, when the island writhed in the turmoil of war, she fought beside her soldiers. No stranger to battle, she stood against cold steel in the hand of another, woman or man, bent upon her death. During the Border War to keep the Mainlanders from encroaching further onto the island, she earned the title "warrior queen." Always then she held steel; she could fight in return, move, run, yell for help.

Never before had all her defense faculties been constrained, made helpless for the vital seconds during which she would live or die. Rendering her unable to help herself, or even take her enemy with her, formed the ultimate cruelty.

Just for a second, a vision filled her mind. She saw Aarvan and other men, stretched in locchot, helpless to stop the swinging paddle and horrible agony. She squelched it. It was unqueenly, as much as her unseemly shivering.

For the mortification of shivering alone, she would slice Ishtabarra into tiny pieces and drop them down a mertan's burrow. She would spill her accursed cousin's blood, let it stain her hands and heart, wear the stain as a badge of honor.

She pictured Aarvan rising with incredible speed. To do so, he had of necessity closed his mind to pain and misery, stretched sore tendons. His long leg flashed across her, broke the outlaw's neck, flipped her into a useless heap. She knew until her dying day she would recall that vision of him, lifting up and over her, like a great bird of prey.

Efficiently, he dispatched the others, not killing but saving for interrogation. She held no doubt each woman lived or died according to his intent. Her guards were known and feared for their lethal competence. He defended against them, without serious injury, even in his condition, as though with no great effort. He dodged a crossbow bolt—who could do that?

She looked at him. He lay on his side asleep, facing her. The flickering light from the brazier lit and shadowed the planes of his face, changed them from one moment to the next. She saw what she had always seen—beauty, innocence, gentleness, warmth, strength that had made her think of the great stag, Aarvan. The great stag, however fast, strong, favored of LaSheena, in the order of nature, was prey. Watching the flickering light outline and change the planes of his face, she saw what she had not before—the lean, hard edges, sharpness of the great eagles—finally, fully recognized the ominous flame burning unseen and formerly unsuspected behind those shuttered eyes. He looked like an eagle, moved with the effortless grace of the tarag cat, struck with the speed of the snattsnake. This man was not prey, but a subtle hunter. Within her beautiful queen's man—beneath the calmness, behind the soft voice, despite the winsome smile—lurked a savage, ruthless predator.

She remembered she feared him in the tent, though only for a moment. Such a creature should be feared, but the realization he strove to save his queen stilled the fear. LaHeeka said he was dangerous, but he posed no hazard to Rejeena. The ancient conjurah had yet to be wrong. LaHeeka favored her queenship, approved Aarvan. The danger in him would be aimed at those who tried to harm the queen.

Suddenly, inexplicably to a queen, she needed something from him, some kind of comfort. She wanted nearer him, to merge with him, become part of him. She shivered again as she saw the knife slash, felt the helplessness.

Sensing her discomfort, he stirred and murmured, "My Queen?" His eyes flickered open, his midnight blue, drowning-deep eyes.

She shivered.

Half asleep, he pulled her to him, turning her so her back pressed against him. He wrapped both arms around her and drifted back to sleep.

She felt his lean body all the way down her back. Comfort flowed from him, like her goose down filled quilt on the coldest winter night, like heat from the braziers spreading and chasing the frost away. The warmth of him pulsated in gentle waves through her, driving away the chill. She pushed against him and felt the hard, strong, muscles like silk-sheathed steel. She had never cuddled with a man before, not even him. His arms encased her, fingers of one hand entwined with hers, breath sliding past her ear in soothing puffs.

Oh, LaSheena, with his strength at my back, curled into his powerful hunter's embrace, I need fear nothing.

The queen slept.

* * *

Secreted in a tiny clearing nearby the camp but out of sight and hearing, Lepka, leader among Ishtabarra's followers, with four horses waited the designated length of time, then another hundred time beats. When Tierga and the others did not appear, she rode quietly away as instructed by Ishtabarra, taking all the horses.

Fury at their failure and dread engulfed her. She shuddered despite being dressed for the night air. LaSheena's Corridor loomed as their only remaining opportunity, that corridor where death stalked the imprudent traveler—a terrifying alternative.

- finis -

Watch For: *Queen's Man: Beyond the Corridor*

AnnaMarieAlt enjoys a passion for writing romantic fantasy fiction, building otherworldly realms and cultures. Her creativity and imagination blossomed during a restrictive, lonely childhood in central Pennsylvania.

At eighteen, she joined the U.S. Army and her two careers, the military followed by civil service, exposed her to varied cultures, races, religions, and beliefs in a number of foreign countries and states—England, Continental Europe, the Far East, the South, North, Southwest, Hawaii and Kentucky, where she resides. This exposure granted her a rounded view of the world and a host of invaluable knowledge that she now brings to her fantasy creations.

AnnaMarie married her true love, a man far removed in creed and action from the hills of her origin. That love grew and lasted until his death. Her lifestyle and journey crafted quite a change from her strict upbringing.

Finishing her college degree as well as surviving and supporting the Women's Liberation Movement launched her understanding of herself as a woman and a writer. She writes to convey her myriad experiences, because she cannot not write—to share the legacy of a lifetime of love, rage, desire, disappointment, humiliation, ecstasy, learning, twisting mores to accommodate new values, and accepting that we are all human.

Out of this driving passion, AnnaMarie has written the Queen's Man series, an adventurous, romantic fantasy, about the Island of Kriiscon, where women rule and men are slaves. The series encompasses the struggle between a domineering but curse-haunted queen and a mysterious, audacious Mainland man. Her words expose the ugly underbelly of the human race and illumine the power of virtue, while following the grinding agony of a culture in the throes of change.

Life's ambition: Fully grown, AnnaMarie wants to be just like Granny Clampett.

Printed in the United States
By Bookmasters